Father Sandro's Money

Father Sandro's Money

K Spirito

Health, happiness,
and most of all
Love!
K Spirito

Writer's Showcase
presented by *Writer's Digest*
San Jose New York Lincoln Shanghai

Father Sandro's Money

Writer's Showcase
presented by *Writer's Digest*
an imprint of iUniverse.com, Inc.

For information address:
iUniverse.com, Inc.
620 North 48th Street, Suite 201
Lincoln, NE 68504-3467
www.iuniverse.com

Front Cover by Sal Spirito Jr.

ISBN: 0-595-13130-1

Printed in the United States of America

To Sal, my forever love.

Heartfelt thanks to Sal, JR, Joy, Cyn, Richard, Beth, Jill, Jo, Pat, and Nellie.

Chapter 1

Without color or fanfare the sun dissolved into the Gulf of Salerno on a February evening in 1910. The rain had ceased—at least for the moment—but clouds were once again breeding, intending another infliction upon the countryside and the cottage nestling against the foothills. When the wooden walking stick raked across the rough-hewn door, Maria Avita LaRosa frowned. That racket had become all too familiar of late. She heaved a sigh then wiped her hands on her apron before plodding to the door. She stood there for a moment, biting the inside of her bottom lip. Then flattening the wrinkles out of the stained homespun, she took a deep breath and lifted the latch. The door creaked open. Father Sandro.

Brown monk cloth swayed back and forth as the youthful cleric fingered a lavish crucifix pinned to the yoke of his alb. Gold chain threaded through the loop at the top of the medallion and encircled his neck. The coarse basket-weave fabric, cinched loosely at the waist with braided cord, befitted his station, but the ornate quality of the adornments gave the priest dominion, a quality rare for his age. Giving a slight tip to his galero, he said, "*Bona sera, Signora LaRosa.*"

Her lips wrinkled into a pursed smile as Maria Avita gave a curt nod. Refusing contact with his piercing gray eyes, she reluctantly stepped aside and motioned for the comely priest to enter. She scowled as he made himself at home at the oaken table next to her thirteen-year-old daughter. "Wine?" spat the woman.

"*Grazie.*" Sandro set his galero on the table while taking great interest in Louisa who was preparing vegetables for the morrow's meal. From the corner of her eye, the young girl peered skittishly at him. When their eyes met, hers quickly reverted to the chore at hand.

The twinkle in his eye and the smirk that twisted his lips irked Maria Avita, but her blood boiled when her daughter's long dark eyelashes fluttered ever so slightly. This man should not come around so often. He toyed much too much with the child's innocence. Slamming a flagon of wine on the table, only inches from his corrupt fingertips, she snapped, "Louisa! Bring those vegetables over here." She stepped over to the set tubs. "I will help you to finish them here. And for heaven's sake, tie back that hair of yours. Hair in the food is not good for the digestion."

"*Si*, Mama," the girl replied. Her head bobbed submissively as she gathered the vegetables into her apron. But a tomato fell to the floor so Louisa hastily bent down to retrieve it. At the same time Father Sandro lunged for it. Suddenly the two were eyeball-to-eyeball, in his hand, the tomato. A Cheshire grin germinated on his lips as he tossed the tomato into the air, up and down like a rubber ball. The pupils of his eyes grew into large black orbs mesmerizing her, salaciously pawing the young girl. Her face flushed. She swallowed hard. But her eyes failed to turn away.

Maria Avita snatched the tomato out of the air and leaping in between the two, put the backside of her five-foot frame to the priest. "Will you be hearing confessions in the morning, Father?" she asked while dropping the tomato into her daughter's apron. "Perhaps cleansing our souls of impure thoughts might persuade the Lord to bless us with better weather."

His mouth opened to respond but the priest choked back his words. The woman had already dragged her daughter off in such a brusque manner that he got the distinct impression that anything he might have said meant less than a good God damn.

Louisa rolled the contents of her apron into the sink, and with their backs to the priest, the mother and daughter proceeded to clean and cut up the vegetables. Maria Avita turned her head slightly to one side and asked, "More wine, Father?"

Fire rose in his eyes. Clearly that old hag was taunting him. "No," Sandro hissed, chugging down his wine.

Noting his wrath, Maria Avita straightened with satisfaction. After all, Sandro was a man of the cloth. It served him well to be reminded of his place. With just a little more than fleeting pleasure, she picked up another vegetable.

"Any letter from your husband today?" Father Sandro scowled.

"No," Maria Avita replied flatly.

"Joseph LaRosa forgets his responsibilities to his family. And to the Church I might add. Tithes have not come from the LaRosa household in quite some time. I cannot understand for the life of me why he has deserted his family in such a manner. Never mind God and country."

Maria Avita clenched her jaw. This conversation came up every time Sandro came to call. Well this time, she was not going to get into it with him. He would only refuse to accept her husband's desire to provide a better life for his family anyway. It was as simple as that. Besides, she asked nothing from the Church—so far. And now, because of Sandro's condescending reminders, she resolved that she never would.

All eyes turned as metal rings screeched across the bar that extended over the opening to the bedroom as the homespun curtain parted. Six-year-old Vincenzo ambled towards his mother with his chin folded onto his chest, peering down at his clumsy fingers fumbling with the ties of his nightshirt.

"Are Seth and Francesca asleep?" Maria Avita asked.

The boy nodded.

Her expression softened. She placed the paring knife in the bowl of cleaned vegetables and wiped her hands on her apron. "Come here, my son," she chuckled and bent at the knees. Untangling the strings of his nightshirt, she tied them again so as not to come undone during the night then kissed the sleepy-eyed boy on the tip of his nose. "When will my little Vincenzo learn to tie his own nightshirt?"

One shoulder shrugged as a trace of a smile lifted a corner of his lip.

She began to fuss over his chestnut hair. "No matter how I cut this hair of yours it never stays put. It always falls in your face." She spit on her fingers and pasted the baby-fine fluff high across his forehead. His doe-like eyes caught hers. Unable to resist them, she smiled. The sober lad never raised his voice nor caused her worry, unlike his oldest brother, Armand, who was short to temper and easily caught up in the adventures that life set before him. Still, Maria Avita missed his husky voice, his naughtiness, and his impish smile that reminded her of a boy who had just stuck his finger into the batter of the Christmas cake and thought he might actually get away with it. No matter how much mischief Armand got himself into, he artfully weaved a charmed web until she had no other choice than to forgive the little bugger.

Maria Avita sighed. Her eight children were all so different. Rom, a mixture of both Vincenzo and Armand, cared deeply about the world around him. For the most part he kept his head when things went awry and sought out ways to make right from wrong. When frustrated in doing so, he had little to say, though he cracked his knuckles relentlessly. But now the place reserved in her heart for Rom and Armand felt so painfully empty. Were they well? And their father? Oh, Joseph. How hard living had been since the three of them had left her and the other six children behind.

Doe eyes shook Maria Avita back to the moment at hand. She scolded herself for daydreaming again. She did too much of it lately. Drawing a deep breath, she nodded approvingly at Vincenzo then patted his bottom. "Come, my son. *Biscotti e latte di capra* before you sleep."

"*Finito*, Mama," Louisa said. Placing the bowl of cut up vegetables on the table, she pretended not to notice the priest's intense eyes while she untied her apron and carefully folded it, draped it across the back of a chair.

"*Buono*," said Maria Avita. "Go and settle the rabbits for the night. Do not waste time, for darkness is upon the countryside. And don't forget to take the scraps of vegetables."

Louisa nodded. Collecting the scraps from the sink into an old tin, she never once glanced back at Father Sandro. With barely a sound, the door closed behind her. Silence befell the house; only slurping and crunching coming from the six-year-old interrupted the stillness.

Moments passed. The priest snorted. His spindly fingers tapped an uneven cadence on the wooden tabletop. Seconds later he turned sideways in his chair and with great flourish crossed his legs at the ankles. His gaze fell upon the paring knife in the bowl of vegetables. Squinting at it, he rubbed his feet together while his cane scraped back and forth along a crack in the fieldstone floor. Manicured fingernails clicked together, but abruptly stopped as Sandro caught sight of little Vincenzo who watched the priest's every move. What a mess that whelp was making, sopping *il biscotti* into the cup so deep that the goat milk overflowed. Damn those blasted eyes. Sandro was sick of their indolent stare, to say nothing about that half-wit kid. Twisting up his face, the priest grimaced so ghastly that Vincenzo sprung from his chair and scurried for the safety of his mother's skirt. Sandro snickered then stuffed his galero onto his head and grunted, "I will continue my evening meditations."

The priest stepped out of the stucco structure to find that the last traces of sunlight had faded into the West. He did not call out *arrivederci*. Neither did Maria Avita. And the door remained ajar. Sandro could not care less about closing the damned thing, for he was angry…very, very angry. "The arrogance of those good-for-nothing guttersnipes. Such disrespect for a man of the cloth."

Halfway down the lane, he ran into Angelo and Paolo returning home with meager armfuls of wood. "*Bona sera*, Father Sandro," the boys called in unison.

"*Si*," he scowled incoherently, distracted by unholy notions whirling about his head. Earthly desires demanded satisfaction, and Louisa was the only one to get the job done. But that old woman…argh! She perpetually stood between him and the one thing machismo craved most. Any day now that bitch and those nasty whelps of hers would go sailing off to America. And take Louisa, too. Without a doubt, she would marry that Bascuino kid. "Undeserving *mendicante*. He will delight in her innocence, not I. Aaurggh, these vestments cling to me like shackles! *I* should be the one to teach Louisa the needs of a man."

He slumped against an eroded outcrop. Instantly, jagged edges needled icy moisture into his vestments and pricked his buttocks. "*Che cosa e questo*?" he blasted as he leapt away from the rock and yanked the robe around to despise the onslaught of wetness. "It rains much too much in this accursed land. I cannot take another day of it!"

Rustling through yards of fabric he found a dry spot and made a few adjustments before sprawling against the outcrop once again. He rotated his head in a vain attempt to release the stress knotting up the muscle in the back of his neck. He snorted. Before him the Tyrrhenian Sea, blackened by dense clouds, reduced a ship's signal to a mere pinpoint in the distance. A shrouded halo circled the lighthouse as the muffled drone of the foghorn brought back Vito's words. "Listen to me, my foolish young godson." His low brassy laugh still irritated Sandro. "Your Mama's greatest desire from her short life on this earth was for you, her only child, to become a priest. On her deathbed she begged of me, your witness to God, 'Swear to me. See that Sandro follows the Will of God.' Those were her very words, I assure you. And I listen good to your Mama. For she insisted that you are truly different from other children. More into your thoughts. Your skin glows fairer, more resplendent. And there is special meaning to the way your bronze hair glows red in the sunlight."

"But the cloth is not what I choose for myself," Sandro had protested.

"*Si, si.* So well I know that," Vito prevailed again with that impudent chortle. "But do this for me, my young Sandro...for your Mama. It will be well worth the sacrifice, I assure you. More than you ever wish for will be yours. Time is short, this I promise you. When I send for you, a parish in New York will be yours. The organization needs a friend within the walls of the Church. I will put you there myself for I, Don Vito, am denied nothing. And you, Sandro...you will likewise never be denied."

The words echoed in the priest's mind. "You will never be denied...never be denied...never denied..."

Yes, it certainly was true. Sandro had never been denied. Under the cloak of the priesthood, he took advantage of situations that would surely raise suspicion against the common man. At any time, the insatiable young male also had his way with the ripening maidens who inhabited the surrounding villages. All were easy to take, like fishes from the sea. But Louisa, she had become a baffling problem to him. "No, she is not the problem. Her mother. There is the problem! Not one single moment does that hag allow me to be alone with *il vergine.* Oh, to get my hands on the cold iron of *il pistori...*"

Father Sandro glared at the LaRosa homestead. The door had just closed behind Angelo and Paolo. Through the graying dusk, his eyes strained to make out the enclosure, where rabbit hutches formed a barricade. Only a short distance from the house, it seemed a world away to Sandro. And behind the enclosure, his ultimate fulfillment, Louisa.

He shifted his weight. His left sandal scuffed the gravel back and forth, building ridges as he envisioned the wench moving about among the cages. His tongue skimmed over his dry lips. Her raven hair cascaded over her shoulders while her arms cuddled a rabbit and her cheek rubbed against its soft fur. She whispered tender words into the animal's ear, though it seemed as though her breath warmed Sandro's ear instead. Her fingertips caressed the rabbit's neck, yet gooseflesh tingled the back of the man's. His teeth gnashed back and forth, filling his head with grinding. His brittle nerves shredded into pulp. Lust set itself free as the priest sprang to his feet and stomped towards the enclosure with clenched fists. "It is time. I will have *il vergine* for myself this very moment."

Rounding the corner of the enclosure, Sandro stopped to catch his breath. His eyes rooted on the unsuspecting maiden who stood in the open doorway of a nearby hutch. Rabbits were taking vegetable peels directly from her hand. "Ah, she hums like an angel from heaven," he muttered under shallow breaths. Sweat beaded up on his brow and upper lip. Saliva began to drivel off his bottom lip. Desires of the flesh had mastered Father Sandro.

Louisa tossed her hair over her right shoulder and closed the door of the hutch. She picked up the empty vegetable tin and turned for home. "Oh…Father Sandro…you startled me."

"*Commo esta*, my child?" He advanced until he and the girl were face to face. When she took a step back, he cajoled, "Until this very moment, we have never spoken alone. Is it not your wish to do so?"

Letting down her guard, Louisa ran her fingers over the rim of the empty tin. "Well, yes, but I…"

Sandro tilted her chin until his eyes peered deeply into hers. "God sends me to you this day."

Her lips quivered. Her eyes lowered, away from his burning trance. "For what purpose, Father?"

The priest toyed with a lock of her hair, coiling the strands in and around his fingers, in and around. "To grant you a tremendous blessing," he whispered. In and around the strands overlapped and shortened. Her shoulder lifted to brush off the hand that inched nearer and nearer to her face. Instantly his fist twisted and locked against her head. There was no escape as he yanked her body against his and crushed his lips upon hers.

"No, Father," she sputtered and with both hands shoved his face away. "This is sinful!"

"My dear child." His voice was smooth and syrupy. "This cannot be a sin, I assure you. God has willed me here this very night to enlighten you, to show you the way. This is a generous service I do for you. Do not pass it up, for after I am finished, you will know exactly what to expect from that young man who awaits you in America. The wedding bed should be one of pleasure."

Her eyes grew wide. Her head rolled side to side as once again, Louisa tried to back away, but her hair, entangled around his fingers, would not give.

Sensing intensifying resistance, Sandro shoved the girl to the ground. One hand kept her pinned while the other ripped aside her skirt then struggled to lift his robe.

In the midst of all this, little Vincenzo had arrived at the entry of the enclosure. Maria Avita had sent him to hurry his sister back to the house. The sky was nearly pitch black. The child froze as his eyes widened from the sight of his sibling struggling beneath Father Sandro. Her clenched fists pounded on the priest while her naked legs kicked at the air. Terror filled the six-year-old. His breath scarcely came and went. Tiny hands clasped together, squeezing, squeezing, forming an ever-tightening ball. His small frame rocked back and forth. All at once his arms dropped and as fast as his stubby legs carried him, little Vincenzo fled back to the cottage. His sister's shrieks pursued him. "Father, n-o! S-t-o-p…"

Louisa managed to worm out from underneath the priest. But the lock of raven hair still entwined in his hand prevented a full escape. She tugged and strained. Several shafts untangled, but the rest plucked from the root, leaving the priest looking at a handful of hair as the girl fled. Shaking the hair off his fingers, he seethed, "I will not be denied." Again Sandro leapt upon Louisa. "Before you go to America, you will give up your innocence to me."

His hand pressed against her mouth as she squirmed relentlessly face-down in a mound of hay. While hardness probed for its mark, screams went unheard. She could not breathe. The world spun so fast that when darkness began to overtake her, she summoned up her last ounce of strength and clamped her teeth down on his hand. Howling in ungodly pain, Sandro withdrew and Louisa filled her lungs. Ghostly hillsides resonated with "Mama!"

As Louisa sucked in another breath, Sandro's full weight fell upon her. Everything came to a standstill, quiet. She choked back air then opened her eyes. Father Sandro did not move. She took several shallow breaths then rolled over. His body slithered off her back and into the muck. Someone was standing above her. She got to her knees and swiped away the mud befuddling her sight. "Mama?"

Bristled with rage, the woman's jaw was set and her black dilated eyes were fixed upon the priest. Her shoulders were square and determined, bolstered by legs spread wide. One hand gripped the mighty weapon, a driftwood club, that had brought the battle to a swift conclusion. Blood dripped from it and splattered into muck. Louisa had never seen her mother like this. "Mama?" Tottering to her feet, the girl slipped and fell forward. "Mama!"

The club dropped to the ground as Maria Avita caught her daughter. They clung to each other, the girl sobbing, the mother soothing her convulsing child…and herself. "Sh…sh, *mia dolce bambina*. Shshsh…"

"Mama?" called a small voice out of the darkness.

Maria Avita gasped. "Vincenzo?" Her eyes scanned the shadows. "Stay where you are, my son. Louisa will come for you." Tracing the muddy swaths that tears had cut down her daughter's cheeks, Maria Avita stroked away the flow and said, "Be brave now. Go to your brother. Take him back to the house and put him in his bed. Vincenzo must not see any more. Then wash yourself and fix your hair. I will be there soon."

Without a word Louisa followed her mother's wishes. Maria Avita listened to the girl's unsteady footsteps slosh in the mud then join with others, lighter ones, and fade away. Alone, she peered down at Father Sandro. His glazed eyes stared off into untold oblivion. What had she done?

Raindrops splattered the muck…slow then faster, heavier, louder. Her own spasmodic breath rose above the din as her fingertips picked at sopping strands of black and drew them away from her face to behind her ear. Her heart thumped so hard that drawing breath had become nearly impossible. Bending down, she slowly extended an arm toward the priest. Her hand trembled like the single leaf that clings to a tree, refusing to give up to winter's blast.

Forcing herself onward, she nudged his cheek, first one side, then the other. "Wake up priest." She choked back the vomit that bubbled up in her throat. "You…you are dead?"

Covering her mouth against the fear that bolted through her, Maria Avita jumped to her feet. Her hands contracted about her head as her eyes wildly contested the storming heavens. "This is a nightmare. It cannot be real. No! But…but there on the ground…right before me—Father Sandro. He is still…dead. *O Dio!* Why do You not wake me from this cursed dream?"

Her eyes darted about the enclosure, leaping from one object to another, searching for something, anything. She knew not what. Just take away this aberration. Her insides screamed, *Joseph! Somebody? Anybody. Help me! What am I going to do? How did I let this happen? Jail! I am going to jail. And surely hang for killing a priest!*

Maria Avita collapsed against a rabbit hutch and stared at Father Sandro, dead in the cold slimy muck. "*O Dio mio, il bambini!* What is to become of them? Joseph? *Caro marito mio*, you are so far away. You cannot save us."

Rain pelted the dead man, washing rivulets of blood away into the muck. And like the blood, her life and the lives of her children were vanishing right before her very eyes. Suddenly the woman spotted his left hand. She gasped. Louisa's hair…entwined around his spindly fingers. The monster had yanked out her baby's beautiful tresses. Deep within Maria Avita, instinct rebounded. She absolutely could not give up. Bolting to her feet, she looked down upon Father Sandro. Contempt mounted. She spat upon the evildoer. "Priest, ha! Devil! That is what you are! You will not make hell on earth for the LaRosa family even if I have to take care of this mess myself." Her foot sprung back to kick him. "Wait a minute…what is that?" Swiping away the rain that streaked down her face, she leaned closer and squinted through the darkness. What was sticking out from under his alb? She got down on her knees. "Paper?" Her forefinger nudged aside the brown monk cloth. Two fingers fished out the object and dangled it close to her eyes. "Money," she gasped. "*Americano.*"

Maria Avita fell back upon her ankles. What was she to make of all this? She squinted at the robe. Bulges. Her index finger poked at them then gingerly nudged the cloth turning it inside out. A hidden pocket…and a wad of bills secreted away in it.

She rummaged through the alb. Another pocket. "Money!" The more she rummaged, the more pockets she found; each and every one filled with currency. In all her thirty-five years, Maria Avita had never seen so much money.

Chapter 2

Several weeks earlier, Joseph LaRosa had tipped his hat against the brilliant East Boston sunshine while exiting Our Lady of Assumption Catholic Church. Crisp, unspoiled wintry air invaded his nostrils, expanding his broad chest to the deepest reaches. Withholding it momentarily, he then forced out the stuffy hour-long Mass in a surge of hot billowing breath. Several more exchanges of musty air for fresh further invigorated his burgeoning satisfaction with life.

The thirty-six-year-old Italian stood tall and proud. His head cocked back, giving a slight raise to a firm chin. A straight nose of moderate length added to his aloof demeanor while hazel eyes, intensified by onyx brows, pierced the souls of all he met. His mustachio, cut evenly across the middle of his upper lip, concealed all emotion and lent to an air of brashness. If it were not for his immigrant clothes, Joseph might have been looked upon as a man of great prominence.

The view of the East Boston landscape from these church steps at Jeffrey's Point pleased him. He twisted the tips of his mustachio. The newly fallen snow bore a whiteness found only in the purest of souls. Crystal icicles, hanging from the eaves of the houses, glistened like the Tyrrhenian Sea on a sun-drenched afternoon. Across the street in Belmont Park, the colors of the American flag fluttered ever so slightly in the benevolent breeze and appeared brighter than ever, promising great things for the immigrant. Off in the distance, only the shallow wake of a square-masted ship disturbed the reflection of the cloudless cobalt sky in the unruffled waters of Boston Harbor. Long forgotten, the blizzard that had raged yesterday.

He had made the right decision to leave Italy, of that no doubt bedeviled his mind. Never would this humble carpenter have been as successful back there as he was here. And in such a short time.

Oh, how Joseph loathed Prime Minister Giovanni Giolitti. The master of *trasformismo* and his government of corrupt politicians made it virtually impossible for god-fearing Italians to put food on their tables and roofs over their families' heads. No wonder that, as each day faded into night, urban workers resorted more and more to violence. Living and working conditions in Italy had become truly deplorable. Joseph predicted that these worker demonstrations were only the beginning. Things were going to get a whole lot worse, and God help the innocents who got caught in the fray, for they would be the ones to suffer the most. As soon as possible, he must get the rest of his family out of Italy.

It pained Joseph every time cousin Luca came to mind. He had warned that rascal not to become involved in worker protests. Nevertheless, boldness of youth gave rise to invincibility...or so Luca had thought. Summarily imprisoned, the twenty-two-year-old was beaten nearly to death. Joseph frowned. Considering the dire conditions within the bars of the jail cell, death seemed more merciful than life. How dreadful that filthy hell hole must be this time of year. Raw and dank, the flea-infested earthen floors served as bed, chair, and kneeler on which prisoners prayed for salvation that would not come on this earth. Joseph shuddered. One window allowed a single ray of sunlight to enter. Set close to the ceiling and out of reach, it was too small and narrow for a man's body to squeeze through. Putrid odors reeked from the corners of the cell where bloodied, unbathed prisoners had relieved themselves. There was neither water nor cup to hold it. A single dented tin, deposited next to the barred door, contained something wormy—food—but only round-bellied green flies and maggots found it palatable.

Joseph cringed as once again the fear that had electrified him when he had first heard of Luca's incarceration bolted through him. Giolitti factions had surely marked for extinction everyone bearing the name LaRosa, whether related to Luca or not. Many a long black night Joseph had spent awake in his bed, afraid to fall asleep, dreading the inevitable pounding on the door by the enforcers. For the preservation of his family, he had concluded that he must leave Italy. There was no other choice. Yet, the day Joseph left Maria Avita and his six young children was the most tormented day he had ever lived. Every doubt that ever existed wreaked havoc on his resolve. He prayed to God to give him strength not to change his mind, for relief at that moment would surely bring disaster to the LaRosa family within a very short time.

Maria Avita had tried to be strong—for the sake of the children. Nonetheless, Joseph could feel her five-foot frame convulse as she clung to him one last time. Terror intermingled with the tears that flooded her ebony eyes. She had no living relatives in Italy to give her support after he left. Her father had been a mariner, lost at sea before she was born. Her mother, who had worked as a servant, had died when Maria Avita was eight years old and was only a ghost that roamed the empty corridors of memory. When and what the woman died of, no one knew. She was dead, that was all. Not long after that, Maria Avita was farmed out as a companion to a rich girl.

Joseph smiled. *Angelatina Mia*. Such a good, strong, Christian woman. Whatever must be done, she would do.

Deeply rooted in the Catholic faith, Joseph prayed daily to St. Anthony. Please watch over the family he had left behind in Italy. Keep them safe while he labored with his two oldest sons to earn enough money to send for them. Accompanying their father on the voyage to America, Rom and Armand had vowed to work hard at the side of their father until the family was reunited.

"*Commo esta, Signore LaRosa?*"

The gravelly voice yanked Joseph from his musings. "Ah, Monsignor DeSilva." He grabbed the prelate's hand and shook it vigorously. "*Buono.* A glorious day, is this not so?"

"*Si.* You are looking hardy. You have heard from your wife?" Monsignor DeSilva asked.

"A letter just this week past," said Joseph while patting his breast pocket that protected her letter. "God willing, I will send for Maria Avita and the rest of my children within two weeks."

Monsignor DeSilva slid his hands into the slits of his ceremonial dalmatica. "Work is plentiful then, eh?"

"*Si.* I could not be blessed with more, for there are not enough hours in the day." Turning to his son, Rom, who followed close behind, Joseph grinned. "And with this strapping young man here, things go much better than I ever hoped."

Giving a nod of farewell, Rom and Joseph descended the stairs of the church and stepped into the street, crowded with Sunday worshippers. There was no other place to walk since snow had been piled into high banks on both sides following the blizzard that had unleashed its fury on East Boston. A dozen inches of new snow overwhelmed the remains of several previous storms. *The Worst Wintry Blast Since 1898*—that's what the morning newspaper headlined. In some places wind gusts of hurricane force blew snow into drifts of twenty feet or higher. Several people, foolish enough to venture out during the gale, were later found frozen to death.

Joseph had never seen so much snow. What a truly wondrous country. Everywhere he turned, there was something new, another unfamiliar sight, another great adventure. "Look over there, my son," Joseph said as he pointed to a man crossing the street just ahead. "What a splendid topcoat *il gentiluomo* wears. See there. Even his hat and silk scarf match!"

"That's a fine cane he carries on his wrist. Do you suppose the handle is pure gold?" Rom asked.

"In my mind I am sure it is. Someday, my son, we will dress like that."

"*Si*. It will bring great relief to give these scratchy clothes back to the charities." Rom scuffed the back of his hand against his brown woolen coat. "These rags label us immigrants. Look at these boots, stiff and turned up at the toes. How is a person supposed to walk in them?"

A perplexed look shadowed Joseph's face. His son was very perceptive for his fourteen years. And strong. Although, curly brown hair gave Rom the appearance of a much younger person. Hazel eyes of the father were also the son's, but the teenager's heart beat with the spirit and determination of his mother.

"Soon all will change," Joseph promised. "We, too, will be successful American citizens, just like that gentleman."

He imagined his wife walking along side of him the same way that elegant lady was walking next to that man, who obviously was her husband. Ah, such fine clothes, shaded like the greenest of Apennine forests. It was good to see color on a woman instead of the drab clothes that most Italian females wore these days. Maria Avita deserved such luxury. *Si*, a day was coming when people would stop to watch or perhaps even shake the hands of Maria Avita and Joseph LaRosa as they too strolled this street after Mass.

The immigrant and his son paused to watch the gentleman help his lady tow a wooden sled on which a silly little girl with spiraling chestnut curls giggled. She wore a green ankle-length coat just like her mother's. Sable fur lined the cuffs as well as the matching muff and bonnet. Joseph thought of his own daughter, Francesca. She was about the same age as that little girl. He wished that he were that man and that Francesca rode on that sled.

A short distance behind the trio, a small boy dallied in the street. Ignoring all parental urgings to keep up, he squatted down to pick up a handful of slushy snow and tried to fashion it into a ball that refused to stick together.

Down the street, groups of boisterous older lads egged each other on with shouts and a flurry of snowballs. Joseph could not decide if the ruffians were just cavorting or being contentious, but there was no time for further consideration, for just then, one poorly aimed snowball missed its mark and exploded on the muzzle of an old mare languidly clopping down the street. High-pitched whinnies echoed throughout the village as the startled animal reared up and dumped her rider onto the cobblestones, glazed with icy slush. Her hind legs flailed out from under her and as she came down upon her front legs, a distinct crack resounded. Splintered bone slashed through the hide just below the right knee joint. With a thud her full weight impacted the ground. Her eyes bulged as a loud guttural wheeze shot hot vapor from her mouth into the frigid January atmosphere. Blinded and winded, the animal struggled to her feet. On three legs she staggered about while the fourth leg swung back and forth without form. Suddenly the riderless horse catapulted forward. Out of control, she stampeded down the street in the direction of Joseph, Rom, and the small boy squatting in the middle of the street, still laboring to fashion a snowball in his tiny hands.

"*O Dio mio!*" Joseph forgot his English as catastrophe loomed right before his eyes. "*Ragazzo! Attende*," he shouted while thrashing his arms about like a madman.

But the lad paid no attention. Oblivious to everything, he continued to slap the snow in his hands.

However, boy's father comprehended the immigrant's Italian outcries. He bolted towards his son, bellowing, "Antonio! Get out of the way!"

Casting a startled look at his father then down the street at the frenzied horse hurtling straight toward him, the boy froze where he squatted. His eyes rounded in horror as people screeched and scurried for safety. Thinking only of self-preservation, they scrambled up snow banks that collapsed under their weight while others slid backwards and tumbled into the street. The closest person to the petrified child, the only one who stood even the slightest chance of saving little Antonio was Joseph.

With no time to second guess, the immigrant turned to his right and shoved Rom into the snow bank, out of harm's way. He then spun around and launched himself in the direction of the boy. Grasping Antonio under the arms, Joseph hurled the child into the open arms of the onrushing father. But as the immigrant did that, his boots skated beneath him. His arms flailed as he tried to catch his balance. It was no use. His feet slid out from under him and up into the air. His five-foot-nine frame somersaulted towards the opposite side the street. His skull bounced on the unyielding cobblestones like a child's rubber ball until it rammed into the snow bank. As his body crumpled upon the frozen cobblestones, the light went out from his world. But not before Joseph LaRosa felt the full weight of a hoof crush his left thigh.

Chapter 3

The sequence of events that landed Joseph and Maria Avita LaRosa on separate shores began on Christmas Day 1907 when long-time friend Orazio Bascuino announced that he had booked passage on the SS Florio sailing to the Port of New York. The sprightly gentleman of short, heavy-set stature with deep-set chocolate eyes planned to leave Salerno with his oldest son, Dominico on January 7, 1908. On numerous occasions he had spoken about leaving Italy but to actually do so caused great distress.

"But Orazio, there is such risk," Joseph protested while half-heartedly stoking the fire. How could this be? Orazio had been a friend—a brother—for so many years. Surely God meant for them to always walk the same ground. If that was not so, why did God take Orazio's mother while giving birth to her only child? Or allow Joseph to survive when his parents and only sibling succumbed to the plague that had ripped through their tiny inland village? For what purpose did Matteo Bascuino come along and take Joseph the orphan to Salerno to grow up with Orazio as if they were true brothers in blood?

"Risk? How can you say there is risk?" Orazio retorted. "The risk is to stay here and do nothing. You are but a farmer, destined to be poor and taken advantage of, but I, I am a businessman, a tailor. Also take in account that I inherited Pa's shop. I should be well off. But look at me,

Joey. I have nothing to show for my many years of hard work. And *cara amico mio*, we both know why."

"Giolitti." Joseph winced.

"Si. That tyrant speaks of making life good for all Italians, but as it goes, he steals from us all that we earn. It is getting where I cannot even afford food for my family. At least you can take food from the field to keep your family alive. I have no fields."

Joseph stared at the dancing flames. Orazio was right. Giolitti's government absconded with everything it laid its filthy hands upon whether it needed it or not. All of Orazio's reasons for going to America regurgitated in Joseph's mind. Yes, he too had many dreams of a better life for Maria Avita and his eight children. But starting over from nothing? In a place he had never even set eyes upon? God only knew that the farmer did not want to make things worse for his growing family. If only he could be sure it the right thing to do. Fear of the unknown quickly swayed Joseph from seriously considering leaving Italy.

"You would leave your Carlotta alone, Orazio? And the children? Think of them," Joseph contended, but the argument felt lame and more with himself than with Orazio. Returning to his chair, Joseph avoided Orazio's optimistic glare while pointing out, "See your little Margaret, born just last August. She still suckles at Carlotta's breast. How will your wife sustain the family without you?"

Orazio leaned close to Joseph and whispered, "Secretly, I have saved money, money that Giolitti knows nothing about. There is enough for two passages and a little extra for Carlotta. It will not be long, I assure you, before I send more. But you, *amico mio*, I know you all too well. You will keep a close watch over *mio famiglia*. Is this not so?"

"*Certamente, certamente*," Joseph blustered.

"You are *paesani*, a true friend and brother to me!" Orazio leaned back in his chair and gestured with an upturned palm. "Wait and see. I will succeed. And after I send for Carlotta and the children, you and *tuo famiglia* must come, too. It will be easier for you since I will already be there and can help you and your family settle much faster and easier than I."

* * *

A month had passed after Orazio and Dominico left Italy when a letter arrived. "Many opportunities exist for anyone who wishes to come to America," Orazio wrote. "Strong people who are not afraid to roll up their sleeves find prosperity in this great land."

Joseph folded up the letter and stuffed it into his breast pocket. He climbed to the hilltop overlooking the Gulf of Salerno. It seemed like only yesterday that the great Tyrrhenian Sea had snatched Orazio away as if it were the hand of death. Joseph sank to the ground. Oh, if only it was possible to go back to the simpler times, carefree childhood days, running through the streets of Salerno with Orazio. Their arms outstretched like great seabirds, *il paesani* soared up into the hills, climbing, climbing until finally, they fell to the ground. Not a single breath remained in their bodies as the golden sun shone down from the cobalt sky above and singed their sweaty brows.

Joseph peered up at the sky. This day, no golden sun burned through the torpid overcast. And there was no Orazio gasping beside him. Childhood was gone. The gloom of cautious maturity had long since replaced the impervious clarity of youth.

Heaving a mournful sigh, he looked around him. Many Sundays after Mass, he and Orazio had brought their brides up to this hillside, lugging baskets of wine, cheese, and bread to loll away long, lazy afternoons until brush stokes of evening blended blue with pink, lavender, and gold across the western sky. After the sun had retired into the Tyrrhenian Sea, they headed home. Their laughter tickled the twilight and echoed throughout the terraced hillsides. "O Dio mio, those days are ended forever. *Finito*."

Joseph drew up his collar against the raw offshore wind that brought rain and the memory of a February day in 1907. While torrential rain etched the hillside above the LaRosa farm and washed away the winding dirt road that led to their two-room cottage, Maria Avita had given birth to their eighth child, Serafino. Agonizing over his inability to provide for his beloved family, Joseph had argued his fate with his God. "Lord, I have always lived as a devout Christian should. I till Your land as You intend for Your flock to do. What more do You wish from this humble farmer? Like men, my twelve-year-old Armand and ten-year-old Romeo labor in the fields and terraced hillsides. Always at my side, they are the best of workers. Why is that not enough for You to ease my burden?"

It took many weeks of backbreaking work to make the land fit to plant. The short growing season produced little, since the mild climate along the flat coastal belt and low slopes kept the summers cool and dry. When the rain did come, the parched hillsides, deforested by past generations, released sweeping maelstroms of infertile stony mud. The LaRosa farm felt the devastation before all others. For weeks on end, Joseph, Armand, and Rom labored from dawn to dusk to grow the *pomodoro, zucchini*, eggplant, and tobacco, only for the state to confiscate most of the harvest. Complaining did little good. If a farmer persisted in doing so, Giolitti's enforcers came during the night. A long time passed before the battered farmer worked his fields again...that is, if he survived the enforcers' visit at all.

So it was that every night Joseph fretted while sitting at the table, sipping his wine, and watching his children as they huddled by the hearth and prepared for bed. Eight-year-old Paolo and six-year-old Angelo grew stronger by the day and helped in the fields as much as their immature bodies permitted. Three-year-old Vincenzo and two-year-old Francesca demanded all of their mother's attention which meant that she no longer leant a hand in the fields. Neither did Louisa, who was twelve years at that time. The addition of Serafino meant that the miniaturized version of her mother bore more responsibility in the household. Still somehow she managed to care for the goats and rabbits. Such animals needed less to thrive on than conventional farm animals. Thank

God that the children had a taste for rabbit meat. Unless traded for chicken, rabbit was pretty much the only meat the LaRosa family ever ate. Maria Avita skillfully prepared it in so many different ways that the family never grew tired of it. She also made wheels of cheese from goat milk and traded them along with the extra milk and rabbit meat at the village store for eggs and other necessities.

During winter months Joseph supplemented the meager farm income with woodcarving. His natural talent allowed him to see things in wood that others did not. By simply whittling away excess material, he produced a work of art so realistic that people stopped to study the intricate detail. Every now and then wealthy inhabitants of the Salerno countryside hired him to etch ornate patterns in the doorways, cabinets, or archways of their palatial villas. Sometimes he carved statues in their exquisite gardens. Chiseling wood near spouting fountains and budding rose bushes renewed his spirit. During breaks he meandered garden pathways lined with privet hedges. Shrubs, shaped like animals and other silly things, and benches interrupted secluded lush lawns. There were times when he lingered in the early spring sunshine and imagined himself the owner of such a place.

Joseph reveled in the thought that the aristocrats paid money for something he perceived as pleasure. Not only that, the government assumed that he bartered his services for goods. Having no idea that hard cash had exchanged hands, Giolitti never saw a single lira. This pleased Joseph to no end. Since Orazio first mentioned plans about going to America, Joseph had saved most of the money, just in case he made up his mind that he too should follow his friend. The seed that Orazio had planted in the farmer's brain sprouted and as circumstances watered it, the dream of a better life grew strong.

A second letter came from America, reassuring Joseph of job opportunities and a better life. "Come, friend of my childhood," Orazio penned. "Together, we will be rich *gentiluomo* in a very short time." Joseph stowed the letter in his shirt pocket along with the first one.

Then in March 1909, Joseph and Maria Avita waved a tearful goodbye as Carlotta Bascuino and her children, Nick, Eleonora, Anna, and baby Margaret sailed out of the Port of Salerno to join Orazio and Dominico in New York. The moment was a sad one for Joseph who faced the loss of the only people other than his immediate family whom he considered close kin. With the rest of the family at his side, Orazio now had no reason to return to Italy since God had called his father Matteo home more than five years ago.

On the other hand it was a moment of triumph. Now, Joseph knew someone who had personally tested the unknown shores of America and proved that a better life waited there. Opportunity beckoned from the other side of the world, convincing the hard-working Christian that God was little by little answering his prayers. Taking His humble servant by the hand, He was guiding the way. With faith and determination, Joseph could also succeed.

As the ship that carried Carlotta and her children disappeared beyond the edge of the world, Joseph drew a deep breath. His mind was set. In order to provide the life he desired for his family, they too must leave their homeland. The dream had flowered.

* * *

Joseph had not planned to leave for another year, but protests by urban workers that summer forced him to change his mind. Giolitti had made several small concessions to accommodate the protesters, but it did not take long before he got fed up with the lot of them and sent in the enforcers. Violence ensued.

Cousin Luca had participated in the demonstrations and along with many others, got himself arrested. Somewhere along the way, Giolitti's enforcers beat the prisoner to within an inch of his life. Joseph found his cousin cowering in the corner of a filthy jail cell, bloodied and half-crippled. Chains bound wrists to shoeless feet, keeping Luca hunched over and unable to escape. The fire had gone out in his eyes though they continually darted about like that of a snared animal. His shirt and pants were tattered, and he shivered mercilessly from the dankness. Or did he tremble from the knowledge of what the future held in store for him? Through swollen, slavering lips, Luca pleaded, "*Cara mio* Joseph. You must take Maria Avita and *il bambini*. Flee Italy. Now. While there is still time."

Two days later, Joseph journeyed once again to see cousin Luca. He brought all the money he had in the world; money he had secreted away for passage to America. Perhaps, Luca could garnish freedom with it. At the very least, he might bribe the guard into providing a few extra comforts while incarcerated in that hell hole.

As Joseph neared the prison, he stopped short. Fresh bullet holes riddled the exterior walls and dried explosions of blood stained the mortar and trickled down into the soil. His eyes widened with trepidation. He wanted to turn and run from what he knew he was about to find. He forced himself onward, his heart palpitating with dread. A surly guard made no attempt to stop him.

"The cells are empty," Joseph said. "Where are the prisoners?"

"I don't know nothin'," the guard retorted.

Joseph knew better than to press the issue. There was nothing else to do. Cousin Luca had vanished without a trace, never to be seen again.

* * *

A rolling fog draped the harbor that day in late September 1909 when Joseph, Armand, and Romeo sailed for America. Joseph had kissed two-and-a-half year old Serafino on the forehead and swore that as soon as he and his two oldest sons found work and a place to live in America, the rest of the family would then join them. No more than one year would pass before the LaRosa family reunion.

Aboard the steamship Liberty, the days passed slowly. It seemed to Joseph that the horizon never changed and remained ever distant. He often glanced back at the ship's wake to reassure himself that the vessel was actually moving. Restlessness quelled only when Joseph studied the translation book that he had purchased in Salerno just before boarding the ship. Finding English difficult to learn, he blamed it on his age, but determination led to success. His sons took to the language quickly, for books were a familiar way to learn since the LaRosa family was too poor to attend school in Italy, a privilege reserved only for the affluent.

When Joseph was a child, Matteo Bascuino had sent him to school along with Orazio. Christianity compelled Matteo to take the orphan in when his parents died, but Christianity went only so far, which meant that Joseph needed to work and contribute to the Bascuino household. Consequently, he missed as much school as he attended and that stymied his education.

Maria Avita had learned to read at a young age while working as a companion for a rich English girl in Salerno. It also gave her a background in the English language. Before her own children were old enough to work in the field, she used this time to teach them reading, writing, and simple mathematics and tell them stories about life in the English household. At least with the ability to read, her children would later in life be able to teach themselves whatever they needed to know.

While working in the field, Joseph had taught his children things he learned from books and lessons in life that God had granted him. Never did it cross his mind that someday he might need to speak English. Now he looked forward to hearing all his children speak English and their being educated in America. All must graduate from high school and perhaps one or two might even go to a university and learn how to make life better for themselves as well as all Italians.

During the long voyage to New York, Rom stuck close to his father's side. Armand, on the other hand, became totally immersed in the adventure. The fifteen-year-old made friends easily, one of which was Aldo Messina who became a close associate. Tall and lanky, the sixteen-year-old came aboard with his father, Gaspare Messina, who thought it best to leave Italy after careful consideration of his connection to *il cosa nostra.* Giovanni Giolitti was quite resolved to rid Italy of this scourge that pilfered the wealth he coveted for himself. Mafia members by the droves fled to the United States, thereby avoiding persecution or even death in the black of night. One such person was Vito Cascio Ferro, the first Sicilian *Capo de Tutti Capi.* In 1901 he extended the arm of the Black Hand to America, filling his New York organization with hardened criminals and fugitives from Sicily.

Gaspare Messina, a small rotund hustler with hooded black eyes that when angered instantly terrorized their victims into submission became a welcome addition to Don Vito's family. He strongly adhered to all the rules of the organization, especially *omerta*, the code of honor and silence. Well aware of the money to be made in the United States through extortion, prostitution, and gambling, Messina foresaw bootlegging entering into the equation. If the United States government thought that people would give up drinking just by enacting laws, it was sadly mistaken. Prohibition was sure to generate waves of illegal activity from which incredible sums of money could be had for the taking.

American gangsters openly flaunted their wealth and power. Not only that, new Mafia chapters sprung up like crabgrass in the springtime, taking control of every city. Many immigrants established themselves as leaders in the New Age American Mafia. Intending to be a don himself, Gaspare set about building his army from muscle he recruited aboard the Liberty. He set his sights on Armand LaRosa, a kid with wavy, jet-black hair and Romanesque features. Built strong and impressively rugged for his age, this ruffian would come in handy in the organization. In addition, friendship with Armand might one day keep Gaspare's only son out of the line of fire. Arrogance tended to get Aldo into hot water much too often. Through Aldo, the future don enticed Armand to come under the wings of the organization.

Gaspare Messina took no interest in Romeo LaRosa since hazel eyes and curly brown hair had branded the kid immature at the outset. Little did the future Mafioso know that an innate sense of right and wrong drove the thirteen-year-old and ruled virtually every decision he ever made. A time would come when Aldo would rue his father's oversight of Romeo LaRosa.

On the second day out of port, Armand happened upon Aldo Messina, a worldly young upstart with flashy eyes and clothes that matched. His jet black hair, in desperate need of cutting, was heavily oiled and slicked back. Skillfully shuffling a deck of cards, Aldo pretended not to notice the naïve kid intently watching the action. Time to do his father's bidding. Munching on a stogie, he squinted through a gray haze that enveloped his head and asked, "Know how to play poker?"

Armand looked around. That fast-talking card dealer talking to insignificant Armand LaRosa?

Aldo gave a slight nod.

Armand swung his head side to side. "Never seen a card before in all my life."

"Shove over there, fellas," chuckled the dealer, his eyes twinkling deviously.

The two other juveniles seated next Aldo rolled their eyes and grunted. Sliding their coins along with them, they made room for another player.

"Piece o' cake," spluttered Aldo from the corner of his mouth. His teeth glistened as they clamped down on the half-spent cigar. "Name's Messina, Aldo Messina. Yours?"

"Armand LaRosa."

"Well, Armand LaRosa, let me educate ya 'bout the rules of the game. Here's a couple o' coins ta get cha goin'." Aldo snatched some coins from a pile in front of one juvenile and tossed them to Armand.

"Hey," growled the juvenile, but with one glare from Aldo, he shrank into silence.

Aldo snickered when Armand caught one coin then went scurrying for the others. "Think ya can keep a hold on 'em, LaRosa?"

"Do my best," Armand said while squatting down in the circle.

Aldo dealt the new guy in and patiently taught him how to set up a hand. The LaRosa kid quickly got the gist of it, much to Aldo's liking. As the voyage wore on and innumerable hands folded, Armand learned the fine art of winning in more devious ways.

It was inevitable that Aldo would offer Armand a cigar. Giving it a try, the thing nearly killed him. From then on smoking came easier. Not only that, the pungent stogies imbued him with a sense of esteem and power.

"LaRosa took that first smoke like a real buster," Aldo told his father later. "He don't never let nobody see him squirm. And he's picked up every trick in the book—even some I ain't got around ta teachin' him yet. No doubt about it, LaRosa's got it in his noggin to be a big-shot."

"This is good. Very good," Gaspare nodded. His lips puckered with satisfaction. "*Il cugine* willingly wades into unknown waters. Go. Fill his head with promises of adventure and wealth, for the rooster is ours for the plucking."

Strolling the deck one evening, Joseph and Rom happened upon Aldo and his gang of pubescent thugs. All were playing cards with burnt-down stogies hanging out their mouths. At first Joseph rejected the sight and turned away. Then suddenly Armand's face loomed up in his brain. His dark brows came together as Joseph looked back. His own son sat among the players. In the kid's hands, a fan of cards. And in his mouth…

Eyes of the father met the son's. Armand yanked the cigar out of his mouth and chucked it behind his back. Snuffing it out against the wall, he stuffed it into his jacket pocket.

"Armand," Joseph snapped. "It is time for the English lesson."

"Yeah, Pop. Comin' right away," Armand stammered. Bumbling to his feet, he followed his father. But just before rounding the corner, the kid glanced back and blinked to his companions. "Back soon," he mouthed.

Aldo smiled and nodded.

"Armand," Joseph sternly rebuked his oldest son. "I wish for you not to do such things nor keep the company of those who do. It is not good for a respectable Christian man and shines poorly upon his family. Use your head wisely, my son."

"Yeah, Pop," Armand muttered with his head bent. He swaggered along, swaying back and forth. He pulled up his collar and stuffed his hands into his trouser pockets. His fingers fondled the coins stashed there.

Staying awake that night was easy since Armand had always been a night owl. He patiently listened for the steady breathing of his father and brother. After a time he figured that they had dozed off, but gave it an extra ten minutes or so. The old man began to snore. Yeah, they were definitely asleep. Time to go. He sat up. His cot chirped. He froze. No reaction from Pop—whew. Wait…what is that? Eyes. Glistening in the darkness, they belonged to Rom.

Armand put his index finger to his mouth and pretended to shush his brother as silently he bent to pick up his shoes. Lifting his jacket from the bottom of his cot, he got to his feet and tiptoed out the door. His hand followed the walls as he ascended the pitch-black stairway.

Once outside, Armand stuffed his jacket under his armpit and put on his shoes. Straightening his clothes and picking off lint the same way Aldo Messina did, he crossed the deck to the rail. He drew out the cigar that he had snuffed out earlier and clenching it between his teeth, cupped his hands against the wind to relight it. Tossing the match into the following sea, the foolish young man belched out a cloud of gray. He gazed up at the full moon waxing over a pewter sea where minuscule whitecaps shimmered like the diamonds he foresaw in his future. Taking a shallow drag, Armand turned and strutted off to join Aldo's all-night card game.

* * *

As the voyage wore on, Joseph became quite concerned about his oldest son. Every time he turned around, Armand was keeping company with that Aldo fella and that bunch of hooligans. No matter what Joseph did, what he said, he could not keep the reins pulled in on Armand. Might those young hoodlums blacken the boy's heart against his father and his family? No, Joseph let go of the thought. That was not possible. His son was God-fearing and respected his father too much to do such a dastardly thing. Both Armand and Rom shared the same deep sense of family that Joseph felt. They knew that for their family to reunite within a year, all three incomes must pour into one bucket out of which dribbled food and rent money for themselves, passage for seven more LaRosas left behind in Italy, and somewhere in the dregs of this leaky bucket, something to send to Maria Avita and the six children on which to live. The three tickets to America that Joseph had purchased for himself, Armand, and Rom left precious little money for Maria Avita. And the rainy season was just beginning.

In spite of everything, high hopes spurred Joseph onward. He intended to send for his family the moment he obtained a furnished home that provided a private bedroom for Maria Avita and himself as well as a bedroom for the two girls and at least one bedroom for the six boys. This would make arrival in America an immediate improvement over Italy. A better lifestyle justified leaving their place of origin and what little family history there was. Joseph vowed to his God to work twenty-four hours a day to see this happen. His family must reunite in as short a time as possible.

Joseph had not spent one night apart from Maria Avita since the day of their marriage seventeen years earlier. At that time he was one month away from his nineteenth birthday and she was a mere seventeen. She was the most beautiful creature he had ever set eyes upon. So petite and innocent to the world around her, her smile lit up his life. Her hair was blacker than the starless night. Her eyes sparkled like the smooth sheen of mined coal.

How life had changed. The love that Joseph and Maria Avita believed was the strongest possible between two people had fooled them. Day by day, year after year, their love and trust grew stronger. Every struggle that they had survived while starting and raising their family drew them closer. Together, they had conquered every challenge until now. Now, a vast ocean was coming between Joseph and Maria Avita. Unable to cleave to each other, only their hearts could sustain them.

Chapter 4

A week out of port, the tempest struck. Time and time again, Neptune pitched the crowded Liberty from one hand to the other while blowing torrents of rain across her deck. With thunderous laughter, he hurled lightning bolts across the dark volcanic sky. Nauseated passengers prayed for an end to his prank. Thirty-six hours passed before the god of the sea tuckered out and sank back into the shadowy depths for repose.

During Neptune's folly, Joseph avoided the living quarters below as much as possible. The times when he had no other choice, his stomach turned from the inescapable odor of vomit, excrement, and human squalor. Most of the passengers, averse to being strapped into cots which prevented the roll of the vessel from dumping them onto the floor, flopped about on the floor or propped themselves up against the walls. With skin pallid and clammy and eyes dark and sunken, the poor souls took on the appearance of death itself. After sixteen days the stench on the Liberty had become so unbearable that Joseph and Rom spent long hours roaming the open deck. Wearing multiple layers of clothing, they tried to keep warm, but still the north wind stole their body heat. The brisk sea air that chilled their lungs kept queasiness at bay, yet no gale could blow powerfully enough to remove the odor that permeated the fibers of their clothing. At times the penetrating blast became too much to bear so Joseph and Rom retreated into the putrescence below deck. Armand was not there. Rarely did he keep company with his father and brother.

Then one day it happened. As Joseph and Rom ascended the dimly lit stairwell into the brightness of day, a shout rang out, "America! America!"

Their eyes met. Could it be? At last?

A cacophony of immigrant voices shouted, "America! America! America!"

Mayhem broke loose. Passengers from the decks below flooded the main deck where only moments before one or two solitary figures had braved the elements. Hats of every description flew into the air and disappeared into Liberty's wake. Endless days of misery drowned with them, never to be resuscitated from a watery grave.

Elbowing through the jubilant crowd, Rom and Joseph stood at the bow and squinted into the bone-chilling wind. Their cheeks tingled, their eyes watered as the speck of New York City in the haze ahead grew larger and larger, closer and closer.

"Pop!" Rom shouted above the hullabaloo. "We made it! Whaddaya think about that?"

Tongue-tied, Joseph nodded. Excitement and wonder welled up and overflowed in the moisture that trickled down the side of his face. He fought back emotion, but the excitement of fellow passengers infected his soul. So as the steamship passed the Statue of Liberty, Joseph laughed. He cried. He cheered along with the rest of the immigrants. Unexpectedly, his eyes fell upon several who had bent their heads in silent prayer. He too must pray. So the religious zealot issued up his prayer. "Thank you, Lord, for smiling favorably upon your humble servants, for allowing Joseph, Armand, and Rom LaRosa to reach this destination unscathed. And may St. Anthony watch over Maria Avita and the rest of my children. Amen."

"Amen," echoed Rom.

With every passing moment the New York skyline loomed taller and more monstrous. The hubbub of tugs, barges, and freighters, weaving in and out of the harbor, left Joseph and Rom awestruck. One massive liner, painted glossy black with white trim, dwarfed the Liberty as it sailed out to the open sea. Red and gold letters of a language Joseph did not know embossed its bow. A diminutive fishing boat became trapped between that ship and the Liberty. With its wind taken, the sails luffed. The untethered boom swung from side to side. Lying dead, the boat pitched about in the chop created by the myriad of vessels. The fishermen struggled to trim sails that had no wind and unsuccessfully navigated a vessel that had no steerage.

"Wanna trade places with those *povero pescatore*?" Rom poked his father.

Ignoring the question, Joseph impatiently asked, "Where in God's name is your brother? He should be with family at a time such as this."

"Don't know, Pop," Rom replied. Hooking one leg over the rail, he raised himself above the crowd and scanned the ship. "Over there, Pop. With Aldo."

"Go and get him."

The steamship with its anxious cargo turned north onto the Hudson River. Shortly thereafter, inspectors from the Immigration Service boarded the anchored Liberty and immediately quarantined the vessel. Several hours passed before they deemed it eligible to dock at Ellis Island. As shuttle boats sidled up against Liberty, the crowd held Joseph and his two sons pinned against the rail. First and second class passengers, dressed in their best finery, disembarked first while cabin hands followed close behind bearing trunks on their backs. Legalized by the Immigration Inspectors in the privacy of their cabins, those passengers never set foot on Ellis Island. The shuttles took them directly into Manhattan.

Yet Joseph felt no resentment that he as well as all others who traveled third class or steerage must go through processing on Ellis Island. No, the privileges given first and second class passengers mattered nothing. The only thing that meant anything at all was that he was here…in America!

The words of several passengers, "Ellis Island, Isle of Tears," echoed in Joseph's ears. "Empowered officers have the right to detain those they deem as undesirable aliens. After interrogation and inspection, anyone they choose can be turned away from America's doorstep." Joseph shivered. The long perilous journey might be for naught. Still, since the overwhelming majority of immigrants processed were eventually admitted, Ellis Island deserved the name, Isle of Hope. "Indeed, it will be 'Isle of Hope' for the LaRosa family," Joseph proclaimed to the wind.

When at long last the steamship Liberty docked, Joseph and Rom scrutinized the island. Three parallel rows of buildings that had to be at least a quarter mile long crossed a perpendicular row on each side and one row in the center. "Some of those structures resemble the Byzantine and French Renaissance architecture I saw in books while growing up in the Bascuino household," said Joseph.

"The buildings look sturdy enough. Probably fireproof, too," said Rom.

"And well they should be, considering the tide of people coming and going all the time." Joseph smiled, pleased that one of his sons had inherited his keen eye for detail.

Tension built. Immigrants pushed and shoved. Children wailed as canyon walls of adults contracted about their insignificant bodies and suffocated them. Men swung the children onto their shoulders and funneled toward the narrow gangways.

"We will stand aside, my sons, and wait until those thoughtless people disembark," said Joseph. "Being anxious is no excuse to forget one's Christianity and cause harm to others."

In the registry room, or as Joseph heard someone call it, the Great Hall, the LaRosa men gaped at the vaulted ceiling high above their heads. The polished Spanish tiles beneath their feet felt smooth and solid, a stark contrast to the rough rolling decks they had become accustomed to throughout the last sixteen days. They soon discovered that if they stood in one place too long, the room swayed as though they were back on board the Liberty. Shaking off the sensation, Joseph pointed to an archway and said, "My sons, walking beneath there marks the beginning of a new life of freedom and opportunity for the entire LaRosa family."

Dirty and smelly from their long voyage, the three LaRosa men stood proud. Just like the three to four thousand other people who had arrived that same day, they eagerly awaited the beginning of a new life in America.

"So many people," Rom said. "Where do they all come from?"

"Places like Italy where God-fearing men are afraid to speak their minds and cannot provide for their families," said Joseph.

A hawkish guard motioned for them to take a place at the end of one of the numerous long lines. Listening to impassive interpreters, Rom nudged Joseph. "Never heard any of those languages. What are they, Pop?"

"German, Spanish, Polish, Italian, Greek, Russian."

"Amazing. They actually understand one another. Can you beat that, Armand?"

Armand was ignoring his brother and father. Instead, his eyes scanned the room searching for familiar faces.

Uniformed physicians of the U.S. Public Health Service thumbed through paperwork then poked and prodded the immigrants. They searched for evidence of harmful diseases, mental abnormalities, or debilitating physical conditions that might present a health menace. At the very least immigrants should not pose any burden to the American taxpayer. All newcomers had to be able to support themselves. Inspectors detained and chalked those whom they wished to examine further. Code letters indicated the reason for the holdover. K for hernia. L for lung. E for eye. H for heart. X for mental disorder.

A cranky heavy-set nurse with stern, bristling eyebrows and a rolling rump herded several dejected newcomers out of the area. Joseph speculated that those individuals would find themselves before a board of review that decided whether immigrants remained in the United States or got sent back to their county of origin. Unexpected fear bolted through his entire being. His stomach turned as if he still rode the stormy sea. Was this also his fate? What if Rom and Armand are accepted but not him? A brusque Immigration Officer interrupted his thoughts. "You there. Seeking religious freedom, political liberty, or economic opportunity?"

Joseph's lips quivered, "Uhm, political liberty, *Signore*," then hastily added, "And economic opportunity, of course."

"Of course," the Immigration Officer repeated dryly.

After completing the medical examination, Joseph, his sons, and scores of others from the Liberty assembled at the opposite end of the Great Hall. Immigration Bureau officers called out names from the ship's manifest. Verifying the list, inspectors asked each immigrant numerous questions concerning gender, marital status, and occupation. Joseph answered the questions, ones he had already answered several times during this long tiring day. "Where were you born? Where did you last reside? Where are you going? Who paid your passage? Do you have $25 on you? Do you have sufficient funds or a relative to sustain you? Have you ever been in prison or a mental institution?"

Difficulty with communication slowed the documentation process to a snail's pace, forcing Joseph and his sons to stay overnight in dormitories that housed would-be Americans. Medical, mental, or financial reasons detained some while others remained for the same reason as Joseph, Rom, and Armand—the day had simply come to an end.

The LaRosa men took showers, the first in weeks. Even though the water was tepid, it felt phenomenal as the sixteen-day voyage sheeted off their bodies and swirled down the gurgling drain. Afterward, they put on clean clothes donated by the missions of New York City. As they stuffed their dirty clothing into the bags containing the extras they had brought with them from Italy, the odor of the ship and vomit overpowered them. "Whew! What a stink," Rom gagged.

"The only thing that stands any chance at removing that nasty odor is Carlotta Bascuino's homemade lye soap," grumbled Joseph.

"Yeah. That stuff could unstink a skunk," laughed Rom.

"All immigrants," an officer hollered. "Form a single line and follow me."

At the entry of the huge mess hall, Rom exclaimed, "Will ya look at this joint! Such a big room just to eat in."

"It will be good to sit and eat with my legs under a table. It has been much too long a time," griped Joseph.

"Aw, come on, Pop," Rom elbowed his father. "All you need is a full stomach and a good night's sleep. Just like the rest of us."

All of a sudden, Joseph felt as though he was the youngster and Rom was the elder. He did not resist for he had no strength to do so. That night, the three LaRosa men slept in cots made up with clean linens and green woolen blankets. It didn't matter that so many others also occupied the room. With their bodies clean, their stomachs full, and their feet on solid ground, the whole slew of them slept like the dead.

The next day, refreshed and raring to go, Joseph, Armand, and Rom returned to the Great Hall. Hours passed. Finally, an officer handed cards to Joseph, Rom, and Armand.

"Says here, 'Admitted,'" Rom said. His face instantly brightened. "Pop! We're in!"

With a mixture of relief and joy, Joseph huffed, "Well, it is about time. Let's get outta here."

After exchanging Italian currency for American, they boarded the ferry bound for Manhattan. Upon arrival, people of all colors and nationalities whom they had never seen before distracted their attention.

"Joey! Over here," waved Orazio Bascuino frantically. Grinning from ear-to-ear, he jostled through sea of passengers who were disembarking from innumerable vessels. Four of his children followed close behind Orazio; two held a death grip on his coattail.

"Keep up, keep up, *bambini mio*. No you losa you faddah," clucked Carlotta Bascuino while jostling three-year-old Margaret in her arms.

When Joseph spotted his long-time friends, tears of happiness welled in his eyes. The bond he shared with the Bascuino family, which had begun in a country quickly fading from memory, remained intact. He threw his muscular arms around Orazio and immediately sensed that his short sprightly friend had put on a fair amount of weight. A good sign indeed.

"How is the tailoring business?" Joseph asked anxiously. "Will there be work for me and my sons? How is it to earn money? Should I rely on carpentry or go to the country to farm?"

"Patience, Joey, patience," laughed Orazio. "No longer do I tailor."

Joseph took a step back. "What? There is no work for tailors?"

"I can tailor, that is if I choose to. But I find my abilities are put to better use in the furniture business."

"Making furniture? But…"

"Me and Dominico, we have just been offered jobs in Massachusetts. East Boston. This from the man we work for since first setting foot upon this wondrous ground."

"Mr. Allesandro Giacopirazzi, that is his name," piped up Dom. "He has recently purchased a warehouse in East Boston."

Orazio elbowed Joseph. "Ey, the boss say to me just this very morning, 'Orazio. Time comes to make my business bigger. You and Dom are the right persons to turn the shell of that waterfront building into a great manufacturing factory.' Dom and me, we know how to make it successful. He say those words right at me. Whaddaya think about that, eh?"

"*Buono, buono, amico mio*," Joseph laughed and heartily shook Orazio's hand.

"You will come, too. And Rom and Armand," insisted Orazio slapping Joseph on the back. "Mr. Giacopirazzi say to me, hire workers I pick myself. So I hire you…and your two strong sons. Right now, this very day."

"This opportunity is extremely unusual," Joseph said.

"Hey, *paesani mio*, this is America. Unusual things happen here all the time."

Joseph pursed his lips and contemplated the words of his trusted friend. A moment later, he nodded. "*Si*. This, Orazio, we do together."

"No, Pop. Not me." Armand shook his head while backing away from the group.

"What?" The smile vanished from Joseph's face.

"I choose to stay in New York with my friend Aldo. Gaspare Messina has already lined up work for him and me. And the others, too."

"No," Joseph sternly insisted. "I say you go to East Boston with me. We will all work there. Do not repay Orazio's kindness this way."

Armand shook his head, "No. New York is the place for me."

"It is not safe for you here!"

"Don't worry about it, Pop. I am OK. Today, I begin to earn money. That's right, today! And I'll send money to you…for Mama and the others. too."

"No, no." Joseph lunged for Armand. Grappling for any piece of his son, he bellowed. "You go with me this moment!"

It was too late. The kid had edged away, far beyond his father's reach.

"Aldo's over there," Armand pointed. "Gotta go. See ya, Pop."

In the blink of an eye, the fifteen-year-old ran off with Aldo Messina who seemed to appear out of nowhere. Several other young punks, all immigrants from the steamship Liberty, chased after Aldo and Armand.

As the great cleft mouth of New York City swallowed up his eldest son, Joseph stood there, helpless.

Chapter 5

In the dusky winter light, snowflakes wafted this way and that as if they had nowhere to go. The weather and lengthy days added to the bleak mood that engulfed Joseph LaRosa since awakening from a death-like sleep. He longed for his beloved Maria Avita and children, but events beyond his control and the passage of time were stealing the image of their faces and his native Italy. He never should have left them. His vacant eyes scanned the musty third-floor bedroom. An inadequate stone foundation had caused the building to continually settle, buckling interior walls and twisting brittle wallpaper until it had split in places. Because the floor sagged, a five-drawer bureau, haphazardly painted an unflattering avocado brown, leaned forward from the far wall. To the right of the bed, a paint-laden door scraped the floor every time it opened and closed. One door of the oak wardrobe remained unlatched and half-opened due to weakened hinges, revealing a meager supply of clothing that scarcely occupied the space inside. Rippled linoleum that had lost its sheen and most of the floral design covered the center of the floor. Along the outer edges unfinished planking invited splinters so Joseph did not dare to go barefoot. No matter. The room was too drafty anyway.

Every time Orazio came to visit, he insisted, "In a year or two, you and me, Joey, we will turn this place into a real palace."

At the risk of insulting his old friend, Joseph avoided telling him that repairing this place was going to be a very big job and take a whole lot of money. Joseph would do what he had to though, for he felt a great obligation to repay Orazio and Carlotta for helping him out during this time of healing. Yet Joseph hated the thought of dipping into the money that he had saved to bring Maria Avita and the children to America. In her letter she had written that conditions in Italy were dire. How could he write and tell her that it was going to take longer to send for them than he had promised?

Joseph fidgeted. He wished Carlotta would come in to talk with him. But she had her hands full with housework, five children, and Orazio. Like everyone else in this industrious society, she was too busy with other concerns than to indulge in idle chatter. When she brought his meals, she always fluffed up his pillows and chattered on and on in Italian about Maria Avita, the children, and Italy. Hearing her speak their native language gave him incredible peace and always made him smile. Once he had asked her why she did not speak English. With a wistful hand gesture, she had brushed off the question in broken English. "In time, in time. I pick it up when I go. That is a way will it be. Is no time for to learn more quick me."

His hand scraped an unshaven chin then plopped onto the bed that held him prisoner. He shifted his weight until his lame bones settled on the dilapidated mattress that sagged in the middle. His leg might heal, but by that time, his back would surely be broken. He punched his pillow into a ball and leaned against it. His mind conjured up the dusty image of the primitive two-room cottage that he and Maria Avita had built all by themselves. Little satisfaction came from the thought as he muttered, "So capable then, look at me now."

Nestled in the shadows of the hillside, the stone and mortar structure overlooked the Gulf of Salerno on the Tyrrhenian Sea. In the heat of summer or in the wind-driven sleet of unforgiving winters, Joseph had trudged the long gravel lane that rambled up to the rough-hewn door that opened on leather hinges. On the other side, sanctuary. Everything wrong in the world had vanished in a heartbeat as the door closed behind him.

On the opposite wall of the great room that served as kitchen and living area, Maria Avita was scurrying about, preparing the evening meal at the open hearth that stretched floor to ceiling and wall to wall opposite the door. Taking down one of the pots that hung from the metal bar above her head, she caused the remaining pots to clang together in a tumultuous sonata. "Ah, to hear that again," Joseph sighed.

He imagined his wife taking bread from the beehive oven, one of the finest ever built in the region. Many countrymen journeyed to this room to view the wonder and ask Joseph how they too might build such a magnificent oven. Maria Avita made it her duty to indulge the visitors with the most delectable baked goods found in all of Italy.

Years of burning wood for cooking and heating had created a thick layer of creosote on the ceiling where a single oil lamp, centered in the middle, provided most of the light. Three lanterns and candles provided additional illumination throughout the house and outside at night.

Off to the side of the hearth, a clothesline sagged with drying laundry and clothes still dripping the day's rain onto the stone floor. Homespun concealed the bedroom where the entire family slept on crude cots that he had fashioned himself. Additional fabric, stretched across ropes, provided a modest sense of privacy between the cots. It wasn't much. Nevertheless, he could lie there with Maria Avita in his arms and listen to the steady breathing of their eight children. He was able to distinguish each one. His two babies, Serafino and Francesca, contentedly squeaked while their tiny fingernails scraped the sheets. Barely discernible, Louisa breathed soft and even, just like her mother. On the other hand Angelo and Armand snored with great abandon, at times disturbing the entire household. Rom snored, but nowhere near as loud. Paolo slept with his mouth wide open and every so often, slurped back the drool that oozed out the corner of his mouth. Lastly, Vincenzo tossed and turned and mumbled in his sleep. Joseph found this strange since the boy spoke very little and was somewhat lethargic when awake. Joseph and his wife filled the darkness with whispers of wonderful things for their children. Things they both knew would never happen. Never happen…never…

Coming back to himself, Joseph gestured toward heaven. "Lord? Will you ever let me outta this infernal torture chamber?"

Joseph scolded himself for not being a good Christian, for Allesandro Giacopirazzi had generously given this house to Orazio Bascuino, the new manager of his furniture business in East Boston. Furthermore, Orazio insisted that Joseph and Rom live on the third floor until Maria Avita and the children arrived. He charged only minimal rent, enough that Joseph would not feel like a beggar. Located less than an eighth of a mile from Boston Harbor, the Bascuino home fronted Maverick Street within minutes of the ferry that crossed the Charles River to the North End. The trip was well worth the cost of two cents. "Two cents," Joseph brooded. "That's all. Except lying here, a broken piece of humanity, I am incapable of earning even a measly two cents. God," he moaned and turned his face to the wall. "Why did this have to happen to me? Now, when I was so close to bringing *tutta la famiglia* together again?"

He had fooled himself into thinking that he could handle this migration without any problem. The separation from Orazio and his family had wrenched apart his insides, but being apart from Maria Avita and his other six children made him feel dead. Will the LaRosas ever be all together again? This had all been one big mistake.

"Hey, Pop. How ya doin'?" Rom trumpeted as he stuck his head in the door.

"Eh…" Joseph winced. His eyes remained unfocused on the faded and tattered wallpaper that had come apart at the seams.

"Pop! Ya made the morning papers." Rom gushed, ignoring his father's gloominess. "Hey, lemme read some o' this stuff to ya. Says here, 'Immigrant saves son of prominent family. Joseph LaRosa, recently arrived from Italy, snatched six-year-old Antonio Messina out of harm's way as a crazed mare that had just thrown its rider bore down upon the unsuspecting child.' Waddaya think about that, Pop? You're a hero!"

"Eh…"

Rom was puzzled. He had never seen his father so downright listless. Not a flicker of the old spark lit the man's sunken eyes and his jet black hair, always neatly combed, was anything but that today. It was oily, tangled, and unwashed, the same as his unshaven face. "Wassa matter witcha, Pop?"

"Waddaya think, eh?" Joseph recoiled as indignant hazel eyes and solid onyx brows hurled piercing vengeance at the son. "How am I gonna send for your Mamma? And your brothers and sisters? Eh? I cannot work like this. See this mangled leg? What am I s'posed ta do about that, eh?"

"Calm down, Pop. Calm down. Listen ta me, will ya? Everythin's gonna be OK."

"Aargh!" Joseph slapped his open hand onto the bed and became more hostile because the blankets had muffled his fury.

"That high mucky-muck Carmelo Messina? He pays all the bills. Medical bills, rent, food, everything. And some extra for us, too. Face it, Pop. A lot of what you earned went for food and rent anyway."

"Humph," muttered Joseph unwilling to admit that the kid was right. "If only that jojo brother of yours was here instead of wasting his time in New York with those hoodlum friends of his."

"Let's not get into that again, OK? What is done is done. Anyway, we got money from Armand just last week. Don't cha remember, Pop? A whole lot of it, too! His entire week's pay; that's what he says in the letter. He'll send more. Just wait and see. Armand wants Mama here, too. You know that." It felt like a slap in the face when his father rolled his eyes and groaned. Rom cracked his knuckles. Frustration built. His eyes fled to the ceiling. What could he say or do to bring his father back to his old optimistic self? He gawked at his father, a limp, dispirited old wretch. "Listen ta me, Pop. Been doin' lotsa thinkin', an' I got this whole thing figured. That leg of yours needs six more weeks to heal, so I will work extra. With my wages and Messina's money, there's gonna be enough to send for Mama and the children by then."

Joseph remained motionless refusing to hear a single word.

Rom's brows came together. Out of patience, he blasted, "You ain't got no faith in me, do ya, Pop?"

Silence.

The kid turned away. His foot scuffed the plank floor while his knuckles cackled. His hands jammed his hips as Rom spun around and faced his father. The fire of his mother blazed from his eyes. "You wait! I'll show ya! You ain't never gonna ever see nobody work as hard as me! I'll show ya!" He flung the paper at his father and stomped out of the bedroom. The oak door slammed, sending tremors throughout the building and making the wardrobe totter precariously.

The clamor shook Joseph from despondency. His eyes fixed on the closed door then fell to the pages of the newspaper strewn about the bed. Stunned by his son's brash behavior, he nudged the pages, one by one, onto the floor. A smile germinated across his face. For a fourteen-year-old, Rom certainly bore the bold determination of a grown man. How quickly he had taken to East Boston and his job at Bascuino's furniture factory. Compared to working on the farm, the generous income was an entirely new concept. Hard cash for long hours of work, free from Giolitti's slimy grasp, gave both the LaRosa men a tremendous sense of accomplishment. At the end of every week, Rom happily turned over every last penny of his pay to his father. There was not one single hint of resentment. Joseph grinned. "Such a good Christian son."

Their arrival in East Boston could not have been timed better. The opportunity to earn good money for the talent Joseph possessed flourished. Through the years, Noddle, Hog, Governor's, Bird, and Apple Islands had been connected and extended through filling operations that made the island known as East Boston a center for the marine industry. Some of America's most famous clipper ships, including the world-famous Flying Cloud which broke the established record for a voyage around Cape Horn, called the Port of East Boston home. Industry had become as diverse and abundant as the immigrants who settled there. Pottery manufacturing, canned goods and preserving, fish-curing and packing, and coal docks employed thousands. The need for more and more workers brought about a great demand for housing. Old sea captains' manses were converted into triple-deckers where immigrants like Carlotta and Orazio opened mom-and-pop businesses on the first floors and lived on the second floors. Quite often, relatives or Italian employees rented the third floors. Carpenters were in short supply, so in addition to working for Orazio at the furniture factory, Joseph took on side jobs. No longer did he till the land. He earned a living in carpentry. But all that had changed in less than a heartbeat. Now, Joseph lay in bed, his leg molded in cement, unable to work.

Drawing a deep labored breath, he reached under the pillow and grasped the letter from Maria Avita. He held the tattered envelope close to his eyes and fingered it as if somehow it was his wife in the flesh. The feel of it, the smell of it became her body. Her melodic voice moved within him, and as it drifted away, Joseph grew more lifeless. Only her caress could heal the broken man. He imagined her hand, its gentle touch penning the words written on the paper. His thumb and forefinger wedged open the envelope and drew out the pages. He laid them flat, careful not to tear the brittle folds that had been opened and closed more often than could be counted. Irrepressible sadness stole over his soul. If he could not touch Maria Avita, at least, he could read the written words that came from her heart. Words that once were a part of her.

November 1909

Mi Amore Joseph,

The cold season comes early this year. The rain falls heavier and more often than in many years. Mud and rock creep steadily down the barren hillside. More than half the fertile ground now lies beneath the flow. The children and I will have much to do before *il pomodoro* and *zucchini* grow next season.

Despite the raw dampness, we are well. Most nights, no fire heats the hearth. Wood has become more scarce than ever. Each day Paolo and Angelo search about the countryside for anything that will burn. They are absent most of the day and return exhausted with only an armful or two of wet sticks that refuse to kindle.

A terrible storm blew through the Gulf of Salerno. The wind and rain lasted for days. The cottage shook so hard that a corner of the roof over the bedroom lifted. I repaired it as best I could but still it leaks. The gale blew out the lighthouse lamp, causing a ship to run against the rocks. The children and I hurried to pick up much of the splinters that littered the shoreline before the villagers learned of it. Now, nothing remains. May God forgive me, for I find myself wishing for another shipwreck so that fire will once again warm our hearth.

Father Sandro comes around often. Perhaps you remember him. He is the young priest assigned to our parish just days before you left for America. A day does not pass that he fails to ask about you. He insists that your reasons for leaving Italy are selfish indeed and does not allow me to forget that when you send money, the Church still looks for our tithe. I tell Father Sandro that I have received no word from you. The one time I did, he told Giolitti's people. Of this I am more than sure, because the very next day three enforcers knocked upon our door and demanded to see your letter.

Grazia Dio, you wrote that you had no money to send me. That made the enforcers angry and they took their leave. Still, our children trembled long into the night. I told our old friend, Rafaele, about the enforcers. He now hides all our mail from everyone including the children. This, because he fears one of them might innocently speak about your letter and it will become the knowledge of the wrong people. Rafaele makes it a point to place the mail in my hand only. He tells me that he does the very same thing for many of our neighbors. We are truly fortunate to have such a postman as a friend.

Father Sandro makes me terribly uneasy. He comes around more often than is necessary and charms our daughter. The fickle blood that inflames the veins of thirteen-year-olds prods Louisa to take to his attention without caution. I constantly remind her that soon she will reunite with Dominico Bascuino in America. Louisa looks forward to that day, this I am sure. But then Father Sandro comes to our door, and once again, the silly girl becomes the butterfly that flits amid blossoms in the springtime.

Mi amore, I miss you more than I can bear. Never have I known such emptiness. Please, Joseph, I beg of you, make our time apart short. It matters not to me that when the children and I arrive on America's soil, the only possessions we have will be the clothes on our backs. We will manage somehow. We always have. You know that, *caro marito mio*. So please send for us without delay. Do not wait one moment longer.

May Saint Anthony watch over you,

Maria Avita

Chapter 6

Night Phantom stole past the primitive two-room cottage nestled against the hillside overlooking the Tyrrhenian Sea. His black cloak mastered the heavens until the final instant when Dawn cast it off and ordered the apparition begone. A bone-chilling day emerged. No sunrise came. Only rain.

Maria Avita left her bed earlier than usual. Sleep had been nonexistent during the long night, for the incessant pelting on the roof seemed to portend demise for the LaRosa family. There were times when she had cried out for Joseph, but his voice never answered. Careful not to disturb the children, she tiptoed into the main room and out of habit slipped on her clothes in front of the hearth. The hearth was cold, like so many times this rainy season. There was not enough dry wood to keep the fire from going out during the night. Nothing warmed the dank homestead. And she was powerless to do anything about it.

Slipping out the door, Maria Avita covered her head with her shawl and scurried to the enclosure. Whipped by the north wind, the driving rain that had scored the stark countryside had changed into raw drizzle. Water pooled over the muddy ground and washed away in streams. No signs of struggle remained in front of the rabbit cage. Nor blood.

She straddled a puddle of water as she dressed off four rabbits; one for the family meal and three to take into town. The meat would provide a pretext for going into the village, though the real mission was to find out the arrival of the next boat to America without raising suspicion. In the past she had often traded rabbit meat, goat milk, and homemade goat cheese for eggs and other things at the store. This time there was no cheese to trade, and the milk she had saved for the children was almost gone. Last week she had handed over all the goats to the government as payment for the right to live on the farm.

Returning to the cottage she cut up the carcasses and let them soak in salt water. Anxiously she waited for the rain to let up before setting out for the village. She busied herself with washing blood and muck from garments worn the previous night. She could not bring herself to mend or wash Louisa's torn skirt. Instead, she poured lamp oil all over it and burned it in the fireplace along with the bloody club. She stoked the fire with every bit of kindling in the house, whether dry or not. When that turned to embers, she searched out other combustibles. Few pieces of furniture remained—the cabinet that held the set tubs, the table, the chairs. Her ebony eyes narrowed. There was Louisa's apron, neatly folded across the back of one chair; the chair where Father Sandro had sat. The vision of the young priest having his way with her daughter once again ignited the furor within Maria Avita. It festered. She stiffened. Her fists clenched. Suddenly she stormed the chair and smashed it against the hearth. She hurled the pieces into the dying embers. Instantly the fire flared, plastering a searing glow upon her face. Abruptly she turned and stomped back to the sink where she grabbed garments and scrubbed. Harder. She crushed them against the washboard. Pounding. Through gnashing teeth, hot breath surged, "Touch my child? No. This is not done. Priest…baahh," she spat into the red mucky water. "No! *Porco!*"

The legs of the metal tub thumped and screeched over the stone floor louder and louder. The pounding of her heart kept beat as the profane concerto swelled to an impenitent crescendo.

"Mama?"

Maria Avita froze in place. Her breath stopped. Louisa! Trying to conceal her madness, she drew a shallow breath and turned. "Louisa…you are awake!"

Pale and silent, the girl stood there hunched over with one arm limp at her side and one hand clutching the blanket wrapped about her shoulders. Her eyes wide and round, she looked as if at that very moment the violation were once again upon her.

Maria Avita avoided going to her child, though her heart ached to do just that. To touch meant revealing the fear laced with anger that quivered her body. Instead, she quickly rinsed and wrung out the clothes. "Here. Help me hang up these clothes, *per favore*."

They worked in silence. When Maria Avita finished, she noticed that Louisa had not yet managed to pin one single thing to the line. In the girl's hand was the blouse she had worn last night. Struggling for words, the mother said, "Here. Give that to me. I will hang it over here where there is more space. Today, you will wear your church clothes. I have noticed that the skirt you wear lately has become too short and there was no hem left to lengthen it, so I tore it into cleaning rags." Maria Avita lied, for her daughter would never see any sign of that skirt again. It had already burned into cinders. "When the rain stops, I am going into the village. Take care of your sister and brothers while I am gone. And make sure the all chores get done. Now I must wash and change my clothes." She kissed her daughter's forehead and ran her fingertips softly across the youthful cheek, devoid of wrinkles but wracked with anguish. Tears swelled when her daughter rested the side of her face in the palm of the mother's hand. Placing her other hand upon the girl's head, Maria Avita was about to whisper words of comfort when banging rattled the door. Their eyes met then riveted on the door. The mother wrapped her arm around her frightened child and whispered, "It will be all right. Open the door. No matter who is there, you must say nothing."

Tenuously, Louisa cracked open the door and took a peek. Two of Giolitti's officers stood there. One tipped his cap and said, "*Buon giorno, Signorina.*"

"Come in," called Maria Avita.

The girl stepped back and pushed open the door. A clutter of saturated wood pulp, where once had been a pile of driftwood, crushed against the wall.

"What brings you out on such a dreadful morning?" Maria Avita asked while wiping her hands on her dirty wet apron.

A short officer with a balding pate rimmed in white entered, followed by a tall, robust officer. Straightening himself after passing beneath the low doorframe, the latter caught sight of the stains on the woman's apron. "We are looking for Father Sandro," he said.

"*Dio mio*. Is something wrong?" Pretending to show concern, Maria Avita was well aware that the officer had detected the blood splattered on her apron. Feeling herself flush with the deception, she quickly returned to the sink where rabbit carcasses were soaking in salted water. Making sure that the officers were watching, she painstakingly removed and placed each piece on a clean cloth. As the cloth wicked up the moisture, it turned pink, so the officer dismissed her spotted apron and directed his attention elsewhere. By that time the heat that had reddened her face subsided, but her armpits had become damp and sticky despite the chilly air.

"The priest is missing," said the short officer. "He did not say Mass this morning and his bed has not been slept in this night past."

"I saw Father Sandro," called an unexpected small voice.

Maria Avita spun around. Paolo! As the eleven-year-old pushed aside the homespun that draped the bedroom door, her heart raced. He was walking toward Giolitti's men. There was no way to stop him. What should she do? What was Paolo going to say? She had to distract the officers. With great clamor she yanked out a chair and spewed, "Here, sit, *per favor*. You are both soaked to the skin. I will make coffee."

"No, no. *Grazie, Signora.*" The tall officer waved her off. "It is imperative that we find the priest." He leaned his gaunt frame over Paolo. "Where did you see Father Sandro, my son?"

"Halfway down the lane, *Signore.* Just last night. He spoke only to himself. Angelo and I waved and called out to him, but Father Sandro acted as though he did not see us."

"Perhaps the priest meditated," the other officer speculated. He looked for agreement from the first.

"*Si,*" mumbled the first officer as he straightened.

Maria Avita watched in horror as the first officer stepped over to the hearth where only embers of the shattered chair and the charred ends of the bloody club remained. He stooped down to pick up the poker to push the pieces together. Toying with them for a few moments, the officer wondered aloud. "Strange. Where does a priest go in such nasty weather?"

A flame erupted. The officer stood up and backed away, quite satisfied with what he had done. In the puddle at his feet, drips from Louisa's blouse were forming pink ringlets. Panic surged inside Maria Avita. She had to draw the officer away from the puddle before he had a chance to look down at it. She took a quick step towards him and waved her hand. "Nobody has any idea where Father Sandro is? I do not understand. Just this past night, he was here, sitting right here at my table. I gave him wine, is that not so, Louisa?"

The officer glanced at the girl. She nodded, but her eyes remained on the floor, one hand clutching the blanket that hid her night clothes. Misreading fear for innocence, he grinned and said, "Your daughter is very respectful, *Signora.*"

Maria Avita managed a nervous smile. "*Si.* Louisa has always been a good daughter."

The officer stepped away from the hearth. Facing the woman, he asked, "Did Father Sandro seem like himself to you, *Signora*?"

Maria Avita thought carefully before replying, "A little quiet. Perhaps a bit more than usual, as I think of it now."

"Did he say where he was going?"

"Umm, no…*uno momento,* he did say he wanted to continue meditations."

The police officer peered at Louisa. She nodded but her eyes still avoided his. He smiled. "*Una timida signorina.*"

* * *

The rain let up around noontime. Shortly thereafter, Maria Avita slogged down the muddy winding lane. Over her shoulder a white cloth sack containing neatly packed rabbit meat. Near the village she caught sight of Rafaele and quickened her step.

"The rain makes me terribly late on my mail route this day," he said. "I do not intend to go out your way."

"No letter from Joseph then." Maria Avita felt as heavy as the weather.

"No letter," the postman repeated.

She trudged onward. At the village store she traded the rabbit meat for flour, eggs, milk, and six pieces of candy. Barter always included sweets for the children. To her dismay no notice of any kind was tacked to the walls but she didn't dare make inquiries. What if someone asked if Joseph had sent money for the voyage? Rafaele knew she had received no mail and might become suspicious enough to inform the authorities. How would she explain her interest in passage if she had no money? They would come and tear the cottage apart searching for money. No, the old postman would do no such thing, for he risked getting himself into trouble for hiding mail that might contain money. Giolitti's enforcers would surely treat Rafaele quite harshly. He might even disappear, just like cousin Luca. Maria Avita shivered. She didn't want to think of that jail where Luca had been incarcerated. She concluded that it was best not to take any chances and left the store.

Her eyes scoured every building. No postings...anywhere. It was getting late. The dusky winter light was fading fast and it looked as though the rain might start again at any moment. Her gait became increasingly unsteady. She passed the church where Father Sandro once heard confessions and caught sight of a rolled up, yellowed paper, secured by only one tack, hanging beside the door. She stopped short and scanned the area. Nobody else was around. She crept up to the church and flattened the paper against the wall. Rising up on tiptoes she read, "'At the Port of Salerno, the Fortuna will accept consignments from merchants and farmers for delivery to Palermo. Making connections with Italian steamer Sannio, scheduled to dock in Palermo within the week. Final destination—Port of Boston, USA.'" Maria Avita sank down onto her feet and mumbled, "The boat will not arrive in Salerno until the day after tomorrow. How will the children and I ever live through two more days? Giolitti's officers will surely continue the search for the priest. How many more knocks will come at the door?"

Maria Avita spent the sleepless night sewing Father Sandro's money into her clothing. She hid it well. No one would ever detect the slightest bulge. There were so many bills that she even had to sew some into the linings of the children's coats.

The next day, she journeyed to Salerno to purchase seven tickets for passage on the Fortuna. It took the better part of an hour to walk one way to Salerno, the opposite direction from the village. The latest bulletin outside the ticket station indicated that the Fortuna was due in later that evening and would lie in port only long enough to pick up products bound for Palermo and America. In the morning passengers would be allowed to board. Maria Avita sighed nervously. Hopefully the LaRosa family could be gone before anyone had the slightest inkling. She wrung her hands. They shook too much. "Take hold of yourself," she commanded. Smoothing out her skirt, she took a deep breath then briskly opened the door of the ticket station. Marching up to the ticket window, she handed the clerk American currency and said, "Seven passages on the Fortuna, per favore."

The clerk took the wad of bills. He seemed to suspect nothing of the very small portion that Maria Avita had found in Father Sandro's robe.

Not far from home, she came over a rise and ran into the same two enforcers who had come to her door yesterday. She could not avoid them. It might look suspicious.

"*Buon giorno, Signora,*" said the tall one.

Maria Avita nodded. "Any news of Father Sandro?"

The men shook their heads no as they passed. They seemed to be in a hurry. Her thoughts began to torment her. Did they search the cottage? Where were the children? By the time she got to the front door, she was running. Bursting into the house, she gasped for breath and frightened poor Louisa half to death. "Did Giolitti's officers stop here?"

"No, Mama." Louisa started to cry.

"*Grazie Dio.*" Maria Avita gestured to the heavens then opened her arms to comfort her daughter. "*Mi dispiaci, bambina mia.*"

Despite the fact that the LaRosa farm belonged to the state, Maria Avita signed over all rights to it that night to a luckless family from outside the village. She also gave them everything that she and the children were unable to take with them. The poor family had waited a long time for a property grant, so Maria Avita had a good feeling that the state would let them stay on the land. Not only that, they had no money to make the smallest of changes which reassured Maria Avita that nothing would be disturbed—especially Father Sandro. When first light cast off the darkness of night, Mama LaRosa and her six children scampered off toward Salerno.

"Louisa, you must hold up your head. No one must suspect," Maria Avita whispered. "And never speak of that dreadful night again. Someone may overhear." Acting as if the nightmare had never happened, mother and daughter guided five children up the gangplank of the Fortuna. Even little Vincenzo appeared to forget. In third class the family stowed their clothes and the food they had packed for the journey. Maria Avita kept the children busy there while the ship slipped out of port. She feared that a person of the suspicious kind might see them if they went up on deck. Not until Salerno disappeared beyond the horizon did she finally let down her guard. When the Fortuna steamed into Palermo, the Sannio had already docked and was scheduled to leave at noon the next day. Maria Avita purchased passage tickets, then secured a room for the night.

"Do you know of an inexpensive place to eat?" she asked the room clerk.

"A small *trattoria* is situated on the back street not too far that way," he said while his finger outlined the way in the air. "It is off the beaten track, in the working-class quarter, but the food…mmm…" He kissed his fingertips, then his hand flew high into the air. "And the wine is truly *magnifico*. Not only that, all can be had for only a modest price."

A short time later, Maria Avita pushed aside the colorful curtain that served as a door to the *trattoria*. The place was empty, so she gave a holler, *"S'e ti aperto?"*

"Si. Si. Avanti." An exuberant waiter with long skinny legs rushed out from the kitchen. "You come just in time, for we are about to close for the afternoon. The evening meal begins at five." Winking at the children, the tall, wiry man motioned for them to follow. They giggled and hid their faces behind their mother as she trailed him across the tiled floor.

"We do not wish to be of bother to you, but we have just arrived on the Fortuna," Maria Avita said. "The children have not eaten a decent meal for several days."

"I will take good care of you and *i bamini*, *Signora*," piped up a short, plump cook whose red face popped out from the kitchen. The stove heat had made her hair a mass of salt and pepper frizz.

"*Grazie*," smiled Maria Avita. No sooner had she and the children taken seats on wooden stools around a massive knotty pine table than the waiter began arranging dishes and utensils on the table. He then brought bread, wine, and a platter of antipasto. With a playful grin on his face, the man dished out the salad onto small plates and handed them to Maria Avita and the children. Without the slightest hesitation, they dug into it. The waiter backed away and clasped his hands into a ball of delight.

The family had yet to finish when once again the happy-go-lucky waiter danced out of the kitchen and set down bowls of full-bodied broth teeming with freshly cut vegetables and a poached egg floating on the surface of each one. He made great ceremony out of sprinkling generous amounts of grated Parmesan on the *zuppa pavese*. For the longest time little Vincenzo sat with his chin cupped in his hands, staring at the yolk suspended in light brown liquid.

Maria Avita and her children had never seen anything so elegant, yet so funny. Laughing at the waiter's antics, the mother marveled, *How wonderful it is to see the children giggle again. Si, it is good.* So she also allowed herself the luxury of laughter as the food kept coming. Homemade pasta, chicken, and fish. Sicilian cake with lemon frosting topped off the feast. It pleased Maria Avita to see the children eat so well. How long would it be before they devoured another decent meal?

Noon, the next day. burly dock workers loaded wheels of cheese, kegs of wine and olive oil, boxes of macaroni, and barrels of lemons aboard the Sannio. This time Maria Avita and her children watched from the port side rail. An hour later the steamer got underway. The voyage proceeded relatively uneventful until just after passing through the Straight of Gilbraltar. At that point things began to change. The sun disappeared into dusty smudges of cloud that boiled up over the horizon. The captain ordered all passengers restricted below deck just as the wind and seas, driven by a hissing westerly, set upon the ship. The gale buffeted the Sannio side to side, forward and aft. Snow mixed with the wind-driven waves that sheeted over the bow and froze to the rigging.

Steerage became a huge sick room. Two hundred and four bodies, including the members of the LaRosa family, lay on the floor, pitched there from their cots as the violent sea tossed the vessel as if it were a mere toy. Francesca became extremely ill. The squalid conditions added to the affliction. She developed a raging fever. Maria Avita found caring for her children extremely difficult when she herself could not bear to stand up most of the time. Days dragged by until the storm finally eased. To Maria Avita's relief, Francesca's fever broke. Still, both mother and daughter were extremely weak and dehydrated. The food the family had brought with them from the *trattoria* was gone.

"Have you seen any food that we might buy?" Maria Avita asked Paolo and Angelo.

"*Si.* Outside of first class, there is a store," Angelo replied. "Everyone has been too sick to eat, so there is lots of food to choose from. Bread, fruit, and chicken that is already cooked."

"But, Mamma," Paolo asked. "Do we have money?"

"A little. Here," said Maria Avita as she reached into her pocket. "Take this. Buy some fruit. Oranges, if there is any. And get some broth…and bread, too. Use the money wisely, my sons, for there isn't much." Guilt rippled though the woman for lying to her sons. But there was no other choice. No one must know about Father Sandro's money. Anxiously, she awaited Paolo and Angelo's return. When they did, they brought chicken soup, bread, and lemons. "Did anyone ask about the money?" she asked.

"No, Mama," replied Angelo. "Why?"

She quickly grabbed the food and mumbled, "Just curious."

The soup and bread soothed their stomachs. Later the family sucked lemons and made faces. Smiles brightened their beleaguered faces. Most of their strength came back in the next few days. Yet ferocious seas continued to impede passage. Finally, the Sannio warped into port two days late. Eighteen days of misery had finally come to an end. Setting their weary eyes upon the skyline of Boston, Maria Avita and her six children contemplated the silent promise of the sunset beyond. The brush-strokes of pink and gold lifted the mother's tired heart. Soon, she and her children would reunite with Joseph, Armand, and Romeo. Never again, she vowed, would she allow any separation of her family.

After the Sannio berthed at the Cunard Dock in East Boston, Maria Avita walked down the gangplank with the children. Her ears picked up a conversation between ships.

"You are indeed fortunate to come into port so late," hollered the captain of the Ragnarock. "My ship was forced to anchor off the light-ship. It took several hours for the dense fog to lift enough for safe passage through the Narrows. We sailed blind since Nantucket and count ourselves lucky to be here."

"I call myself fortunate to have arrived at all," returned the captain of the Sannio. "Never have I navigated such a disagreeable crossing. It was as if the devil himself wanted to send us to the bottom. My ship is now in sore need of a great deal of repair and cleaning. She'll not be putting out to sea in the foreseeable future."

Maria Avita shivered and prodded the children to keep up with other immigrants headed to the Immigrant House on Meridian Street. Using her limited English skills to register the family, she was unable to pen her youngest son's name so it was legible. One particular customs official had faced this same dilemma many times in the past, but he was nowhere to be found. Instead, an inexperienced hyperactive underling struggled with the writing. The only letter he understood was s. Maria Avita pronounced the name several times, then other Italians chimed in until finally, the official threw his hands into the air. "You all speak so quickly." He pondered the wide-eyed little boy. It was at that very moment that Serafino LaRosa acquired the name that stayed with him for the rest of his life. "Sounds like Seth to me. A true Biblical name. Seth was the third son of Adam and Eve," the assistant official declared with much satisfaction for his vast wealth of knowledge. "Well, Seth it is then. And may God bless you, Seth LaRosa."

Several passengers from the Sannio failed to meet the physical requirements to enter the United States. The immigration officers gathered them up and herded them out of the room. Ultimately, the rejects returned to Italy on board the Sannio. Maria Avita cowered while gathering her children close. The rough voyage and seasickness had caused those poor people to become so sickly. Thank God for Father Sandro's money. The food the boys had purchased with it had restored their health. Otherwise, she had no doubt that she and her children would have been shipped back to Italy, too. Only God knew what was waiting back there.

Leaving the Immigrant House with her children, Maria Avita had no idea where to find Joseph, Romeo, and Armand. The only clue was an address scribbled on the back of an envelope. The haste to leave Italy had left no time to write Joseph that she and children were on their way. Besides, the letter would have come on the same ship as they did. Raw mist blew in off the ocean and clung to the street lamps, forming murky halos that absorbed the light and making them look like Giolitti's henchmen that stalked the night. She was glad that she had told the children to put on all their extra clothing, but still they clung to her skirt as they wandered through the shadowy streets of East Boston. At what seemed to be the center of town, they ran into an elderly gentleman who spoke their dialect.

"*Si*, I know Joseph LaRosa well. Such a fine man indeed. The people of East Boston speak high praises of him. Come with me," he said while motioning down street. "That house over there is the place where Joseph lives—above that store. I will take you there myself."

The old man knocked on the side door. They waited. He knocked again. Then footsteps became audible on the other side. The door cracked then flew open. There stood Carlotta Bascuino. "*O Dio mio*," she exclaimed. Her hands waved wildly in the air as she continued to speak in Italian. "Maria Avita! My dear friend, how on earth did you get here? And little Francesca and Serafino! Vincenzo, look how big you have grown. And Paolo and Angelo. Louisa, let me look at you. How beautiful you have become. Wait until my Dominico sees you. But look at me, I have no manners. *Avanti, avanti*!"

Pandemonium broke loose as Carlotta rousted the entire household. The Bascuinos surrounded Maria Avita and her children, hugging and kissing and shouting. The last one through the kitchen door was Joseph; the one person Maria Avita yearned to see most of all after so many long lonely months. To her surprise her husband supported himself with a cane and appeared so much older. His hair and beard had grown so long and unkempt that she was reminded of a picture she had once seen of Leonardo da Vinci. Despite his haggard bearing, the children yelled, "Pop! Pop!"

All but Vincenzo rushed at their father and nearly knocked down the bewildered man. The boy wavered, his eyes focusing on the cane. Maria Avita set down her bags and nudged him. "Go to your father, my little Vincenzo."

Slowly, he plodded towards Joseph who immediately mussed up the boy's fine hair. It spiked with static electricity and everybody laughed.

The sight of the children, finally reunited with their father, overwhelmed Maria Avita. Tears trickled down her cheeks as she bit her lip and nodded her head. Surely, the hand of God had saved her and the children from the wickedness that the priest had wrought. Her eyes met Joseph's. His lips quivered. The corners slowly lifted and teeth began to gleam. Suddenly, a full-fledged grin burst across his face. A tiny squeak erupted from within the woman as she rushed to her husband. At last, Joseph and Maria Avita LaRosa held each other in their arms where melding of bodies renewed their weary hearts.

CHAPTER 7

The arrival of Maria Avita and the children gave Joseph reason to climb out of bed. Determination returned and so did his sense of responsibility. Responsibility the husband and father could touch, see, and hear. Except for Armand, who remained in New York with his hoodlum friends, the LaRosa family was at last reunited. The welcomed encumbrance spurred Joseph onward. His chest filled with air as if he had not taken a breath in months. He was whole again.

"I cannot understand for the life of me why my Joseph allowed himself to become so run-down," Maria Avita commented to Carlotta. "His cheeks are so hollow. And his skin, it looks so sickly and gray."

Carlotta shrugged as she placed a basket of the day's laundry on the table. "I fussa and fussa over Joseph quite so much. If I no do it, I find out later he eats no my food. For the matter, he no even wash."

Maria Avita placed her hands on her hips. "But Mr. Messina paid all the doctor bills and replaced Joseph's lost income."

"*Si*. And little bit for us all. Such a generous man that Mr. Messina." Carlotta handed two corners of a sheet to her friend for help in folding it. "Your Joseph, he should be proud. People in East Boston say he is…uhm, how you say…*eroe*…Aah…*si*. Hero! Little Antonio no can get out of horse way in time."

"It is truly baffling."

That evening Maria Avita studied her husband's withered face. A faint smile lightened it when he discovered her gaze. That moment it dawned on her. During those long bewildering days of the pilgrimage to America, Joseph had longed for her just as much as she had longed for him. They were two people not meant to be apart.

The next day, she sat him down on a kitchen chair and cut off months of scraggly locks. Time had stolen much of its curl. Completing that monumental task, she parted his hair down the middle and combed each side back, forming waves high enough on his head so as not to crush when he donned his hat. Using a straight-edged razor, she shaved off his scruffy beard, leaving behind the mustachio that she loved so much. As Joseph drew up his chin for her to shave beneath, he mumbled through pursed lips, "I am curious, *Angelatina Mia.* Passage money? How did you come by it?"

The unexpected question paralyzed her; the straightedge angled into the skin of his neck. Her heart skipped a beat as their eyes met. For one eternal moment all was quiet, then conscience found its voice and screamed, *Tell Joseph. Tell him everything!* Clearing her throat, she opened her mouth to speak, but the profound faith that Maria Avita had come to know as often harsh and unforgiving reflected from his face. Suddenly aware of the razor she held against his neck, she dropped her hand. She stepped back and straightened herself. "I, uhm…I sold everything. The rabbits, too. The rainy season brought many litters."

Dizziness and nausea overpowered her. Never before had Maria Avita lied to Joseph. Quickly she removed the cloth that covered him and while endeavoring unsuccessfully to avoid letting the cut hair and whiskers fall to the floor, rolled it up. She went to open the window to shake out the clippings and leaned into the brisk wind that fanned her face. Sucking in a deep cleansing breath, she prayed to Joseph's God to absolve her soul of that terrible deed and give her strength to tell her husband the truth. She cleared her throat and returned to Joseph. "There," she said lightly. "Hold still. Let me take a look at you." Gripping his chin, she shifted his head side to side. Satisfied with the inspection, Maria Avita stepped back and nodded. "*Si*, now, you are the husband I once knew in Italy."

"*Grazie*." Joseph got to his feet and took her head in his hands. Adoringly he gazed into her eyes then kissed her forehead. "Here, take this old cane and cook it in the fire. No longer is it of use to me, for next week, I will go back to work." The man had easily dismissed his wife's explanation concerning passage money. In his mind Maria Avita was indeed a miracle worker capable of making the most amazing things happen when all seemed lost and hopeless. "I gave careful consideration to the money Rom and I saved," he said. "We will use it to rent our own place. Orazio heard some talk about a sea captain's house that overlooks Boston Harbor from Jeffrey's Point. I sent Rom off to find the owner and set up a time for us to take a look at it. If the place is to our liking, we will not need to change parishes, for it is just beyond Our Lady of Assumption."

Several days later, an exceptional spring day dawned. A playful breeze cooled the intense sunshine. With Maria Avita at Joseph's side, the world reverted to perfection once again. Their leisurely stroll wound up in front of a large brick townhouse trimmed in forest green. They gawked at it in awed silence. The place was magnificent, something even their wildest dreams could not have imagined.

Cylindrical brick posts reinforced the black wrought iron fence that bordered an expanse of lush green lawn. Apple trees were beginning to bud, bringing shade to each corner. Next to the porch, crocuses bobbed their heads above the earth. Petals from the delicate purple and white flowers dropped one by one to the ground and soon the myriad of daffodil spikes would choke out what was left. Sparrows flitted among the trees and shrubs, noisily chirping their insistence for the intruders to leave their sanctuary.

Joseph lifted the latch on the gate and pushed it open for Maria Avita. Reverently, they climbed the front stairs as if each step brought them closer to the gates of heaven. The front porch faced south overlooking the bustling Port of Boston. Steamships, fishers, vessels of every size and description crisscrossed each other's wake. To the West, the masts of hundreds of sailing vessels pricked the sky above the Charleston Navy Yard. Bunker Hill Monument loomed beyond, rising majestically into the azure sky broken only by a single cirrus cloud. Directly across the harbor, Castle Island stood as a stark reminder of America's struggle to free itself from English tyranny.

Footsteps distracted the couple. Captain McKay, a descendent of a well-known East Boston shipbuilding family, marched up the steps. Bearing the stern visage of his ancestors, the fetching man wore ankle-high sea boots, navy-blue woolen pants with matching pea coat, and a deck cap of the same color. Snow-white muttonchops insulated his face, weathered by untold years at sea. Despite his age, he stood tall and stalwart, like a mighty mast against the wickedest of gales. Tipping his cap, Captain McKay nodded a silent greeting. Keys, laced on a large brass ring, jangled as he unlocked the door and turned the brass knob. Pushing open the door, he stepped aside and removed his cap that revealed a snowy crown. McKay used the cap to motion for Joseph and Maria Avita to enter.

The couple started in but suddenly hesitated. They felt unworthy to set their bedraggled immigrant shoes in the living where the sun streaked in through floor-to-ceiling windows and settled on the oak floor so highly polished that the exquisite furniture reflected in it. A crystal chandelier consummated the living room, creating a kaleidoscope of brilliant prisms throughout the room. To the left, a massive brick fireplace vertically bisected the pastel blue walls. White chair rail meandered horizontally around the room, dividing the walls in half. Crown molding bejeweled the ornate white metal ceiling. Adorning the space above the mantle was a portrait of a youthful Captain McKay and his lovely lady.

"*Que bella,*" Maria Avita murmured while envisioning a future winter's Sunday with a crackling fire dancing in the marble hearth. The chill had fled the room as Joseph reclined in that high-back wing chair. The children were surrounding him, listening to him read the funnies from the Sunday newspaper. At his feet Seth and Francesca were sprawled upon their bellies across the Persian rug.

Joseph delighted in her wonderment, though in his breast he worried about earning enough money to cover the rent on such a fine home. Just yesterday, he had taken a second job on Porter Street. Converting the three-story single-family brick house into several apartments meant steady income for many weeks to come. Money might be tight, but perhaps it was possible.

Their unbridled admiration of the house didn't seem to faze Captain McKay the slightest. Yet beneath the surface, the Italian couple fascinated him as he regarded them from the corner of his eye. Was it their innocence that drew him to them? Or was it their pride in the face of adversity? Whatever it was, the spirit that surrounded the couple filled McKay with a hope and optimism that he had not felt in a very long time. He speculated that they would not wear immigrant clothing for very long. Those rags certainly did not fit their nature. The Captain stepped around the couple and blustered, "Come, come." He led them through the living room and into the kitchen. "How long have you been in America?"

"I have been here since October last," Joseph replied. "My two oldest sons also. My wife arrived just days ago aboard the Sannio."

"There's a coincidence." McKay's eyebrows lifted. "I sailed past the Sannio just East of the Boston Light on the fishing schooner Rob Roy. Luck brought me to port, because the steering gear had been badly damaged."

Maria Avita winced. "Crossing on the Sannio proved extremely treacherous. Many times I feared we were all going to the bottom. The bow lifted high up time and time again then slapped down into the waves. Boom! The entire ship shuddered and the noise was deafening. My six children and I became so frightened and ill. If I never set foot on a ship again, it will be too soon for me."

Captain McKay studied Maria Avita. What a brave woman to attempt the long journey from Italy all by herself. And with that many children. He cleared his throat. "Several months ago, my dear wife passed on. We weren't blessed with children. I see no reason to keep this house, especially since I have another home in Newport. That is where I spend most of my time. Too many memories roam these halls.

Maria Avita glanced the Captain. How sad, not to have children. This poor man was destined to spend the rest of his life without his own blood. Compassion quickly vanished when she spotted the eat-in kitchen. Fully equipped with all the latest features and cookware, it echoed with space. She imagined herself there, scurrying about, cooking for family and friends.

"Louisa will love this kitchen," said Joseph.

Maria Avita nodded as her fingers ran across the shiny jet-black stove. "This shines like her hair."

"And yours, *Angelatina Mia,*" he said and turned to the Captain. "Our older daughter does not work. She helps her mother keep the family fed and clothed. She is a good cook and seamstress and intends to be a full-time homemaker after she and Dominico Bascuino wed. He is the son of my lifelong friend, Orazio, who runs Giacopirazzi's furniture factory."

"Is that so?" Captain McKay said. He liked these people, quite decent and friendly, they were. He felt as if he had known them all his life.

While the men went on and on about family backgrounds, Maria Avita remembered a conversation she had with Louisa just that morning. Dom earnestly sought to renew their relationship, but it seemed the girl wanted no part of him. Nor any other man for that matter including her father.

"You barely speak to Dom," Maria Avita had said.

Louisa shrugged.

Right away the mother knew that her daughter carried a torment brought on by Father Sandro. Not wanting the girl to carry that kind of fear, Maria Avita had insisted, "Louisa, you must put the past behind you and get on with your life. Father Sandro and his wicked ways have no right to interfere with your life; no more than he did in the first place."

"Any day now," Maria Avita heard Joseph say to the Captain. "I expect Dom to send Orazio to ask permission to marry Louisa. It is just a formality. Orazio and I arranged the marriage when the two were mere infants in Italy."

"I have seen such marriages," said the Captain. "Some work well, others wind up on the rocks."

"I am quite sure that the young man is dependable and will support a wife and children quite adequately," said Maria Avita.

Joseph nodded. "Recently, Dom was promoted to the position of foreman at Giacopirazzi's furniture factory. Before the end of the year, Orazio and I will set the marriage date." He chuckled. "Now there is a pretense for you. Maria Avita, Carlotta, and Louisa will have the final word on that."

Maria Avita rummaged about the kitchen. How wonderful it would be to see her elder daughter smile again. When would she be herself again? The innocent child the mother had once known might never reappear. Already, Maria Avita noticed an unplanned maturity created by the ordeal. Trust would never again come easily for Louisa.

Surprised to find herself alone in the kitchen, Maria Avita hurried to catch up with Joseph and the Captain. But in the living room she stopped short and glanced about the sun-streaked room. Her eyes rested on the fireplace that in her mind still blazed. She stepped over to it and ran her hand across the cold marble. Given the chance, she could easily warm this mantle. "Joseph's pay is hardly enough to cover the rent and ordinary living expenses. Nothing will be extra." She turned around. The splendid room took her breath away. "But the LaRosa family needs this home!" She bit her lip. All seemed hopeless. "Father Sandro's money!" Her hands fled to her mouth. Her eyes darted about the room. Did anyone hear? No, she was alone. Heaving a sigh of relief, Maria Avita pondered the money. If she used a little here, a little there, surely Joseph would never notice the difference. "This house is worth the risk," she said as she crossed the glossy oak floor and stared out the sun-streaked front windows. There must be a way to tell him about striking Father Sandro's head with the club of driftwood. She still did not believe that she had struck the priest hard enough to kill him. What would her husband think of her if he knew she killed someone? Not just anyone, but a holy man? Joseph…such a devout religious man. Everything he believed in would be destroyed. And Maria Avita…Joseph thought she was so innocent…his *Angelatina.* If he learned of her sin, he might turn away from her. And never again set his eyes upon her. A satanic murderer, that is what he would call her. "Perhaps it is best never to reveal the secret at all."

Besides, she had already used a portion of Sandro's money to order muslin underwear for the entire family. Buying from the JC Penney catalogue was an entirely new experience; so was underwear, something the family rarely wore in Italy where no money existed for such luxuries. "Hmm," Maria Avita deliberated. "Speaking of luxuries, how on earth did Father Sandro come by so much money? Priests take an oath of poverty, is this not so?"

"Maria Avita. Are you coming?" Joseph called.

His voice startled her. "Uh. *Si*, Joseph, *si*." She lifted her skirt and rushed up the stairs. She found the men in the master bedroom. She stopped short. How beautiful.

"I see how much you both appreciate the furnishings," said Captain McKay. "If you wish, I will sell the entirety to you. Surely we can come up with an agreeable price. You may pay it at a later date, if you like. I am at odds about moving it anyway."

Her eyes growing wide, Maria Avita communicated without words to her husband how much she coveted the furniture. The couple owned nothing, not even the bed they slept in at night. Joseph squeezed her hand and declared, "We will take it all."

They climbed up to the widow's walk where the majesty of the Port of Boston came to life. Square-riggers sailed out of sight beyond the eastern horizon. Fishing boats returned to port from their early morning quests while hordes of sea birds trailed, hovering then diving into the following sea for the entrails that the fishermen threw overboard. At Castle Island Pier a boatload of future mariners made a poor attempt at docking and one unfortunate novice fell overboard when the vessel made unceremonious contact with the pier.

Joseph turned to his wife. "I always dreamed of building a house for you."

"But Captain McKay's house is perfect, Joseph. More so than anything we can ever afford to build ourselves. We will have our own private bedroom. And there are three others for the children to share. Please, *mi amore*, I will be contented to live here for the rest of my days."

Pretending not to hear, Captain McKay gazed westward and smiled. How nice it would be to see a family like this breathe life into this sterile old house that only two people had ever occupied. Pity that he and his deceased wife never had children. Without looking back at the immigrants, the Captain interceded in their amorous bickering. "You may do as you wish to the house."

"My husband and I love it exactly as it is," insisted Maria Avita. "There is nothing that needs changing, I assure you. When is it possible for us to move in?"

Chapter 8

Joseph's reputation as a high-quality carpenter grew. So much work came his way that he made the break with Mr. Giacopirazzi's furniture company and Orazio and started his own carpentry business, renovating old houses in Maverick Square. Saving young Antonio Messina from that crazed mare contributed to his visibility and respect, so people hired Joseph without ever considering anyone else. Then one day Carmelo Messina approached him with plans for a new home in Orient Heights. Joseph was the only man Messina trusted to do the job.

Romeo joined his father who now needed more hands for his thriving business. What a relief to finally leave the furniture business. The strong bond that existed between the two helped ensure success in East Boston. Communication was more often understood than voiced. Day in and day out, they tirelessly worked side by side.

Since the LaRosa family had fared so well in this new land of opportunity, Joseph was eager to make the dreams of others also come true. He hired two immigrants, Luigi Spanucci and Alfonso Venditolla who had come with their wives and children from Torino. Each had four children. Joseph and Maria Avita took the new arrivals under their wings and into the Captain's house while the wives hunted for places to live. Both families ended up in Revere, since housing in East Boston had become scarce.

Joseph never regretted hiring the hard-working builders. They preferred masonry, which they were accustomed to in Italy. Combined with Joseph's woodworking skills and Rom's endless energy, LaRosa and Sons Construction Company erected homes of a better and more permanent character than other builders. Not only that, the structures looked nice, too.

By the spring of 1912, the fledgling company began to turn down work. The men completed their second single family home in Orient Heights, an area that Joseph loved. He especially doted on the backyard gardens of lush grass, flowers, and small plots of vegetables. The garden behind Carmelo Messina's new home influenced Joseph to redesign the one behind the Captain's house. He built a gazebo in the center and painted it white. Maria Avita planted multicolored petunias in the rail boxes and impatiens on the ground surrounding the structure. Blazing roses, Joseph's pride and joy, covered white trellises that gave entry to a lush green lawn bordered by privet hedges. In the far corner meticulously carved evergreens sheltered a statue of St. Anthony from the heat of the summer sun and the fury of winter.

For a time Joseph resisted Orazio's efforts to teach him card games. But once he started, he was hooked for good. One day while playing out a hand, Orazio spoke of a seventeen-year-old man named Tommasso Cacace, a blacksmith from Naples. "An excellent husband for my oldest daughter," he said. "You should hire him, Joey."

"Just because you want him for your son-in-law?"

"Meet with Tommasso. You might even want him for your little Francesca."

"I will hear nothing of it. He is much too old for my seven-year-old."

"Just hire him, Joey. Do it for me, *tuo paesani*."

Tom Cacace reminded Joseph a little of himself, except that Cacace had made the journey to America all by himself. "*Signore* LaRosa, I need work," Tommasso insisted. "I work hard for you and learn quick too.

You see. But even you no hire me, with the grace of God I will find suitable work and living quarters. I bring my family to America real quick."

"I have already told you that you are hired," Joseph said.

"*Si, grazie, Signore* LaRosa. I send for my parents and my two brothers and three sisters. My brothers and sisters, they are all younger than me. Did I tell you that?"

"*Si*, Tommasso. Several times."

At every opportunity Seth watched his father work. Construction fascinated the six-year-old, and Joseph enjoyed the novelty of training his youngest son who still had the hands of a child. Often on late afternoons the residents of Jeffries Point caught sight of the man and his kid lumbering home after spending the afternoon together at a construction site. Blessed with abundant dark curly hair, like his father once had, the boy possessed the engaging smile of his mother. Onyx eyes peered up at Joseph, the same fathomless pools that the man had drowned in the first moment he had laid eyes upon Maria Avita in Salerno so many years ago.

In September, Seth and his seven-year-old sister Francesca entered the first grade at St. Mary's Parochial School in Orient Heights. Francesca had finally acquired adequate English skills that allowed her to enter into the mainstream classroom. The little girl with button eyes the color of the cinnamon rose and spiraling chestnut curls did well in school, but her biggest happiness came from sewing. Her small nimble fingers helped her mother make clothes for the family from fabric purchased at the shops of Boston's North End. Maria Avita spared no expense. Only the best materials went into LaRosa clothing.

The family worked hard all week long then spent weekends together indulging in relaxing activities. Quite often after the 8 o'clock Mass at Our Lady of the Assumption Catholic Church, Joseph and Maria Avita trekked behind their children on the way to the Bennington Street Station to take the trolley with Carlotta and Orazio and all their children. One particular Sunday, their destination was Wood Island Park at the far end of East Boston. As usual twelve-year-old Angelo was bragging about himself. This time he was spouting off his mastery of the English language. His teacher had recently reported that his extraordinary vocabulary revealed no discernible accent. This made Joseph and Maria Avita extremely proud, although Angelo continually rubbed it in his siblings noses.

"Not everyone finds school easy like you," whined Paolo as they loaded onto the streetcar.

"You might do better if you were not as lazy as the day is long," jabbed Angelo.

"I am not!"

"Are so!"

"Are not! I try hard. Even Pop, he say so, *si*, Pop?"

Joseph chuckled and looked out the window, refusing to be drawn into the argument. However, he was not entirely blind to the fact that Paolo was just getting by in school. The man looked back at his third oldest son. Small and somewhat frail for his thirteen years, Paolo would never possess the strength of a carpenter. Joseph decided to encourage the boy to spend his free time studying under the watchful eye of his mother. Hopefully, something might come along that was right for Paolo. Angelo, on the other hand, well…he possessed all the right ingredients necessary to fulfill the father's dream of at least one LaRosa offspring attending college.

"Even Vincenzo, who hates school, does better with English than you," Angelo glared directly into Paolo's eyes. "And he's only in the second grade! Hah!"

"No true," Paolo blasted right back. "He still speak more old country than English."

Vincenzo cringed in his seat. The quiet eight-year-old never got involved in the nonsensical bickering of his siblings and hated being the subject of it.

"Look at Vincenzo. He sits there as silent as the rock that Father Sandro sat on after you and I passed him by that night in Italy. And then, whaddaya know. The priest vanished, pfftt, just like that," Angelo said, snapping his fingers.

Maria Avita's heart stopped. She glanced at Vincenzo who had gasped and taken on the bearing of a cornered animal. Suddenly, he bolted from his seat and darted to one just behind the conductor. His chin dropped on his hands. His fingers dug into the metal safety bar. He looked so terrorized, yet forlorn. Did the boy remember that night?

Joseph turned to Maria Avita. "All this time, you have not mentioned the priest."

She grimaced. Before she got the nerve to speak, Angelo and Paolo eagerly poured out in great detail how Giolitti's officers came to the farmhouse in search of Father Sandro.

"Why does a priest disappear in such a way?" Carlotta shot a questioning glance at Maria Avita. "S'pose he ever turned up?"

"I dare not say," Maria Avita replied. Turning away, she squeezed her eyes shut. Just when she thought all was forgotten, that devil reared his ugly face again. Her heart somersaulted. *What if someday somebody discovers Father Sandro's bones? Oh, God. Please! Do not let that happen. No, he will not be found. That is the end of it…never!*

"Come to think of it, you wrote to me of Father Sandro." Joseph leaned close to his wife. "Did you not, *Angelatina Mia*?"

"I do not remember," Maria Avita lied. She wanted to yell at him to stop calling her that name. She did not deserve it. "Oh, look! Over there next to the bathhouse. The picnic tables under the trees have not yet been taken. Hurry, Joseph! Go and save them."

Joseph leapt to his feet and was the first to disembark the trolley. Orazio was right behind him. Maria Avita heaved a sigh of relief as Angelo and Paolo dashed off to join the foot races on a nearby track. Angelo kept up easily with the runners, but Paolo lagged behind. After the first lap the weaker boy gave up and dropped exhausted onto the grass beside the track.

"Come on, Orazio," said Rom. "Pop and I are going to lift weights in the gymnasium."

"No, no, my son. Not today," Joseph waved him off. "I have lifted enough bricks and lumber for one week, *grazie*. No weights for me."

"Count me out, too," said Orazio. "How about a game of bocci, Joey?"

"Sure, but it is a real shame that we are not at Fenway Park this day. Smokey Joe Wood is on the mound." Joseph sulked while swinging a make-believe bat as the two men walked to the bocci court.

"He has won ten in a row now, right?"

"*Si.* What do you say we get tickets for the September 1st doubleheader?"

"Why that game?"

"Smokey Joe will pitch against Walter Johnson of the Senators. You know, Johnson won sixteen in a row before losing."

"Don't worry about it. Smokey Joe can take him."

"Would mean a thirty-four-win season for that sommanagun."

Maria Avita watched the two men walk away. Opening the picnic basket, she said pensively, "Talk of the Red Sox brings to mind the Titanic. My crossing might have ended that way."

"*Si.* Strange twist of fate, is it not? Great ship sinks the same day Fenway Park opened," said Carlotta. She took the corners of the green checked tablecloth that Maria Avita handed her and helped to spread it over the wooden picnic table.

"It doesn't make any sense to me, Carlotta. The weather was incredibly bad during my crossing, but the captain still kept the boat afloat. The Titanic sank on a clear night. And the sea was smooth as glass. Why did someone not see that iceberg?"

"*Si*, something no right with that. Perhaps government investigation will get the truth. *O Dio mio*. Many people dead. Tsk, tsk, tsk." Carlotta shook her head as she thoughtfully palmed the wrinkles out of the tablecloth.

"Your English is getting better."

"*Si*, er, yes," Carlotta said proudly. "I try, I try."

It took Maria Avita and Carlotta the greater part of an hour to set up the two tables for the picnic—spuckie rolls, cold cuts, cheese, what not—enough food to feed the two families for an entire week. Somehow though, everything managed to disappear before it was time to go home.

"Come and eat," Maria Avita called. Everyone ignored her. Several more times she called. Happily frustrated, the woman threw gestures into the air and issued slurred Italian-English screeches that neither Italians nor Americans understood. The younger children delighted in her antics. The twinkle in her eye and a concealed smile revealed that the scolds meant nothing. Seth and Margaret hid behind the trees and giggled while waiting for her to yell again.

Not until the LaRosas and the Bascuinos had grown hungry did any of them stagger back to the tables, exhausted from their activities. Joseph looked about the two tables. He loved these family outings. What more could a man ever want? Good friends and a healthy happy family. But then Armand crossed his mind. That jojo was the only one missing here today. He had a mind of his own and continued to go against his father's wishes. No matter how much his parents, family, and friends pleaded, Armand refused to leave New York. He and his friend, Aldo, worked for Gaspare Messina, Aldo's father. "In the construction business," is what Armand told everybody. Little did the LaRosa family know that Armand was actually part of a covert system that controlled the issuance of building permits in New York City. This had become very lucrative since building in Manhattan was booming. Contractors paid enormous bribes to organized crime that controlled city hall and the issuance of building permits. Occasionally, a defiant builder needed a little unpleasant persuasion before submitting an envelope filled with currency. Generally, once was enough.

*   *   *

One exceptionally warm September day, the LaRosas and Bascuinos ventured out to Revere for a frolic at the beach and amusement park. They caught the ferry at Lewis Street and made connections with the Boston-Revere Beach and Lynn Railroad. The children loved the train, especially the tunnels. However, the elders found this mode of transportation with all its clanging and crunching a bit unnerving and uncomfortable.

As Carlotta watched her daughter play in the surf with Seth, she said, "Serafino and Margaret are very close, a definite bond. They will not argue the arrangement of marriage. Do you not agree, Maria?"

"*Si.* They are meant for each other; it is plain to see. Both are strong and smart. Many healthy and intelligent children will be theirs. Did I ever tell you, Carlotta, that Serafino was the smallest born of all his brothers and sisters? But stronger than all of them put together. At three weeks he turned over in the cradle. Three weeks!"

"You say same thing every time those two play together!"

After returning to East Boston that evening, the children met up with school chums in Maverick Square and dallied there. Joseph and Maria Avita parted with Orazio and Carlotta at the Bascuino doorstep and strolled homeward. Sunbeams raked at low angles while lavenders and pinks pervaded the sky over Charlestown. With the season drawing to an end, crickets chirped more urgently. Fall was in the air.

"You are quiet this evening, *mi amore*," commented Maria Avita.

"I still see in my mind the game that Smokey Joe pitched last week." Fanatic satisfaction plastered his face.

Maria Avita chuckled. "I am glad you and Orazio took the boys to see the game."

"*Si.* Imagine that, *Angelatina Mia*," Joseph said whimsically as only a baseball fan does. "Looks to me like the Red Sox and the Giants will go head-to-head in the World Series this year."

The contented couple turned the last corner to the street they loved so much. Their eyes eagerly sought out the magnificent brick house they called home as if they still could not believe their eyes. They squinted. Something was laying across the front steps.

"Is that a blanket?" Maria Avita asked.

"No, it looks to be a figure of a man," said Joseph. "Perhaps, he has drunk too much *il vino* and has passed out on our doorstep."

"Who does such a thing?"

When Joseph did not answer, she glanced at him. His face had turned white as a sheet. He dropped the picnic supplies and gasped, "Armand." Making a mad dash to the house, he lifted his son's broken body onto his lap. "What has happened to you, my son?"

Armand was wearing only one shoe. Two toes were unmistakably crushed. Blood stained his tattered clothing. His left eye was blackened and the side of his face swelled into a large red and blue oozing mass. His arm was broken above the elbow. Too weak to speak, he relived that night, cursing the fact that he was not by nature more cautious. A contractor had gotten the drop on the young Mafia soldier while making rounds. A baseball bat delivered the message that he had no desire to hand over extortion money that the organization solicited. Confronting that heavyweight alone was not the wisest thing to do.

Recognizing his own mortality, Armand hightailed it for East Boston. The mob thought their trusted *soldato* had gone home only long enough to heal, but Armand's intent was entirely different. He no longer wished to be a part of Don Vito's crime family. Whacked into the realization that he was not invincible, he saw his life passing by right before his very eyes and wanted to be with his own family. "A staging, Pop," he mumbled. "I fell off a staging."

Denying all reason for doubt, Joseph cradled his son's head and asked, "Why did your boss not fix you up? How come he sends you home like this?"

"Forget about it, Pop. In no time *Mamacita* will patch me up…better than anybody."

Chapter 9

Conversation around the LaRosa supper table on a June evening in 1914 centered on war, one kind or another. Outrage ruled all sensibility since Rom had heard that a Serb terrorist had murdered the heir to the Austro-Hungarian throne, Archduke Franz Ferdinand, and his wife in the Bosnian town of Sarajevo. The assassination proved to be the spark that ignited World War I. Quickly the great powers of Europe became involved and eventually, the majority of other countries around the world. More than eight million soldiers were destined to lay down their lives in the Great War.

Rom and his friend, Nick Bascuino, viewed warfare as a chance for the most glorious and exciting experience of their lives. Not wanting to miss out on this window of opportunity, running away to war ruled their minds.

"This is not the time for war," admonished Joseph from the head of the table while filling his glass with burgundy. "This is a time to celebrate, for the LaRosa family has grown with the birth of Louisa and Dom's first *bambino*. Now that your Mama and I are proud grandparents, we do not wish for any son of ours to be lying dead in some God-forsaken European countryside."

Rom braced an elbow on the table and propped up his chin in the palm of his hand. His expression softened as he set indignity and lust for adventure aside, but mind you, only temporarily. At times a little hotheaded, the hard-working seventeen-year-old knew that this was not the time to push the issue. His family had just gotten on their feet after their migration to America. Still, this stuff going on in Europe really grated on his nerves.

"*Mamacita*, you haven't told us the name of Louisa's *bambino*," said Armand over the clamor of knives, forks, and spoons. Except for a slight limp, his broken body had healed and he was back to his old feisty self.

"Your Mama is too bashful to speak of it," Joseph spoke up. "Avita Maria Carlotta Bascuino, that is the child's name."

"And a fine name, indeed," said Armand winking at his mother.

"But you know, Armand, it is a good thing that we finished Dom and Louisa's new house on Eagle Hill. It will fill quickly with many more little feet."

You are wrong, my husband, thought Maria Avita. *It has not been easy for Louisa to accept Dom's advances. The new bride cries to me that in the darkness she sees the evil face of Father Sandro and not the love of Dominico.*

"The layette needs a dress," Francesca mused. Her cinnamon eyes tracked her fingers as they caressed the delicate tatting on the baby bonnet she had brought to the table. "It's the only thing we didn't make. And I think it should match this sweet little bonnet."

"It will be quite some time before *il bambino* Avita is ready for dresses," Maria Avita chuckled. "But the next time your father goes to the North End, we will go with him. The dry goods store on Salem Street should have gotten in a new supply of material by now."

Pouring more burgundy, Joseph elbowed his youngest son and said, "Speaking of war, one broke out this very day right here on the streets of East Boston. Is this not so, Serafino?"

"Aw, come on, Pop," protested Seth. "You know how it is with those punks from Central Square. They think they can shove the whole world around and get away with it. Well, I taught them a thing or two."

"Fighting is not good, my son," admonished his mother. "It only leads to more."

"Nobody pushes *my* Margaret around and gets away with it, not with Seth LaRosa around! Speak disrespectful to my Margaret, I'll not have it! So I ran them off with their tails tucked between their legs."

"*My* Margaret," exclaimed Rom. One eyebrow arched as he nudged Joseph. "Gee, Pop. Looks like more little feet for the LaRosa family! How old are you, *piccolo fratello mio*? Seven? Eight?"

"My age matters little. Here! Stand beside me," Seth jumped to his feet. "See for yourself. Already, I am the man that you are!"

Rom sighed. He braced his hands on the tabletop and pried himself up from his chair. Standing beside Seth, he said, "I see that Serafino speaks truthfully." Roughing up his brother's curly black hair, he sprung a headlock on him. "You grow up while I look the other way."

Seth rotated and landed a mighty punch right in Rom's gut. Saliva spewed as the older brother doubled over in pain.

"No longer will I be treated like a silly child. And my name is Seth! Remember that. All of you." He stood there, hands on hips, ebony eyes ablaze. From that day on he commanded the respect of a grown man. Furthermore, the word on the street became abundantly clear. Margaret Bascuino was the undisputed property of Seth LaRosa.

* * *

On April 17, 1915, more news of Mother Italy energized Rom. The Italians had taken Col di Lana summit in the Alps. The day he found out that the Germans sank the Lusitania off the coast of Ireland was the last straw. One hundred and twenty-eight Americans were dead. Bursting through the back door, the eighteen-year-old scared his mother and Vincenzo half to death. Maria Avita grabbed for his arm. "Rom! What in the world are you doing home in the middle of the afternoon?"

"Haven't you heard, Mama?" He shook her off. "Those bastards sunk the Lusitania! Time has come for Rom LaRosa to go to war!"

Maria Avita gasped, "Such language!"

Rom didn't hear her words. He had already run out of the kitchen. Taking two steps at a time up the stairs, he slammed his bedroom door so hard that the windows rattled.

"Vincenzo! There is not much time," Maria Avita fretted. "Run to the construction site. Bring your father and the boys. Tell them that your brother packs for war and refuses to hear his Mama's words. *Adiamo*!"

When the menfolk arrived, Joseph sat Rom down at the kitchen table and tried to quell the raging storm. Nothing worked. Rom slammed his fist on the table and complained, "President Wilson remains too damned neutral. What's the point?"

"He keeps the trade channels open, my son," Joseph calmly replied.

"Hasn't worked." The hotheaded young man turned sideways in his chair. "Germany uses submarines to fight their war and spits in Wilson's face every time he warns that they will be held to 'strict accountability' for the loss of American lives if they sink any of our neutral supply or passenger ships."

"Even so," Armand interrupted. Standing in the kitchen doorway, one hand braced against the frame, he attempted to halt this father-son confrontation. "Why do you wish to fight? You owe no allegiance to America."

This lack of patriotism infuriated Rom. "You should be ashamed of yourself! You lack all appreciation for the land that gives the LaRosa family a new beginning. No longer are we subject to the tyranny of Giolitti."

Armand threw his hands into the air and scoffed, "There is no reasoning with pig-headed *fratello mio*. I gotta go. *Cidiamo*, Pop."

*   *   *

May 23, 1915. Italy declared war on Austria. Italian-Americans crowded into Maverick Square daily to debate the politics of their two countries. Rom and Nick Bascuino were counted among them. When news reached East Boston that Italy had captured Cortina d'Ampezzo in the Alps and had also taken Monfalcone, an Austrian port on the Gulf of Trieste, the men threw their caps into the air and cheered. Wine flowed in honor of all the brave Italian soldiers. Victory at Plava came next. Then on July 25 the Italians took the Austrian island of Pelagosa in the Adriatic Sea. Months passed. Victories stacked up for Italy. It became increasingly difficult for anyone to disparage Rom from fanciful notions that war meant great adventure and stature. "Consider the big picture, will ya, huh? This war will be all over and done with by Christmas, if only we just get at it," Rom reiterated, over and over again.

While men caroused Maverick Square, four more months of bloody wins and losses ensued. August 9, Italy took Gorizia, north of Trieste. Before the end of August, Romania declared war on Austria, Italy on Germany, and Germany on Romania. On September 15, 1915, Joseph and Maria Avita's wedding anniversary, Britain declared war on Bulgaria. The next day France declared war on Bulgaria. Two days after that, Italy declared war on Bulgaria. All hell was breaking loose in Europe and Rom itched to be there.

In May 1916, the Germans agreed to abandon unrestricted submarine warfare and promised Wilson safe passage of American ships. However, on October 7, 1916, a German U-53 submarine reached Newport, Rhode Island. The next day, it torpedoed five ships off Nantucket. The unrestricted use of German submarines against neutral and allied shipping inflamed American opinion about the war. With the slogan, "He kept us out of the war," Wilson sought reelection in 1916 and won by a narrow margin. In April 1917 he asked Congress for a declaration of war by vehemently asserting, "The world must be made safe for Democracy." The Selective Service Bill, forced through Congress in May, resulted in the drafting of 2.8 million American men by the end of the war.

Boston became a patriotic city in 1917. Recruiting tents sprung up at the Lafayette Mall. The term slacker characterized any young man who didn't rush off to put on the uniform of his country. Love of his new country and the prosperity it created for his family compelled Rom to join the armed forces. He and Nick Bascuino could have fought in either the Italian or the American Army. They chose the United States Army.

Although Joseph and Maria Avita feared that their second son would not come back from this first war of the world, they had no choice but to support his decision and wave a tearful good-bye. October newspapers blasted devastating headlines, Italian Lines Pulverized in Battle of Caporetto. Retreating to the Piave River, Italy also lost Gorizia. As Joseph read the headlines, his teeth pulverized the ends of his stogie into stinky black ooze. Maria Avita scrubbed the daily dishes much harder and longer than necessary while agonizing over her absent son so far away.

Over the next five months, many losses occurred. More than a million American troops subsequently augmented the allied armies during 1918. Coordinated efforts finally turned the balance against the Germans.

On September 12, 1918, Rom and Nick's outfit joined the attack on both sides of the St. Mihiel salient. Rain and mud were incessant as Allies, exhausted by the long marches through rugged mountainous terrain, dodged thousands of indiscriminately fired German gas shells. Mortar fire often punctured sleep while phosphor flares lit the night sky to expose enemy positions. The Huns made numerous efforts to rally, but in the end were forced to retreat. Allied Forces captured town after town. Pinching out the area, they captured fifteen thousand enemy personnel. One afternoon, Rom and Nick were marching a trio of prisoners through the muck towards a waiting troop carrier. Gray fog, that smelled of gunfire, sulfur, and burnt flesh, hung heavy over the battlefield.

"We've been over the top, Rom, m' boy," Nick snorted. His eyes squinted as his cigarette smoke billowed back into his face.

"Sure's been an experience. Not at all what I expected," Rom winced as his brain flashed back to an awful blur in time. Once again he was indiscriminately firing his machine gun at the unseen enemy, emptying more than two dozen clips, twenty shots each. "Amazing, never once thought of gettin' hit."

"Shish. That latest barrage was a doozy, wasn't it?" Nick grunted. "Noise and smoke was bad enough, say nothin' about the gas. Hear me pukin' my guts out all night? Damn enemy shells, they kept on comin'. And all's that was goin' on in m' mind was keepin' this ol' Italian ass o' mine movin' forward."

"Guys all 'round us kept on droppin' like flies," Rom shuddered. "But you and me? We kept on mowing those cussed Huns down. Can you beat that?"

"Knock on wood, *amico mio*." Nick rapped one of the prisoner's metal helmet. "Remember when we hit that trench? Don't know what was worse, the shellin' up top or the gas floatin' in that damned hole."

Just then, machine gun fire cracked. The soldiers and their prisoners dove for the ground. Bullets whistled overhead, one plinked off Rom's helmet. Then the battlefield went quiet once again.

Nick doddered to his feet. "Tried to write home last night."

"Yeah?" Rom snorted while nudging one of the three prisoners with his foot. "Dead. Hmph. OK, the rest of ya, on your feet. *Schnell*!"

"My hand…Damn…Shook like hell. Pencil wouldn't stay put in it."

Mortar shells thundered. One hit close, and like a rag doll, Rom somersaulted into a shell hole. Only slightly winded, he got to his feet, but his ears rang so loud that hearing was impossible. He shook his head violently. The world spun. He smacked his head to make it stop. No matter what he did, the clanging inside persisted. "I give up," he huffed. Taking a deep breath, he crawled out of the hole. Spotting one of the prisoners, he cursed, "Damn. Another one bit the dust. Where the hell's the last one?"

The third prisoner was lying ten yards from the second. Blood gushed from his mutilated body. His left arm was just barely affixed and his left leg was gone entirely. The German screeched out in excruciating pain, but Rom heard only muffled sounds. "Oughta shoot the bastard 'n put him outta his misery," Rom muttered to himself. He poked a finger in his ear and shook it furiously. "Hey, Nick," he called while knowing full well that if an answer came, he couldn't hear it anyway. The search for his old friend did not take long. Rom froze at the sight. "*NICK*?" His knees quaked. Falling to the ground, Rom whimpered, "Oh no...Nick. Don't tell me ya went and got yaself killed. For crying out loud, look at cha. Ya don't even know what hit cha."

Rom was only a couple yards away from Nick Bascuino when the merciless hand of Satan slapped the battlefield. Now, holding what was left of his friend in his arms, Rom blinked up into driving rain as his clenched fist shook skyward. Bitterly, he cursed His Maker. "Why Nick and not me? Damn You! You turn Your eyes from those who fight Your righteous cause." He collapsed upon his childhood friend, sobbing, "I am *so sick* of this *despicable* war, Nick. Even *God* wants no part of it. How did we ever think that war is just another glorious adventure?"

*   *   *

For the next few weeks, Rom stood vigil over the grave of Nick Bascuino who would forever sleep in the soil of France. Only when his body gave out did Rom close his eyes. He didn't eat. Anger, sorrow, exasperation, then more anger overwhelmed him while he fought off hate-filled urges for revenge. No wonder that for some war swiftly descended into madness.

Rom was forced to squelch his grief when orders came for him to link up with American forces thrusting northward through the Argonne. He became a member of a mobile machine-gun detachment, organized to keep up with the retreating Germans. More than thirty vehicles with three men each operated north of the Vesle. None sighted the German infantry. Uncertain of just where their advance might lead, the outfit carried supplies of food and equipment that enabled them to pursue the archenemy of humanity for quite some time. At the same time the

British were moving eastward toward Cambrai and farther north toward Lille. The goal was to cut off the lateral German railway and force a general withdrawal. The rain and muck continued. Advance became painfully slow, slower than anyone had originally expected.

Another miserable waterlogged day. Pinned down for a time by their own barrage, Rom and his detachment moved up to a slight rise. Just as they got there, a mortar shell shrieked into the their midst. The blast catapulted soldiers into the air. Rom looked to the heavens and grumbled, "*Deja vue*, huh Nick?"

Shrugging it off, he got to his feet. Ten yards away, the kid who carried the American flag lay mortally wounded. Life slowly slipped away, but he still held Old Glory in the air. When it began to sag, Rom rushed to grab the pole just as death loosened the bearer's grip. He stuck the pole into the muck then took off the dead soldier's jacket. He stood up and looked down at the man. "Ain't no more 'n sixteen," Rom winced. Covering the flag-bearer with his jacket, Rom stood there studying the mound before him. His mind devoid of thought, he drew a deep breath and turned away to do whatever he could for injured survivors.

That evening, Rom noticed black and blue marks all over his body. "Amazin'. Skin ain't even broke, Nick." For the life of him, he could not understand how he escaped without so much as a scratch. So many of his fellow soldiers had premonitions of death, but not Rom. Death was not in the realm of possibilities.

Bombardment slackened through the night. Next morning while mopping up a nearby village, the remainder of the detachment ran into a nest of Boche machine guns. Bullets came so thick that Rom beat it on his stomach for a shell hole. No sooner had he toppled in when he heard a thud. Lying on his belly, he turned—another doughboy who had sought sanctuary in the same precious space.

"Any others make it?" the doughboy panted.

The conflict above ceased. Rom listened. Silence. He rolled over and lit up a cigarette. "Don't know."

"I took one in the thigh," wheezed the doughboy. His teeth clenched as his hand tried to plug the hole, the size of a fist. Without so much as a wince, Rom tore off his belt and used it as a tourniquet. Tightening it just above the wound, he fell back on his elbows and took it all in stride. The atrocities of war benumbed him.

"What're we gonna do now?" asked the doughboy.

"Lob a grenade, I s'pose."

"Might do the trick," agreed the doughboy.

"Yeah," mumbled Rom skeptically. "Tossed the ball around a bit back home, but that nest's a bit farther than even I can throw."

Painfully the doughboy lifted himself up to the edge of the trench. His flaxen head rose above the level of the dark muck, which set off a burst of machine gun fire zinging above him. He dove for cover. "Whooowheee! Nasty bunch of hornets, ain't they? Well, maybe I got it in me to tear up their happy little home. Gimme a grenade, will ya, coach?"

Rom eyeballed him. *Coach? Hey, what the hell's up with this guy? Is he off his rocker or somethin'?* Something inside told Rom to unhook a grenade from his belt and toss it to the doughboy. The flaxen-haired kid caught the grenade with one hand and playfully tossed it into the air a time or two, thinking, thinking. Kneeling in a modified pitcher's stance, the likes of which Rom had never seen before nor would ever see again, the doughboy spat on the ground. He rubbed the grenade as if it were a baseball. His right index finger reached out to the earthen wall and drilled, pinpointing an invisible batter. The lefty adjusted his crotch then brought the ball, clutched in both hands, up to his chest. He paused…checked the runner on first then zeroed in on the strike zone. An eyeball went back to first. There's the windup. His right knee came up off the ground. He pulled the pin. There's the pitch…Flash! Blam! A mighty report. Several times it thundered back at them. Then, there was only silence. Rom and the doughboy weaseled a look. The force of the blast had ejected the enemy out of the nest. Bodies and pieces of that damned machine gun littered the surroundings. Nose-to-nose, Rom and the doughboy made eye contact. Rom's left eyebrow arched. "Done this before, haven't cha?"

The doughboy cleared his throat. "A time or two."

* * *

From the Vesle northward over the plateau, the Germans stripped everything of value or use and easily moved in the path of their retreat. Everything else they burned or destroyed, that is, if they had the time and means. This was in direct contrast to the great stores of supplies and ammunitions left behind due to the hasty withdrawal from between the Marne and the Vesle. Allied engineers quickly repaired roads and small bridges, allowing the mobile detachment to continue the pursuit. Rom drove past Allies on the move, some on foot, some on horseback or motorcycles. Others drove mule teams. Then there were trucks. So many trucks, most loaded to the hilt with soldiers. All headed in the same direction to rout the German Army. Through pocked grain fields overrun with weeds, they trekked into skeletons of villages with shells of homes ravaged by gunshots and mortar. Rom saw nothing of military value, only dazed and starving residents wandering through the remainder of all that they had once known. Occasionally he caught the glimmer of apprehensive eyes peering back at him from the shadows of blasted-out doorways and windows.

* * *

General Ludendorff panicked when he heard of allied victories and the surrender of Bulgaria. He demanded that the government of Germany initiate armistice and peace negotiations. On October 5 King Ferdinand of Bulgaria abdicated his throne and Germany sent the first peace note to President Wilson. Three days later, Wilson replied requesting the withdrawal of German forces from all foreign soil. Within the week Germany sent a second peace note to President Wilson. In reply Wilson demanded that all inhumane practices stop and that Germany change its form of government.

Meanwhile, Italy took Durazzo, Albania. Joining British forces, the Italians advanced across the Piave River. The battle of Vittorio-Veneto was long and bloody. November 2, 1918, they invaded Austria and the next day took Trent.

Americans cut the main German line of communication by taking Sedan on November 7. German seamen revolted at Kiel and Hamburg. On the 10th German Emperor William II fled to Holland and the British advanced in Belgium to the Mons Canal area.

Hostilities ceased at 11:00 AM, on the eleventh day of the eleventh month of 1918, the moment Germany signed an armistice. On the 21st the German fleet surrendered to the British. The last German forces in East Africa surrendered on the 25th. The beginning of December, American troops marched into Germany. So did Rom LaRosa…without Nick Bascuino.

Chapter 10

One muggy Saturday afternoon in late August 1918, Seth LaRosa and Margaret Bascuino were strolling down Meridian Street after seeing "Johanna Enlists" starring Mary Pickford at the Gem Theatre. Mature and articulate for their age, the couple had become quite an item on the streets of East Boston. Consideration of others had earned them a great deal of friends and respect. Easygoing by nature, both demonstrated a sense of humor that at times turned heads. Their laughter often interrupted the humdrum of the otherwise stodgy neighborhoods of East Boston. No one doubted for a moment that upon reaching the age of consent, Seth and Margaret would marry. Brimming with excitement, she said, "Gosh, I wish I could enlist."

Seth stopped in his tracks. "Now, why on earth would you want to go and do a crazy thing like that?"

"Oh, it would be so wonderful!" She held out her hands and rotated dreamily. "If only I were a nurse. You know nurses are needed really bad in this awful war. And doctors, too. Bet you don't know that over 4,000 nurses are over there at this very moment."

"Well, I'm sure glad you're not a nurse," Seth postured. "Geez, you might get killed or somethin'. And then what am I gonna do, huh?"

Margaret giggled and grabbed his arm. She dragged him along until he loosened up and went willingly. At Packard's Drug Store in Maverick Square, Seth tugged her toward the door then opened it. As she stepped into the store, a playful breeze caught a lock of her hair, blowing its feathery sweetness into the face of the pubescent male. Embryonic maturity suddenly turned to mush. He stumbled into the store behind her and hastily removed his cap. "I-ice cream soda…" he stammered. "Uh-huh…That will top off my birthday present to you, Margaret. Movie and ice cream. Can you believe it? Now, you and me, we are both twelve years old. How 'bout that?"

"You know, Seth, it won't be long before our parents stop us from keeping company like this," said Margaret as she crawled up on the last stool at the farthest end of the counter.

"But Margaret, we're not really alone," Seth whined. He threw his cap on the counter and slid onto the stool beside her. "Your Mama always sends those two sisters of yours along. They tail us everywhere we go. For crying out loud, what does she think we're gonna do anyways?"

Margaret twisted up her face and shrugged, "Thank heavens, my sisters met up with their friends. They'll leave us be, at least for a little while."

"What'll it be, folks?" asked the soda jerk who seemed quite amused by the secretive young couple secluded at the far end of the counter.

"Two root beer floats, if you please," Seth said without taking his eyes off the young beauty next to him.

The soda jerk paused. He eyed Seth, then Margaret. Neither was paying the slightest bit of attention to him—nor anyone else for that matter. The smile melted from his face. "Sure," he said blandly. When he returned, the soda jerk set the soda glasses down in front of the amorous couple and stood there for a moment. Again, neither girl nor boy acknowledged him. Heaving a big sigh, he shuffled off.

Sipping through red and white spiraled straws, Seth and Margaret continued to gaze into each other's eyes. He placed his hand lightly on hers and said, "Your eyes laugh. You know that?"

"Now, how could I know, you silly?" Margaret looked away and peered into her soda glass. Avoiding his intense onyx eyes, she mindlessly studied the effervescence that bubbled up as she jabbed her straw into the melting ball of ice cream. "Do you think I'm pretty?"

Seth pushed his glass close to hers. Their faces nearly touched. Totally smitten by this radiant young beauty, he secretly wished to kiss her. "You are the most prettiest girl in the whole wide world." His root beer breath touched Margaret like a soft summer breeze and she dropped the straw into her glass. Her chocolate eyes grew big and round as she looked up at the handsome young man. "And someday, I'll marry you," he murmured. "This I swear 'cause you're the only love I will ever ever have in all my life. Never, never, ever will there be anybody else but you."

For a long, lingering moment, Seth stared into her eyes. His heart raced. Rubbing his sweaty palms on his pants, he scoured the store. Nobody looked his way. So for the first time, he kissed his Margaret. Her lips were soft, moist, everything his imaginative adolescent mind had presupposed. "Happy birthday, Margi," he whispered.

Margaret blushed. "Margi? You've never called me that before."

"I surprise myself," Seth choked for breath. "I guess I couldn't get out your whole name. Sorry."

"Oh, don't be sorry. I like Margi. Call me that from now on!"

"Really?"

"Sure. If I decided to pick out a nickname for myself, Margi is the one I would choose. It's so, so perfect. Better than Margie.

"Uh-huh, the hard g does make it sound a whole lot different, doesn't it?"

"Yeah. Margi," she breathed dreamily. "I'll hear you whisper it to me forever. Especially when we're not together. And today…I'll always remember…"

"Do you think of me at nighttime?" Seth ventured as he avoided eye contact and sipped his root beer float.

"You know I do." Her voice was soft, innocent, seductive.

His empty soda glass sputtered, "Glub, glub, glub." When he didn't notice, Margaret burst out laughing. "Your soda's all gone, you silly!"

* * *

When Seth arrived home that night, his mother and father were sitting on the front porch rocking chairs, watching storm clouds bubble on the western horizon. Fanning herself with the evening paper, Maria Avita paused for a moment and peered at her returning son through half-glasses caught on the tip of her nose. "Did you and Margaret have a good time?"

"Uh-huh."

"And Carlotta and Orazio, are they well this evening?"

"Uh-huh..." Plopping down on the top step, Seth dreamed of Margi and the first kiss they had ever shared. It seemed as if she was right there with him at that very moment. Her soft mouth was brushing against his as her dark eyes gazed innocently into his. Then she smiled, wide...those teeth, so snowy-white...The young lover tingled all over.

Maria Avita and Joseph exchanged glances and beamed with quiet amusement. Their son's thoughts certainly did not include either of them. At that moment the rumble of distant thunder drew their attention. A dark blanket of clouds rolled nearer as heat bugs chirped louder, challenging the impending storm. "By the look of those clouds, we are in for a good blow," Joseph speculated. "Rain should cool things off a bit."

"I certainly hope so," Maria Avita sighed.

"Did you read the paper today?" Joseph asked.

"No. I put it to better use," she pouted while continuing to fan herself with the newspaper. "The heat takes all my strength."

He glanced sympathetically at his wife then patted her hand. "Poor *Angelatina Mia*. Well, there is an article that claims sailors are coming into port from other countries and bringing with them a new sickness. Spanish Influenza, that is what they call it. Thousands of soldiers at Fort Devens are coming down with it."

"Is that so?"

In all their wildest dreams, Maria Avita and Joseph could not have imagined that within the coming weeks, the Spanish Influenza would race through the city, through the state, through the country, and through the world. The contagious wildfire would decimate families and close theaters, clubs, lodges and other public gathering spots until further notice. By the first week of October, city officials would have no other choice but to shut down all the schools.

Needless to say, the Championship game at Fenway Park went on as scheduled on September 11. Joseph and Orazio counted themselves lucky to be in attendance and saw the Red Sox triumph over the Chicago Cubs 2-1. It was the last time the two men would have any peace of mind for quite some time.

Standing elbow to elbow with Carlotta Bascuino and other women of East Boston, Maria Avita tended the legion of poor souls afflicted with the Spanish Influenza. They conjured up poultices of raw onions and garlic, remedies they had brought with them from the old country. They invented other recipes out of the desire to do something…anything to alleviate the horrific suffering. Every three to four hours, they applied poultices to the feet, under the knees, and around the necks of stricken individuals. If the sickness invaded the lungs, they mixed a bit of lard into the paste and spread it on the victim's chest. At times the poultices seemed to do the trick. More often than naught, they failed.

Time and time again, Maria Avita coaxed grieving family members off sealed coffins in which deceased loved ones were immediately placed after drawing the last breath of life. No one was ever allowed to reopen caskets. Burial was immediate and final.

Maria Avita stopped tending to others when Seth came down with the grippe. A day later so did Vincenzo. Within a week Francesca and Joseph took ill. Worry gave Maria Avita more of a burden than the influenza. Aspirin and remedies from the old country helped Seth and Joseph, perhaps because they were so strong and healthy to begin with, but that was not the case for Paolo, Vincenzo, and Francesca who always took so much longer to get over even the slightest illness. As Maria Avita fussed over a poultice mixture brewing on the stove, she lamented to

Armand, "They sweat so hard and the fever rises in spite of all I do. *Mio bambino* will not last much longer. We must get a doctor."

"But *Mamacita*, doctors are just about impossible to find these days," Armand said as he leaned against the door jamb between the kitchen and living room. "Pop and I have tried, but we do not have enough money to sway one single doctor to come."

Last-ditch desperation took control of Maria Avita. She quickly removed the poultice from the stove and set it on the table to cool. Shoving Armand aside, she charged through the living room. "Wait here," she commanded.

Armand watched his mother disappear up the stairs, and then something crashed over his head. His eyes riveted on the ceiling. It sounded as though she was rustling through the bureau in her bedroom. Moments later, she stumbled down the stairs and back into the kitchen. All out of breath, she jammed a wad of Father Sandro's money into Armand's hand and squeezed it shut. "Here, my son," she wheezed. "Put it with the money your father gave you. I beg of you, do not come back without a doctor."

Armand gawked at his hand. His jaw dropped open. "*Mamacita*... Where on earth did you get all this?"

"Never mind. Just go. Go!"

With her head filled with anxiety, Maria Avita continued to sponge the fever from Francesca, Vincenzo, and Paolo. Hoping to quell their coughing fits and chills, she hummed fitfully. What was taking Armand so long? When finally she heard the front door open, she wedged blankets up under the chins of her desperately ill children and fled down the stairs. Armand stood before the open door, swaying uneasily. Reluctantly he stepped aside. His thumb pointed over his shoulder. "*Mamacita*, Dr. O'Shea has come to see the children."

Maria Avita stopped short. An Irish! No Irish had ever set foot in this house. Joseph would not like this at all. Her fingertips scraped nervously together. What was she supposed to do? She swayed back and forth. Was she to turn away the last hope for her children? Or honor his ridiculous prejudices? But the children's lives were in jeopardy. To hell with Joseph. She reached for the doctor's arm and said, "Come in, come in."

Avoiding her grasp, the Irish stepped back and donned a facemask. "Take this as no offense to you, my dear lady," explained Doctor O'Shea with thick Irish brogue. "This I must do before entering your lovely home which I can see is clean enough to eat off the floor, if I took a mind to do so. But it is more than vital for me to minimize the danger to myself of falling victim to this devil scourge. City Hospital does this very same procedure, wouldn't you know, since Dr. Leen himself died of the sickness, may God rest his soul."

"I understand," Maria Avita nodded. "Please. Follow me." In the sickroom she whimpered, "My Francesca and Paolo do not seem to respond at all. They cough and cough. And little Vincenzo, he had two sinking spells during the night. I cannot think of anything to do."

The Irish doctor stepped over to the basin and washed his hands. Without a word he examined the two boys, then the girl. Teetering on edge of hysteria, Maria Avita followed O'Shea's every move. He stepped back to the basin and again washed his hands. Wiping them, he turned to her. His face was grim. He tossed the towel next the wash basin and said. "None of the children have developed pneumonia, as yet. That is a good sign, if there be any in all of this." His thick left eyebrow arched. "Have they had the nose-bleed?"

"No."

O'Shea pondered the answer then nodded, "This is what I will have you to do. Send that brawny son of yours off for some good Irish whiskey. Keep these children soaked in it."

"But my children, they are not allowed the drink."

"What does any of that nonsense matter now?" Doctor O'Shea shook his head side to side as he reflected on the hopelessness of the situation. "It is the only thing to be done. You have already tried aspirin. Here, give them this quinine. I have known it to be of some help. That is all I can do for them…and for you, my dear lady." The Irishman picked up his hat and black bag. He started to leave but then turned back. "You've done a good job, as much as anyone I have seen to this very day," whispered Doctor O'Shea. He stuffed the money Armand had given him into her hand. "Keep the sick ones isolated from the rest of the family. Many refuse to do even that. And continue to let in the fresh air and sunshine. It is of my own opinion that proper ventilation and light chases sickness from a house. For that matter I cannot see how it can hurt one wee bit."

"Everything I do seems so useless," Maria Avita sobbed while her palm, filled with Father Sandro's money, cradled her cheek. "My Armand and I are the only ones in this house who have not caught the illness."

Frowning, the Irishman noted the fatigue on her face. He wanted to touch her, to reassure her with a friendly arm about her shoulder. But times prevented such action. Instead Doctor O'Shea reached for the doorknob, and though he was not known to be of the praying sort, he turned and said, "May St. Anthony watch over you and your family, dear lady."

* * *

Carlotta and Margaret stopped by daily, bringing meals that most often went untouched. No one had yet become sick in the Bascuino household. Carlotta tended the boys while Maria Avita got some much-needed rest. Margaret kept watch over Francesca. The fevers lingered on for what seemed to be an eternity. The Spanish Influenza finally took down Maria Avita. She suffered worst of all. Throughout the ordeal the woman who had cared so much about others had ignored her own health and became rundown. By Christmas, she developed pneumonia.

Meanwhile, the epidemic began to diminish, and although the suffering continued for many months, schools reopened. Children returned to classes without a sibling or two only to find empty desks where school chums had once sat. Boxing matches and schoolboy football games resumed. Boston was dazed by more than two hundred deaths. Joseph thanked his God that so far every member of the LaRosa family survived, "But please, *Dio mio,* spare *Angelatina Mia.*"

The Spanish Influenza left the Bascuino family unscathed. People called it a miracle, but Carlotta claimed it was her fine homemaking skills and cooking that produced such a healthy family able to fend off the malady. She celebrated too soon, for the message came from the War Department that Nick Bascuino had been killed in Europe. That was only the beginning. Within the next few months, the Bascuino and LaRosa families came to believe that a grain of truth existed within old wives' tale that bad things come in threes.

Chapter II

Just before Christmas 1918, Rom got a message that Colonel Parks wanted to see him. As he lifted the flap of the colonel's tent, cigar smoke billowed out. Squinting through the stagnant haze, Rom saluted then asked, "You sent for me, sir?"

Colonel Parks gave a weak hand signal that swept the cigar from his mouth at the same time. "Hear ya speak some pretty mean Italian there, LaRosa."

"Yes, sir," Rom coughed.

Gripping the cigar between yellowed fingers, the colonel used the slimy stump as a pointer. "Got a communiqué here. Says the Army needs volunteers who speak fluent Italian, *pronto*. Seems the Italians got their hands full over there in Vittorio-Veneto."

"Sure, why not."

Even though the battle occurred more than a month earlier, Vittorio-Veneto still reeled from the after effects. Fragments of families delayed the burial of victims by insisting to view decayed remnants of flesh in hopes of finding missing loved ones. Refusing to give up, survivors had no shelter; food was in short supply. Rain and mud didn't help matters. They mixed with human excrement, producing a sloppy filth that became the breeding ground for countless ailments.

Just after Rom passed the roadblock into Vittorio-Veneto, an exasperated Italian soldier pressed him into service. Short in stature and nerve he grabbed Rom by the arm and tugged him towards a sodden unbathed peasant woman who held a death grip on a young girl's hand. She dragged the child along while badgering the Italian soldier who shielded himself behind the American. Face to face with the middle-aged matron, Rom wasn't at all sure what to do. The determination that filled her ebony eyes overflowed into her stance reminding him of his own Mama, ready to fight at a moment's notice for what she deemed right.

The Italian soldier behind Rom continually spat hasty pleadings in a dialect that Rom didn't quite understand. Dropping his duffel bag into the muck, the American placed his hands on his hips and tried to concentrate. But the words came much too fast. "This is going nowhere." Rom spun around and flailed his hands in the face of the blubbering soldier. "Wait, wait. You must speak slower, so I can understand you. OK? I speak southern Italian."

"*La Signora*," the Italian squawked. "She refuses to relocate to the relief center. There she will find shelter and food, but here…this place…there is nothing for her and the girl. We simply cannot care for them here."

"Calm down," Rom put his arm around the exasperated man. "I will try to make the lady understand."

"This is the only home I have ever known," fumed the ragged dowager while her head and arms flagellated like a centipede gone amuck. "My little one here, the only child I have left in this god-forsaken world, was born in Vittorio-Veneto. You cannot make us leave. I will not go! And that is that!"

"What is your daughter's name?" Rom asked.

"Anna Maria."

Rom nodded as he tried to hide the pain. Anna Maria was the name of Nick's girlfriend back in the States. Clearing his throat, he asked, "And your name, *Signora*?"

"Maria Rinaldi."

"Ah. Maria. My own dear Mama's name is Maria Avita."

The woman's thick dark brows arched as her eyes pierced his. "There is much sadness in your voice. Your Mama means very much to you."

"*Si, Signora*," said Rom. "I miss Mama *mia* very much…her and Pop…all my family."

Commonality grew between the peasant woman and the American soldier. They exchanged family histories and names and even discussed the difference in food between northern and southern Italy. The strangers found great joy in each other, and also great sadness.

"You see, *Signora* Rinaldi, I truly understand your plight. I myself left Italy for America with my Pop and oldest brother many years ago. How frightening it is to have no money, no home, and to be in a strange place separated from family, not knowing if they are all right or not. And then my Pop got hurt and could not work."

It took quite some time, but Rom finally brought Maria Rinaldi around to his way of thinking. "The best thing for you to do is take your Anna Maria to the relief center and when the reconstruction process is complete, return to Vittorio-Veneto if you wish."

When the peasant woman nodded, Rom kissed the back of her hand then stuffed an American dollar into it. He folded her fingers around the bill and winked at her. She smiled. He patted the child on the head then turned to the Italian soldier. "Do whatever you can to make *Signora* Rinaldi and her daughter comfortable for the journey to the relief center."

So it was that Romeo LaRosa took on a sense of a great responsibility towards all displaced Italians. Determined to help, he quickly learned the northern dialect and put in more than his required time. He became drained, pale, and gaunt. One day, an Italian superior forced him to take a fourteen-day leave. Having no place to go, the American took the road south. Heavy rain pelted him as he slogged along. Soaked to the skin, he swiped at droplets that continually dangled from his nose and chin, while repeating, "Walk. Just walk. Five or six days one way. Five or six days back. Nothing else for two weeks."

At a curve in the road, his ears picked up the rumble an oncoming vehicle. Not wanting to interact with humankind, he stepped off the road where no trail existed. Immediately his boot mired in the muck. He struggled to pluck it out and hid behind some overgrowth. The vehicle passed. The soldier heaved a sigh of relief. Adjusting the canvas straps of his Army-issue backpack, Rom moved on. He figured that he was probably the only one to tread this lush woodland in quite some time. An hour or so later, thick mist had replaced the driving rain. He came upon a fallen tree trunk and collapsed. Emptying the water from his boots, he tied them together and slung them over his shoulder. He wrung out his socks and looked ahead to a fog-shrouded clearing. The vision of Nick Bascuino, wasted on the battlefield, loomed. Artillery fire exploded. Again…Again…Rom squeezed his eyes shut, but eyelids could not hide the potency of memory. Terror molested him worse now than the moment it had happened. He shielded his ears and his socks dropped in the mud. The war inside his head raged on until he bolted to his feet. "I can't take it anymore!"

He ran, blinded by the insanity, barefoot, gear jouncing on his back. He sideswiped a tree and spiraled around and around. His bare foot caught a root, tripping him up and he somersaulted onto the sodden ground. His lungs struggled for air as his teeth ground together fighting off the demons that haunted him. An eternity passed, it seemed, before the terror eased and began to fade. Rom got to his feet and pretended not to care…pretended the carnage of the battlefield did not happen. It had changed him. He was tougher now, impenetrable. Nothing could hurt Rom LaRosa ever again.

The dawning of the second day brought dazzling sunshine that greeted him as he pushed aside the flap of his tent. "Thank God, no rain."

The air was dewy and cool. Puffy fair-weather clouds drifted past at the same unhurried pace as the journey through the pristine Italian countryside that day. He looked for his socks. They were not in his backpack, so he put on his boots and left the laces loose and untied. At nightfall his tent became a mat to lay under a canopy of stars and relive those endless nights when the only sound that broke the eerie silence of the battlefield was marching soldiers changing guard. The unnatural silence created an emptiness that craved fulfillment. So did the loss of Nick Bascuino, a real person, with a girl back home, with dreams just like anyone else. Freedom came at an exorbitant price.

On the third afternoon Rom followed an ill-defined path, created by wild goats, that zigzagged up a steep ridge southwest of Treviso. The rocky terrain loosened beneath his feet. Working up a sweat, he paused at every open ledge to catch his breath. Before his eyes two rivers carved silver ribbons in the carpet of green that stretched for miles. It all came to an abrupt end at the base of the sheer gray rock of the Apuan Alps. The mountainsides were white in places, not from snow, but from residue of marble mining. Since the time of Emperor Augustus, these mountains had furnished the world with marble. Michaelangelo's David had been set free from there as well as columns and balustrades…and simple white crosses…like the one that marked Nick Bascuino's grave in France.

The wandering soldier slumped against a lonesome oak near the edge of the rocky snout where the ascending terrain ended abruptly. It was getting late, but finding shelter for the night would have to wait. All he wanted at that moment was to rest and forget about everything. Releasing the straps of his backpack, Rom massaged the tracks out of his shoulders. His feet ached. Going without socks had its disadvantages. Rubbing his feet was much too painful, so he laid back and faced westward where amidst a myriad of lavenders and pinks, the sun had almost vacated the aqua sky beyond the pristine mountains. So painfully beautiful, it reminded Rom of East Boston and the evening skies over Charlestown. A curious blend of sadness and renewal drifted over him. Incredible beauty existed in this world. Why was it that his life was surrounded by devastation?

Rom bolted out of his daydream. Was that a baby's wail that disturbed the stillness? "Where are you?" It must be lost. Or maybe abandoned? Leaping to his feet, Rom fetched binoculars out of his duffel bag. Scanning the area below for the source of the forlorn cries, he worried. The hour was late. No child should be left alone in these woods at night.

The Great War had taught the soldier to not take chances so cautiously he descended his perch. The steep scree-strewn hillside gave way beneath his feet and he veered into the brittle undergrowth. Fighting his way through it, he made his way up a grassy knoll. He got down on his belly and crawled to the top. His head slowly levitated. There, on the other side of a small clearing, was a child of perhaps one or two years old, whimpering, sucking on a strand of her own dark curls entwined in her tiny fingers. From the look of her, he knew her cries had come from hunger.

The bushes behind the toddler rustled. Rom ducked then raised his head again. Before him stood the most beautiful woman he had ever seen. Hold it…she had not come out of bushes. That was a pile of brush, stacked in a fashion that created a crude shelter. Cooing softly, the statuesque creature enraptured the American. With the grace of an angel, she swept the whimpering child up into her arms and paced back and forth, rocking back and forth. Moments later, she paused and gazed down upon the sleeping child's face, the way only a mother does. Rom had seen this same sweet look upon his own Mama's face many times. When the woman and child disappeared into the shelter, the world became an empty, silent place. He rolled over and stared up at the fading sky. Heat radiated from his body. He felt sticky in spite of the cold, damp evening. Sweat glazed his palms. He wiped it onto his uniform and sighed.

It wasn't long before the little girl's plaintive wail began anew. He waited to see if anybody else came to or from the brush pile. The evening light strained into darkness. Stars appeared overhead. No further activity, only the hungry cries. Compassion urged the soldier onward. Scanning the area one last time, he got to his feet. For a moment Rom stood there, cracking his knuckles, swaying back and forth. Then noiselessly, he stepped towards the shelter. Brush covered the small opening from the inside. If it were not for the whimpering child, nobody would have known that anyone was in there.

"*Buona sera, Signorina,*" Rom spoke softly.

Abruptly the crying stopped. Silence.

"*Buona sera, Signorina,*" he called again. He listened. What was that? Choking? Alarmed, he shoved aside the brush and strained to see into the darkness. Crouching in the farthest corner of the wretched hovel, the woman trembled. Her eyes grew wide with mounting fear as each second passed. Her hand was covering the mouth of the squirming child.

"I am a friend. *Americano,*" Rom spoke in Northern Italian dialect. "Please do not smother *il bambino*. I mean no harm to either of you. Here." He tossed a can of c-rations to her then backed off. "Give this to her. She is hungry. You take some, too."

The woman lunged for the can and keyed it open. After giving small bits of food to the child, she choked down the rest without so much as a taste. Rom offered his canteen, "Here, better have a drink with that." She eyeballed him, then the canteen, then him. He smiled reassuringly and beckoned with the canteen. "It's OK. Take it. Please."

Clutching the child to her breast, she slowly crawled within grabbing distance of the canteen and snatched it away. Quickly she retreated into the corner where she held it to her little one's lips. The babe suckled loudly and much too fast. She began to gag. The mother tore the canteen away and took several long gulps herself. When there was no more, she tossed the empty container at the American.

"I don't understand," he said. "Why on earth do you hide like this? Don't you know? The war is over. You can go home."

The woman shook her head. In the northern Italian dialect that Rom had come to know so well, she said, "There is no home for me."

"Why. Where do you come from?"

"Gorizia."

"That is a far distance. How did you get here?"

"Germans." She defiantly spat on the ground.

"I don't understand."

Fear blanketed her face. She turned away. Horror paralyzed her tongue.

"Your little one sleeps."

Looking down upon the sleeping child, the woman brightened.

"What is her name?" Rom asked.

"Isabella."

"And yours?" he asked.

"Rachele."

Rachele. The name moved within every fiber of his being and transformed into a rising symphony that seduced his mind and robbed his breath.

By noon the next day, his supply of water was gone and no more than three days of rations remained. He knew Rachele must take Isabella back to civilization but to leave the only security they knew? He doubted that she would go for it. But the mother and child would surely starve to death if he left them there. Rom gnawed on a piece of grass and marveled at Rachele doting over Isabella. What a great mother. Spitting on the fabric of her skirt, she tenderly washed her little girl's face. An idea came to him. "Not far from here, I passed a lake. We can get water for my canteens. And I have soap. Here, look!" He held up the bar of soap. "You can give Isabella a bath."

Rachele fingered her child's matted and tangled hair. "Do you also have a comb?"

Rom nodded and rummaged through his duffel bag. He held up a brush and a wide-toothed comb.

"We will go now," she said.

The distance was farther than Rom remembered. They had to go back up the hillside the way he had come the night before. After that it was a least another hour. Luckily, Rachele didn't seem worried. When she grew tired, she surprised him by letting him carry Isabella. When the lake finally came into view, Rachele squealed and broke into a dead run. Throwing off her shoes, she dove headfirst into the water, clothes and all. Rocketing up out of the depths, she swished her head from side to side then splashed more water onto her face.

"Hey, Rache, you forgot the soap!"

Effortlessly, she caught the bar that Rom threw at her. Tossing back her wet hair, she laughed with glee. Never in his entire life had he heard a lovelier sound. After washing, Rachele trudged out of the water; her clothes clung to her sleek body. Her dark eyes and ethereal smile sent chills to the very heart of him. She proceeded to strip off Isabella's clothes and scrub away weeks of grime. The child loved the water as much as the mother did. For more than a half an hour later, they splashed in it, then Rachele wrapped the babe in a green Army blanket. No sooner had her mother washed her tiny clothes and hung them on the bushes for the afternoon sun to dry than the child was asleep.

"Here's a shirt," Rom offered. "Wash your clothes, too."

Rachele looked at him suspiciously.

He waved his palms in front of him. "Hey, you got nothing to worry about. I am a gentleman, a man of honor. Mama *mia* taught me not to peek at naked girls."

That same beguiling grin flashed across her face again. Unexpectedly her tongue wagged at him. Rom didn't know what to make of it. Her smile grew wider. Suddenly the terrible war no longer existed. They burst into laugher and like a couple of innocent school children, threw off their clothes and frolicked into the water.

A while later, Rachele was sitting on a rock opposite Rom and he was skimming pebbles across the surface of the water. He pretended not to notice the Army fatigues that he had given her. With rolled up sleeves, the shirt hung off one ivory shoulder and reached mid-thigh. It fit her terribly…terribly wonderful. How could it be? She looked so ravishing. That woman could not have looked better in an evening gown. She was combing her long coal-black tresses, tossing her head from side to side, releasing the moisture from within the thickness. Sensing his eyes, she locked into his trance. "Last night, you asked how it was that I came to that place in the woods." She continued to comb her hair in long thoughtful strokes.

Rom gave a slight nod.

"The Germans invaded Gorizia." She paused. "Not long after that, they marched through my village. My husband fought them, but they captured him…and all the other villagers, too. The Nazis separated the men from the women. We were on one side of the street, on the other, the men. Machine guns jabbed at the men to make them kneel on the ground…even the boys. Then…a line of German soldiers marched in between us. They raised up their machine guns…The men…murdered right there…for all of us women to see. My poor Mama…She saw Papa get shot dead. Mama fell upon the ground and refused food and water from that day on…and…and then…Mama…she died…" Rachele buried her face in her hands and wept uncontrollably.

Rom went to her and knelt in front of her. His hands cupped hers. Tears streamed down her cheeks as anguished eyes searched his for reason. "The dirty pigs chose the girls they liked. One of them took me to Vittorio-Veneto. A month or so later, the leech found out I was pregnant and kicked me out of his tent. He screamed at me, 'Go home. Go home!'"

"The invasion of Gorizia happened a long time ago," Rom said. "Isabella his?"

She shook her head. "No, I was late when the Germans invaded my village, but I think that Nazi thought the child I carried was his and that is why he kicked me out instead of killing me."

"Where did you go? How did you deliver?" Rom asked.

"I hid in the countryside for a long time. One day, monks found me. I was very weak, and so they took me to their monastery. It was west of Bassana del Grappa. That is what they told me. When my time came, they found a woman who helped me. Isabella and I did very well there. But then Italian soldiers came to the monastery. They asked for food for the army that was fighting the Germans in Vittorio-Veneto. I became so frightened. The Germans will win again, that's what I thought, so I ran away from the monastery to hide with Isabella."

"How long ago was that?" Rom asked.

Rachele shrugged.

Chapter 12

Joseph believed that God had truly blessed him. The entire LaRosa family had survived the Spanish influenza and a letter from Rom reassured him that his son was still alive in Europe. Armand had summoned Doctor O'Shea for Maria Avita—against the father's wishes. Throughout the worst of the deadly illness, the Irish had never left his patient and had even slept in Seth's bedroom. Needless to say, when all was said and done, Joseph felt beholden to O'Shea. Could it be that his preconceived notions about the Irish needed further reconsideration? A good Christian man certainly would have done just that, but there was no time to do so on this outstanding day in January 1919. Joseph had other plans, an outing to the North End for Maria Avita and Francesca. He pictured himself tagging along with them through specialty shops and purchasing the imported lace that Francesca had pestered him about long before the sickness took hold of her. Usually Joseph found such outings quite tedious, but today, he promised himself, things were going be different. He would show more interest in the silly things the women buy. By mid-afternoon how hungry he would be. Hotel Napoli came to mind. The most delectable food was on the menu there. In addition, listening to the orchestra render classical selections was incredibly relaxing. Well, that was that! Hotel Napoli for lunch.

At 10:45 Joseph gave Maria Avita and Francesca a hand onto the train that took them into the North End. Just before North Station, the metal wheels of the train rounded the precarious double curve, emitting the most ungodly screech. From there the brakes took over, squawking until the train came to an unsettling halt at the platform. Joseph glanced at his fifteen-year-old daughter. Her hands were clasped against her ears and her eyelids were squeezed so tight that a tear budded outside the corner of her eye. The sourest look plastered her face. A he helped her to disembark the train, he chuckled, "Only one thing can sweeten *piccola* Francesca *mia*."

"And what is that?" Maria Avita asked with a twinkle in her eye.

"*La cioccolata*."

Anticipating the taste of thick, luscious chocolate melting in their mouths, the trio traipsed over to the Samoset Chocolate Factory on Hanover Street. Like they had done on previous outings, they foraged through endless trays of hand-dipped creams, caramels, and fruits. It was impossible to make up their minds. "Come on, you two. Pick out an assortment," Joseph pleaded. "The day is wasting away."

Outside, Francesca stopped. "I have an idea. Let's close our eyes and reach into the bag. That is the only way to choose."

"If that is what you call it," Maria Avita laughed as her hand plunged into the bag.

After Francesca drew a chocolate surprise out for herself, she handed the bag to her father, but he refused to take it. "I will wait." Joseph had other ideas. At Quincy Market he stopped at a pushcart that sold fresh oysters and cherrystone clams *al fresco* and indulged himself. Alternating squirts of lemon with dashes of pepper sauce on the raw shellfish, the man drifted into a heaven made on earth.

"Hey, Pop," giggled Francesca. "You complained at the chocolate factory that Mama and I were wasting the day. We can say the same thing about you now."

His mouth packed full, he could not reply. His finger signaled "wait" as hastily, he chewed and swallowed. Wiping his chin and mustachio with his handkerchief, he sputtered, "*Si, dolce piccola* Francesca *mia*. We go, we go right now."

Meandering through Haymarket Square, Joseph proudly tipped his hat to passers-by, most of which he did not know. He felt like a true gentleman. With money in his pocket, fine clothes on his back, and a beautiful lady on each arm, he was in his glory. They stopped at Boston's United Fruit & Produce Company where Joseph inquired, "Are these fruits and vegetables fresh?"

"Shipped in just last evening from South and Central America," bragged the vendor.

"If not for this company," Maria Avita said while thumbing tomatoes, "Boston would not see such a variety at this time of year."

"Look at those poor immigrants over there," Francesca pointed.

"*Si*," Joseph whispered and pressed his daughter's finger down to her side. "It is not polite to point, *cara mia*." When her cinnamon eyes dropped to the ground, he patted her head and said, "All is well. Forget about it. Those hungry souls wait for handouts of vegetables and fruits that are wilted or do not look so good and cannot be sold."

"But little trim here, a little trim there, and a free meal fills their bellies," Maria Avita said.

"How gaunt they are," said Francesca.

"*Si*. God surely blessed the LaRosa family," said Joseph. "Such bad times did not befall us after arriving in America."

Maria Avita took his arm. "Let's go down to the docks. The fishing boats must be in by now. I want to take some *baccala* home with us."

"But Mama. I don't like to go there," Francesca stamped her foot. "It smells so disgusting. Besides, you make salted cod much too often. I swear, I cannot stomach another bite of it."

Joseph blinked at his wife. "Come, *dolce piccola* Francesca *mia*. The wind blows from the West."

Maria Avita leaned close to her husband and whispered, "It is so nice to hear our daughter whine like that again."

He nodded and took Francesca's arm. "After we buy *baccala*, we will head up Commonwealth Street and you will smell the docks no more, no, only the delights that the chef at Hotel Napoli cooks up."

"Now listen to me, *marito mio*. We cannot linger," insisted Maria Avita. "The clock tower says ten minutes after twelve and my stomach calls out to me that it is in sore need of filling."

"*Si, Angelatina Mia*, mine also," he said while marveling at how wonderful his wife looked. Her appetite had returned and she grew stronger every day. The only other time she had been this thin was when she first arrived from Italy. He boldly concluded that Maria Avita was healthier than ever.

It didn't take long for Francesca to change her mind about the docks. The handsome young fisherman who waited on them caught the maiden's eye. She curled a strand of chestnut around her finger as her cinnamon eyes charmed him to death. Maria Avita and Joseph pretended to look at the lobsters in a wooden vat filled with seawater. "The fisherman and our daughter are entranced with one another," Maria Avita whispered out the corner of her mouth. "Did you hear him tell Francesca that his name is Joe Belladonna?"

"*Si*," Joseph chuckled. "Joe. A good sign, is that not so?"

When the bell in the clock tower tolled, Maria Avita spoke up, "Twelve-thirty. Come now, Francesca. It is time for…"

Thunder, the likes of which nobody had ever heard before, echoed throughout the streets as the ground shook under their feet. "What in God's name…" Joseph gasped while searching for the source of the blast. Little did he know that beyond his vision, *Malavita*, Lord of the Underworld, had risen within an elevated storage tank at the United Liquor Company. His fury exploded from his containment. Fragments from the fifty-foot-high, ninety-foot-diameter tank plus the contents of two million gallons of molasses blasted high into the air over 529

Commercial Street and rained down upon North End Park, filled with lunch hour activities. Black goo, used in making alcohol for smokeless gunpowder, roared down Commercial Street, ripping buildings from their underpinnings and crumpling them like houses made of cards. Iron supports beneath the tracks of the elevated railway groaned and gave way to the weight of the rolling maelstrom that surged murderously southward. Directly in its path was the unwitting throng at the fish market, including Maria Avita, Joseph, Francesca, and Joe Belladonna.

"Run!" voices shrieked as the rolling black wall, so high it sent chills up and down the spine, roared at them.

"Come on, Joseph. We must get out of here," Maria Avita yelled. But fear had paralyzed Joseph. She grappled for his hand and towed him down the side alley towards the Charles River. They ducked behind a wood-framed storage shed just as the river of molasses swept past.

"Mommy! Help," choked a tiny voice. "Mommy…" Tiny fingers reached out.

"*Dio mio*! It takes a child," Maria Avita screeched and extended her hand. Her fingertips were only inches away from the tiny hand. She stretched…more. She got it. "It is too slimy! I cannot hold onto it! No…" she shrieked as the hand slipped through her fingers. Losing her balance, Maria Avita fell forward, but Joseph,'s strong arms snatched her from the brink and held her against his body as the rolling molasses gobbled up the child. One little hand clutched at the air then disappeared. Maria Avita buried her face in her husband's chest. Suddenly, she looked up him. "Joseph?" Her eyes grew wide. "We are moving."

His brows came together. "That cannot be." The shack nudged his heels. He stepped away. The next thing he knew, it plowed into him, nearly knocking him off his feet. When he saw Maria Avita lean all her weight against the wall and dig her feet into the ground, Joseph braced his palms into it and gritted his teeth. As they struggled to keep it back, Joseph cried, "It is no use. Our strength is not enough to stop it."

The couple was the mercy of *Malavita* as the shack swept them toward the Charles River. It gathered speed. Abruptly it stopped. The unattached tin roof lurched forward and hovered in mid air until gravity brought it crashing down...down upon Joseph and Maria Avita. Sprawled underneath the peak, she rose up on her elbows. "We are trapped! Joseph?" When he did not answer, she looked at him. "Oh, God! You are unconscious. And molasses it is rising around your head! No," she cried and shook him violently. "Joseph, wake up." But he did not respond. She struggled to her knees then yanked on his arm. "You must sit up!" She fell back on her ankles. Bile bubbled in her throat. "Your leg is stuck," she whined. She picked up his head and held it to her breast. Rocking back and forth, she whimpered. "Wake up, *mi amore.* Please. You must wake up."

Searching the cramped space that held them prisoner, Maria Avita discovered a broken crate. With one hand she shoved away debris then slid it under his head. At least for a little while, the molasses could not steal his breath. She patted his slimy hand while fretting, "Wake up, Joseph." No use. She dropped the lifeless limb. Sweet sticky molasses splattered into her face and mouth. She spat it out as if it were the venom of the viper. "Joseph, you are going to drown if you don't get up this minute!" No response. "What am I going to do?" Maria Avita scanned the narrow confines then raised her voice skyward. "Help...Somebody help us!" Suddenly, she felt a draft on her cheek. "Air," she wheezed. Where...?" She spotted a tiny gap in the mound of rubble just above her shoulder. Tearing into the debris, she found it too compacted; not a single piece would budge. She leaned back. *Malavita* was rising relentlessly. Her hand gestured toward the heavens. "Is there no way out of here?"

Desperation spawned a terrible rage. Only one other time had Maria Avita been this incensed. In her brain she saw the sinister ooze transform into the evil priest. Yet this time, no matter how she battled, he continued to have his way with her loved one. Inflating her lungs to capacity, the woman screamed for all she was worth, "Leave us alone! I will kill you! You cannot do this!"

"Why do you holler so, *Angelatina Mia*?"

She spun around. "Joseph!" She gasped. "Joseph, you woke up!"

Relief filled her senses, but then he mumbled, "We must think of happier times. Pray to God for our salvation."

Her breath stopped as her eyebrows knitted. "God? *GOD?* To hell with your God," she blasted. "We will save ourselves for it does not seem He has a mind to. Your foot is stuck. Work it free. This minute! There is too much left for us to do in this life. We will get ourselves out of here. That is all there is to it!"

* * *

While sitting at the open window of his second story flat, Armand sipped his first coffee of the day and watched the children at play on Hull Street. People were going into the café across the street for lunch. He felt at home here among closely built tenements where mornings found laundry cascading from lines strung to buildings across the street. At all hours background clatter of life going on around him gave him a sense of peace, even when he slept. From his vantage point he could see the Old North Church down the street. Its obvious presence leveled Armand in ways he was at a loss to understand. Only occasionally did he attend Mass, and that was for family rites. Church was just not in his blood.

Suddenly, a blast nearly shook him off his chair. "What the hell?" he thundered and leaned out the open window. The children in the street below scattered like flies. Heads bobbed in and out of other tenement windows, searching out the annoyance. People began to shout. Some were running towards Commercial Street. Armand slammed the window shut and bolted down the stairs to the street. He grabbed the arm of a man charging at him from the direction of the waterfront. "What's going on?"

"Molasses tank blew," panted the man who was covered with black gooey grime. He shook off Armand. "Gotta get help!"

Armand joined the crush of people at Commercial Street. The scene confounded the senses. Such things were not possible. A thick black river of molasses coagulated with warped steel and splintered wood into twisted mounds of debris around which dazed victims wandered about, bleeding, faces gashed, limbs broken…or missing. Demolished automobiles, overturned wagons, and carts with no wheels littered the scene. Trolleys, lifted off their tracks, rested against remnants of buildings, shoved off their foundations. There were scores of dead or injured horses, dogs, cats—even pigeons, sparrows, and seagulls. Groans of disbelief issued up from the crowd when an adolescent emerged alive from the sticky goo that had hurled him upside down and sideways along its path. Wobbling in an aimless stupor, he tripped and fell across a child lying dead against the Bay State Freight office. Horror blanketed his face as he looked at her. Black death had heartlessly slammed the tiny body there and if that were not enough, the fiend had impaled a metal shard into her heart.

"Poor kid," Armand winced then turned from the sight, but his mind held the vision of the coils of long chestnut hair. "Same color hair as Francesca's." The utterance somersaulted in his gut. "Pop! *Mamacita*! Christ, Francesca! They're here today. Nah, they can't possibly be in all that mess." He forced himself to believe that but…"Come on, they're on Salem Street. Having lunch." He yanked his watch from his pocket. "12:45." His chest heaved. "Better check on 'em anyway." He started out for Salem Street. At first he contained his instincts but as he searched the crowds and shops, panic built within him. "Where'n hell are they!" Sprinting back to his apartment, Armand grabbed the phone. "Damn! Out of order." Slamming down the receiver, he bounded down the stairs and made a mad dash towards Faneuil Hall. He almost ran past the pay phone at the corner. He dropped in a coin. Dial tone. "Great, it's working." He dialed the Captain's house. It rang and rang. And rang some more. "Come on," he snorted. "Answer. For Crise-sakes, answer!" It rang several more times.

"Hullo?"

"Vincenzo," Armand spat. "Get the guys together and get over here. *Pronto!*"

"Where? What is wrong?"

"Not far from my place. Molasses tank exploded. It's all over everything and I can't find *Mamacita* and Pop."

"Whaddaya mean, ya can't find Mama…?"

"Shut up and listen to me, will ya? Come by car; the train tracks are out. Go down Washington Street then take Salem. Don't take Commercial…do not go that way, ya hear me Vincenzo? Do not go that way! Nobody's getting' through." Armand slammed down the receiver and raced back to the cataclysm. "Dammit, Vincenzo, ya better get this right." At times that kid gave Armand the willies. Vincenzo lived in a world all his own. Nobody ever had an inkling of what the hell he was thinking. What was wrong with him anyway? Deep in thought, Armand crossed Salem Street. Out of nowhere, a Red Cross Ambulance blared past him and nearly mowed him down. "Pay attention, LaRosa," Armand muttered. "Won't help nobody if ya go and get yaself killed."

At Commercial Street he waded into the ankle-deep molasses and slogged toward South Station. He climbed over the mountain of debris that the tide of the molasses had created and plunged unwittingly into a knee-deep pool of black goo where dazed victims raised themselves up as if the resurrection had come at last. He helped some of them to their feet and peered into the whites of their eyes while asking. "Who are you?"

More often than not, the shocked victim could not find his tongue. So Armand wiped the molasses from their faces with his handkerchief until it became so slimy that it was of no further use. He tossed it away and continued the search. All sensibility became lost. He wandered without understanding where he was and what he was doing. The remains of the building next to him suddenly ruptured and a man, coated in a mix of dirt and molasses, bulldozed himself out, scaring the daylights out of Armand. Shocked back to reality, he bristled with the thought that a similar fate had befallen his parents. Only they might not be able to get out like this guy did. Armand stopped dead in his tracks and bellowed, "Pop! *Mamacita*! Where are you?" He listened...only the dripping of his clothes, his own desperate gasps, and the sounds of agony. An eternity passed. He called again. Still no answer.

"Armand?"

He spun around. "Seth!"

Vincenzo, Paolo, and Tomasso Cacace caught up with Seth, behind them, Luigi Spanucci and Alfonso Venditolla. Armand clutched his youngest brother's shirt with both hands. "I can't find 'em! I just can't find 'em!"

"Calm down, will ya?" Seth grasped his brother's wrists. "We'll find 'em."

"Gotta spread out," wailed Armand; his arm swept out into a huge encompassing circle.

"OK, OK," agreed Seth. "Tell us where to start."

Armand stopped short. Gaping into the thirteen-year-old's questioning eyes then at his own hand that had become white from clutching the kid's shirt, he came to his senses and released his grip. He flexed his stiffened knuckles and said. "A few of ya go back to the shops on Salem Street 'n fan out. Weren't there before, but double-check anyway. Could've missed 'em. Vincenzo, Paolo, you two go down to the end of Commercial. And don't forget the side streets to the water." Armand grabbed Seth's sleeve. "Come with me, 'K? We'll check the fish market and docks."

As they sloshed through the molasses, Seth hollered to the right, "Pop? Mama?"

"Pop! *Mamacita*," Armand bellowed to the left. "Dammit, Seth, you ain't gonna believe the people buried under all this shit."

Beneath the mountain of rubble and tin roof that entombed Maria Avita and Joseph, they heard the desperate calls. Unfortunately, they had hollered for help so intensely and for such a long time that their voices had become barely audible. "They will go right by us, if we don't do something," Joseph squeaked. "If only I could pry this leg of mine loose."

Feeling utterly useless, Maria Avita rolled her eyes. Her mindless gaze rested on twisted pieces of pipe. "Over there," she pointed then lunged for them. "Here! Bang them together! Like this." She clanged two together.

Seth froze. His open palm slammed into Armand's stomach. "Sshh…listen!" They were almost out of range, and the rising clamor of sirens, shovels, and hysteria muddled their hearing. "There it is again! Did you hear it?"

The brothers spun around in the direction of the clanging. They searched each other's eyes. "And there it is again," said Armand and led the sprint in the direction of the clanging. Halfway there, they zeroed in on a mountain of rubble.

Breaking a mad dash, Seth hollered, "Mama? Pop?"

When the clanging became more rapid, more intense, Armand cried, "*Mamacita*, we're here. Hold on, ya hear me? We're gonna get ya out of there!" With their bare hands, the brothers tore at the rubble. Moments later, Tom, Luigi, and Al came back from their search of Salem Street and Armand screeched, "Pop and *Mamacita* are at the bottom of this mess."

"You sure it's them?" Tom asked.

"Sure I'm sure!"

Nobody stopped to agree or disagree. Someone was under there, that's for sure. What seemed like hours passed as they dug into the heap. At last the roof lay before them. "Take a look under there, Seth," said Armand, "while the rest of us lift this corner."

As they elevated the roof, to their surprise Maria Avita scrambled out like a sand crab. Getting to her feet, her lungs sucked in fresh air, "The debris…it holds your father by the leg."

"We need somethin' to hold up this corner," hollered Armand. That done, he said, "There. Now, lemme under there for a look." He wormed into the confined space. The old man didn't look too good, but Armand was not about to say it. Instead he said, "It's OK, Pop. Just relax. We'll have ya outta here in no time."

Joseph nodded.

Armand surveyed the debris that refused his father his freedom. He yanked on Joseph's leg. It did not budge. Backing out of the hole, Armand stood up and tried in vain to find something on which to wipe the molasses off his hands. "Couple o' two-by-fours got a hold of Pop just above the ankle," he said swiping his hands across the front of his shirt. "Gotta get that roof up another four or five inches before Pop can free up that foot."

"There's not enough of us to lift this thing that high," Tom winced.

"Yeah. I know," Armand shrugged. His hands jammed into his hips as he studied the roof. The others gathered around waiting for the next command.

"We gotta do something," Seth insisted. "The molasses is starting to congeal with the cold air drifting in off the ocean.

"Oh what the hell…everybody grab a piece," Armand snorted and threw his hands up in the air. "And *Mamacita*? I'm sorry, but ya gotta go back under there. When some of the weight's off, see if ya can help Pop pry himself loose. OK, everybody? On the count of three. One…"

"Hold on there a minute!" The hunched over men turned to see several sailors running towards them. One called out, "Wait. We'll lend a hand with that."

Tom shouted, "More hands! Just what we need."

With renewed hope Armand shouted, "OK, fellas! Let's get this thing over and done with! One. Two. Three!"

The men grunted. The roof inched up and when Maria Avita saw that the timing was right, scooted back into the molasses-filled hole. "Come on, Joseph. Pull your leg out of there," she commanded.

As the man struggled to free himself, the roof cracked and buckled. His eyes shot upward then at Maria Avita.

"Forget about that. Come on, we can do it." Anger and determination, the likes of which he had never seen before, flared in her eyes. "This is not the way to die." She clenched her teeth and yanked on his leg. "Pry that junk off with your free leg and yank harder on the other one."

"*Si*," Joseph huffed. "If I have to tear these old bones apart, we will not die here today."

The roof gradually moved upwards. That was all that he needed; his leg sprung from the demon's grasp like a rubber band recoiling. Seconds later the roof buckled again—worse than before. It dangled precariously, snapping, splintering, sagging. "Dig your heals in and shove yourself backwards," hollered Maria Avita. "I will help you." Little by little, she dragged Joseph out of the hole. A section of roof caved in, barely missing his feet. At long last strong arms pulled her out the rest of the way and she fell against Armand while Seth and Tom plucked Joseph from the black viscous grave. The other men let go of the roof. It came crashing down, belching forth a thunderous cloud of dust and molasses.

Seth and Tom helped Joseph to his feet. With a wide grin on his face, Joseph held out his arms and Maria Avita rushed to him. "Look, *Angelatina Mia*. My ankle. It is not broken." His foot twisted this way and that. "Not so much as a sprain."

Everyone crowded around to see the miracle. In the midst of congratulating each other for a job well done, Paolo elbowed his way through the crowd. "Mama. Pop," he muttered. "It's Francesca. You better come."

Maria Avita covered her mouth. Her eyes grew wide in horror. How could she have forgotten all about her little Francesca?

The cacophony of wailing emergency vehicles, barking rescuers, screaming victims, and hacking pickaxes and shovels dwarfed the morbidity in which the group, led by Paolo, Joseph, and Maria Avita, hastened down Commercial Street. They stepped in the congealing goop, two to three feet deep in places, and passed by rescuers. Eventually, twenty-one bodies were extracted from the bogs of molasses and debris that day. Molasses covered victims so completely that identification was nearly impossible.

A shot rang out. Off to the right, a cop had just shot a horse that was stuck like a fly to flypaper. Nothing else could be done for the poor creature.

The fish stand where Joseph and Maria Avita had bought the *baccala* was gone. Like a scaled fish, nothing was left of the entire market area. Just beyond, Vincenzo huddled with several others. His coat covered a heap on the ground before them. Joseph and Maria Avita stopped in their tracks. She covered her mouth. Holding back her terror, she clutched her husband. Vincenzo stood there with both hands in his pockets. His head bowed. When he saw his frightened parents clutching one another, he turned away and began to sob.

Joseph grasped his wife's arms. Slowly he backed her away from him. Dread surged through his body. He took one step then another. Standing above the garment, he clenched his fists. Apprehensively he bent down. A trembling hand lifted the coat. Color drained from his face as he fell to his knees and moaned, "*Dolci piccola* Francesca *mia!*"

* * *

Joe Belladonna had tried to protect Francesca, but his body was not enough to ward off the black death. As the maiden's cinnamon eyes locked with his ebony eyes and her small nimble fingers entwined his, *Malavita* snuffed out their lives.

Chapter 13

On a mild afternoon in late February 1919, Seth caught up with his teacher on the way back from lunch. "Mrs. Russo," he exhorted. "I don't know if you noticed or not, but Margi's not feeling too good. She seemed OK this morning, but by the time noon rolled around, she wasn't at all herself. She didn't eat a single bite."

"You worry too much about Miss Bascuino. She's a big girl. I'm sure she can take care of herself quite adequately."

"But look at her, Mrs. Russo. Don't she look all dragged out and kinda ashy?"

"Take your seat, Mr. LaRosa," Mrs. Russo brushed him off without so much as a glance at the girl hunched over on one elbow at her desk.

Reluctantly Seth took his seat, but he kept a watchful eye on his Margi anyway. The afternoon wore on. No sooner did he redirect his attention to a problem in his math book than a shadow crossed his desk. He looked up to see Mrs. Russo, as white as a sheet, hastening towards Margi. Surely his eyes deceived him, for there was Margi sprawled across her desk. Her head lay on top facing the windows unsupported by arms that dangled at her sides. She looked like a puppet without the puppeteer. Bedlam broke loose in the classroom as Seth sprang his feet and sped across the classroom. "What's wrong Margi?"

"Go back to you seat," commanded the teacher quite harshly.

"But..."

Pointing her index finger at him, her lips pursed and her eyes meant business. Seth slunk back and collided with other students who pressed forward for a better look. The teacher crouched down and wrapped an arm around the girl. Without raising her head, Margaret feebly twisted her body until she faced Mrs. Russo. They whispered words that Seth could not hear, and then the teacher coaxed Margaret to her feet. Bearing most of the student's weight, Mrs. Russo took Margi out of the classroom. An eternity passed before the teacher returned. Looking quite grim, she avoided his inquisitive stare and said, "Let us return to our mathematics lesson, class."

Seth was beside himself. What's the matter with that dumb ol' teacher? She knew full well that for him concentration was impossible. Well that's it then, he was not going to stay in that stupid classroom one moment longer. He had to find Margi. Just as he slammed his book shut, the dismissal bell rang. The young man raced out of the classroom and searched the halls, finally catching up with the love of his life outside the girl's restroom. The school nurse had all she could do to exit with her charge. Limp as a rag doll, Margi teetered with every step. Her glassy eyes failed to acknowledge him. "Margi? It's me. Seth. You don't look too good at all."

"Mmm." Her voice was muffled and weak. Running her dry, pasty tongue over her cracked lips, she stammered, "I'm so thirsty. And my muscles…hurt bad. I…I can hardly stand u-u…" She reeled and fell against him.

Seth dropped his schoolbooks and caught the stricken girl around her waist. Holding on to her for dear life, he gaped at the nurse, what to do? Abruptly the young man bent his head and lifted Margi's arm over his shoulder. Her body heat blazed through him like a forest fire. "My God! You're burning up!"

The nurse placed her hand on the girl's forehead then quickly withdrew it. "She grows more feverish with every passing moment!"

"Hey there, Seth," hollered Margaret's two sisters in singsong unison. "Boys are *not* supposed to touch girls. Better get away from Margaret this very instant or we're gonna tell our Mama."

"Go right ahead and tell her," he bellowed. "Margi's sick, you dummies. Can't you see? I'm bringing her home and nobody's stopping me."

Margaret's eyes rolled back and the little color left in her face vanished. Terror swept the faces of the two sisters when their sister's head fell backward and Seth nearly caved in from the unexpected dead weight. His weakness angered him and he took it out on Anna and Eleonora. "*Go!*" he thundered.

The panic-stricken girls tore off for home while he scooped Margi up in his arms and sprinted off after them. His cap flew off. Somberly, the school nurse picked it up and his books.

Margaret's nose started to bleed. Blood trickled down the side of her cheek and onto his shirt. "This ain't good," Seth moaned. His legs refused to carry him as swiftly as his mind dictated. "Come on legs, faster. Faster!"

Maverick Square had never seemed so far away. At last he rounded the grocery store at the square and smacked head-on into Carlotta Bascuino. He reeled against the brick building, panting.

"Tell your Mama what is the matter, *bambina mia*," she spoke softly. She brushed the back of her hand across her daughter's forehead and gasped. "Margaret, you burn like an August day! *Rapidamente*, Serafino, we must get Margaret to her bed." Carlotta dashed ahead, waving her outstretched arms and screeching Italian. The churning multitude scattered. Seth struggled onward, cradling Margi against his chest. Carlotta shoved Eleonora and Anna out of the doorway as he stumbled up the front steps. From here on Carlotta spoke only Italian. "Careful. Do not drop her. This way. Come on, come on!"

Barely had Seth laid Margi down on her bed when her mother bulldozed him out of the way. His breath gone, he quaked from head to toe as he backed into the wallpapered wall and slithered to the floor.

Carlotta rubbed Margaret's arms, patted her cheeks, slapped her hands while over and over, pleading desperately, "Come 'round to me, *mia* Margaret. Mama's waiting for you." The stricken girl did not stir. "Eleonora! Anna," Carlotta ordered without turning. "Wet some towels and bring them to me. We must put down the fever." She threw off Margaret's shoes and socks then unbuttoned the blood-spattered blouse. Slinging the lifeless body over her shoulder, the mother ripped the sleeves off her daughter's arms. "Serafino, go get that doctor. The Irish. You know—the one that brought your Mama back. What in God's name did he call himself anyway? Aarch…never mind. Just go and get him. And hurry, for I fear that time is not with *bambina mia*."

Seth scrambled to his feet and dashed out of the bedroom. His arm scraped the door casing. His body ricocheted across the kitchen and into the living room. He skidded into the credenza, causing treasured breakables inside to rattle just as violently as his traumatized brain did. He leapt into the street, never setting foot on a single stair. "Please, God, don't take my Margi. She's the best thing in my life!" He brushed away blinding tears, resenting such childish things. "No, God, don't! It's not fair."

* * *

Dr. O'Shea stepped out of Margaret's room and without a word crossed the room to the sink where he washed his hands. Carlotta closed the bedroom door quietly then turned and leaned on it for support. Worry riddled her short stout being. Eleonora and Anna went to her; each took one of their mother's hands. Maria Avita stood in the archway between the living room and the kitchen. Seth shielded himself behind her. Like everyone else, he was afraid to ask, afraid to know. The Irishman slowly turned. Drying his hands, he searched the faces. These poor tormented souls…must he once again utter those dreaded words that no mortal on this earth dared speak aloud? He cleared his throat.

"Spanish Influenza. The dear girl has herself come down this very day with the scourge."

"No," Carlotta screeched and collapsed to the floor. "*Non vero! Cio malattia e non piu. Basta!*" Doctor O'Shea looked bewildered.

Maria Avita spoke up, "She says, 'It cannot be. That dreadful sickness is done with. Over.'"

The doctor hung his head and shrugged. "To be sure, I wish it were so, though I m'self possess only a wee understanding of the dreaded malady."

Seth withdrew from the house. The wind had been knocked out of him as if a bully's fist had impaled his gut. He collapsed on the front steps. His vacant eyes stared into the street and the stark gray sky beyond. Time blurred. "My Margi's got the flu...Margi's got the flu...got the flu..."

Into the night Seth kept vigil on the steps outside the Bascuino home. That's where Joseph found his son slumped against the brick wall, head angled against it. The tearstained face revealed only a hint of the child Joseph once knew. At thirteen his son had grown into a man. "Come, Serafino," Joseph coaxed. "I take you home."

"No, Pop. I must stay."

Joseph did not argue his son's resolve. No one had torn him from Maria Avita's side while death stalked her not so long ago. No one would have dared. "*Si, caro* Serafino *mio. Si,*" Joseph whispered and hunkered down beside his son. He gazed into the dark empty street where shadows leapt like demons as clouds passed in front of the sylvan moon. Strange, this street teemed with activity during today, but this night it was deserted, allowing Satan free reign. From time to time Joseph shifted his weight on the cold brick step. Eventually, he got to his feet and plodded home. A short time later he returned with a tapestry pillow from the parlor sofa stuffed under his arm. A homespun blanket from the steamer trunk in the hall closet was slung across his shoulder. He tucked the pillow between the brick wall and the boy's head then draped the blanket over him. Kissing his son's head, the father laid one hand on the mass of dark curls and the other he lifted skyward while issuing up a fervent prayer. "Thy will be done, *Dio mio*. But this I pray to You, think this decision once again. If the girl does not live, all will not be well with *piccolo figli mio*, Serafino." His heart heavy, the solitary figure trod homeward.

Before sunup the next morning, Maria Avita and Louisa nudged Seth awake. As one eye peered out from under the blanket, graupel snow rolled off and dusted the ground like granules of sugar. "Come into the house," said his worried mother. "You must eat."

"No, Mamma, I…"

"Listen to your Mama. She knows what's best," Louisa insisted.

Seth stood up. His young bones were chilled and stiff. In the house he refused all offering of food and took only steaming coffee. His frozen hands failed to sense the singe of the stoneware. The quietness and the smell of the house turned his stomach. It felt like death itself. He had to get out. His mother had tried to keep him indoors but to no avail. Throughout the day Seth maintained his vigil on the front steps of the Bascuino home. Every so often he peered through the panes of colored lead glass. The living room was dark and empty. Beyond, he occasionally caught a glimpse of his mother and sister going about household chores. Their lips barely spoke at all. It was not so long ago that the LaRosa family had lost Francesca to *Malavita*. To be at such a juncture again, so soon, was beyond all reason. Invariably Seth crept back to take up his post on the top step where the times he had spent with Margaret played over and over in his head. When was there not Margi? She had been there since his mind first had memory. He wanted to love her forever…to grow old with her…to have many children, just like Mama and Pop. The young man aimed to build for this girl the finest house, the likes of which East Boston had never yet seen. He recalled that perfect summer day they had spent together and how her hair had brushed his cheek as he opened the door of Packard's Drug Store for her. Their first kiss. Her eyes, so round, soft as sable fur. And her moist lips…"My

God!" Seth leapt to his feet. "This is all my fault. Margi got the sickness from me! I shouldn't have kissed her again last week." Pacing back and forth he chastised himself. "The newspaper warned about kissing. I just got over the sickness myself…I must have given it…*I* did this to Margi."

He sank back down on the step and moaned. Day passed into night. Daylight came. Still Margaret burned with fever. And Seth burned with guilt. The Irish doctor came and went, more often than he did to homes of other patients. Furtively he mumbled to the vigilant young man, "No change, m' boy."

Day passed into another night. Another day. Dr. O'Shea exited the house and donned his cap. Seth jumped to his feet, searching the man's face, but the Irish evaded the anxious eyes and passed by with not so much as a word. The sullen doctor shuffled down the street with shoulders overburdened by an imperfect profession.

Seth looked back at the door. The panes of glass, red, green, blue, divided by thin strips of tarnished metal were too colorful for a house in peril. There was the worn brass knob. How many times had Margi touched it? Should he? His eyes twirled. He stepped over and turned it. Adjusting to the dimness inside, he made out his mother slouched across the kitchen table, dabbing her cheek with a tatted handkerchief. "My friend of so many years is filled with the grief that only a mother can know," she sobbed. Louisa was also crying while halfheartedly wiping off the table. "Now, I must comfort her. But how can I when I myself cannot find comfort in my own loss?"

"Mama?" The voice was barely audible.

Serafino. She swallowed hard. How could she look upon his suffering?

"Margi?" Her name stuck in his throat.

"Not good, my son. Pneumonia…" The word strangled her. She motioned for him to come to her.

"Please, Mama," he murmured. "I wish to see my Margi."

"No, my dear son. It is not proper."

Seth knelt at his mother's feet and held her hand against his heart. His onyx eyes penetrated her soul. "Please, Mama. I beg of you. Let me see my Margi."

Traversing her youngest son's face, Maria Avita heard the unspoken beckoning of the gravely ill girl beyond the bedroom door. Seth and Margaret meant so much to each other. Maria Avita glanced at Louisa, who nodded slightly. Getting to her feet, the mother went to the bedroom door. She hesitated then straightened her dress and drew a deep breath. She turned the knob and slipped inside. The door closed silently.

Carlotta Bascuino was leaning on her elbows, braced against the edge of the bed. She clutched black rosary beads halfway around the strand while murmuring passionate Italian supplications. In the far corner Eleonora and Anna clutched each other's hands and whimpered. Orazio's dark form stood at the window as if looking out, but the curtains were drawn and let in no light. Halos glowed around candle flames that surrounded a wooden crucifix placed on the bed stand. Blessed incense pervaded the room.

Maria Avita placed her hand on her friend's shoulder and spoke the language of the old homeland. "With all respect intended, my son, Serafino, has made a request to see your daughter."

Carlotta drew back. *This is not done* was written all over her face. Then, as if the gravely ill girl had whispered to her, she looked down upon her daughter. The mother's eyes grew soft. Her head nodded.

Bowing slightly, Maria Avita backed away and opened the bedroom door. She beckoned to Seth.

At first he stood there, his body paralyzed. The scourge of their lifetime taunted him. Did he have the courage to look upon Margi's ailing face? No, that fiend would not keep her from him. Seth forced himself onward. First one heavy foot moved. And then the other. *God, the bedroom is dark. Not a breath stirs the air.* His eyes searched out his love. Like an angel in the darkness, her image materialized and drew him to her. His insides cried out, *Margi, you lay so still. And your breath comes too fitful. Don't fold your hands like that, you look to be dead.* His heart ruptured within his chest as great unseen hands crushed his chest so he could not breathe. This was all one big bad dream. He must awaken. This cannot happen. Urgently he mumbled, "Margi. It's me. Seth."

Did her eyelash flutter just then? Or did he just wish it so? Clutching her frail hand, he drew it to his lips as he fell to his knees. "You can lick this thing, Margi. I know you can." Her hand was without warmth and did not fold around his the way it had always done before. A well of tears burst forth. "I'm so sorry. I did this to you. If you forgive me, we can forget about all this and make things like they were before. You've always been there for me, Margi. You know how to make me smile, even when I'm angry or sad. What'll I do if you go away?" Abruptly Seth straightened. His brows knitted and he shook her hand. "No, you won't leave me! We grew from babies together; I won't let you go! I'll not hear another word of it."

Waiting for her to speak, he grew silent. The distant ticking of the clock on the living room mantle intruded. Futility overcame him. He began to sob inconsolably. "Stick around, Margi. Just a little bit longer. And love me. I'll show you how much I love you. You'll see."

How long he had kneeled at his Margi's bedside was lost to the ages. His vision was murky as he sensed his mother's presence. She lifted him by his elbow while whispering softly, "Come, Serafino. It is time we should go."

Hours passed. The dawn came. Margi was gone…leaving Seth behind forever.

Chapter 14

The battleship New Jersey and the steamship America cut through fog-cloaked Boston Harbor followed by the USS Mt. Vernon and the Agamemnon, formerly the German liner Kaiser Wilhelm II. A myriad of smaller vessels weaved in and out, blowing whistles and horns to welcome home the returning Yankee Division. Eager doughboys jammed the rails, hoping to spot the faces of flag-waving loved ones among the throngs assembled on Castle Island and Commonwealth Pier.

Over on Tremont Street, Commonwealth Ave., and all the surrounding streets crowds waited. The dank cold April day in 1919 failed to deter their enthusiasm. Hats flew into the air and flags waved as the parade of triumphant young men in khaki uniforms marched the five-mile serpentine route in military precision...well, perhaps not quite military precision.

"Eyes front," barked officers again and again.

Few obeyed the command. Actually, neither did the officers who had issued the orders, for they too scanned the grandstands trying to spot those special faces waiting for them there.

"There he is," shrieked Maria Avita. Clutching her husband, she steadied herself. Tears of relief and pride streamed down her cheeks.

The sight of his second son prompted Joseph to look skyward and whisper a silent prayer, "*Grazie*, St. Anthony, for returning Romeo into the love and safety of his family's arms."

Not long after the four-hour parade concluded the LaRosa home and yard in East Boston overflowed with family and friends. The arrival of the guest of honor was close at hand.

"Will you please calm yourself, *Angelatina Mia*." Joseph's voice feigned worry, but his face beamed with delight. "You run around like a chicken with its head cut off!"

"Now you listen to me, my husband, right here and now," Maria Avita hyperventilated. "Things must be just so for our son's homecoming. I will not hear another word out of you."

"But there's enough food here to feed the entire Yankee Division," taunted Joseph. He poked his finger into the marinara, then into his mouth.

"There'll be none of that," she said and playfully swiped a ladle at his hand.

Just then a shout rang out from the front room, "They're here!"

Exchanging anxious glances with her husband, Maria Avita gasped, "Oh. Oh!" Flinging off her apron, the nervous mother straightened her dress and her hair then scurried into the living room. Joseph and the crush of family and friends swarmed behind her.

Seth held the front door wide open. Armand, who had picked up Rom at the Army depot, strutted through the doorway, proud as a peacock. One would think he was the returning patriot. He waved an introductory gesture in the direction of the door and announced, "Ladies and Gentlemen. For your listening pleasure, I present to you the long-absent, the hardest-headed of all the hardheaded LaRosa sons, Romeo LaRosa!"

Clapping, cheering, and whistling raised the roof as Rom walked through the door. Before he got the chance to set down his duffel bags, his mother's arms enveloped him. Months of agonizing worry flowed in her tears. Suddenly she pushed herself away from him and ran her hands over his face, neck, and arms. "Thank God. You are still in one piece." Her fingers snagged on three bronze stars that decorated his uniform. She peered into his hazel eyes and once again started to bawl.

"Mama, I'm OK," Rom reassured her and dropped his bags. He stretched around her and shook hands with Joseph. "Hey, Pop. How ya doin'?" Without waiting for an answer, the returning soldier reached outside the door. "Mama, Pop, everyone…meet Rachele…my wife. And…" He bent down and picked up a dark-eyed curly-locked two-year-old who hid behind her mother. "As soon as possible," he paused and winked at Joseph and Maria Avita. "This little one will officially become your new granddaughter, Isabella LaRosa."

When little Isabella covered her face with her hands and peeked through her fingers at all the strangers, Maria Avita clasped her hands to her heart. Her emotions got the best of her as her arms opened wide to welcome the new members of the LaRosa family. Laughter and gaiety filled the air. Only one person balked—Joseph. Even his worst nightmares didn't leave him this aghast.

"We got hitched at a monastery just West of Bassana del Groppa." A broad grin pasted Rom's face.

Joseph withdrew; his mind vehemently protested. How could this be? Another man's woman? Another man's child? His sons and daughters were to join in marriage only with spouses untouched by all others. Only LaRosa seed brought forth LaRosa lineage. He decided to speak to the Monsignor immediately and have this marriage annulled. Thinking that this unholy union was easily rectified gave him great satisfaction. On the other hand, he could not ignore the fact that Maria Avita had enthusiastically accepted that woman. And the child. They acted as if they had known each other forever. What was he to do about that? And what about all these friends and family? They took to that woman much too easily. His own daughter had also betrayed Joseph, for she had brought little Isabella to Francesca's bedroom, left without an occupant now for only a few short months. Louisa had no right to do such a sacrilegious thing. Upon their return, the child clutched the rag doll that

Francesca had brought from the old country. It was all Joseph could do to restrain himself from savagely ripping the plaything from the child's grasp. Quickly he turned away. His eyes seared Rachele. Just as surely as Satan stalked the fiery depths of hell that unchaste jezebel had tricked his son into marriage!

Hush fell over the room when Rom caught sight of Nick Bascuino's parents. Head bowed in sorrow, he wormed his way to them through the crush of people. He was still unable to come to terms with the loss of his friend whose toothy grin and devil-may-care attitude brightened every place he went. "I'd give anything for Nick to be here today. He was standing there, right next to me," Rom whimpered while bobbing side to side. "It makes no sense. The battle was over. Finished. He was telling me about a letter he was writing home. Next thing I knew," Rom gasped and pointed to the floor as if it were the battlefield. "Nick? Ah, geez, there's Nick."

"You could do nothing," Orazio laid his hand on Rom's shoulder.

"Nick and I saw too many atrocities," Rom rambled on while cracking his knuckles. "War's not the great adventure we thought it was. No. Everywhere, blood and muck. Wounded. Dying. No matter where you looked there was death."

"Do not torture yourself so. My Nicholas, he is in Heaven with *la dolce* Margaret," wept Carlotta. She held the returning soldier as if he were her own son. Looking into her eyes, Rom nodded. Nick would not have taken his sister's passing well—no, not at all. Always babbling on and on about his first rate family, Nick's pride and joy was little Margaret. *Mia dolce piccola Margaret*, that's what he called her. My Margaret. Those words interrupted Rom's train of thought. his hand massaged his arm. And that punch, the one that Seth laid on him years ago for teasing him about *his* Margaret. "Seth, remember when…Hey, where's Seth?"

"Probably up at Eagle Hill," Armand replied.

"How come?"

"The kid hangs around up there all by himself. After the grippe took Margaret, he ran off and nobody could find him. Pop and I tracked him down there."

"Gimme your keys, I'll go get him," said Rom.

"Nah. Let the kid be. He'll get a hold of himself in time."

Seeing how deeply the discussion was upsetting Carlotta, Orazio changed the subject. "What is all this we hear about Mussolini and his Fascist party? Is it good or is it bad?"

"Too soon to tell," Rom shrugged. "He says he cares about the Italian people and promises to make school mandatory for all people, not only for the rich. Time'll tell, but in my mind, it doesn't look good."

"Hey! Don't worry 'bout it," interrupted Armand. "It's about time we canned all this morbid talk. We're here together, that's all that matters. And because Rom participated in the Great War, he now becomes an American citizen automatically. A toast! To the new *Americano*!"

Glasses clinked. "*Salute*," resounded throughout the house. Chugging down his drink, Armand asked, "What're you gonna do now, *piccolo fratello*?"

"Well." Rom took deep breath as he put his arm around his wife. "Rachele and I talked about it quite a bit and well, with all those pay-checks I sent home to Mama plus my separation pay, there's enough money to put a sizable down payment on a farm."

Joseph's brows lifted. "Farm?"

"Yep."

"Where?" Maria Avita asked.

"I was thinking about Reading."

"Come on, I can't believe you wanna be a farmer," Armand scoffed.

Rom shrugged. "Just want some good ol' fashioned peace and quiet. After all, that's what all the fighting's for, isn't it? The old homestead and Mom's apple pie?"

"Yeah, but making a living at farming?" Armand argued.

"I know, I know. More'n likely, I'll have to fill the gaps with something else. What's the prospects of a job?" Rom glanced at his father. Surely, Pop had a job for him.

Joseph stammered, "Well, er." He wiped the palms of his hands on his pants. "Things are slowing down right now, with the war over and all." The old man knew full well what his son wanted. Well, Rom was not about to get one blessed thing from Joseph. Flashing a murderous look at Rachele and her little one, the pious man clenched his teeth. Uh-uh, not until that woman and that kid got their heathen souls out of the picture.

"Mayor Peters is taking the rap for the slowdown," Angelo interjected. "He's a good man, but his timing's bad. Too many of you warriors returning home, looking for something to do."

Returning vets were not the only problem. The cost of living had doubled since 1914. Contributing to a general uneasiness, incomes failed to make much headway. Like everyone else, nine hundred Boston policemen sought better hours and higher wages and joined the American Federation of Labor in the fall of 1919. An enraged Police Commissioner dismissed those men whom he considered responsible for organizing the union. In support of their coworkers, the rest of the Police Force walked off the job. That night, Boston streets became a war zone. Vandals struck everywhere. Smashing windows, looting stores, the criminal element knew there was no one to stop them. The following morning Mayor Peters called out the State Guard. Later that afternoon the man whom some claimed was weaned on a pickle, Governor Calvin Coolidge, gained national attention when he stated, "There is no right to strike against the public safety anywhere, anytime." With that, he called up additional regiments of the National Guard to maintain law and order for the next three months. On December 21, 1919 an entirely new Boston Police Force took over and relieved the last National Guard Unit. Young men recently discharged from military service became Boston's Finest. Romeo LaRosa stood among the ranks.

In the meantime the FBI cracked down on suspected anarchists and Communists in response to the opinion of many that there were just too many foreigners up to no good. Never should they have been let into this country in the first place. As a result three thousand foreign born, including Italians, found themselves paraded through the streets of Boston like cattle, some innocent and some not so innocent. This worried Gaspare Messina. Was his Boston organization in jeopardy? Motoring to New York, Messina voiced his concerns about the Red Scare raids to Don Vito.

"Similar *problema* plagues *tutta la famiglia*," claimed the Don as he offered a mahogany box of cigars to his visitor.

"Perhaps, it will serve us well to put our heads together," suggested Messina. He pretended to study the fine carvings on the box before he opened it.

"I sense that you have already hatched a scheme to rid us of our common *malattia*."

"*Si*, a remedy that is sure to take the heat off the organization."

The Don lit his cigar. He sucked in a full chest of smoke and stared at the ceiling. Slowly he exhaled then nodded for Messina to speak further.

"*Il Mafioso* resorts to robbery and murder only as a last-ditch resolution to its own internal problems. So much secrecy cloaks such acts that they draw little or no attention. The authorities are wise to this."

Vito's thick eyebrow lifted. What Messina said was true.

Tapping ashes into a silver ashtray, Messina drew a deep breath before continuing. "In my mind if a robbery comes to pass, the authorities will naturally become outraged if that robbery involves ripping off one of their own. So waddaya think? Who will the Feds and cops go after?"

"The anarchists and other hard-core criminal elements," expounded the Don.

"Nobody else," Messina said flatly. With an air of satisfaction, Gaspare chewed his cigar and watched Don Vito shuffle over to the window. Damn, the Don was getting old. Still, who was Messina to talk? He too felt the years. Hacking violently, Gaspare ripped the cigar from his mouth and silently cursed the black slimy pulp. This death stick was doing nothing for his health.

"Who's trustworthy enough to do the work?" asked Don Vito.

"Phil Buccola," said Messina.

"*Si*, Buccola. His name has reached my ears," said the Don skeptically. "He is a man of methods beyond those sanctioned by the organization. He rises quickly to the surface and might prove dangerous to our survival."

"That is why Buccola is perfect for the job. Already, local cops know him as a renegade of the organization. If anything goes wrong, they will search out Buccola. The family will disavow his actions and can insist that he acted without our consent or knowledge."

"Still, I cannot trust a man who does not live by *omerta*."

Messina knew not to speak. Don Vito was thinking.

"You and me, we will plan this and..."

"We...?" Messina started.

Surprise blanketed Don Vito's face. Rarely, did anyone interrupt him. Or question him for that matter. Even regional bosses knew their places. No further words came from Messina. The Don continued, "Only those who actually carry out the details will have knowledge of it."

Ultimately, Phil Buccola was out of the picture as Messina and Don Vito concocted a payroll robbery in Braintree, a small industrial town south of Boston. They tagged the Morelli Gang for the job that went down on April 15, 1920. The heist netted fifteen thousand dollars. Unfortunately, a guard and pay officer were killed. That was not supposed to happen. Don Vito hit the ceiling. He sent word to the Morelli Gang, "Clean up this unholy mess!"

Eyewitnesses reported that there had been five robbers who appeared to be Italians. Based on several descriptions, the police set a trap in a seedy section of Boston but those suspected in the Braintree heist didn't show. As the cops prepared to scuttle the ruse, Nicola Sacco and Bartolomeo Vanzetti entered the picture. Although the two men did not fit any witness description, they stumbled into the wrong place at the wrong time. The cops needed someone to quash their animosity, so hey, what the hell, they frisked the two Italians and discovered guns stuffed in the waistbands of their pants. Eyebrows raised. Well, well, well. Concealed weapons was enough to make any man suspect, so the cops hauled them downtown where Sacco and Vanzetti lied about their anarchist backgrounds. The authorities found out, of course. So innocent or not, they arrested the two men and used them as examples to others of similar persuasion by throwing the book at them. An open-and-shut case was hastily built; prosecutors demanded the death penalty for Sacco and Vanzetti.

Sometime in the early morning hours after the arrest, with only a fingernail of the moon to light the way, a solitary dark figure stole through the back alley of the police station to a door conveniently left unlocked. The unknown individual went directly to the evidence room, also unlocked. With sinister precision the rogue switched Sacco and Vanzetti's guns with those actually used in the Braintree robbery and tampered with fingerprint files. In another part of town, witnesses who claimed they had seen Italians pull off the job were either paid off or otherwise induced to identify Sacco and Vanzetti in a police lineup. The fate of two innocent human beings was sealed.

Chapter 15

In 1920 short skirts and high prices became the fashion. Women hiked their hemlines closer to the knee than the ankle, and playing cards sold at six packs for a buck. A decline in business brought unemployment and the collapse of prosperity. Americans blamed their troubles on President Wilson and the Democratic Party. Republicans charged Wilson with extending the powers of the presidency at the expense of the legislative branch. They wanted their own man in office, but Warren Harding had never drawn a great deal of voter support. However, his plea for a return to normalcy for the country made him a favorable candidate for the presidency. Throwing his hat into the ring, Harding tapped Governor Calvin Coolidge of Massachusetts as his running mate. The Democrats nominated Governor James M. Cox of Ohio for president. Franklin D. Roosevelt of New York ran with him for vice-president.

Since 1916, Gaspare Messina, the first boss of the Boston organization, spearheaded one of the most prominent families in the American Cosa Nostra. Don Vito welcomed the new business venture. Not only did new territory come under the domain of organized crime, but also Gaspare dispatched generous monthly tributes to his mentor. New York coffers swelled and this set well with the Don.

His newly acquired prominence caused Gaspare more worry than ever, not for himself, but for his son, Aldo, who had great potential, though at times plunged headlong into situations without the slightest regard to either the cost or his personal safety. A day might come when such brash behavior might prove lethal. Messina needed someone to keep the reigns pulled in on Aldo. The only one with that kind of ability was Armand LaRosa. Since their days on the boat, Aldo had grown to trust the LaRosa kid. They had similar ways of thinking too, but where Aldo was weak, the LaRosa kid was strong and vice versa. During their days in New York, things got done without too much dust. Aldo, although a strapping young man, was not quite as intimidating as Armand who had grown taller and more broad-shouldered since the boat. LaRosa's stomach was flat and hard, whereas Aldo could never weather a barrage of punches. Armand carried himself proudly like a noble Roman soldier despite a slight limp from a battle over kickbacks. Aldo, a hot-shot pinhead, ran off at the mouth without any muscle to back him up. The fire that blazed within the onyx eyes of Armand LaRosa hid a calculating vigilant mind. Aldo's eyes wandered just like his brain. Women and rumors ruled his life. Other matters took the back seat.

For all these reasons, after placing Aldo at the head of the loan sharking branch of the Boston operation, Gaspare persuaded his son to make Armand his right-hand man. The thought of working with *il capodecina* whom he had personally molded pleased Aldo. To Armand the lucrative offer made the money he earned working for LaRosa and Sons look like peanuts; the work wasn't as hard either. Not a person to live by the clock, Armand relished the thought of not having to go to bed just when nightlife got under way. Every day Boston grew and changed and he liked the idea of to being a part of the scene. The rapid expansion exhilarated Armand, but Joseph hit the ceiling when informed that his oldest son was leaving LaRosa and Sons Construction Company. Nevertheless, the Messinas succeeded once again in sucking Armand LaRosa back into their organization.

Bootlegging made headlines daily and Armand LaRosa was in over his head. From the get-go he had quickly become a big earner, impressing Don Vito and the Messinas with each morning's receipts. Because of this, they allowed him to branch out from the loan sharking end of things into buying and selling homemade liquor. Within a couple of years, Armand had an overabundance of alky cookers at his disposal, which provided him the base to set up numerous swanky speakeasies to distribute the alcohol. The outside of these establishments resembled laundries, shoeshine shops, or churches, but inside the nightlife flourished, which was Armand's cup of tea. So the handsome young upstart made more money than he spent. He splurged on expensive baubles for his mother though she rarely wore them, and bought an automobile for his father. At the same time, he bought one for himself. The long black Packard plus the ability to drive it on hard-surfaced roads increased his mobility and sense of independence. On the other hand, too many horse-drawn carriages still lumbered along the cobblestone streets. Streetcars, tracks, and electrified trolleys added to the clutter. He cursed them one and all whenever he was in a hurry, which was usually the case. This led Armand to rent an apartment on Hull Street in the North End. Not only could he keep a close eye on his business interests, but he was also close enough to East Boston just in case his family needed him. Little did he know that when the Great Molasses Flood struck, his family would need him more in the North End than in East Boston.

Armand also took good care of his siblings. Paolo bought a barbershop with two cutting chairs, thanks to his oldest brother. Angelo managed to hook up with an apartment near Boston College, but only after his oldest brother applied a little persuasion to an unwilling landlord. After Angelo graduated from East Boston High School, he informed Joseph that he intended to become a lawyer. He planned to work his way through college and live at home, but Armand would hear nothing of that hogwash. "You are the first LaRosa to attend college," Armand said with genuine admiration. "You must devote all your time to studies if you want to be successful. Use your extra time playing football. That joint wants high school jocks like you. Plus the broads will flock all over ya, more than they ever did in high school."

"Gee, you make a hard argument," laughed Angelo.

Deep down, Armand envied Angelo. What was it like to sit in a classroom? Cripes, the only book learning he had ever gotten came from *Mamacita*. "Whatever you do, don't waste your time traveling back and forth to East Boston. And don't listen to any of Pop's religious mumbo-jumbo either. That stuff will make you question every damn thing you learn."

There wasn't much Armand could do for Seth. His youngest brother did just fine without any assistance from big brother. No longer the smallest child in the family, at fourteen years of age, he stood even with Armand's shoulder. Judging by the size of his hands and feet, the kid still had quite a ways to go. Yes, he was good with his hands, like the old man, and wanted to learn everything about LaRosa and Sons Construction Company. Seth believed everything Pop told him, such as a man who made his living by the sweat of his brow was closer to God than any other. Well, considering his present state of economic well-being Armand found that philosophy a bit hard to swallow. It had taken longer for Seth to get over Margaret Bascuino than Armand had expected. Big brother began to get concerned. Little by little though, the kid came around and buried himself more and more in his schoolwork or long hours working with Pop. He did well in school, a real whiz in math. Armand constantly kidded teased him, "Of course it is easy for you to learn so many things since you head is still so empty!"

On top of everything else, Seth picked up the business end of LaRosa and Sons as, one by one, his siblings found other things to do with their lives. That was okay with Armand. Someone had to stick by the old man.

*   *   *

Friday night—boys' night out. Armand LaRosa and Aldo Messina got all decked out in white linen suits, white patent leather shoes, and gray spats. White fedoras, ringed with gray headbands, topped off their slicked back manes. The hangout of choice this evening was one of Armand's smoke-filled speakeasies in Southie. The place looked like a church, but the rites inside were anything but religious. The two cocky studs swaggered in and took a table next to one with an intricate card game in progress. Aldo scrutinized the action and snickered, "Stakes ain't high enough."

Their attention shifted to the ladies, several quite inebriated, indulging in wild behavior near the jukebox. Before this decade men rarely saw the opposite sex dressed in such skimpy garb. It certainly left nothing to the imagination. Not even in New York City did Armand and Aldo see young ladies act so wild and free. Perhaps, Armand speculated, the reason for this was that women had won the right to vote thereby giving them a sense of independence to act and dress any way they pleased.

"Take a gander at those flappers!" Aldo's eyebrows twitched. His clenched fist poked back and forth as his lower body rocked with a naughty phallic thrust.

"Hey, these are the Roaring Twenties," laughed the skimpily clad waitress who came over to take their drink orders.

"House special." Armand held up two horizontal fingers.

"Do me the same." Aldo never took his eyes off the flappers.

"Whoa, get load of that sassy bleach blond," Armand pointed his thumb at the chick with the bobbed hair earnestly doing the Charleston. "Taking that one home with ya, Aldo? It's Friday night ya know, man's night to howl."

"Damned right, LaRosa." Aldo slugged down his double shot and slammed the empty glass on the table. "Gotta get it while the gettin's good. As we speak, my ol' man's arranging marriage between me and that whiny brat of the Providence *capo*. Good for business, bad for me.

No doubt it'll put the skids on Friday nights with the *comare*. Gonna take a little time to get the new *sposa* used to the idea. How 'bout you, LaRosa? Which one's straightening the beast?"

"Pondering the options," Armand said but a classy dame at the end of the bar had already captured his imagination. Sitting cross-legged in a low-cut powder blue dress that complemented her coloring and petite hour-glass frame, she wistfully stirred a mixed drink. A high hemline allowed ample appreciation of her slender legs. His hormone level soared with visions of the upper edge of those silk stockings and the other treasures playing hide-n-seek beneath the tissue-thin garment.

"Aw, come on, LaRosa. Take it out and dust it off," Aldo nudged Armand and offered him another double. "Let's see what kind of stuff you're made of."

Through the years Armand had gotten wise to Aldo's uncanny ability to egg him on. To summon up courage, Armand would drink like a fish and before long, Aldo could talk him into doing things that nobody in their right mind would even remotely consider. This time Armand ignored the taunts. Aldo was just a big kid, full of himself. Instead Armand focused on the young lady in the powder blue dress. Her luscious strawberry blond hair was finger-waved tight to the head and drawn into a glittering beaded clasp at the back of her long, slender neck. Waves of golden tresses cascaded freely between her shoulder blades and down her back. Armand felt an urge to leap right over there and grab a handful of it. He imagined crushing the thickness against his face, its perfume wafting up his nostrils, its softness soothing the anxieties in his life, like a child finds comfort from a freshly washed security blanket.

Armand scoped out the scene. No one put the moves on the striking redhead, so after a while, he excused himself, "Gotta hit the can." On the way back the inamorato strutted up to the bar. Leaning his six-foot frame against the deck, he rested his foot on the brass foot rail below and once again ordered two fingers of the house special. "Tab it," he said and casually turned toward the strawberry blond. Acting as if he just noticed her sitting there, he winked. "Hey. How ya doin'?"

"Good," she replied. That single whiskey-warm utterance nearly laid Armand out on the floor. Her ivory fingers circled the rim of the crystal popcorn bowl as their eyes met. Emerald eyes pierced his puffed-up facade and his anatomy instantly reacted. The smoke-filled speakeasy, full of rambunctious patrons, blurred leaving only the sharp image of the strawberry blonde with green eyes who wore the powder blue dress.

* * *

The next morning Armand feigned sleep as Kathleen quietly slipped out of his bed. It didn't take him long to come to his senses. Pop would never approve of this hussy. Why, the old man didn't approve of Rom's wife. And she came straight from the old country. "That woman's used goods," Joseph constantly complained to Armand behind Rom's back.

"It ain't Rachele's fault the Kraut's killed her husband," Armand countered. The old man would hear nothing of the kind, but as far as Armand was concerned, Rachele was OK. Whew! A real looker, too. Not only that, it was as plain as the nose on your face that Rom and Rachele were head over heels in love. What more could anyone want? Besides, *Mamacita* liked Rachele. And little Isabella too. But Kathleen…an Irish? *Mamacita* accepted the Irish doctor, so maybe…but Pop? Uh, uh, uh, an Irish lass ain't never gonna meet with Pop's approval.

The bedroom door opened. Nudging it closed with her bare foot, Kathleen was wearing the button-down shirt that Armand had worn the night before. He raised himself up on one elbow. His insides frothed. Look at those legs. And that shirt. Holy mackerel, she filled it out better than any man could. Kathleen carried a tray with two steaming cups of coffee on it and some biscotti that she found in the kitchen. Without a word she gave Armand his coffee and laid the plate of biscotti on the bed between them. Only a hint of a timid smile brightened her youthful face.

"How old are you?" Armand asked.

"Seventeen."

"No, you're not. You're not a day over fifteen."

Kathleen said nothing. Those emerald eyes gazed at him. Armand slugged down his coffee and put the empty cup on the night table. Oh, shit, now what was he gonna do? That girl was some kinda looker, that's for sure. But fifteen? He could get arrested for that! But then the midnight hour before wafted across his brain. Whew, what a romp! Kathleen took real good care of him. And she didn't yammer on and on afterwards like most broads. Aargh, what does it matter? Marriage didn't suit his plans anyway. Grasping the gorgeous creature by her hips, he pulled her to him. The biscotti dish fell on the floor and broke. She looked at him with uncertain eyes. He broke into a wide grin and they both laughed while her hand massaged his washboard stomach and his fingers slithered up the front of the shirt, unbuttoning it with swift precision. The shirt slipped off Kathleen's slim white shoulders. She fit him like a glove.

*　　*　　*

That afternoon Armand took a seat on one of the wooden chairs lined up in the front window of Paolo's Barbershop. Waiting his turn, he gloated, pleased with himself since he had contributed a significant amount to putting Paolo through the New England School of Barbering and setting up this shop. The waterfront of East Boston was the perfect place. Lots of foot traffic. He watched his brother, an artist at work. Paolo thoroughly enjoyed this hair cutting stuff. When he announced that he wanted to be a barber, Pop happily gave his blessing. "Paolo does not have the physical ability to do carpentry work," the old man had told Armand. Barbering satisfied the old man's moral requirements. "It is a steady Christian job, and Paolo can make a fair and honest living at it." Yet Armand knew that it would also keep Paolo in East Boston and under the old man's thumb. According to Pop, "Paolo could not survive anywhere else because his mind is slow and he speaks only enough English to get by."

Armand stretched. Oh well. What's it matter anyway? Look at Paolo. He's certainly in his glory. He and that old bugger, Sal, sitting there in the cutting chair, bantered back and forth in the language of the old country. Leo, another broken-down piece of reprobate, slouched next to Armand. From time to time the loudmouth put in his two cents worth, jarring Armand out of a snooze. The topic was sports. Gaston Chevrolet had taken the checkered flag at the Indianapolis 500 with an average speed of 88.6 miles per hour. Harvard won the Rose Bowl defeating Oregon 7-6. And never, never would it *ever* be forgotten that the Red Sox sold Babe Ruth on January 5, 1920, for $125,000. A curse on those stinkin' Red Sox!

Against Armand's better judgment the subject of the Prohibition came up. Not in the mood to play along, he only nodded his head or pursed out his lips when they tried to draw him into the discourse. Sal, Leo, and Paolo had no idea how deep Armand was into the illegal sale and distribution of alcohol.

"These laws control our drinking, we don't need 'em. Know what I mean?" Sal grunted in a gravelly voice. He got up from Paolo's chair and leaned close to the mirror. He scrutinized his hair, this way and that. "*Buono*."

With a stub of a stogie bobbing in his mouth, Leo dribbled, "Only reason Prohibition got through Congress is 'cuz of a handful of Senators and Reps claim that brew's what the Boche are famous for. Holy smoly! Raise the American flag on that one, why don't cha! These here United States tolerates nothin' German. Not even beer. Nope, not after the Great War."

Paolo patted the back of the cutting chair and eyeballed his sleepy brother. Finally it was Armand's turn. Draping a cape over his brother, Paolo said, "Prohibition don't cure alkies. I see more of 'em now than ever before. Difference is, gangs make all the money from the booze these days."

"And they got their own territories, too," Leo agreed. "Look at Capone. Ices anyone who even thinks about horning in on his liquor business. People can't walk the streets, even in the light of day. Might get caught in the crossfire of those Chicago typewriters." Leo held an invisible machine gun in his hands and made slurpy gunfire noises. He lowered his arms and said with a sarcastic grin, "Sucha nize boys."

Sal slithered up to Paolo and stuffed several bills in the barber's vest pocket. "We got a right to live by our own code of what is right and what is wrong. We should do what we want to," said Sal as he put on his jacket. "That's how come we came to this country in the first place. Fer Crise sake, men fermented *il vino* long before Christ and He turned it to blood in the last supper."

"*Si*," Paolo agreed. He took a black comb from the jar filled with blue disinfectant and tapped the moisture from it into a white towel.

Putting on his cap, Sal shook his head. "Gangsters, sheesh! They are all small potatoes. Take my old woman. Ha! Capone could learn what true brutality is from her. So. I find it necessary to shove off or you will all read about me swimming with the fishes in the morning paper." With that, the bell over the door jangled and Sal left the barbershop. Leo followed right behind him. The shop became quiet. After several moments, Paolo asked, "*Commo esta*, Armand?"

"*Buono, buono.* And business?" The conversation changed to Italian. It was easier and quicker for Paolo, but every so often, Armand yanked a bit of English out of him.

"Cleared twenty bucks a week for a month now. With that kind of money, Maddalena and I set the date."

"No kidding. When?"

"Next summer. By that time I should trust her brother to run the shop while I go away on the honeymoon that you are going to give to us as a wedding present, is that not so?"

Armand snickered then asked, "When is Filippo getting out of barber school?"

"Two weeks."

"Bad idea," Armand shifted the talk back into English and rolled his eyes. "No matter how you look at it. *Piccolo fratello mio*, you are much too young for marriage."

"Whaddaya mean, too young? I am twenty-five, for crying out loud!" Paolo shouted in English while pointing the scissors at Armand. "You should talk, you...you old *scapolo*. Wassa matter? Nobody will have ya?" Just then Paolo caught the gleam in Armand's eyes. "Hah! Ya jolly joker ya!" And he punched his brother square in the arm. Moments later, Paolo asked, "Hey, you seen Mama and Pop?"

"No. Goin' there after I get outta here."

Pensively Paolo tap-tap-tapped the black comb on his chin. "Strange thing happened this morning."

Armand perked up. His brother wasn't all that observant. If something was strange to Paolo, one took heed.

"Two men, Mafia types, showed up this morning. Waited for me to open up. Clipped one of 'em while the other one paced back and forth looking me up and down, real mean like. What a greasy mop that guy had."

"What's their beef?" Armand asked.

Paulo shrugged thoughtfully as he parted Armand's hair on the left. "The guy in the chair, he didn't sit still worth a plug nickel. Asked what village in Italy I come from. I tells him and whaddaya know? He says rumors been floatin' around about the place."

"Whaddaya mean, rumors? What kind of rumors?"

"Seems a farm was dug up to make way for some rich mucky muck's house. They uncovered bones. And vestments of a priest."

"No kidding."

"Well, I says that I remembered a Father Sandro. He dropped outta sight before we came to America. Never heard one way or another if he ever turned up. You remember Father Sandro, don't you?"

"Nah. Must've come along after Pop, me, and Rom left Italy," replied Armand. "But I don't get the connection. Those two goons sniffing around here? What's the deal?"

Paolo nudged his brother's head forward and pasted shaving cream across the back of his neck. "All they says is, the place might be the farm we lived on." Paolo shivered.

"Our farm?"

Paolo nodded as he pulled a strap out from the wall and raked a straightedge razor over it. "Anyways, that's the reason I asked if you stopped by Pop and Mama's. Maybe they heard talk of this rumor at one time or another."

"Don't worry about it. No way it's our old farm."

Chapter 16

The Captain's house reeked of frying sausage, boiling cavatelli, and simmering tomato sauce spiced heavily with garlic and oregano and keeping a watchful eye over the evening meal was Maria Avita. A gingham smock of pink and blue flowers protected her navy dress accented with a white tatted collar. The years had rounded her small frame and added wisps of gray to her long dark hair, braided then encircled within a black crocheted snood. Armand kissed her on the cheek and asked, "Where's Pop?"

"Playing cards with Orazio and the bunch of 'em down at Mizzulo's," she said. "I kicked the old buzzard out. He makes me crazy with all his garl-darned moping over Captain McKay. Here, taste this," she said as she jammed a steaming ladle of sauce into his face.

"Mmm, *perfecto.*" Armand smacked his lips while wiping them off with the back of his hand. "So, the house is yours and Pop's now."

"*Si.* Just like the Captain told us he was gonna do. 'Cause Pop and I took such fine care of it for all these many years. Captain McKay fretted so much that distant relatives were going to sell off this place to just anybody, and that did not set well with him at all. Sit, sit. I make you some pasta."

"No, *Mamacita,*" Armand shook his head and patted his stomach. "Not hungry."

"Come on. You gotta eat! Whassamadda, you sick or somethin'?"

"No, no, *Mamacita*. I'm not sick," Armand insisted, but she set about making a bowl of pasta, sausage, and sauce anyway. He grimaced. *Mamacita* had a mind of her own. Not of the mind to argue a lost cause, he said, "Captain McKay. Who'd have thought. He looked the picture of health at your twenty-fifth anniversary shindig." Armand had a long conversation with to the long-time family friend, a true gentleman. Dressed to the nines that day, McKay had taken great pleasure in watching the festivities at Mizzullo's Restaurant in Maverick Square. He went on and on about the fine job Joseph and Seth had done with the remodeling of Mizzullo's and claimed the place resembled a fine museum he had seen over there in Florence, Italy. And Donato Mizzullo was showing off the improvements too, going as far as taking guests through the bustling kitchen of harried cooks and steaming pots. Armand remembered how his face had lit up when all the LaRosa kids showed up at his restaurant, wishing to make arrangements for the anniversary celebration. He laid out a meal for over one hundred family members and friends and refused to take any payment. "Joseph did too fine a job for Donato Mizzulo to accept one red penny from his children," he boasted.

Maria Avita placed a huge bowl of pasta in front of Armand. He looked at it and fidgeted. "When's Pop comin' home?"

"Not so soon, if I have my way," she said while hurrying back to the stove to stir the sauce. She rapped the ladle on the rim of the pot. "It's so quiet and peaceful around here. What is so important with you?"

Armand pushed the bowl of pasta away. "Just wanted to pick his brain about Father Sandro."

The ladle dropped from her hand and bounced across the floor. "Father Sandro?" she shuddered.

Armand's eyes widened. His mother was white as a sheet, "You knew about the priest?"

Maria Avita wiped her hands nervously on her smock. "Well, uhm…he did not show up for Mass one morning a very long time ago. What have you heard?"

"He turned up." Armand watched his mother intently.

"Where?"

"Italy. Our farm, to be exact."

Maria Avita sank into a chair.

Something was terribly wrong. "*Mamacita*?"

Her terror-filled eyes met his. Her lips quivered.

He took her hand. "What frightens you so?"

"I did it."

"Did what?"

"Killed the priest." Her eyes darted away. She took a deep, tremulous breath.

Armand backed away in disbelief. "Come on. You could never do such a thing."

Her face twitched as she held back her anguish. "I cannot live with his ghost any longer. I…I…" Abruptly she stopped. Her eyes shot to the door. "Singing," she gasped. "It's your father!" Lurching away from the table, Maria Avita fled into the bathroom and slammed the door behind her. Leaning against it, she gasped for air while one hand tried to still her pounding heart. "Oh, God. I should not have told Armand. Now he will tell Joseph."

Footsteps chafed the back steps and across the porch. The door swung open.

"Hey, Pop. *Comma esta*?" Armand casually asked. His arm slung over the back of the chair, he covered up his agitation. After years of working for the organization, one took on that ability.

"*Buono*. Where's Mama?"

Armand pointed his thumb over his shoulder, "In the bathroom."

Crossing the kitchen, Joseph kicked the ladle. "What is this?" he muttered and picked it up. Studying the ladle he called, "I am home, *Angelatina Mia*." When no answer came he pounded on the bathroom door. "You in there?"

"*Si*," came a muffled voice.

"I have drunk too much of the *vino*, so I go to lie down. Wake me in a little while?"

"*Si*."

Joseph tossed the ladle into the sink then plodded up the stairs. Armand peeked around the door jamb and watched his father disappear. When he heard the bedroom door latch shut, he tiptoed to the bathroom door and tapped. "Pop's gone, *Mamacita*," he whispered. "Come out. 'K?"

The door cracked open. Ebony eyes, swinging back and forth like pendulums, peered out.

Thud!

The bathroom door slammed shut.

Armand looked up at the ceiling. "It's Pop, *Mamacita*. Just taking off his shoes."

Thud.

"See?"

When the door slit open, Armand reached in and took her hand. "Come on out of there." He led her to the table and seated her next to him. Without letting go of her hand, he said, "Talk to me."

"Father Sandro. He forced himself on Louisa. And I caught him at it."

"Where?"

"Behind the rabbit hutches."

"What did you do?"

"I hit him."

Armand's brows shot up. "You hit him?"

She nodded.

"With what, *Mamacita*?"

"Driftwood. *Si*, for the fire. Well, I pick it up and say, 'You evil priest, you do not do this thing to *bambina mia*.'"

Armand's eyes grew wide. "You…you killed him?"

"*Si*. I did not mean to hit him so hard. I just wanted him to stop."

"What did you do with him?"

"He is in the ground."

"Where?"

"Under the rabbits."

"*Mamacita*, I don't understand."

"Where the droppings fall. Dung covers Father Sandro. It was easy for me to dig there—a very deep hole. Father Sandro will not be found for a very long time. In the morning I look. Fresh droppings cover the ground and the rain washed away all the blood."

Armand got up and leaned against doorframe of the bathroom. His brain screamed *No! This can't be. Not Mamacita mia. Una assassina?* In shock he stared at his mother. Obviously she had not told Pop. *Nah, how could she tell him? So set in his stinking ways, who knows what would happen if Pop ever learned about this.* "Louisa?"

"We never speak of it. It never happened."

"But *Mamacita*, it did happen," exclaimed Armand. "Who was Father Sandro anyways?"

"Sandro Ferro."

"Ferro? As in Don Vito Cascio Ferro?"

"*Si*, his godson."

Don Vito's godson! Horror sliced through Armand like a steel blade just taken from the blacksmith's forge. The Don would stop at nothing to avenge Sandro's killer. His hounds already had a scent. Armand had to divert them—but how? "Listen, Mamacita. I want you to pour yourself a nice cup of coffee and go sit in the living room. Don't worry about it, you hear me?" he said kissing his mother good-bye. I will take care of this, I promise. So relax, OK?"

She gave a pitiful nod, though fright plastered her face. She wrung her hands and watched Armand dash out the back door, jamming his white fedora with the gray headband onto his head. His hand held it against a cold blast. He had to put the kibosh on any vendetta against *Mamacita. Pronto*!

* * *

Armand's connection to the Mafia was no secret, though the LaRosa family never openly acknowledged it. Maria Avita constantly feared for her oldest son, more so since she had told him about Father Sandro. What's more, Joseph did not approve of the lifestyle at all. His oldest son had many associates but few true Christian friends. The old man had vehemently opposed Armand leaving LaRosa and Sons to strike out on his own again, yet realized the danger to his family and business if he openly opposed Armand's involvement with such powerful men. The Boston organization controlled construction permits in New England, though essentially, it stayed within the commercial construction arena. The majority of Joseph's work was residential. However, LaRosa and Sons Construction Company received no opposition when requesting the occasional commercial permit. In addition Messina never solicited Joseph for the customary fee associated with obtaining paperwork. The old man would not allow himself to admit that his company received any special treatment due to the unholy alliance between Armand and Aldo Messina.

On a dazzling Saturday afternoon in September 1920, Aldo showed up at the LaRosa home. Across his arm he bore a huge basket of fruit for Joseph and Maria Avita in honor of their wedding anniversary. Aldo did this every year, hoping that his generous gift might convince the family—especially Joseph—how much they meant to him. Joseph gave Aldo the usual cold, silent greeting. Aldo wondered if the old man would ever warm up to him. Armand had said that *Mamacita* had persuaded Joseph to let bygones be bygones after the organization sucked their son back into the ranks. Must be nice to have a woman like that around. Aldo had never known the warmth of a mother's touch.

He felt at home at the LaRosas. Friends were always dropping by, and the food and wine never stopped. Static from an RCA radio or phonograph needle always pervaded the background while they hashed over events of the day or played cards. More times than Aldo could count, he had dunked warm bread that Maria Avita had just taken from the oven into wine that Joseph had made in his basement, one barrel at a time. The old man drank wine with all his meals and encouraged his children to do so too, especially since the epidemic when Joseph got it in his mind that wine makes the body resistant to disease. Aldo's mouth watered whenever he saw a loaf of bread or a carafe of wine. Domestic scenes like this were not possible in the fortress that Aldo called home. At any moment someone on the rise within the organization might send renegade soldiers over the cement walls with machine guns ablaring.

"Haven't seen you around in a while," said Armand. He chomped on the bread he had just dipped in wine.

"Just got back from New York," said Aldo as he took a seat next to Armand under the grape arbor. Many a stifling summer afternoon or balmy eventide, Aldo had relaxed under here where overhead, as autumn neared, clusters of green grapes slowly matured into fragrant masses of purple. The vines had come from clippings that Orazio Bascuino had brought with him from the old county. Joseph and Seth had built the beautiful hand-carved arbor seven years ago. Aldo wished he and his father could do those kinds of things together.

"Oh yeah," Armand grunted. He forgot that it was the middle of the month when Aldo delivered tributes from the Boston organization to Don Vito.

Extremely careful not to engage in any conversation that might offend either family, Aldo asked, "Hey, *Signore* LaRosa. How 'bout some of your delicious brew?"

"Come on, everybody," Louisa called from the gazebo. "Mama, Pop. Time to cut the cake and open the gifts."

Joseph held up his right index finger. "OK, OK. Be right there." He filled Aldo's glass to the brim then topped off Armand's and his own. Lumbering out from under the grape arbor, he met Maria Avita halfway to the gazebo. Together they climbed the stairs.

Aldo chugged half the glass of wine and sloshed it around in his mouth. Swallowing it in one noisy gulp, he ground his teeth together in a toothy grimace. "You haven't by any chance caught wind of a couple of Don Vito's dogs sniffing around, have ya?" he asked while stretching his long, skinny legs across to Joseph's empty chair.

Armand coughed. "Can't say as I have. What's the deal?"

"Someone snuffed out a priest back in Italy a while back."

Armand shifted nervously. Why didn't Gaspare tell Aldo about their meeting concerning Maria Avita's confession? Should he bring it up or not?

"I've never seen anyone talk with their hands as much as your family does," Aldo chuckled.

"Yeah," said Armand, carefully concealing his agitation. He wanted to stick to the subject at hand. He needed more about Don Vito's intentions concerning the dead priest.

Aldo continued, "Don Vito says it's been months without any word from a couple of sniffers he put on the trail of the killer."

Armand acted disinterested. "Think I ought to check it out or what?"

"Might not be worth the time and effort."

"How's that?"

"Father Sandro."

"Never met the guy."

"Not missing much."

"So you knew him."

"Yeah, he was Don Vito's godson. We all knew each other back in Italy. He wasn't only a year or two older than me. If ever a man was not cut out for the priesthood, Sandro fit the bill."

"How come?"

"Couldn't keep his grubby paws off the wenches."

"He got away with it?"

"Sure. He was the Don's godson."

"So, some virgin's old man laid Father Sandro down for stealing his daughter's purity?"

"Perhaps." Aldo looked around to see if anyone was in hearing range. Then he leaned on his elbow and whispered behind the back of his hand, "The Don's missing dogs showed up at our house and grilled my ol' man about the priest. They got nothing out of him. Later, my ol' man explained me how Sandro played both ends from the middle and Giolitti got wind of it."

"He crossed Giolitti?"

"Yeah. Made off with Church funds, too. And, not only that, listen to this. According to my father, Sandro was ripping off Don Vito. Whatever you do, keep that one under your hat, 'cause the Don don't like people badmouthing his family. Besides, Vito always thought the sun shone up Sandro's ass."

"Whew. That guy sure had balls."

"Hey, Armand, Aldo, come on," Louisa called. "Mama and Pop's cutting the cake."

Armand squinted at his sister, cuddling her nine-month-old daughter, Concetta, who was sucking on her thumb like there was no tomorrow. Dom's left arm draped over her shoulder and his right hand held six-year-old Avita Maria. Meanwhile, their son, Nicholas, terrorized the festivities the way three-year-olds do.

Louisa looked radiant. So did *Mamacita*. With Pop's hand over hers, she smiled up at him like a new bride as they cut the cake. Armand tried to visualize his mother angry. Not the angry a scolded child saw, but *angry*. Angry to the extent that she actually picked up a club to harm another person. This was not the *Mamacita* he had known all his life. At that moment the faceless image of the priest gyrating on Louisa flashed in Armand's brain. Suddenly the mother's anger became the son's. It surged. It festered. If only he had been there. Sandro would have met the prince of darkness with Armand's bare hands gripping his filthy throat.

"OK for you," Joseph hollered. "Cake's all gone."

"Yeah, yeah, Pop. We're comin', we're comin'." Armand got to his feet. If Pop only knew. Then again it's a good thing he didn't. The old man was too much of a religious stuffed shirt to stop this thing from destroying him and *Mamacita*. If Louisa told Dom, it might destroy their marriage also. Come to think of it, the whole damned family would go straight down the toilette. Jesus Christ, what a stinking mess! All because those things that dangled between Sandro's legs lusted for satisfaction from innocent little girls. Why didn't he get himself a whore? Don Vito would blast hotter than the worst day in hell if he knew what a scum his godson really was. And what's the deal with Gaspare? Why didn't Gaspare tell Aldo that Armand had gone to see him about Sandro? Armand considered telling Aldo what *Mamacita* did to the priest, but by then they had gotten too close to the gazebo and someone might hear. *Nah. Not now. Another day, another place. Another time.*

Chapter 17

Based largely upon circumstantial evidence, a jury of anyone but their peers found Nicola Sacco and Bartolomeo Vanzetti guilty of murder and robbery on July 14, 1921. The sentence: Death by electrocution. The case polarized the nation and the world. High-ranking American leaders deplored this trial by atmosphere.

From the very beginning Romeo LaRosa had guarded Bartolomeo Vanzetti and came to believe that the two men had been railroaded. Certainly no jury would ever convict them, but when the guilty verdict came down, the Italian-American cop was stunned. After returning the devastated Vanzetti to his cell and still wearing his BPD uniform, he sought out his father in East Boston. Joseph was puttering around the backyard.

"Judge Thayer pointed his finger at Nicola and Bartolomeo and called them dagos and sons of bitches, Pop." Rom cracked his knuckles and paced. He wished his father would put down the hedge clippers and listen more attentively. "Right there in the courtroom. I heard him with my own ears—everybody heard him! He didn't allow one single Italian-born witness to testify on Vanzetti's behalf. And then—your not gonna believe this—Thayer had the nerve to say he's unbiased…unbiased!"

Joseph continued to trim the privet hedges, knowing full well that no words could pacify his son's consternation. "All is not the way we had prayed for it to be in this great new country we live in," he said dryly.

"The attitude especially," Rom winced. "Everybody thinks immigrants are dirt, the problems that other countries are happy to get rid of. They label Italians thugs, criminals. But Pop, most of us live good, decent lives. Look at me. I fought their war. I'm a cop. Doesn't that mean anything?"

Joseph stepped back and pretended to inspect the hedges. He wiped the sweat from his brow. These questions his son posed were ones he had asked himself more than once throughout his many years. How much he and Rom thought alike. "There has always been intolerance. Always will be, I suppose," Joseph sighed. "Perhaps Judge Thayer crossed paths with one or two bad Italians at one time or another. Still, that does not mean we are all bad."

Rom couldn't agree more. Look at the difference between him and Armand. His own brother, up to his eyeballs in Mafia business. How did that happen? One brother swore to uphold the law; the other flagrantly defied it? "From where I stand, I see criminal elements in every nationality. Just look at the Irish. 'Cuz they got here first, they got more muscle. They set territories against all other immigrants. You know as well as I do that the Irish got the North End fenced in, and if they squeeze hard enough, the Italians will have no other choice but to get the hell out. Irish control Boston, not Italians."

"*Si*," Joseph nodded and handed a burlap bag to his son. "Here hold this open, while I stuff the clippings into it."

His father's apparent apathy riled Rom, but beneath the calm exterior, days of long ago pestered Joseph. He relived the terrible things Giolitti's enforcers had done as if it were only yesterday. Enforcers, gangs, what's the difference what they called themselves? They were all the same. Look what they did to cousin Luca. The fear that Giolitti created drove Joseph and many others from Italy. And now it seemed that history was repeating itself. Two innocent men were about to die. Italians might also desert the North End just as they did Italy. Someone must put a stop to all this death and running away. Was there nobody to stand up to evildoers? Joseph pursed his lips while making a silent promise. No matter what, he would never leave East Boston. He was done with running.

Still, times were difficult. Many lived a very austere existence in East Boston. Crowded into three-deckers, family lived with family because living on their own was unaffordable. The LaRosas had experienced very little of that kind of hardship. Joseph and Maria Avita lived in the captain's magnificent house and all but Seth and Vincenzo maintained their own households. The family counted their blessings and shared them with their community. When they saw a need, they lent a hand, regardless of race or ethnicity.

Not long after that conversation with Rom, Joseph learned that prejudice ran deeper within him than he cared to admit. It happened the afternoon that his granddaughter Avita Maria received her First Communion. Watching his grandchildren running around the backyard, he still grieved the loss of Francesca, but he could not help but believe that God had blessed him and had answered many of his prayers. His world and family was growing and prospering in America. Just the week before, Vincenzo had spoken of his desire to become a priest. Joseph was ecstatic, to say the least. Imagine that. One of his sons, a priest—a dream come true for the religious old patriarch. The sad truth about it was that he had actually given up on Vincenzo a long time ago. So withdrawn, the kid hardly ever spoke. It was like prying open the teeth of a dead man to get a decent conversation out of him. But now Joseph understood. People who have close links to God were often reclusive.

On the other hand Maria Avita was not as thrilled. "Vincenzo is too young," she complained.

"*Caro Angelatina Mia*. We must let our son follow his heart. The final decision is not in his hands or ours. Only after he spends many hours in pre-seminary counseling will a final decision on the matter be made. And that will come from the Church and God."

Maria Avita relented. The next day, Joseph went to St. John's Seminary to set the wheels in motion.

Seth was also contributing to Joseph's sense of well being. Taller and more muscular than his father, he was entering East Boston High School in the fall. All along he had done well in all his studies and had his pick of many professions. Nevertheless, Seth had made it known just this morning that upon graduating from high school, he intended to work for LaRosa and Sons full time. He wanted his father to teach him the ins and outs of the construction business and all the fine woodworking skills Joseph possessed.

Satisfied with his lot in life, Grandpa Joseph lounged under the grape arbor while the grandchildren tugged on Nona Maria Avita, wanting her to join their dance circle. She tried to resist since she was in the process of putting food on the table, but the oldest grandchild, Avita Maria, persisted. She held tightly to her grandmother's hand and would not let her go. The child was the spitting image of both her grandmother and mother and was just as stubborn. Finally Nona tossed off her apron and joined the children.

"You are a truly fortunate man to have so many grandchildren, Pop," said Armand.

"*Si*," Joseph smiled.

"Soon, you will have more," said Rom with a twinkle in his eye.

"You do not have to brag about it," Paolo laughed. "We all know Rachele is expecting."

"You don't know the half of it," Rom laughed and reached out to Rachele. As he drew her close, they gazed into each other's eyes as if they were lovesick teens.

"What? Are you expecting twins, Rachele?" Maria Avita asked, all out of breath. Somehow she had managed to set herself free of the grandchildren.

Rachel giggled. "No, no."

"Come on, you are all too funny," Rom teased.

Joseph and Maria Avita exchanged glances. What in the world was their son talking about?

"Remember that fire a month ago? In Central Square?" Rom explained.

"A Lithuanian man and his wife died in it," said Vincenzo.

"They had a couple of kids but only one made it—a boy. He took in so much smoke that no one had expected him to live. The little *tigre* surprised everybody and beat the odds only to end up without anybody wanting him."

"Poor little man," said Maria Avita.

"Yeah. That's why when Rachele and I heard about it, we decided to adopt him. We signed the papers yesterday afternoon. We're going to pick him up in an hour."

"Why, Rom," Maria Avita clasped her hands over her heart. "How wonderful!"

Joseph clenched his fists. His anger built until he struck a mighty blow upon the table, launching dishes and silverware into the air. Abruptly, all conversation halted. Startled children scurried to the safety of their mothers. All attention flashed toward the crazed man who slowly, deliberately, hoisted his infuriated frame from his chair with stiffened arms. His jaw was set and his face grew redder with each passing second. "No more outsiders in the LaRosa family. I forbid it," he lathered. "Two used *mendicante* washes the blood as it is. But, a Lithuanian? No! Absolutely not!"

"Joseph," shrieked Maria Avita. "Rachele and Isabella are not beggars! Shame on you for saying such a thing." Disbelief and confusion stifled her words.

Awkward moments passed then Rom growled, "Is that what you think of Rachele and my daughter, Pop?"

"She is not your daughter," spat Joseph. "Your *child* is in that woman's belly!"

"That woman's name is Rachele LaRosa, Pop."

"Bah," Joseph spat and crossed his arms. Pursing his lips, he tossed his head back. "The marriage should have been annulled."

"You mean to tell me that you don't accept Rachel as my wife?"

Joseph turned his back.

Rom grabbed his father's arm and spun him around. Eyeball to eyeball, Rom demanded, "Is that the reason you don't greet her nor Isabella the way you do everybody else? Is that the reason you don't speak to them, Pop?"

Joseph remained silent, cold. The pupils of his eyes dilated so large that hazel was barely discernible as they pierced his son's, equally intense. Moments passed as the two men stood there glaring at each other. Then Rom stepped back. With a blanket of disgust sheeting his face, he said, "Come, on Rache, let's get out of here."

With eyes riddled with pain, Rachele watched her husband gather up Isabella and stomp out of the yard. She looked to Maria Avita. Surely, there was an ally. When the confused old woman didn't speak, Rachele burst out sobbing and ran after her husband.

"Mama...," Louisa whined. "For heaven's sake," she spouted as she shoved little Concetta into Dom's arms and darted after Rachele.

At the corner of the house, Rom stopped and yelled back, "As of yesterday, little *Joseph* is my son."

"Little Joseph?" Maria Avita whimpered and glanced at her husband. Like the devil of darkness, he stood there with his arms crossed and a look of evil satisfaction spread across his face.

"Joseph LaRosa, Pop. That's the name of my little Lithuanian," hollered Rom. "LaRosa! Just as Isabella is my daughter. Isabella LaRosa! Just as the child in Rachele's womb is mine—a LaRosa. I will teach each and every one of my children that their grandfather is a religious man. He preaches tolerance and love but does not live those words himself!"

Vincenzo and Seth took their brother's arm and tried to bring him back. He shook them off. "No," Rom said emphatically, "I will have an apology before I set foot here again. It will come from Pop, not Mama. My wife and children must hear words of remorse only from his lips."

Louisa came back alone. She wrapped her arms around Maria Avita and cried, "Rachele and the children are family, too…"

"No, Louisa, you are family," Joseph interrupted. "You have always done things the way they are rightfully done. You went into marriage untouched."

Louisa and her mother held on to one another in terror. Was this the way for the truth to come out?

"Pop. You don't know about…" Louisa started.

"I know all I need to know. You stay home and raise your family as a decent woman should."

"As a *decent* woman *should*?" gasped Maria Avita. She let go of Louisa and stepped towards Joseph.

"*Si*," the old man said smugly. "Women—telephone and telegraph operators, clerks, bookkeepers, stenographers, secretaries and sales persons…blah! They have no right to those jobs. Not one of them! They steal the livelihoods of men. Decent women stay home and see to it that children are raised properly."

Joseph had just said the wrong thing. There was now no place for the man to run, no place to hide as the wrath of Maria Avita fell upon him. "*I* stayed home, Joseph. *I* raised your children. Does that mean *I* am better?" She stood in her husband's face. Her small frame became that of a fearsome towering giant. Her heavy black eyebrows formed one solid line that overshadowed the fire of hell blazing in her eyes. "No, Joseph. Take a better look. Who did the accounting work for LaRosa and Sons? Was that person not me? That means I too worked while raising your children. Or perhaps that does not count because you gave me no wages? Just as you give me none for the work I still do. I take away some man's livelihood, do I not? You should fire me. Aargh, never mind, I quit. Hire an accountant. A male accountant! Right this very moment."

"*Angelatina Mia*, I did not mean it that way," Joseph whined as he reached out to her.

"Don't soft-soap me, Joseph. That's exactly what you meant!" Ripping off her apron, Maria Avita threw it at him. "And do not call me *Angelatina Mia* no more. Not until you bring Rom and his family back to me. I will see you talking and kissing on Rachele, Isabella, and little Joseph…oooh, poor little Joseph. We don't even know him yet. No! You will hold Rom's two *bambini* on your lap, the same way you will hold the one on the way and all our other grandchildren. Until the day comes that I see you do this, you call me *diavolotina*, for your sinful soul will live in the hell I make for you and your unchristian ways." With that Maria Avita stomped into the house. The door slammed behind her. Needless to say, the party was over.

Chapter 18

Countless nights passed since Rom LaRosa first took up the post outside the death row cell that incarcerated Bartolomeo Vanzetti. They shared quiet conversations, mostly of Vanzetti's great love for the northern Italian village of Villafalletto from whence he came. Some revealed his personal philosophies related to Tolstoi, Saint Francesco, and Dane. A few were trivial ruminations meant to pass the sleepless nights.

Rom gained tremendous respect for the unassuming Italian immigrant and adamantly contended that Sacco and Vanzetti had not received a fair trial. The whole sordid affair had been blown out of proportion, brought on by the failed attempt of the police to capture a comrade of the two defendants. If it were not for the anti-immigrant sentiment prevalent at the time, combined with the Red Scare, the trial, much less the conviction, never would have taken place. Rom chewed the injustice over again and again in his mind. He dreamt of it and lived with a mounting guilt that he didn't know what to do with. The evidence was highly suspect—something he was at a loss to prove. And this so-called American Red Scare had no basis whatsoever. Sacco and Vanzetti were just pawns, caught in the war between patriotic ideals and radicalism. No matter which side won, the two men were innocent casualties. Their fate, death by electrocution, went against everything Rom believed. Even the atrocities of the Great War had not prepared him for this kind of barbarity.

So the years passed following the conviction. Appeals were made. All failed. One particular night, Bartolomeo Vanzetti became unusually withdrawn. Rom peered into the cell numerous times. Vanzetti remained seated on the edge of his bunk, head bowed, hands folded. The heavy bone structure of his broad forehead lined with heavy coarse eyebrows shadowed his dark eyes. Despondent by years of imprisonment, failed appeals, and an extended hunger strike, the man appeared to be consumed in prayer. The cop could not bring himself to disturb the prisoner. Instead, he took up his post once again on the straight wooden chair outside the cell. The night wore on. Rom became quite uneasy with the silence. Finally he ventured to ask, "*Commo esta?*"

"*Non so.*" His voice was somber. The convicted man did not rise from his bunk. His eyes remained fixed to the floor, his large hands clasped together.

"What troubles you this night?"

After a time Bartolomeo whispered, "We have enjoyed deep *conversaziones*, you and me. *Si?*"

"*Si.*"

"Both born of the same Italy, you and me—you, from the south and I, from the north. We have come to be *paesani, si?*

"It is so. Why do you ask me such a thing?"

When Vanzetti failed to respond, Rom cracked his knuckles. Why didn't the man speak?

At last Bartolomeo's voice. "Through the endless hours we have spent together, we have each come to know the man that exists within the other. My heavy heart cries out to that man."

"For what reason?"

Vanzetti looked up from his hands. Coal black eyes, outlined by long dark lashes, affixed to those of the young policeman. "You know that I am a man of much faith. I have no fear of death, though I will continue to fight to the bitter end for my right to live...and to be free.

My innocence is in the hands of *Dio mio*, but I am destined to lose this battle. *Dio mio* deems it so."

"You must not speak that way." Rom tried to be encouraging, not only the Vanzetti but also himself. "More appeals are coming down the line."

"They will do no good. Things are stacked against Nicola and me."

"But this new lawyer, Thompson. He submitted new arguments. Surely..."

"All useless," interrupted Bartolomeo as his hands unfolded then wedged against his knees. Slowly he got to his feet. His shoes scraped the floor as he shuffled to the door of the cell. Thick, heavy fingers encircled the bars. "Thompson has it in his mind that not only must Nicola and I be defended, but respect for the law must also be defended. He feels nothing for our case, only that it meets the standards of the law. He refuses the political defense. Such methods cannot stop the wheels already set in motion."

"You must not lose hope," Rom implored.

"Can it be otherwise? Evidence exists that several witnesses for the prosecution lied. Nothing comes of that. And let us not forget Celestino Madeiros. He confessed to the crime but Thayer refuses to hear his words."

"*Si*," Rom shook his head. "Even the Morelli Gang's involvement has come to light."

"All rejected by Judge Thayer. He refuses to allow any new trial. He knows Nicola and I will not be convicted again." Bartolomeo rubbed his discretely curved Roman nose then turned away and trudged back to his bunk. Wrapping himself in a green Army blanket, he sat down once again. His eyes closed as Vanzetti resumed the position of prayer.

Moments passed. Rom shifted his weight from one leg to another. His knuckles clicked amplifying within the jailhouse silence. Focusing on the iron bars, his eyes followed them up to their entry into the ceiling. "*Non capisco*, Bartolomeo," he stammered. "Is there something you wish me to do?"

Vanzetti's head lifted. His eyes shot hopefully at the young cop. Underneath his coarse mustachio, wide lips quivered. "You will help me?"

"If it is possible. But how?" Rom winced and looked toward his prisoner. "My hands are tied."

Arising from his bunk, Bartolomeo spoke no words as once again he crossed the jail cell. At the bars he whispered, "Get word to Vito Cascio Ferro."

"Don Vito?"

"Si."

"That is no small order."

"Please. I wish a personal favor from him," said Vanzetti.

"He won't come here. You know that. He keeps great distance from you and the anarchists, so the authorities will not hassle his organization."

"This I know only too well. That is the reason I ask the favor, for I hold the cards that can deal out much trouble for Don Vito."

"Let me see what I can do. It may take some time."

"As you see, *cara paesani mio*, I go nowhere."

* * *

Shortly after 3:00 A.M., Romeo LaRosa exited Charlestown State Prison. Dense fog had rolled in from offshore and enshrouded the street lamps with an eerie amber-gray glow. He lifted his collar to the raw night air and took a deep breath. The chill removed the stagnant jailhouse air from his lungs but not his spirit. Instead of heading home Rom drove down the cobblestone streets of the North End and parked block away from Armand's Hull Street apartment. He scanned the deserted street. At the end the Old North Church stood watch over Little Italy—the place of great hope for Italian immigrants. Ironic that his night owl brother lives so close to a church. And considering the business Armand was in made it even more so.

After several knocks, the door cracked open. Wearing a full-length royal blue smoking jacket and matching slippers, Armand immediately plucked the Garcia Alonzo Cigar out of his mouth and swung open the door. "Rom! What in hell are you doing here?" Grabbing the uniformed policeman by the arm, Armand hauled him into the apartment. He checked the hallway, up and down. Nobody. Good. The door closed. Inside, Armand stood with his hands upon his hips. Questions wrinkled his face.

"Sorry to get you out of bed," muttered Rom. "Something's come up that I gotta talk to you about."

The bedroom door clacked. The cop's eyes slitted toward the noise. A redhead…peeking through the narrow opening. He leaned close to his brother and rolled his eyes toward the bedroom. "In private."

Armand turned to see emerald eyes. Immediately he went to the door and without a word, pulled it shut. Motioning Rom to the farthest corner of the room opposite the bedroom, Armand poured two fingers of black market hooch into a couple of etched ruby glasses.

The cop took a seat. Breathing on his cold hands, he rubbed them together while wishing he had put on his overcoat.

"What's so damned important to bring you around here at this hour?" Armand demanded as he handed his brother a drink. "And in those duds. Ya wanna get me killed or somethin'?"

Rom slugged down the whiskey and said, "Bartolomeo Vanzetti."

"Vanzetti?"

"He wants to see Don Vito."

"Can't be done." Armand snorted with a wave the hand

"Hey, I know as well as you the way this business works. Bartolomeo says he will speak with either the Don or the Feds."

"He told you nothing else?"

"Only that he knows things—things the dogs will have a field day with if he spills the beans."

"Bartolomeo. Sounds like you and this man are *paesani,* eh?"

Rom shrugged. "*Paesani.* Hmm. I s'pose. One way or the other, prospects are that the guy is not getting out of Charlestown alive. Thing is, it's all a setup. I'm sure of it. Others are too. Unfortunately, all sides are in the wrong, but to cover their asses, Vanzetti and Sacco must die." Rom tipped his empty glass then handed it to his brother.

Armand hesitated. Did he correctly read the signal for another drink? Rom was not a drinker. When the cop kept his arm extended, the older brother took the glass and went to refill both of their glasses. "I'll look into it," Armand said skeptically as he handed Rom the hooch. He offered a cigar but it was declined. "Now that I do for you, *fratello mio*, you do for me."

Rom shot a puzzled look at Armand. What on earth could he possibly do for big brother, a man who had everything? Not only that. Armand? Asking for favors? He'd rather die first. "Uhm, sure. Name it."

"Gaspare Messina croaked," Armand sat down and puffed on a newly lit cigar.

Rom nodded. "I heard."

"A new leader of the Boston rackets is in the works. Aldo doesn't want to stick around to fight it out, so he got Don Vito to send him down to Miami to keep a check on business interests there."

"You and Aldo are pretty tight. You goin' with him?"

"Nah," Armand scowled. "He's gotta learn to take care of himself sooner or later. Anyway, with Aldo out of the picture, Phil Buccola's strong-armed his way into the organization."

"Buccola? The boxing manager?"

"That's just a front."

"For crying out loud, the guy's just off the boat!"

"Didn't take him long, did it?"

"Wow. Who would have thought?"

"Yeah, well. The bugger's messing with trouble, and there's no doubt in my mind that the heat's gonna come down hard on Boston operations. In no time both the locals and the Feds will be gunning for us all. And I'm smack in the middle. That's why you gotta arrange a position for me within the police department."

"Informer?" Rom gasped.

"Rat, snitch—call it what you like, but when the big one goes down, I'm going with it. I'll be the disgrace of the LaRosa family and Pop will have nothing to do with my memory, that is, unless it comes out I was working for the cops."

"Don't remind me about Pop's sanctimonious drivel. Wasn't all that long ago that Rachele and the kids didn't fit into his way of thinking either."

"Sheeesh. Think Pop goin' off on you was tough? Wait till he gets a load of..." Armand pointed his thumb over his shoulder. "What's in that bedroom over there will definitely kill the old man."

Rom scrutinized the door. "How come?"

"That dame you saw? Name's Kathleen...Kathleen Kelly."

"An Irish. My God, Armand," Rom wheezed. "You're right. Pop'll blow a stack! How long's she been hanging around?"

"Two, three, four years. Crise, I don't know. What's it matter anyway? She's on her way out any day now. Soon's I find her a flat in Southie with her own kind."

"She know you're looking to get rid of her?"

Armand shook his head side to side.

"Must mean something to you if you kept her around this long," Rom speculated.

"It ain't safe for her. Best thing is a wide berth between her and me. I'm going down someday, and nobody's goin' with me."

"That's no way to talk," Rom winced.

"Listen, it ain't no big deal!" Armand's hands flailed. "You gonna arrange things or not?"

"Sure, sure. But there must be something else we can do," insisted Rom. "We'll go to Mama...She got Pop untangled from those old notions of his. He made things right with Rachele and the kids."

"Nah. I don't feel like messin' around with it. Like I said, the fewer connections the better. You know, when I left New York and came back to East Boston long ago, it was for *Mamacita* and the family, not the Mafia.

"*Mamacita*," Rom echoed. "Where'd that tag come from?"

"Knew a *senorita* in New York. She called her mama that." Deep in thought about days gone by, Armand refilled their glasses for the third time, but the cop made no move to drink his. "I let myself get sucked back into the mob again. Messina ran the show then. I felt safe. Now, I don't."

"You can't quit the Mafia," warned Rom. "They'll kill you first."

"I know that." Armand brushed off his brother's concern. "I kept thinking that maybe next month, next year, someday, I'd get a new life. But too many years have gone by and I know too much. Finally got it through my thick skull, there's no way out for me. That's why we gotta make sure that when it all goes down, I'm working for the cops. Pop won't think bad of me, and all of East Boston won't spit on my grave."

* * *

Noon the next day, Armand paid a call on Phil Buccola. It was against his better judgment, but if he wanted to stay in Boston, he had to find some sort of common ground with the upcoming boss of the Boston underworld. Vanzetti's request startled Buccola. At first he resisted the mere suggestion of contacting New York. On second thought it could be a way of clarifying to Don Vito that he was now the undisputed boss of the Boston family. Buccola jumped on the opportunity and sent word to Don Vito that Vanzetti wanted a sit down.

Word came back surprisingly quick. A meeting outside of New York was completely out of the question, much less at a Boston jailhouse. Instead the New York mobster threw everything back into Buccola's court, much to the dismay of the new boss. Don Vito commanded that Buccola give Vanzetti whatever he wanted. Just keep Vanzetti quiet! Alone in his office, Buccola raved on, "The insolence of that bastard…ordering me, Phil Buccola, around like that!" He sucked on his cigar as if it were a nipple to pacification. Suddenly, his eyebrows arched. "Like flies on a dead man's carcass, this Vanzetti deal makes the old Don squirm. Something more than meets the eye is going on here."

* * *

Many a night Don Vito had agonized over Sacco and Vanzetti's fate. He never expected them to turn into heroes, men of courage whom he came to respect like none other. Blaming himself for the two *paesani* taking the fall for the Braintree heist, the Don cursed the day that he and Gaspare Messina put their heads together and concocted the scheme. It was the greatest screw-up of his entire life. But why? He just couldn't understand it. Many times similar games had been played out, all successfully. Why didn't the Braintree heist come off as planned? Now the eyes of the world looked upon all *Italianos* everywhere as hoods, gangsters, anarchists. Immigration quotas from Italy had been slashed. Suddenly Don Vito felt a weight that his many years could no longer bear.

* * *

Phil Buccola tapped Armand LaRosa as negotiator for the sit down. Since it was his brother with whom Vanzetti sent the message, LaRosa was the ideal go-between. If anyone saw the cop's brother hanging around the jail, nobody would take notice. It also made getting into a meeting with Vanzetti easier. Besides, something's rotten here and Buccola didn't want any connection to it. His plan to show Don Vito who was in charge of the Boston rackets had backfired. If the deal got botched with Vanzetti, Buccola was going to take the heat for it, not the Don. Arrangements were made. Late the next Sunday night, while the good citizens of Boston closed themselves up at home with their families, Rom secreted Armand into the Charlestown State Prison. Vanzetti contemplated the two men standing at the bars of his cell. "*Interessante…due Italiano fratello—Uno polizia, uno Mafioso.*"

Ignoring the comment, Armand said, "I have been sent here by Phil Buccola. He sincerely regrets that he and Don Vito find it impossible to meet with you. Your unfair situation gives them cause for great sorrow. However, they insist you must also consider their position. To come to such a location would cast undeserved suspicion upon them and place them at the hands of their enemies. Nevertheless, they wish to help in any way they can to make you comfortable. They send me, Armand LaRosa, to hear your words. In what way may *la famiglia* be of service?"

"It is well known that I have never taken a wife. For a short time there was a woman. Where the relationship may have gone is lost. Perhaps, we may have married. But we spent too a short time together for that kind of decision."

Armand shifted. *What's this got to do with Don Vito?*

"Because you are here, Armand LaRosa, reveals to me that what I surmise about Don Vito is indeed true. He would not have sent you if I was wrong."

Armand tried to act nonchalant. *This guy reads minds. Obviously, he's no dummy. Yeah, Vanzetti's got something figured out, something the rest of us with our noses buried in the muck have not.*

"Things Don Vito wishes for me not to make public will remain within my soul. That is, as long as my request is granted before I take my last walk."

"Your request?"

"The woman I just spoke of, she sent a mutual friend to me. *Una bambina*, a girl, was born of our time together and is now several years old. The woman struggles. She has no money. Her family has discarded her and *il bambina*. It is my wish that a marriage be arranged for this woman to a good and honorable man who will take care of her and *il bambina*." Vanzetti squeezed his eyes shut and turned away. His head dropped. He did not want to give up the woman—nor the child. His shoulders expanded, forcing his words to come more quickly. "Whoever is chosen must never know that *il bambina* is Vanzetti. The man must never know of the relationship between me and the woman. Neither should *il bambina*. She will grow up educated, an *Americano*. However, I wish for her to know and respect our great Italian heritage."

Armand gritted his teeth. *Damn. Is there no way for men and women to come together in this godforsaken world?* He handed Vanzetti a Cuban cigar, "It is done, *paesani*."

CHAPTER 19

For the sake of peace at home, Joseph decided to squelch his misguided beliefs and make peace with Rom, Rachele, and the children. In the process he surprised himself. He actually enjoyed Rachele. She turned out to be quite an intelligent individual. Many winter afternoons, he huddled close to the wood stove in Rom's parlor as the blaze that flickered behind the grates cast a warm glow upon his wrinkled face. Maria Avita sat in the rocking chair in the front window and smiled contentedly while crocheting. Before long Rachel brought mulled wine and homemade bread, which instigated deep conversations. The Great War or the politics and landscape of Italy versus this new land of constant change absorbed the man and daughter-in-law for hours. Rachele, hungry for family attachment, showed great interest in discussing his beliefs and had a way of differing from them without riling the old man too much. More often than not, the growing of crops was the topic. She possessed an exceptional understanding of the land and how to entice Mother Nature into giving up the finest fruits and vegetables Joseph had ever seen.

Isabella and little Joseph also gave great joy to the old man. Before the day ended, they usually crawled up on Grandpa Joe's lap and snuggled close, begging to hear stories of the old country and the immigration of the LaRosa family to America. Oft times the graying man recited Italian folklore and stories from the Bible that came alive with his fiery voice.

He was pleased, for Isabella and little Joseph loved Grandpa Joe as if they had sprung from his own blood. Then along came Rom and Rachele's baby, Celestina. A gift from heaven, she reminded Joseph and Maria Avita of their own sweet infant, Francesca. With button eyes the color of the cinnamon rose, her smile warmed the place in their hearts left empty so suddenly.

The strong bond that grew within the LaRosa family extended outward. One day, Joseph even shook Aldo's hand and patted him encouragingly on the shoulder. Young Messina was beside himself. It was a miracle. After all this time the old geezer finally had set aside ancient grudges. So it was that when February 1926 rolled around, Joseph and Maria Avita looked forward to her fiftieth birthday celebration at Mizzulo's Restaurante. The golden bond of friends and family awaited.

"Joseph, we are late," whined Maria Avita while weaving a pearl-headed hatpin into her green felt bonnet. "Everyone will be at the Mizzulo's before us. Why is it that you mope about so?"

"I did not sleep well last night, *Angelatina Mia*," he half-lied. Lately the pains in his chest came more frequently and were terribly uncomfortable. Last night, they disturbed his sleep and just now it felt like a great hand was crushing his chest as he fumbled to put on his long woolen coat. The old patriarch had avoided mentioning anything about the discomfort. He was glad he did. How foolish he would have felt after running into Doctor O'Shea in Central Square the other day. "My dear man, it is only indigestion," the Irish had said flippantly. "Stay away from the hot peppers!"

On the other hand the pain was unbearable today, and Joseph sweat more than he should. He needed to sit more often, just to catch his breath. Taking shallow breaths, he wormed his arm into the sleeve of his dark green coat. Was the coat heavier today than before? Must be his imagination.

"Let's walk to the restaurant," bubbled Maria Avita. Her hand extended into the air as she stretched black lambskin gloves onto her fingers. "It is chilly, but there is no wind. And the sun is so bright. Armand will give us a ride home later on."

The old man did not have the strength to argue. Descending the front steps she said, "Careful, some of last night's glaze has not yet melted."

"Here, take my arm," he said. Joseph viewed this as a sign of a true gentleman. So long ago he had stood on the steps of Our Lady of Assumption Church and taken notice of Carmelo Messina and his wife. Now Joseph possessed the same stature as he and his beautiful Maria Avita strolled arm in arm. Yet with every step, the old man clung to his wife, more for support rather than for manners. The chest pain intensified and slowed him down. So much so that Maria Avita fussed, "Joseph, why is it that you poke along so?"

"What is your hurry?" he mumbled. "You yourself made it plain that this is a perfect day to walk. We should enjoy it, every last moment of it."

"You are right, my husband. Mizzulo's is not that far anyway. There is plenty of time."

The street was deserted except for a highly polished black Buick just ahead of the couple. Parked close to the curb, it glistened in the sunlight while exhaust fumes sputtered from the tailpipe and circled up into the frigid air. A trio of males, wearing long dark coats and caps pulled down to their thick dark eyebrows, milled about, idly smoking hand-rolled stogies. Two of them stood at the rear of the seven-passenger automobile; the third leaned against a wrought iron fence opposite the car, studying the ashes at his feet. As the couple approached, the three men stiffened. The one near the fence flicked his burnt-down cigar onto the ground and crushed out the glow. In a heartbeat his powerful arms snared Maria Avita and his huge hand stifled her terror. He plucked her from Joseph's arm and dragged her away from the Buick. The other two thugs drew .38's. Cold steel jabbed into the old man's belly while the butt end of the other revolver came down hard at the base of his skull. As Joseph crumpled, the men grabbed his arms and crammed him into the back seat of the idling vehicle. They piled in behind their victim and slammed the door. "Time has run out, *Signora* LaRosa," growled the goon who restrained her. "This day, you pay for Father Sandro. *Felice Compleanno*!"

With that he cast her to the ground and scrambled into the front passenger seat of the black Buick. Tires whirled on the slick cobblestones, and as the car fishtailed down the street, the passenger door opened and closed like a pectoral fin.

Disoriented and winded, Maria Avita raised her head. Her fingernails dug into the cobblestones. "Father Sandro?" Did she really hear that heathen's name? After all this time? Fear congealed her blood. "Father Sandro. They know!"

Her eyes skimmed the cold, silent street, devoid of person or vehicle. She spotted Joseph's black fedora crushed beside the curb. A vision loomed before her. Two men were stuffing Joseph into a black car while smoke from the tailpipe wafted up into the air. Her husband, covered by his dark green overcoat, lay in a heap on the floor. The car door closed. "Joseph?" His name froze in her throat like ice crystals suspended in the wintry air.

Maria Avita staggered to her feet, but her injured hip resisted her weight as she hobbled towards Mizzulo's Restaurante. With every arduous step the ragged drumbeat of the Charleston grew louder until finally she toppled against the door. Crashing through, the woman tripped over the threshold and tumbled onto the dining room. "They took Joseph," she bawled.

Silverware stopped clinking. Dancing stopped. So did the music as Seth and Armand rushed to her. Lifting her to her feet, she yelped and sagged against them. The injured hip refused to support her weight any longer. Orazio grabbed a chair and slid it under her, then Seth and Armand gently lowered her onto it. "Whaddaya talkin' about, *Mamacita*?" Armand demanded. "Who's got Pop?"

"Mama! Your knees," Louisa shrieked. "They're bleeding!"

Maria Avita pushed her daughter aside and latched onto Armand with both hands. Jostling him back and forth, she cried, "They took your father! They said today I pay for Father Sandro. They know, Armand. They know!"

"What's she talking about?" Seth charged as his narrowed eyes searched his brother's face.

Unhooking her fingers from his jacket, Armand shifted her hands to Louisa who was frozen in terror. "Take care of *Mamacita.* Come on, Seth. You and me got business."

Just as the two brothers turned to go, Rom burst through the door. The crowd gasped. Blood was splattered all over his uniform. "Paolo's in tough shape," he panted. "Goons worked him over to within an inch of his life. Used his head as a battering ram, smashed the wall mirror to smithereens."

"*Dio mio!* Where is my Paolo?" Maria Avita wailed.

"At the Relief Station."

"What'd he do to deserve this?" Seth railed.

"Goons drilled him about a priest named Sandro. Paolo didn't know nothing, but they weren't about to take no for an answer 'n kept on beating him 'ntil the lookout spotted a uniform comin'.

"Their gonna kill all my family," sobbed Maria Avita.

"No, Mama," said Rom hesitantly as he scanned the restaurant. "Looks like the rest of us are all here. Pop's the only one they got. Paolo's under heavy guard, and I've called in for reinforcements."

Louisa sprung to her feet. "Rom!" Her apprehensive eyes darted around the crowded dining room. "Vincenzo's not here!"

"They're not gettin' away with this," seethed Armand. *Mamacita*, tell me, quick! Which way did the car go?"

"This way. It came this way."

"But Mama," Seth argued. "I got here just before you and I didn't see any cars, especially speeding ones."

"Must've turned off," Rom spat.

"Either on Bremen or Chelsea," Armand nodded. "But which way?"

"Not down the wharves," said Rom cracking his knuckles. "Too busy this time of the day."

"Yeah, had to be the other way," said Armand. "Maybe out to the railroad junction or Breed's Island." Instinctively places the Mafia chooses for executions, which were meant to send a message, popped into Armand's mind. The rail yards were right next to Chelsea Creek. The swift current was sure to carry a body out to sea in no time. "No, wait!" he stamped his foot and whirled around. "Too simple. Just too damned simple! They're tryin' to throw us off. While we waste our time mucking about in more obvious places, they're doing the work elsewhere."

Armand paced. He studied the floor as if the answer lay at his feet. The reservoir at the top of Eagle hill? Nah. The excavation for the new East Boston High School had just begun, but that place wasn't ready yet for cement. Suddenly he stopped short and viciously slapped his temples with the butts of both palms. "Airport flats off Jeffries Point. That's it," he snarled. "Runway's ready for paving. Perfect place to dispose of garbage."

"No," screeched Maria Avita.

"Listen to me, *Mamacita.*" Armand got down on one knee and patted her hand. He kissed her broken fingernails that stuck out from her torn glove. "I don't want ya worrying now. I'll bring Pop and Vincenzo back to ya in no time at all."

"And what if you're wrong?" Rom demanded.

Armand got to his feet. "Keep your fingers crossed, *fratello mio*. Plus a hell of a lot of praying won't hurt none."

"Well, just in case, a bunch of us will scour the docks," Rom said as he motioned to a few guys to go with him. "If we come up empty, we'll hustle out towards Chelsea and scout out the rail yards. Catch up with you and Seth later."

Family and friends who had come to Mizzulo's Restaurante for Maria Avita's fiftieth birthday celebration instead joined a manhunt.

Word on the street spread faster than grains of sand blown by March winds. A priest had turned up dead in Italy, and for some reason the LaRosa family was up to their eyeballs in his demise.

* * *

The hostage-hauling Buick arced around street corners then bounded over railroad tracks. Joseph's vision cleared enough to make out the intersection of Addison Street and the Eastern Railyard just before the bridge that passed over Chelsea Creek. Once again the great invisible hand squeezed his ribcage and robbed his breath. Though his focus blurred, he was still aware of the Buick accelerating and braking, taking unnatural turns first this way then that. Metal grated against metal as the car sideswiped a guardrail. Moments later, it grazed a utility pole and the thug in the front seat hollered, "Hey, knucklehead, watch it, will ya?"

Suddenly the car screeched to a stop. Joseph pitched forward and jammed into the back of the front seat. Crumpled on the floor, his muscles were powerless to right himself. Next thing he knew, two goons grabbed him by the arms and hauled him out of the car. They dumped him onto the frozen ground as if he were a mere sack of chicken feed. The toe of a shoe wedged under his belly and rolled him over. "Get up, old man," a voice barked.

Joseph struggled onto one elbow and strained to ascertain his whereabouts. Some sort of construction site. A blast of wind brought the odor of the low tide to his nostrils while dark clouds overhead sprayed icy mist into his face. His tongue sought out the moisture on his lips. Salt. He winced with the pain that spread from his neck into his shoulders. He was cold and clammy, yet he sweat like a pig. As two thugs opened the trunk of the Buick and dumped a naked body onto the ground, horror bolted through Joseph. "Vincenzo!"

Severely beaten, the young man's feet and hands were bound together making it impossible for him to stand. Moisture beaded his bruised and bloodied forehead despite the frigid temperature. One of the thugs removed the gag and held up Vincenzo's head by his hair. "Your son here informs us that you know nothing about the priest," he sneered.

Joseph shook his head weakly, "What priest?"

"Tell him, kid. Tell *tuo padre* the thing that your dear sweet Mama has done."

Vincenzo hung his head. His lips quivered. The thug yanked back his head. Still the unclad young man refused to speak. The thug kneed Vincenzo in the kidney and barked, "*Parla*!"

Wracked with pain, Vincenzo coughed, "Pop." Red matter spewed from his mouth. "Pop. Mama killed Father Sandro."

Joseph shook his head violently and moaned, "No." Pain spiraled down his neck and infested the rest of his torso. His right arm went numb. "No! That cannot be!" He could not breathe. His world spun around and around. "*Angelatina Mia*…she can do no such thing!"

"Tell him, kid," the goon shouted and threatened to kick Vincenzo again.

"It's true Pop. I saw the bloody stick in her hand."

"There, *Signore* LaRosa. Now you know the reason you and your son will die this day. Death is retribution for Father Sandro, Don Vito's murdered godson. When the Don learned of your wife's heinous deed, he found himself vastly adverse to whacking a woman. But after much thought, he concludes that it is fitting that *Signora* LaRosa lives a long life, for she will suffer the loss for many years, the same as Don Vito has suffered these past years. You and the kid will only partially satisfy the rage that burns within Don Vito's breast. The rest of her sons will also feel his wrath." The kidnapper grappled Joseph's chin side to side. With his head cocked sideways he sniggered, "Whassamadda, ol' man? You no looka too good."

* * *

Back at Mizzulo's Restaurant, an armada of automobiles lurched away from the curbside and out of alleys, speeding off in different directions. Armand's Packard raced down Chelsea Street. Its tires squealed as it swung onto Maverick Street and headed towards the airport. Seth stared straight ahead as he asked, "Gonna tell me who Father Sandro is or not?"

Armand glared at his youngest brother. He looked back at the road and shouted, "Fer Crise sakes! In all your nineteen years, ya never caught wind of Sandro?"

"Come on, Armand."

"Shit!" Armand waved his left hand wildly then bashed it against the steering wheel. "Why me?" Filling his chest full of air, he hissed, "Back in Italy, *Mamacita* caught Father Sandro forcing himself on Louisa."

"Our Louisa?"

"Yeah, yeah, our Louisa. Beat that one will ya. A priest doing the nasty."

"Before we left Italy?"

Armand grunted.

"Why's it surfacing now?"

"Actually, rumors got started a few years back when some bones turned up. Damn. Thought I had a handle on the situation."

"You?"

"Long story kid."

"I don't understand."

"Sandro's Don Vito's godson."

"Oh."

Nearing the construction site, Armand slowed to a crawl. The temperature had dipped. Icy glaze layered the windshield. Everything blurred. The wipers were useless. Seth and Armand rolled down the windows and craned their necks outside for more visibility.

"Gotta watch our asses," Armand grunted. "Lots of holes for an ambush." Weaving the car in and out of the construction shacks and mounds of dirt, he wondered if Rom was right. Yeah. Pop and Vincenzo were probably safe and sound in *Mamacita's* arms at this very moment.

"Hold it," Seth shouted. "Back up."

Armand stomped on the brakes. The tires spun in reverse.

"Over there."

Armand stopped. "I don't see nothin'."

"Behind that bulldozer, see?" Seth pointed.

Spotting the rear end of a black Buick sticking out, Armand lathered, "Oh, yeah." One finger spun the steering wheel as his foot jammed the gas pedal to the floor. "Brace yaself, kid."

Squealing tires alerted the goons. Immediately .38s opened fire at the long black Packard side-winding at them. The hail of bullets didn't faze Armand. It only served to rile him even more. He pulled a Browning automatic out of a secret compartment under the dashboard and slung it out the window. "Duck," he hollered back and blasted away.

Seth hit the deck just as the windshield shattered above him. Bullets pinged off the hood and zinged overhead. Blood splattered inside the car. He looked up in time to see Armand yank the gun into the car and throw it onto the seat. It smoked and smelled hot and pungent. Seth could not believe that this was his bother. Fingering the wound on his right arm, Armand howled, "It'll take more than that to bring down Armand LaRosa, ya bastards."

Sleet turned into hail. With virtually no visibility Armand spun the wheel to the left and slammed on the brake. The car skidded sideways on the icy surface, but when it hit an unfrozen patch it rose up on the two left tires and hung there for a moment. As the Packard came crashing down on all four tires, Armand grabbed the Browning and vaulted out. Using the open door as a shield, he strafed the fog bank with indiscriminate fire. Suddenly other vehicles slid to a halt on both sides of the Packard. Rom leapt out of his police cruiser. The fog billowed away by the disturbed air, giving him a chance to get off three well-aimed bullets. The first slug disabled the kidnapper closest to Joseph; the other two took down the goons off to Vincenzo's left.

Grimacing in pain and astonished anger, the thugs spun around; their legs buckled. Grasping their wounds they sought escape as Armand emerged from the protection of his car. His eyes blazing with diabolical hatred, he stood spread-eagled in the pelting hailstorm. "Die, you fucking pricks," he raged and pumped bullets into the backs of the fleeing goons. An eternity seemed to pass before the barrage of gunfire stopped. Silence…except for the ice pelting the carnage.

Armand tossed away the empty gun. It sizzled when it hit the ground. "Got 'em." He puckered his lips then backed away. Clutching his shoulder, he collapsed against the hood of his Packard.

Cautiously, men stepped out from behind their cars. No one spoke. Not since the Great War had Rom witnessed such a bloody massacre. Only on two occasions during his years on the Boston Police Force had he drawn his weapon. Even then, he didn't feel compelled to take a life.

Seth raised his head above the dashboard of the Packard. Through the bullet-riddled windshield, he beheld his unconscious father, covered with ice, lying prostrate on the frozen ground. In a fetal position next to him was Vincenzo, shivering mercilessly and sobbing like a child lost in the wood.

Chapter 20

"Come on. Shake a leg, will ya?" Armand hollered from the passenger seat of the unmarked car. Moments later, the station attendant handed a couple of bills through the open driver's side window. Rom snatched them away and tossed them on the seat between him and Armand. He popped the clutch on the revving engine and the car, now with a tank full of ethyl, sped off towards the North End. Pulling up next to a black Ford coupe parked in front of the Seaman's House on Hanover Street, Rom gave a head nod. Carmelo and Antonio Messina acknowledged. As the Ford bolted away from the curb and accelerated down the dimly lit street, Armand barked, "Floor it."

Outside of city limits, the two cars gathered speed and disappeared into the black winter night. Their destination, Don Vito's compound, outside New York City. Just over the Rhode Island border, Armand glanced at Seth and Angelo in the back seat.

"They asleep?" Rom asked.

"Yeah."

"Mama know what we're up to?"

"Nah, she's got her hands full with Pop." Armand gazed out the passenger side window.

"Think he's gonna make it?"

Armand shrugged.

"Strange," said Rom. "They lettin' Paolo and Vincenzo out so soon."

"Didn't have a choice."

"Whaddaya mean?"

Armand motioned to Messina's car.

"Ya gotta be kiddin'."

"Messina says it's the only way. We all gotta do this.

"But Paolo and Vincenzo aren't in any shape for this."

"Gonna have to be."

"But..."

"Listen, I got a handle on the situation."

"Heard that one before," Rom scoffed.

Hours later, Messina's Ford skidded to a stop in front of ornate cast iron gates. Rom stomped on the brakes, stopping within an inch of Messina's bumper. Half a dozen sleepy guards leapt to attention and aimed machine guns at the cars that still rocked from the abrupt stop.

"Whoa, Sammy. Come on, it's me. Armand," he signaled with his left hand and got out of the car. A sling cradled his right arm that had taken a bullet just above the shoulder joint during the scuffle at the airport construction site. Sammy briefly lowered his machine gun while the other guards remained poised for action. Reinforcements gathered behind them. A second later, Sammy took notice of the large number of male passengers in both cars and quickly raised his weapon once again.

"Calm down. Calm down, Sam the man," said Armand. "Let's all keep a cool head here." With one hand waving above his head, he walked up to the guard. "Gotta see the Don, Sammy, m'boy.

"Too late. In bed by now."

"Come on," Armand pleaded with open palms. "It's important. Life or death important."

Sammy glanced dubiously at the other guards. Their dark eyebrows lifted. Their shoulders twitched indecisively.

"Hey, have I ever asked ya for anythin' in all the years ya known me?" Armand lowered his voice and his hands. "Rub us down, if ya have ta, but we're clean and ya know it. See for yaself. Only, if we don't get in to speak to Don Vito, innocent people will die."

Sammy appeared to yield.

"Please," Armand pressed. "Tell him, Carmelo and Antonio Messina and *il sei LaRosa figli* come here tonight filled with the greatest of respect and beg this uncommon courtesy. He will know the reason. Once again I say to ya, this is a matter of vital importance."

A long uncertain moment passed. Sammy and Armand scrutinized one another. Sammy finally relented. "Wait here," he grunted. His gun dropped to his side. "Keep an eye on 'em, boys," he commanded to the dozens of guards surrounding him. "Any one of 'em so much as bats an eyelash, plug 'em, 'specially this one," he pointed at Armand. He parted the throng and disappeared around a curve of the dark cobblestone driveway.

Armand went back to the unmarked car. Ignoring the occupants, he leaned against it and crossed his legs at the ankles. The oldest LaRosa son felt the guards eyeballing his every move as he reached into his pocket for a cigar. He bit off the end and spat it out. Striking a match against the car, he lit up the cigar and puffed circles of smoke into the frigid night air. A while later, his shoe ground the butt into oblivion. About to put the match to another cigar, Armand shook out the flame when he saw Sammy returning, signaling with his head. Armand stuffed the unlit cigar into his pocket and jumped back into the car as two guards opened the gates. He glanced at Rom. "It's now or never."

Slowly the automobiles entered the compound and spiraled up the long driveway to the mansion where a male servant opened the car doors. Carmelo and Antonio hoisted Paolo out of their car. The mangled barber grimaced with pain as they propped him up over their shoulders. Hiding his fury over Paolo's condition, Armand muttered, "Seth, you and Angelo give Vincenzo a hand." As everyone bunched up around Messina's Ford, he whispered, "Nobody opens their yap, hear me? Not unless the Don speaks directly to ya."

The housekeeper at the front door took their coats and hats. Several brutes frisked them while *il consigliere* watched, after which he led them down a long, dark hallway to the study. A grandfather clock throbbed somewhere within the dimly lit room. On the opposite wall the muted portrait of an Italian matriarch overshadowed a great mahogany desk where Don Vito slouched in an overstuffed upholstered chair. He wore a burgundy smoking jacket made of imported silk that picked up insignificant reflections of the late hour. The matching scarf, wrapped about his short, thick neck, had been hastily stuffed into the jacket collar. The Sicilian *Capo de Tutti Capi* was ruminating over a small black leather pouch lying on the great mahogany desk before him. He glanced up as the group of ragtag individuals assembled before him. Before meeting their end, his crew had worked two LaRosas over pretty good and did some damage to Armand. Ah, the casualties of battle.

The door closed and latched with barely a sound. Armand waited for the Don to speak. It would have been disrespectful to do otherwise.

"What is it you want?" Don Vito rumbled in a low, breathy voice. The palm of his right hand stroked the black pouch as if it were a cat.

"With so much respect," Armand bowed his head slightly. "We are aware of the lateness of the hour. For this, we humbly apologize."

Don Vito waved his left hand. Rolling it impatiently, he urged Armand to continue.

"Based upon the advice of Carmelo and Antonio Messina, we, the sons of Joseph and Maria Avita LaRosa respectfully come here tonight. Here, my youngest brother, Serafino. And there, Vincenzo, Paolo, Angelo, and Romeo."

The Don scrutinized the LaRosa men. Were they all heathens like their mother?

"Don Vito." Attention immediately zeroed in on Antonio Messina. Armand was horrified.

Carmelo hastily grabbed his reckless son's forearm and said, "Forgive my son's foolishness, Don Vito. He speaks out when he should not."

"Come on, Father," Antonio persisted. "Don Vito knows you and I always did substantial business for him in Boston. Even after Uncle Gaspare's death, we still continue to follow Phil Buccola. We do not question Don Vito's decision to put him in charge instead of you."

"My son, say no more," gasped Carmelo. Nervously he turned to the Don, "I say again, forgive my son. It is my fault, for I myself have failed to teach him to control his passions."

Armand had all he could do to contain himself. *Antonio better shut up or this whole thing's gonna get blown to smithereens.*

"The family has prospered from the great contributions you and your son have made," Don Vito conceded. He wished Carmelo had picked up where Gaspare left off, but that damned Buccola controlled too much muscle. To fight him would have meant an extended and very bloody war, which could have resulted in great losses of income for the family. "And all these years, the Messinas have asked for only inconsequential things. That has not gone unnoticed."

"With that in mind," Carmelo saw his opportunity. "May we respectfully make a request of sizable magnitude?"

Reluctantly Don Vito nodded. Loyalty needed its reward.

"Find mercy in your heart for Maria Avita and the LaRosa family. We beg of you, hear us. Spare Joseph from an unjust death. He is a pious man who works with his hands. Never has he done harm to others."

"When I was a mere child of six," Antonio interrupted once again.

Armand rolled his eyes. *That's it. We're all done for.*

"Joseph LaRosa threw himself in front of a crazed horse and saved my life. Don Vito, you must remember the occurrence."

Yielding to the memory, the Don nodded his head. He ran his index finger along the outline of the rigid object within the leather pouch as Antonio continued, "Joseph never had any knowledge whatsoever of Father Sandro's fate," Antonio continued. "*Signora* LaRosa told me herself that she intends to reveal all the details to her husband—that is, if he survives the devastating heart attack he took as a result of all this."

Don Vito shifted uncomfortably. He himself experienced such pain in his chest. Aargh, what was he thinking? Here he was thinking of himself while Sandro's soul drifted with the restlessness of an untimely death. The Don's heavy eyebrows knitted. "You, Antonio Messina. You know of my Sandro?

"I filled him in," Armand spoke up, knowing full well that he went against protocol. But what the hell, nothing could make this night worse than it already was.

The Don inhaled and exhaled heavily. Images of the savage and senseless assault, driven by nothing but hatred, loomed in his head and fueled his desire for revenge. "Fill me in also, Armand LaRosa."

"I see." All eyes tracked Vincenzo who was now limping towards the mahogany desk. He faltered before the dreaded inquisitor.

Armand clenched his teeth. *For crying out loud, another one gets mouthy. What's that little milk toast gonna drone on and on about now? How the goons scared him? Great. Any time now, the Don's gonna call the guards, and by dawn, eight bodies will float on the East River.*

Impatiently Don Vito dissected the beaten and bruised Vincenzo. One eye was swelled shut and his bottom lip was split and drooped. His shirt was bloodied, disheveled, and buttoned unevenly. It took *molti caloni* to stand before the Don looking like this.

"Parla!" charged Don Vito.

"I was barely six years old," Vincenzo cleared his throat. "Each day, the sun no go down until Father Sandro come to *nostra casa* to taste *il vino*. One day Mama and Louisa, they prepare the vegetables. Then Mama, she say, 'Louisa, go tend the rabbits.' Louisa left and after a time, Father Sandro, also." Vincenzo drew a shallow trembling breath but no words followed.

Armand noticed Don Vito rubbing his thumb on the pouch. *The old man's gettin' real fidgety. Come on, come on, wrap it up, Vincenzo!* Suddenly Armand found himself locked in Don Vito's cold black stare. It mandated that something must be done about this needless waste of time. Armand took a step towards Vincenzo, but then his brother began to speak once again. This time the words came faster, more urgent, more fretful. "Then Mama, she say to me, 'Vincenzo, go, bring Louisa back, for she plays much too long with *i conigli* and so I go. But you know I get scared and run back to the house. 'Mama,' I say. 'Mama, Father Sandro lay on top Louisa and she cry. Her legs kick at the air.'"

Armand's jaw dropped. Did he hear that right? Vincenzo saw it all? What else was there to all this?

"Mama, well, her face go white. She stand kinda strange. And then she rush out and forget to close *la porta*." Vincenzo hesitated and took a deep breath. "I follow."

Seth and Rom stepped up to Vincenzo and put their arms about his shoulders. Don Vito's eyebrows lifted. The show of brotherly love impressed him.

"I see Father Sandro on top Louisa. He no move no more." Pain and horror engulfed Vincenzo. His entire being quaked. "And Mama…she stand above. In her hand the club of driftwood from the sea. *O Dio, il sangue*…I see blood. It splasha the mud." Vincenzo held his head between his hands. His body rocked to and fro. "Then, Louisa, she crawl from under Father Sandro and fix her skirts back to her knees. I see her clothes, they are torn. Louisa, she hugga Mama *mia* and cry. I hear Mama. She cry too, and I say, 'Mama?' So, Louisa come and take my hand. We go back to the house." Vincenzo heaved a ponderous breath. "She cry and cry and cry. I ask why but Louisa no speak at all to me. She just put me in my bed. All night long it rain and rain and Mama and Louisa, they cry behind the curtains and I never see Father Sandro again."

The Don's face contorted. This boy, this family bore great pain. Sandro, what a manipulative young man. Beneath an angelic exterior, many earthly desires festered. Don Vito had always suspected in his gut that this was the case. Nevertheless, he adamantly rejected salacious gossip that repeatedly reached his ears regarding the priest's less than saintly activities. Even when relatives and associates who journeyed to and from the old country confirmed the rumors, he refused to believe. *Stupido! Was there no way to control yourself, Sandro?* Was there nothing Vito could have said or done to convince the impetuous youth how much his godfather would have given him? If only the priest had patience. Now what should be done? There has been so much suffering already. His fist constricted around the rigid object within black pouch. Was revenge absolutely necessary because a peasant woman protected her own? But Sandro's mother…on her deathbed…She made Vito swear that her son would become a priest. Well, that promise had been kept. Sandro did become a priest, but shamefully, met his end doing the devil's work. Exasperated, the Don raised the leather case to eye level and scowled at it. His knuckles whitened. His mind settled on a course of action. "These things, all of you swear on your father's life to be true?" His voice was flat, not angry, not pleasant.

As Vincenzo nodded, Armand understood at last. No wonder the kid acted the way he did. He was floating in Limbo. He couldn't go back to make things right and yet, he couldn't go forward until they were. Once again Armand became aware of Don Vito's gaze. "Er, *si*," he stuttered. "*Si. Mamacita* told me the story. I have also spoken to Louisa this very day, and her words agree. Never have I heard Vincenzo speak of this before tonight, but his words about that night are the same."

Don Vito yanked out the center drawer of the desk and tossed the black leather pouch into it. Metal clanged against the back of the draw as he rammed it closed then rose from his chair. Waving his hand, he exhaled, "Go. *Non dubitare.* I grant Maria Avita and the LaRosa family a pass."

As the Don shuffled out of the room through a side door, the LaRosas and Messinas questioned each other without words. That's it? Yes. No more vendetta. A low sigh of relief drifted throughout the room. *Il consigliere* came in through the side door and closed it behind him. He motioned to the visitors, and through the door they had come in earlier, Armand and Rom followed him out of the study. Behind them, Paolo hobbled out supported by Carmelo and Antonio Messina. Vincenzo walked unsupported, his heavy burden lifted. Seth and Angelo were last in line. At the end of the hallway, they gathered up their belongings from the housekeeper and left New York. As the Boston skyline rose on the horizon before them, daylight overtook the canopy of darkness.

Chapter 21

Joseph recuperated for several weeks at the East Boston Relief Station. His heart attack, though extremely serious, could not have happened at a more crucial time. His abductors had no idea what to do with their victim who was apparently already dead on the cold ground before they even got the chance to kill him. "Might be a good idea to pump the old geezer full of lead anyway, just to show Don Vito we done the work," one kidnapper suggested.

Their haggling over the dilemma gave the LaRosa boys time to find them at the airport construction site. Then all hell broke loose. Joseph never heard the hale of bullets streaking over his head nor saw the slaughter that his oldest son wrought. Conversely, Vincenzo lay half-frozen on the ground and suffered through the entire nightmare. Although shame more than injury or fear kept him pinned down, for he had betrayed his mother. How on earth could he ever tell her that he was the vile creature who had set the hounds upon her and the rest of the family? It took quite some time for Seth to finally convince him that everything was over and hoist him to his feet. But for the beaten and broken Vincenzo, it was just another chapter in his unhappy life.

* * *

Maria Avita faithfully tended her husband every day at the East Boston Relief Station. Harping on the fate of Father Sandro seemed the only thing that kept Joseph going. The stubborn old Catholic persistently probed for information but his wife continually put him off, saying, "This is not the time nor place for such a discussion."

The day finally arrived that he was well enough to go home. His daughter and six sons gathered around him as Maria Avita wheeled him out to Armand's car where Joseph asked, "New car?"

"Yeah, Pop," Armand replied.

"A Caddie?"

"Yeah, sure hope it don't end up like the Packard."

The next morning dawned cold and blustery. Spring refused to come. Just like the weather, Joseph was just as obstinate, for another day would not pass before every last detail of this secret was laid bare before him.

"You must not upset yourself," implored Maria Avita as she fluttered about him. Pretending to be too busy for talk, she poured the last of a bottle of milk onto his bowl of Wheaties. "Your heart is still sick. It is not ready for troubling thoughts."

"Tell me! I demand to know this moment," Joseph forced an impotent shout. His full weight sloped onto the table for support.

"*Si,* we will talk. But first, sit. Calm yourself. You will make yourself sick again." Maria Avita went to help him sit down, but his arm repelled her and knocked the milk out of her hand. The bottle spiraled across the kitchen floor and shattered against the cast iron stove. Glass flew everywhere. Looking at the mess, she took a trembling breath. Tears welled up in her eyes.

It didn't dawn on the couple that Vincenzo was upstairs in his bedroom and was listening to the rancorous discourse. The hollering, the shattering glass, all added to his guilt. His hands clamped over his ears, but still the noise reverberated in his head, growing ever louder and louder. He panicked. "Gotta get out of here!" Bursting out of his room, he stopped short at the top of the stairs. His mother's voice floated up the stairwell. "At first Father Sandro came around only once in a while."

Vincenzo heard broken glass being swept into the metal dustpan. Shards dropped into the trash can as he slowly descended the stairs. With every carefully placed step, he strained to hear her words. "Then every night the walking stick rapped on the door. He looked at Louisa in ways a priest should not, but I never thought…I wished so much for Father Sandro to go away and not come back. She took so to his attention." When Maria Avita paused, so did Vincenzo's steps. His brain echoed with the sound of Sandro's cane upon the door. "The night it happened I sent Louisa out to the enclosure to bed down the animals for the night. Father Sandro did not like it one little bit that I sent her away, and that made me feel good. He left. Then she did not come back to the house but I did not worry. You know how she always amused herself with the rabbits. But darkness came and there was no moon to light her way back to the house. So I sent Vincenzo to hurry her along and…" Maria Avita gasped and Vincenzo leaned against the living room wall for support. "He returned, all out of breath and shaking. His nightshirt was all muddy. I will never forget his little voice. 'Mama, Father Sandro makes Louisa cry.' I bent down and shook his shoulders. The things he said I did not want to believe."

Vincenzo quaked to his knees on the living room floor. His hands pounded his head. Every last detail blasted in his brain as his mother continued, "'He lies on top of her, Mama. Her skirt does not cover her legs and Louisa kicks at the air. Make Father Sandro stop, Mama!' My eyes suddenly fell upon the driftwood beside the door. I grabbed a piece and ran out of the house. The next thing I know, I look down on Father Sandro, my face burns with anger. The priest is dead and I do not know what I should do. So I move the cart, the one that catches the droppings under the hutch. He is buried under it. The ground was soft and easy to dig. I set the cart back and…" For the first time since her confession began, Maria Avita glanced at her husband. Old and haggard, he sat so still. He didn't speak. She worried. Did her husband take another heart attack?

Contempt grew and spread across his face. For as long as Maria Avita lived, that look never faded from her mind, neither did his words. "You killed a priest? A man of God? Your soul is damned, lost in hell forever!"

"Never you speak to Mama *mia* in such a way."

Maria Avita reeled around. Vincenzo stood in the doorway. His shirt was buttoned wrong; his fists were clenched into white-knuckle balls. Though fury reddened his face, he trembled like a child of six. "I wish to God and all the saints above that I kill Father Sandro."

"Vincenzo, no," sobbed Maria Avita as she rushed to him.

"Mama, *mi dispiace.* I tell the kidnappers you…you kill Father Sandro. *Mi perdonerai se?*"

"There is nothing to forgive, *cara mia*, Vincenzo. You had no choice." She wept while refastening his buttons.

His fists relaxed, and gently his hands wrapped around hers. He pulled them to his lips and kissed her open palms. "You no cry no more." He kissed her forehead and smelled the sweet essence of her thick black hair. Still braided from the night, it hung over her left shoulder. "So many night, I wake from sleep with the vision of *il diavolo* on Louisa. She scream and I cannot stop it," Once again Vincenzo covered his ears. His hands slowly dropped. His fingers flexed. "Time go by and I am now old enough and understand the thing Father Sandro do to Louisa. I get angry. So angry," Vincenzo raised a clenched fist to the heavens. "I wish I kill damned priest myself, then no one else ever get hurt. Don Vito get revenge from only on me. And so Pop and Mama no fight like now. Filthy priest, he no deserve no more thinking. Never!"

Vincenzo lumbered over to Joseph who sat speechless in his chair. The son towered over his father. Rampant bitterness reflected on both of their faces. "You left us, Pop. You desert us. There was little food and Mama sell *e capre* for us to stay on the land. And rain…it come and come. Mud wash away so bad. Mama no grow food without you and Rom and Armand. Vincenzo turned and shuffled over to the window. With blank eyes he stared at the starkness outside. "Days and days,

Paolo and Angelo look out for armfuls of wet twigs that no burn until dry inside *la casa* many days. Still the wood bring no warmth to that old place. It only smolder and cast off smoke, so bad we go outside in the cold and rain to fill our insides with clean air. And you know what?" Vincenzo turned back to Joseph. "That fire never last till morning. We so cold, Pop. *Freddo!*" Vincenzo jammed his hands into his pockets. "And that lustful priest come again and again. He no care nothin' for us. He no bring food, no wood, nothing. But he always come there and drink *il vino* and scratch *il pavimento* with his cane."

Denying the sight of his father, Vincenzo's mind returned to the hovel nestled against the hills by the Tyrrhenian Sea. "*Non so capisco* why Mama no like Father Sandro. She no herself when he come and know what, Pop?" Suddenly Vincenzo was right in Joseph's face. "You no there, you no protect Mama *mia*. And Louisa. So you got no right to judge Mama *mia*. No, not when you run off to America and leave her and us to *il diavolo* that roam the hills of Italy." Vincenzo walked away then looked back at Joseph for understanding. None came. He drew a long steadying breath. His hands grasped the back of a kitchen chair. He needed the support to defy his weakness, to defy his father, to defy the pain. "Pop…Bah! Sucha religious man. Who are you to judge Mama *mia*? You carry same guilt she carry. More!"

The fire dissipated within Vincenzo and he sank into a chair next to Joseph. His hands squeezed together in a ball until his fingernails lost their color. "Father Sandro is reason I no take the vow of the priesthood."

Joseph's mouth dropped open. His eyes, his soul begged to know, *My son, what is it you say?* But his lips did not move.

Vincenzo quivered, "Father Sandro come back to me when I take counseling from Father Roberto…"

* * *

Five years before. St. John's Seminary. The first day of counseling, Vincenzo took the stairs to the rectory two at a time. Always a quiet sort, the fifth son of Maria Avita and Joseph LaRosa was not known for this type of flippancy. But this was something Vincenzo wanted. He was going to become a priest. Peace and joy filled his heart.

An old lady answered his rap at the door and led him through a musty dark hallway. She knocked softly on the massive oaken door, heavily stained to a highly polished honey surface. A muted response came from within and she opened the door. The woman stood aside and motioned for Vincenzo to enter.

"Come in, my son," Father Roberto smiled and got to his feet. He was taller than Vincenzo had expected and more athletic-looking than any priest he had ever known. His black robe fluttered like drapes in the summer breeze as he rounded the desk and shook the visitor's hand. "Sit down. Please. Your father informs me that you wish to enter into the priesthood?"

"*Si.*" Vincenzo contained his happiness. The door closed behind him as he took a seat.

"Why?"

Why? Vincenzo thought. Nobody had ever asked him that. "I serve *Dio mio*." Quite satisfied with his answer, Vincenzo relaxed.

"There is much more to the priesthood than serving God, my son. Your whole heart, your whole soul, your whole life enters into it. The commitment is monumental, for the independence your brain is accustomed to will be lost forever. You will come to think and live as a holy man. Vincenzo LaRosa will not exist anymore."

"It is desire in my heart," Vincenzo insisted in a low firm voice.

Father Roberto did not reply. He contemplated his hands folded upon the huge oaken desk. Moments passed. Only the ticking of a distant clock disturbed the silence. Vincenzo wondered if the priest was praying, but suddenly Father Roberto placed his hands firmly upon the top of the desk and stood up. Offering a hand to Vincenzo, he said, "You may start reflections tomorrow."

The months that followed revealed to Vincenzo unexpected knowledge about himself. For one thing he had always been a loner and even though he had five brothers, he never really opened up to them. In addition he felt more comfortable in solitude than with crowds. The vacuity of a church after Mass let out gave him security and peace.

Most of the time, the future disciple was convinced that he had made the right decision. Other times the dark abyss of doubt overcame his soul. For some unknown reason Vincenzo wanted to run away from all of this and hide so nobody might look upon his undeserving face.

One day, Father Roberto greeted him at the door of the rectory. "On this truly glorious day we will drive out to Brighton. I have arranged an audience for you with William Cardinal O'Connell."

As the two men drove up the hedge-lined driveway of a lavish estate set atop a grassy knoll, Vincenzo could not believe his eyes. Where was the oath of poverty?

The prim brunette receptionist led Vincenzo and Father Roberto through the home adorned with fine furniture, tapestries, and works of art. She swung open a pair of French doors revealing a private golf course and the Cardinal making a putt shot. Dressed in the latest garb for the sport, O'Connell certainly did not look like a holy man. "So. You found me," Cardinal O'Connell said quite unabashed in a thick Irish brogue. "I have been patiently awaiting your arrival, for I am anxious to have our meeting done with so I may leave for my estate in Marblehead. I plan to spend the fall there, and by Christmas I will be in the Caribbean. Tsk, tsk, New England winters are much more than I can bear. Tell you what, you gentlemen have a seat right here in the sun. Miss Shaunnessy, please bring our visitors a cold brew. I will go quickly to change into something more fitting for this momentous occasion."

Vincenzo refused to touch the alcoholic beverage and pastries that Miss Shaunnessy set in front of him. It seemed highly improper to do so. These were Prohibition times. Times of great poverty and hunger, too. But Father Roberto made no qualms about it. Instead he soaked up the sunshine and sucked down his beverage within moments and even asked Miss Shaunnessy for a refill. While he waited he feasted upon the pastries.

Unsettling questions raged within Vincenzo. What did Pope Pious think back in 1911 when he made O'Connell his Holiness, the head of the Archdiocese of Boston? Is this the way the Pope expected the Cardinal to carry on the Lord's work?

Quite some time passed before Cardinal O'Connell pranced back out to the back yard. Checking his gold wristwatch to see how much time he had until his departure to Marblehead, he said to Vincenzo, "I am required to evaluate your readiness for the priesthood."

Vincenzo became incensed. Evaluate *his* readiness? Did that mean sporting expensive clothing like that white linen suit that O'Connell wore? How about donning a derby hat? Or swinging a gold-knobbed cane? Did such things make a better candidate for the priesthood? Every hour of the day, indigents staggered into Boston City Hospital with self-inflicted wounds in order to get free food and shelter. Meanwhile this Cardinal who had taken the oath of poverty lived and dressed in the lap of luxury? And drank bathtub gin? All this went against everything that Vincenzo believed.

But that cane. Vincenzo's eyes kept darting back to that cane. Throughout the interview, something about that cane…

During the drive back to East Boston, Father Roberto prodded Vincenzo. "Why did you look upon his Holiness so strangely?"

Vincenzo stared out the side window. Infinite vacuum blurred disconnected visions that flashed in his head.

"Your answers to the Cardinal's questions were so shallow. I know you better than that, Vincenzo. What on earth happened?"

The young man did not answer.

"You kept looking at him, his clothes. And your face contorted every time your eyes fell upon his cane. What thoughts did you have, my son?"

The cane bloated in Vincenzo's mind. Warping. Liquefying. The gold knob gleamed, blinded. Father Sandro's cane had no gold knob. It was a twisted piece of oak that made noises upon the door in the bleakness of winter. Without warning the past became an unbridled monster that crept up on Vincenzo and crushed him like a shoe upon an insect. Once again he stood at the entrance of the enclosure. Terror seized him. Louisa screamed and wriggled beneath Father Sandro. Her milky-white legs were naked all the way up her thighs to where the priest's body met hers. His feet dug in for leverage, banking the mud as he thrust himself at her time and again. Vincenzo scrambled through the muck. With everything he had in him, he ran. He fell. For a time he crawled then got up and ran some more until his little boy hands smashed into the door. It burst open and slammed into the wall. "Mama, Mama! Father Sandro lies on top of Louisa. She cry."

"Vincenzo. Vincenzo!" Father Roberto tugged on the young man's shirtsleeve. "What is wrong?"

Vincenzo gasped for air as if he had just run a great distance. He sweat profusely. His eyes focused momentarily on Father Roberto. "Nothing." His body convulsed. Turning away, he mumbled, "Nothing."

The remainder of the journey back to St. John's Seminary was silent. Never again did Vincenzo meet with Father Roberto.

Chapter 22

The next few months were troublesome ones for Maria Avita. Tending to Joseph and tormenting herself about the events that led up to his illness caused her to become tremendously rundown. And Vincenzo's revelations made matters worse. What was to become of her reclusive son? He lacked direction, motivation, faith. Worst of all, a wall of resentment now separated father and son. On one side, unquestionable faith, on the other, disenchantment. Since each man knew the other's routine, they went out of their way to avoid all contact.

Time dragged for Joseph as well. Rarely did he exchange words with his wife, but when he did, his voice burned with sanctimonious revulsion and bitterness. He blamed her for everything bad that had happened to the LaRosa family since Father Sandro's murder and maintained that God had punished the entire family for her wickedness. Armand had run off to the Mafia because she killed the priest. God took sweet Francesca because her mother killed the priest. Yes, for everything that went wrong, Joseph laid the entire blame at Maria Avita's feet. The hopes and dreams, which the patriarch had prayed for his family, had not come to pass because of her. His faith provided no solace. Instead it seemed to only prolong the agony. Prayer and attending Mass became empty and at times even painful.

Orazio did his best to draw out the festering anger that consumed his childhood friend. He tried everything, including baseball, to get Joey's mind off his troubles. In the past the two rabid fans had reminisced for hours on end about the days they had spent at Fenway Park. Perhaps that would work. "Hey, Joey," he ventured. "Remember the time that Ruth out-pitched Johnson, 1-0?"

"God curse the Red Sox for trading *Il Bambino*," spat Joseph. "I want no part of any of those traitors." The conversation skidded to an irreversible standstill. Orazio's plan had failed.

After long moments of silence and not knowing what to say, Orazio picked up his hat and said, "Gonna play cards down at Mizzulo's. Comin'?"

Joseph shook his head no.

To everyone's relief the grouch finally went back to work. At first it was for only a few hours each day, then gradually the hours increased to full time. Carpentry renewed his sense of worth. Seeing the results of his own handiwork, his face slowly lifted into the smile Maria Avita cherished and he began to speak to her in more civil tones.

During the recuperation Maria Avita had occasionally babysat Louisa's latest arrival, Dominico Junior. It gave her daughter a chance to do some odds and ends as well as errands for Dom Senior, who was now the proud owner of Bascuino and Sons Furniture Sales. More importantly, the bubbly child gave his grandmother some much-needed levity and distraction.

Carlotta showed up regularly on the LaRosa doorstep. She had always been a good friend to Maria Avita. The two women had seen each other through some terribly vexing times. Seeing Maria Avita so unhappy and worn down gave Carlotta great distress. Chattering about trivial matters was the only way that she could think of to lighten her depressed friend's mood. One morning she burst through the screen door at the Captain's house and happily announced, "This day is so warm and pleasant, we must spend it away from these four walls."

"Oh, I am not up to it," mumbled Maria Avita.

"*Si, si.* We must. First we leave off Joseph's lunch, and then we go to Belmont Park. While little Dom takes his nap, we will bask in *la bella luce del sole* before the summer turns it hot."

Maria Avita shrugged while mindlessly wiping off the stove that needed no cleaning.

"Ey, come on, *amica mia*," whined Carlotta. *"Dobbiamo togliere odora pantaloni."*

"Carlotta, please. Such talk." A hint of a smile lifted Maria Avita's face.

Carlotta grinned sheepishly. "Come on, whaddaya say?"

Maria Avita relented, and the two women proceeded to pack the baby carriage so full of food and supplies that Nona Maria Avita was forced to carry little Dom in her arms. This was no terrible chore, however. The little guy did not weigh much, and she loved to hold him anyway. Nobody else seemed to want to touch her anymore except little Dom. His pudgy arms always opened wide and reached out to her without any question or hesitation.

As the two women rounded the block next to the construction sight, Joseph noticed his wife carrying his newest grandson. He smiled. As usual Carlotta was babbling on and on without taking a single breath while pushing the packed baby carriage. Maria Avita's head bobbed up and down. More than likely, not one single word was sinking into that brain of hers. He waved then while replacing tools in his canvas apron, hollered, "Come on, Seth. Your Mama has arrived with lunch.

"Be right there, Pop." Seth's voice came from the rooftop as the old man swung his leg over the top rung and started to climb down the ladder.

"Joseph is more himself these days," muttered Carlotta. Many times in recent months, she had wanted to shake Maria Avita and somehow, some way, get it into her thick skull that people treat their dogs better than her husband treated her. Nevertheless, Carlotta bit her tongue and tried to be a good friend, but her insides churned. *That mean old excuse for a man is too sarcastic, surly, and domineering for his own good.*

It matters nothing to him who sees or hears his tirades. For a man who believes in his God so much, Joseph is incredibly slow to forgive his wife and grant her a second chance.

"*Si*. Things are much better," Maria Avita agreed. "Lately, my Joseph opens up more. His fun-loving ways will return in no time at all—this I am sure. He will become the attentive husband soon."

Little Dom gurgled and Nona smiled down at him. His eyes were glued to the right. She followed his gaze to the alley next to the construction—an English bull terrier…headed in their direction. His slavering red tongue flopped about from a cavernous muzzle. Spiked canines glistened. In no time the brindled dog would intercept Maria Avita who was carrying her grandchild in her arms and Carlotta who was still yammering on and on in her own little world. Apprehension surged through Maria Avita. To her horror, little Dom let out a squeal of delight and clapped his tiny hands. The dog's ears pricked and one bulbous eye focused on the child and then the other. A low, throaty growl sent a sickening wave of nausea washing over Maria Avita. As the dog mounted an attack, panic seized Mara Avita. Her hair stood on end as she clasped little Dom close to her breast and screamed, "Carlotta!"

Dashing behind her friend for protection, Maria Avita overturned the carriage, stuffed with their lunch. Food, dishes, and other picnic supplies littered the sidewalk and street as a whirlwind of lighter items scattered at will. "Look at what you have done, Maria" gasped Carlotta. "What were you thin…"

Carlotta turned and came face to face with the charging bull terrier. It pounced upon her and knocked her to the ground. As mighty jaws sank into her forehead, the woman's shrieks drove the dog into a heightened frenzy, tearing and ripping.

By that time Maria Avita had put distance between her and the dog. Suddenly the animal picked up the sound of little Dom's fright. Its jaws, still clamped into Carlotta's skull, froze as one bulging eye rolled about its socket, searching for the source. Chills ran up her spine as Maria

Avita whimpered, "*O Dio mio*, it looks this way." Little Dom was too heavy for her to run to the protection of the parked cars on the other side of the street, so she put her back to the dog, hoping it would not see her grandson. "Shsh, quiet, my little Dominico," pleaded Maria Avita, but he let out an ear-piercing screech.

The dog's jaw opened. Slowly, meticulously, it placed the head of its unconscious victim on the ground and backed away. Snorting red matter out its nose, the animal worked to rid bloody scalp and coarse black hair from its tongue.

Maria Avita muffled her grandson's mouth with her hand. The desperate act only made matters worse. He squirmed for air and wailed even louder.

The terrier's keen sense of hearing was not to be denied. Alert ears riveted in the direction of the child as fierce black pupils probed the exact location. Finding the mark, its legs bent back as the animal set itself to spring.

"No," Maria Avita bellowed. "No!" Her right arm fended off the attacker. As massive jaws crushed bone, she screamed from the excruciating pain and fell to the ground. Her body shielded little Dom against the powerful muzzle that whipped her arm side to side. Canines viciously tore at her, trying get at the bawling child. She struggled to keep her back to the animal and Dom close to her breast. Suddenly a roaring grizzly shadowed her. "Joseph!" she screeched.

His arms flailed like a madman as he kicked and bellowed. Nothing had the slightest effect on the dog. Joseph fell to his knees and grasping it's muzzle in his mighty carpenter hands, pried at the monstrous jaws that would not budge. Snarling vicious defiance, the man strained for all he was worth. His fingers dug deep as his teeth gnashed back and forth. Still the animal held fast. "Aargh!" Joseph released his grip and violently shoved the animal. His hands battered the air with frustration. Then seizing the dog's neck, he squeezed, constricted. "Die, *il diavolo*, die!"

The dog choked but maintained its hold. The man rammed his forehead into its skull again and again. Blood pulsed from his brow and streamed down his face as Joseph staggered to his feet. Cursing and kicking, he continued the barrage.

Maria Avita had never witnessed such malevolence in her husband. She wasn't sure which frightened her more, the dog shredding her right arm or the man's rage. Suddenly his hand gripped his pocketknife. He began hacking at the animal. Again and again. All to no avail. He backed off, gulping for air. "There must be a way to kill this demon," he cried while scanning the area. He searched his person. "Ey, I got ya now, ya sommanabitch," he cursed and drew out a 32-ounce machinist hammer from his canvas apron. He swung it out to arm's length. Suspended in mid air for a long powerful moment, down it came. Again. And again. And again. Finally the English bull terrier expired. Its eyes rolled back. The massive jaw quivered then opened. The shredded right arm plopped onto the ground.

A stranger darted out of the crowd that had gathered to watch the spectacle and pulled Maria Avita and her screaming grandchild to safety. Several others had formed a barrier around Carlotta, just in case the dog set upon her a second time. Nobody dared to move the unconscious woman. Her severe head injuries required more than they could give. Blood splattered into their faces and onto their clothing as Joseph continued to hammer on the dead animal. Crimson covered his entire being, giving him the appearance of Satan himself.

"Come on, Pop. It's over," Seth shouted and pulled his father away. But Joseph broke loose and returned to the dead animal. Kicking and whacking, he swung the hammer time and time again. Seth ducked as the hammer whooshed inches from his chest. Latching onto the tool, he wrenched it from his father's grip. "Hey, enough is enough!"

Yet even without a weapon, Joseph was a man possessed. With bare fists he continued to pound on the dead dog. Each blow released angry moments he had endured in his life. Bam, bam…for the time he was torn from his parent's grave. Whack, whack...for the moment that damned horse broke his leg. Bash, bash...for the day his beloved Francesca drowned in a tidal wave of molasses. The instant he learned his wife had murdered a depraved priest named Father Sandro...smash, smash!

"Joseph, stop," Maria Avita screamed. "The dog is dead. Joseph! Please. Stop!"

His fists and knuckles were completely devoid of skin by the time Seth, Tom, Luigi, and Al succeeded in hauling him away. Pinned against the hood of a car, the old man struggled savagely even as Seth jerked on his bloody shirt and bellowed, "Pop! It's over. Pop! Come out of it, will ya?"

Maria Avita placed her screaming grandchild into the arms of the man who had pulled her out of harm's way. With her broken and shredded right arm dangling at her side, she tottered towards the demon that raged before her. Her heart cast aside all fear and spurred her onward. She was the only person capable of bringing Joseph back from the brink.

"Mama, stay away," hollered Seth.

Nudging past her son, Maria Avita spoke softly as she put her arm around her husband. "Joseph, it is me, Maria Avita."

Eyes of the gecko glared at her. Suddenly Joseph cast her off.

"Do not come near, *Signora* LaRosa," Tom Cacace shouted. "Satan's evil grasp holds him fast."

Again she drew near, softly soothing her husband. "Sh...sh..." Her fingertips stroked his bloodied face. "Shshsh..." She hid her fear as his face lathered and froth bubbled from his mouth as if he were a rabid dog. His chest heaved like rogue waves at sea. "Shshsh...sh..." she whispered.

Slowly his eyes revolved in their sockets. His facial muscles relaxed and hazel returned to his eyes. As his full weight toppled against her, Joseph came back to Maria Avita. "I am sorry...*Angelatina Mia*...for everything."

Chapter 23

In July 1927 the Massachusetts Review Commission upheld the guilty verdict of Nicola Sacco and Bartolomeo Vanzetti. The order came down forthwith. For the murder of a guard and a pay officer during the Braintree payroll robbery, the convicted killers must suffer the penalty of death by means of electrocution on August 23.

Asserting that the two Italians had received a fair trial, Governor Fuller chose not to intervene. The community, the nation, and even the world did not agree. Sentiment that Sacco and Vanzetti had been railroaded ran rampant. Bombs exploded in New York and Philadelphia. World leaders, such as Benito Mussolini, Premier of Italy, pleaded for the men's lives, but to no avail. In front of the Massachusetts State House, protesters gathered daily. Additionally, two thousand people staged a demonstration on Boston Common. Despite the fact that the rallies remained orderly and nonviolent, the driving forces behind the conviction feared the worst and took precautions. Governor Fuller activated the National Guard. Heavy guard encircled his house. The entire Boston Police Force and the FBI were put on high alert. Vacations and leaves were canceled. Work shifts doubled. Furthermore, police and FBI formed special details to monitor the whereabouts and activities of individuals suspected of belonging to various anarchist groups, Mafia, and adamant supporters of Sacco and Vanzetti. Authorities did not rule out countless reports that many of these people plotted incidents intended to provoke mass riots following the execution and during the Parade of Sorrow.

Violence was exactly what covert factions within the law enforcement community wanted. To make sure it did happen, they devised their own schemes so that killing the seditious lunatics would be entirely legal and justifiable, no questions asked.

Meanwhile, militant anarchists targeted high officials within the Boston Police Department as well as the FBI. In addition, judges, lawyers, and others deemed enemies to the cause became assassination targets.

On every opposing front addresses and activities became widely known. The minute the slightest trouble broke out whether at the execution or along the funeral procession, blood would flow all over the great Commonwealth of Massachusetts and flood into the streets of America and percolate throughout the world. By the same token, Phil Buccola had come up with his own agenda. Shortly after hearing that the execution date had been set, he called in his trusted soldiers, Armand LaRosa among them. Packed into the poolroom of Buccola's palatial home, they waited for their boss to speak. Clenching a burnt-down cigarette between his front teeth, he squinted through the smoke as he leaned over the pool table and made a clean break of the balls. He stood up and angled his next shot. "Our family has many enemies, most within the legal community," he said. "But we must also remember that we have enemies within opposing underground organizations who connive with the dawn of each new day to steal our territory." He took the shot and stood up to chalk the tip of his stick. He paid no attention to cigarette ashes that fell on the table. He bent down and let fly until the cue ball pocketed the last mark. His hands flew victoriously into the air and the stick bounced across the table. Defiant that nobody could match his prowess, the boss of the Boston *Cosa Nostra* spat his cigarette butt into the middle of the pool table. "Let us also not forget that years overtake the current dons," he said smugly. "New leaders rise above the horizon. Winds of change and opportunities for vast wealth are coming. We must prepare ourselves."

Buccola reclined in a red velvet high-back chair. He took on a regal appearance in the black satin smoking jacket and slippers he wore. Long bony legs outlined the thin fabric of his pants as he crossed his legs and arrogantly lit up another cigarette. His eyes squinted, scrutinizing the room. This well-equipped army of his, which he had hand-picked himself, was just the right size and quality. All impeccable choices, he might add. Young and strong, and most of all, loyal to a fault. They would be useful to him for many years to come.

"Sacco and Vanzetti's executions provide the cover we've been waiting for. At hand is the perfect opportunity to eliminate every last one of our enemies," Buccola sniggered. "Yeah...And when the dust settles, we will all join the outcry against those damned anarchists, for it was they, we will claim, who caused the disrespectful atrocities during the Parade of Sorrow. Time to act, *paesani mio*."

Armand stirred uncomfortably in his chair. A power struggle such as this was not going to improve the already sad image of the Italian community. The Sacco-Vanzetti affair had stunk up the air, giving rise to the suspicion that all Italians were murderers and thugs. Reading the faces around the room, Armand saw total commitment to Buccola's cause. Without question all these soldiers would follow their unbalanced leader to the death. He peered up at the vaulted ceiling, certain that all hell was about to break loose on the streets of Boston.

Hatching his sinister plot, Phil Buccola handed out makes. Extremely meticulous with the details, he knew the best button for each clip. In the end not one don or immediate family member would be left standing.

It was almost midnight when the meeting adjourned. However, Armand's work had just begun and it had nothing to do with advancing Phil Buccola's cause. Quite the opposite, as a police informant, LaRosa's first priority was to alert Rom. After that he motored out to Dedham and shortly after 3:00 a.m. found a phone booth to drop a nickel to Don Vito in New York.

"What the hell is Buccola thinking of?" exploded the Don. "That idiot will blow the lid off each and every one of the organizations, not only in Boston, but New York and all across the entire country! Feds will come down so hard that this thing of ours will come to an end with a single beat of the heart. *Finito*!"

"No doubt. But ya gotta know, Don Vito, my neck's really stuck out," Armand winced. Visions of himself taking a full magazine dirtied his brain. "If it leaks out…that I'm the rat? My goose is cooked for sure."

"*Si*, you take great personal risk in this matter. Understand, however, I am not blind," said Don Vito. "You have always been a trusted member of my family. From your days on the boat, I have known of your friendship with my nephew Aldo. It is one of great respect and love. I myself have also become very attached to you. As part of the family, trust is of the thickness of blood. I strongly reminded myself of that the night I pushed my anger aside and gave Maria Avita LaRosa and her family a pass."

"You make me a humble man, Don Vito." Many times through the years, Armand regretted his involvement with Aldo Messina and the Mafioso. Nevertheless, it was quite apparent that this affiliation with Don Vito's family became the deciding factor that had saved his mother and family. Anything less than that the LaRosa family would have been history.

"Gaspare Messina molded you into a trusted *soldato*. Ah, but with his death…" The Don paused then his raspy breath filtered through the telephone lines. "The thought of your loss to the organization caused me great concern. To my infinite happiness you remained. Your continued loyalty will not be rewarded by putting you in peril."

* * *

Not one week had passed before Phil Buccola called in his crew for the second time. Clearly, his volcanic anger verged on eruption as he seethed, "*Il traditore* exists within our midst."

Silence electrified his office. Soldiers fidgeted. Eyes nervously hunted about for the yellow dog. Armand feigned the same reaction. It was inevitable. This day was coming down the pike sooner or later. The informer for both the cops and Don Vito would have been stupid not to prepare for it. In which case nobody—not even Phil Buccola—detected anything other than innocence.

Unable to ascertain the guilty party, Buccola banged his fist on the desk and roared, "It's a matter of time, *babbo mio*. The one among you who enlightened New York will find such actions extremely costly. And let me assure *il traditore*, as well as everyone else in this room, Don Vito does *not* make the decisions in Boston. *Phil Buccola does!*"

Hearing of the insolence, Don Vito blew up with an intensity that Armand had never witnessed. The Don rarely lost control, especially in front of others. A man in his position simply does not reveal true feelings. "Conniving, cold-hearted thieves, pickpockets, and murderers," raved Don Vito. "*Dannare* Buccola! *Dannare Americano Cosa Nostra!* Respect and benevolence exist no longer. Neither does the code of *omerta*. No more Moustache Petes." Don Vito caught himself. Setting his jaw, he calmed himself. In a smooth, controlled voice, he said, "Don't worry about it, Armand LaRosa. Power-hungry Buccola meets his match."

The receiver had barely rested on its cradle before Mafia heads throughout the country were informed of Buccola's intentions. It did not take long for them to form a united front and organize the troops. The higher echelon of the Boston underground was going down with the first attempt to wrest control from the current families.

Back at the Charlestown State Prison where Sacco and Vanzetti remained incarcerated, riot squads and machine gun sharpshooters manned strategic positions. All law enforcement pounded the streets up to the night of the execution and during the funeral that followed.

Shortly after midnight on August 23, officials for the Commonwealth of Massachusetts marched Nicola Sacco and Bartolomeo Vanzetti down the corridor of death and into the chamber at the end. They strapped the two Italians into electric chairs while a priest mumbled supplications to the Lord. The handgrip of the impotent breaker was unclasped. Slowly, deliberately, it was arched over the hinge that held the contraption to the wall and jammed into the service clasp. Current surged to the chairs and through Sacco and Vanzetti.

For three days their bodies lay in state at the Sacco-Vanzetti Defense Headquarters on Hanover Street. One hundred thousand mourners passed through the building, wearing down the marble steps at the entrance more than a quarter of an inch.

Sunday morning, Joseph and Vincenzo met in the kitchen for a rare outing together. Seth joined them. They were going to board the subway to Tremont Street and witness one of the greatest funerals ever held in the North End. "Wait, I am going with you," called Maria Avita as she rushed into the kitchen. Her left hand struggled to weave a hatpin into her black Ecuadorian Panama. She never regained total use of her right arm and fingers after the dog attack.

"It is not right that my wife should go to such a thing," argued Joseph.

"Pffft! You and your old ways," she sputtered. "I feel just as strongly about this as you. I am going and that is the end to it."

"Here, Mama, let me do that for you," Vincenzo said and zigzagged the pin into his mother's hat.

Joseph's eyebrows bristled. Men did not do such things.

The train was not due for another twenty minutes when the LaRosas arrived at the Maverick Street Subway. Seth waited for Paolo to show up while Joseph, Maria Avita, and Vincenzo went to a nearby pastry shop. Taking a seat, Maria Avita said to the waiter, "Nothing for me."

"Two coffees, *per favore*," Joseph said while signaling a thumb pouring liquid. "*Zuzu*."

"This is not the day for that sort of thing," protested Maria Avita.

Ignoring her, he dragged a chair noisily from another table and sat down just as the coffee came. Both cups stunk of home brew. Joseph raised his cup and said, "To Nicola and Bartolomeo."

Reluctantly Vincenzo raised his cup. The cups clinked together. And so did many others of those who overheard the toast.

Later, not far from the Tremont Street Theater, Joseph and Maria Avita lingered in the heavy drizzle. Vincenzo stood a few feet away. Even on a sad day like this, the barrier that separated the father and son refused to chip and crumble.

Maria Avita blinked through the mist, searching for Seth and Paolo, lost somewhere in the waves of people coursing into the area to view the Parade of Sorrow. Her eyes rested on the theater billboard across the street. "'Honeymoon Lane', starring Eddie Dowling," she mumbled. "Hmmph. Honeymoon, happiness and new beginnings. Such a shame. This street I stand on is only a soggy road of unhappy endings."

"What is it that you say, *Angelatina Mia*?" Joseph leaned toward her.

"Nothing," she said. Her mind was haunted by another soggy road that she and six of her children had tramped along in the early hours before dawn, fleeing Italy and an unhappy ending.

Time passed. The drizzle let up, leaving oppressive heat in its wake. Crowded together, shoulder to shoulder as deep as the streets and storefronts allowed, two hundred thousand people sweat. Scores wore red ties and armbands printed with the words, "Remember! Justice Crucified August 23, 1927." Others wore pins on their lapels bearing the likeness of Sacco and Vanzetti.

Men, women, and children rubbernecked from second-, third-, and fourth-story windows and balconies. Others weighed down stairs of fire escapes to the brink of collapse. Little did anybody know that hundreds of the strangers in the midst were cops and Feds disguised as common folk. Ordinary jackets concealed their weapons. Equally armed Anarchists and Mafia soldiers from across the United States also infiltrated the crowd and also wore everyday clothing. Then there was Armand. Scanning the growing sea of humanity, he picked out Buccola's soldiers. Not far from them, he spotted a number of wise guys from New York. All of these people awaited *il imbroglio*. This was going to be a blood bath. He had absolutely no idea how he could protect himself...and his family...lost in the surging crowd.

Two o'clock. Hush fell over the scene as a solitary figure in black bore a giant flowered heart down Tremont Street. Waves of men removed their hats. People crossed themselves. More wreathes followed, so large that two bearers were needed to carry each one. Flags rippled from the front fenders of the black hearse that bore the bodies of two martyrs. Alongside was Romeo LaRosa, Vanzetti's *paesano*. For seven years the cop had stood guard at the cell door. Now excruciating wretchedness weighed him down as he accompanied his ward to final rest. His left hand clung to the cold steel door handle as if it were Bartolomeo's hand. Seeking strength one last time from *il paesano*, Rom subdued his grief. With his right hand falling open at his side, he appeared relaxed, confident, professional. In actuality he had braced himself, for at a moment's notice, circumstance might arise for him to reach for the handguns stuffed beneath his uniform jacket. The secret conspiracy, instigated by unnamed individuals in the law enforcement community, was about to play out. Who was the real enemy here today? The ideals Vanzetti stood for? The corrupt legal system? The Mafia? There was no way to stop the bloodshed. The only thing needed now to incite the massacre was the excuse. Numbness swept over Rom. Somewhere in this crowd was his parents and his siblings. Anticipating the worst, he waited for the riot to commence. Then, there was nowhere to run...nowhere to hide.

Meanwhile, Buccola's soldiers had disappeared from the crowd. The New York organization had snatched them one by one and taken them to a central location near Scully Square. Buccola's army became quickly educated to the fact that the daily routines of their wives and children were not secret. Unfortunate things could at any time happen to them. Fortunately, the renegade soldiers had the power to prevent such things. All they had to do was back off their current course of action and fall into line with Don Vito and his cohorts. After all, only best wishes extend to loyal soldiers and their families who choose to follow the Don.

The crowd folded in behind the funeral procession and followed in close cadence to Forest Lawn. Because no cemetery in Massachusetts chose to accept the bodies of Sacco and Vanzetti, the Italians were cremated. Their commingled ashes were divided and put into four copper urns. Only one of the four ever made it back to Italy.

At the conclusion of the Parade of Sorrow, transformed soldiers were released and tramped back to Phil Buccola with a message from Don Vito. The current families intended to stop at nothing to remain in power. If Buccola valued his position and his life, he would honor their leadership and learn to control his greed and lust for power.

That evening, Joseph and his sons lingered on the front porch of the Captain's house. The old wooden rocker creaked as the aging Italian gazed sadly to the west where the sky grew black with rain that did not come. It seemed to him that the clouds had darkened from the Maker's sadness as He welcomed the souls of the two men, set free at last from seven years of agonizing imprisonment. "Terrible day for Italy," he muttered. "Even more so for this adopted country of ours. No longer is America innocent."

"Yeah. So much for truth and justice," Rom winced while cracking his knuckles. He got up from the glider and braced his leg upon the porch railing. If only he could wash Bartolomeo out of his mind. A human being with such intelligence and compassion as Vanzetti had so much to contribute to this turbulent world. Now he was dead. What did that accomplish? It certainly did not improve the image of American justice. Nor the cops and Feds for that matter. Worst of all, not only

Italians but also immigrants of all nationalities bore the brunt of the injustice. The cynical policeman wondered if it was all worth being a cop. If only he could have done something to save Bartolomeo. Some small elusive piece of evidence or maybe a purebred American witness, anything. Cops get at the truth. Why didn't he? He had failed in his job. He had failed Bartolomeo Vanzetti.

Armand flicked his cigarette butt into the street then wedged himself against a post with his legs stretched across the top stoop. Thank God this day was over and done with. Nobody got hurt...well, except Phil Buccola. Armand could just hear the boss ranting and raving right now. He ain't gonna take Don Vito horning in on his territory lying down.

"It is a great tribute to the multitude of people who showed up today that no trouble came as a result of Nicola and Bartolomeo's deaths." Joseph heaved a great sigh. "So my sons, the war over who is right and who is wrong will come again some other day. But this day people set aside to honor those two men and their valiant struggle to live."

Armand glanced up at Rom. The informer and cop exchanged knowing glances. Within their weary eyes and souls, a sense of uncertain relief prevailed. Indeed, the unseen wars that festered in Boston would surely see another day.

Chapter 24

The year 1928 was good to the LaRosa family. Armand, rugged man-about-town, turned thirty-four. Brother Seth, twenty-one, virile, and sought after by the opposite sex, hung around East Boston for the most part. Both men were still single. Dismissing his concern, Joseph insisted that the right woman had just not come along yet. Not to worry, any day now…just wait and see.

During the day Seth supervised employees at LaRosa and Sons Construction Company. Late afternoons and early evenings found him at the office doing paperwork. He spent the better part of Saturday mornings with Louisa at the East Boston Branch of the Boston Public Library. For the last eight years now, they had volunteered as readers in the Children's Story Hour sponsored by the Americanization Committee. The effort familiarized immigrant children with the customs and language of the United States. Boys packed into the basement of the building while a smaller number of girls met in the Adult Room. Occasionally they all congregated in the auditorium to hear Mary Cronin, the great storyteller. Her silken voice held children as well as adults spellbound.

The marriage of Paolo and Maddalena produced a son, Rocco, who turned two years old in June. Another little one was in the oven, due out in early '29.

Six days a week, clientele jammed Paolo's Barber Shop. So much so that profits piled up, more than enough to purchase the building. The shop took over the entire first floor; the two new barbers Paolo hired and their families rented the upper two floors.

Louisa and Dom Bascuino celebrated sixteen years of marriage. Their daughters, Avita Maria, a freshman in high school, and Concetta, a third grader, did extremely well with academics. Nicholas was in the seventh grade and quite often accompanied Uncle Seth to construction sites. Little Dom resembled his grandfather to a T, both in looks and temperament. The rascal tormented his older sisters with his endless three-year-old demands and insisted on picking Joseph's roses.

Avita Maria, now fourteen years old, looked more like her grandmother with every passing day. It frightened Joseph to think that when he had wed Maria Avita she was only seventeen. Yet his oldest granddaughter, quickly approaching that age, was still only a baby.

Nine years sped by since Rom and Rachele had become one at the monastery just west of Bassano del Groppa. In addition to eleven-year-old Isabella, ten-year-old Joseph, and eight-year-old Celestina, the couple took in a set of five-year-old twins. The girl and boy were born to Italian immigrants who had lived in East Boston for less than three years and faithfully attended Our Lady of Assumption Catholic Church. Then tragedy struck. The mother succumbed to tuberculosis; the father ran off, and the children fended for themselves in a second floor flat two blocks from the church. Rent came due and the landlord discovered the children cold, alone, and hungry. An urgent plea for help came during Sunday Mass.

"Those poor *bambini*," whispered Maria Avita. "Orphans. You remember them, don't you Joseph?"

"*Si.* Such a handsome young family. The father's soul is forever blackened for deserting his children like that." Stirred by anger and compassion, Joseph took it upon himself after Mass to let Rom and Rachele in on the children's plight. When an extensive search turned up no relatives, Joseph and Maria Avita gained two more adopted grandchildren who joined the others to wreak havoc on Joseph's roses.

Erich Marie Remorque's *All Quiet on the Western Front*, published that same year, brought powerful realism home of the devastating realities of the Great War. Rom put the book down before finishing it. Too many painful memories stirred within him causing flashbacks that bolted him awake sweating and trembling in the darkness of night.

Angelo practiced law from his North End office. Joseph and Maria Avita bragged about their college graduate son to everyone. However, after several years of dealing with the same old shoot-em-up cases and civil squabbles, the twenty-eight-year-old lawyer became increasingly bored. He wanted more. But what? The answer came just before the stroke of midnight on New Year's eve.

"Come on, come on, woman," Angelo nagged.

"But the children, Angelo," whined Heather.

"Let the goddamn baby-sitter deal with them," he barked and threw her coat at her. "Now here, let's go!" Angelo was so sick and tired of his sniveling wife that he thought he could ram his head right into the wall and feel less pain in doing so. He had met Heather while attending B. U. Law School. Hell's bells, what a man-eater! So liberated, lively, and bright. She loved to talk politics and was good for a whole night's romp in the sack. Not only that, Pop accepted her on the spot even though she was half-Irish, half-Italian. What a surprise that was. Then those kids came along and screwed up everything. All Heather cared about was them. A time or two, Angelo had given her a good smack, just to get her attention. That didn't work. It only made the damned bitch even more frigid and whiny. Angelo sulked. God only knows how long it had been since he got a decent screw out of her. Oh well, that's her loss. For quite some time now, Miss Babs Flaherty took ample care of that end of things. Hah! A lawyer could not ask for a more efficient secretary.

Shortly before eleven, Angelo and Heather arrived at Mizzulo's Restaurante. The ride had been cold and without conversation. He immediately dumped her with Maria Avita and the rest of the old hens and joined the good old boys in the back room. The instant he walked through the door, the fragrant aroma of all-Havana tobacco bowled him over; he had to have one immediately. There's Armand. He's always got top of the line Havanas on him. "Hey, Armand. Bum me a cigar, will ya?"

"Sure, kid," Armand sniffed as he tossed one to Angelo.

Lighting it up, Angelo sucked in the mildness, letting it take away all his cares. He glanced at the eternal card game. Other Italian mustaches stood around smoking stogies, drinking cellar wine, and talking politics of both old country and new. The rumbling voice of Donato Mizzulo bemoaning the dull political year caught Angelo's ear. The Mayor's seat and two senatorial vacancies were up for grabs and the same career politicians vied for the spots. "We need *il paesani* in the Senate who feels the needs of the Italian people and brings them to the front burner. The interest of Italian immigrants must be advanced," exhorted Donato.

"Yeah, times are tough," said Tom Cacace. "Few immigrants get into the country these days, not many of 'em Italian. And most ain't educated. Who's gonna hire em? Nobody."

"My point exactly," spouted Donato. "How can our people ever advance unless someone comes along who knows his way around the system? A person like this will stick up for us in Washington."

"And let in more from the old country," Tom added.

"So where do we find such a person?" Orazio asked.

"There," Joseph pointed with his cigar. Without looking up from his fan of cards, he said, "My Angelo. He is everything you speak of and more. Angelo will make a fine senator."

The whole room focused their attention on Angelo. He choked on a mouthful of cigar smoke and straightened himself. Senator? Angelo LaRosa? His lips jerked into a crooked grin.

"Yeah, Pop," shouted Armand. "Angelo's our man!"

With that the whole room leapt upon Angelo, slapping him on the back, shaking his hand, shouting, "*Si*, Angelo's a shoe-in for the job!"

In the blink of an eye, the jubilant supporter ushered the fledgling politician into the main dining room where Donato Mizzulo shouted, "Ladies and gentlemen, I present to you Angelo LaRosa! Our next United States Senator! Happy 1929!"

Angelo glanced at his father standing proudly beside his mother. *That Pop, the old son-of-a-bitch. Hah! Quite the manipulator all right.* Their eyes met and suddenly any misgivings Angelo had quickly vanished. From that point on he rode the roller coaster ride of his life. His campaign raised more money than any other senate hopeful. In essence Angelo had the election wrapped up long before the process had even tested him.

Joseph immediately called in his chips. Scores of people knew and respected him, not only for the fine work of the LaRosa and Sons Construction Company but also for his religious and charitable work. The Church stood squarely behind him and the future senator. Not only that, many still considered Joseph a hero in the runaway horse incident many years ago. In due course he reeled in countless votes for his budding politician offspring. The campaign meant a lot to him. Angelo, always the good son, would make a fine Senator. Indeed, God must be pleased.

Maria Avita vigorously sought out unregistered voters. She knew that to win this race, a general outpouring of support by the Italian community was necessary. Without any second thoughts she doled out Father Sandro's money. Call it bribery, call it taking care of one's own kind, call it whatever, she was the first one to admit that she purchased food and clothing for scores of unfortunate individuals and paid the rent they were unable to pay. All this in exchange for their vote in the November 1929 election. What better way to use the heathen priest's money?

Rom finagled the backing of the Boston Police Department, while Paolo plastered the windows of his barbershop with posters and talked up his brother's candidacy with all who sat in his chair. Large groups of *paesani* came in and offered their votes in blocs to one candidate, Angelo LaRosa.

Even Vincenzo emerged from his self-imposed shell. Angelo's platform represented true concern for the wrongs that accepted society reeked upon the peons. So Vincenzo helped Louisa and her children hand out hundreds upon thousands of flyers that bore Angelo's perfect toothy grin. Posters plastered virtually every open space in East Boston, the North End, and the entire district. Amplified red, green, and black letters shouted, "Elect LaRosa for U.S. Senator."

Unbeknown to Phil Buccola, Armand motored to New York to seek Don Vito's backing. "Victory for Angelo will give the organization access to certain political favors," said Armand. "Favors that now remain out of reach."

The Don mulled it over. Handsome sums of money kept the pockets of judges, police, and local politicians filled, a necessary evil for looking the other way so numbers rackets remained lucrative and traffic of black market liquor and other goods continued uninterrupted. Yet success always hinged on cooperation at the local level. Every so often some young upstart cop or city hall candidate came along wanting to make a name for himself. Crime was an easy sounding board to get elected. Business became shaky until that person was adequately disposed of or otherwise brought into line. "Perhaps, *il paesano* in Washington could provide a higher degree of political protection for the family," mumbled Don Vito.

"A few new ambiguous laws won't hurt none either," said Armand, though the real motive for being here was to eventually expose the whole system of organized crime and how payoffs effect the decisions of those in high places.

"*Si*," said the Don. "I see places of benefit."

"Solidarity provides protection," Armand pressed. "With high-powered bankrolling from the family, Angelo's a shoe-in. Nobody else can come close to raising that kind of money. Trust me, Senator Angelo will someday be useful to all of us."

Armand returned to Boston a happy man, confident that Angelo was going to someday blow the lid off corruption. Within days organized labor came out in support of Angelo. What's more, money showed up unexpectedly in campaign coffers. Where it had come from nobody knew. Nobody asked.

Unfortunately, Phil Buccola got wind of Armand's meeting with Don Vito and was not at all happy about the slight. "LaRosa bypassed me, the boss of the Boston underworld." Buccola chewed on a slimy Havana. "Hmm…pieces come together." Certain events in the past had seemed unrelated, but now? How many times had New York squelched Buccola's activities and attempts to rise to the top? Yet the person who had squealed remained in the shadows, that is, until now. "Yeah, LaRosa's the rat," Buccola crushed out the stogie. "He's the one who made me a puppet to New York. This needs attention. Real soon."

The campaign went according to plan. Angelo kept up on all the grassroots issues and never forgot a face, especially any that benefited his candidacy. The flamboyant campaigner easily won formal debates and spur-of-the-moment challenges that arose while campaigning the streets. When opponents questioned his inexperience, Angelo used his uncanny ability to change the subject from himself back to them, slandering them with their own weaknesses. He knocked on every door, kissed every baby, and shook every wrinkled hand. On numerous occasions dogs chomped on his legs, but that didn't matter. Not since his gridiron days at B.U. had he been the center of attention like this. He was in his element. Everybody loved Angelo LaRosa.

September 3, 1929, Boston baked. The temperature of ninety-seven degrees set records, the hottest ever for that date. Joseph had campaigned the North End in the blistering heat all day long. His feet hurt. The soles of his shoes, worn thin from months of intense campaigning, allowed pavement heat to sear the bottom of his feet. There just had not been the time to shop for shoes. The old buzzard had just come from the North Church where the pastor had unexpectedly asked for Angelo to speak that night. The candidate would be pleased to see the very active Episcopal congregation back him. The wilted old man thanked God when he finally reached Angelo's office. He planned to take his shoes off immediately and rub his tired, swollen feet. The door was ajar. For ventilation, he assumed, and nudged it open. His deduction was confirmed. The air in the office was incredibly stagnant, hot, and muggy. Miss Flaherty was not at her desk. Must've taken the afternoon off. Who could blame her for not wanting to work in this kind of heat? He crossed the room and admired large black letters painted on the door. "Angelo LaRosa. Attorney at law. Private," he quietly read aloud then gloated, "My son the lawyer. Soon to be my son, the Senator from the great Commonwealth of Massachusetts."

Joseph crooked his knuckles to rap on the opaque glass, but voices stopped him. Undefined shapes moved on the other side of the glass. Angelo had a client. The weary old man let his hand drop. He half-turned when an unexpected blast of hot summer air whirled up the front stairwell, through the office, and blasted open the partially-latched door. He glanced into the room ready to apologize for the interruption only to see there on the desk, Angelo's bare bottom gyrating on top of Miss Flaherty. Her long slender white legs girdled his waist. Her face bore the look of throbbing ecstasy until Babs opened one eye and saw the old man standing there motionless, his mouth agape. She screeched like a barn owl and dumped Angelo onto the floor. She yanked down her skirt and gathered up her nylon stockings, girdle, and shoes. Making a swift exit out the back door, Miss Flaherty never once looked back.

"What the hell…" Angelo cursed and stumbled to his feet. "Pop!" He snatching up his pants and covered his nakedness. The old man was the last person on earth he expected to see.

Joseph endeavored to speak. No words came. Abruptly he turned and fled.

"Pop! Come back!" The outer door slammed. Angelo rammed his foot into the metal desk. "Fuck!"

An hour later the phone rang at the Captain's house. Maria Avita answered. "No, Angelo, your father has not come home yet."

"Tell him to call me, OK? I'm still at the office." Abruptly the phone went dead and Maria Avita pensively set the earpiece back on its cradle.

"Everything OK, *Mamacita*?" Armand asked.

"That was Angelo. He is looking for your father."

Something about that phone call just didn't click, so Armand got to his feet and kissed her. "Well, I gotta go. A couple of guys are waitin' up for me in Maverick Square." That was his excuse. Instead, he headed to Angelo's office.

"What the hell was ya thinking of?" Armand roared within inches of his brother's face. "You of all people. College graduate. Beautiful wife. Great kids. For crise sakes, ya got it all, fella. And ya piddle it all away on some cheap trick!"

"Don't give me that crap! I've heard that all my life. 'Angelo's the smart one.' 'Angelo's going places.' Angelo, this. Angelo that. Angelo, Angelo, Angelo. I hate that fucking name, Angelo. Well you know, I got needs, too!"

Armand could not believe his ears. This hot-tempered brother of his was nothing but a self-centered volcano that percolated with rage for those who carried only the highest regard for him. Armand should be so lucky to have such respect. He backed away from Angelo. "Nobody forced ya to do a thing."

"Well, *nobody* ever left me alone either. Especially Pop," countered Angelo, bracing his knuckles on the corner of his desk. "Push, push, push. Every time I turned around he was in my face. I had to live up to his lofty expectations. But who are you to talk? You yourself ran off from the old windbag. Hah! Wish I had guts like that."

"Not guts, stupidity. Been paying for it ever since."

"What are you talking about?" Angelo stood erect.

"Where's Pop?"

"Who knows."

"We better get out there and find him."

"No. You find him." Angelo pointed a finger at his oldest brother.

Armand's patience ground into ashes. With deadly accuracy, his right fist landed a peremptory blow into his brother's diaphragm. Pain bent Angelo in half. He choked for a breath. "Now listen here, *piccolo fratello mio*." Armand lifted his brother by the scruff of the neck. "No more of this idiotic sniveling. Time has come for ya to straighten up, hear me? If ya don't, your dear old brother is ready and willin' give ya a couple of lessons on what true unhappiness feels like." He set his brother down and smoothed out his clothes then straightened his tie. "There, Senator LaRosa. Ya look a lot more presentable." He put his arms around Angelo's shoulders and said. "Now. You and me? We gonna take a little walk. The streets of the North End have never seen such dignity the likes of me 'n you. We're gonna find Pop. And when we do? You grovel to that old man and beg for his forgiveness. Is that clear?" Satan himself embodied Armand as black fiery eyes charred Angelo to the marrow.

Realizing that he bit off more than he could chew, Angelo nodded and the two bothers took off down the street. They found their father's car locked and packed full of election paraphernalia. Joseph was nowhere to be seen. Armand and Angelo continued on squinting into coffee shops and stores and asking people they met if they had come across the old man. No, nobody had. The two bothers tramped down to the Charles River and scoured the docks. Armand let out a frustrated sigh. His fingers dug into his hips. The last time he searched this place, thick black molasses floated on the water. "Tide's goin' out," he said.

Angelo grunted and flicked his cigarette into the river.

Armand glanced at his brother who stared mindlessly off at the distant islands. "You wasn't here that day."

"What day? What the Christ you talking about?"

"The molasses flood."

"Nah, I was taking a friggin' law exam or somethin'."

Armand's dark brows came together. Sure. That's what the kid says now. "Perhaps if ya faced the actual loss of *Mamacita* and Pop. Or saw Francesca...your attitude might o' been different now."

Angelo sniggered, "Yeah. Right."

Armand turned away. "Hard to believe the same blood flows in our veins," he sighed as he scanned the Boston skyline riddled with ever rising towers. The shimmering white spire of the Old North Church snagged his eyesight. Day by day, the ancient structure on Salem Street was becoming more and more lost among skyscrapers. "Come on, let's go. I know exactly where Pop is." In front of Sacred Heart Church on North Square, he said, "Get your Italian ass in there. Make peace with the old man. Or Angelo? Don't you ever come out."

An hour or so later, Joseph and Angelo emerged. The incident was over, forever to remain locked in the souls of the three men, insulated from public stench and contamination. Unfortunately, the enormous pride that Joseph and Armand long held for Angelo vanished like immigrant caps tossed into the following sea.

Twenty-four hours later, the saucy and quite provocative Miss Babs Flaherty found herself relocated elsewhere, far from the hub of Boston. As if nothing had ever happened, the campaign proceeded without a hitch.

Chapter 25

October 23, 1929. This blustery fall day, Angelo reassured supporters that upon his election to the Senate, prosperity would quickly return. Little did he know that a relentless liquidation had begun on the Boston and New York Stock Exchanges. By mid afternoon, trading reached epic proportions. He got edgy. Then news came that John D. Rockerfeller and J. P. Morgan were attempting to prop up the market and put a halt to the decline. Angelo wallowed in a false sense of security that the crisis was over right then and there. To his horror the effort failed. At close the next day, tickers in Boston and New York ran more than two hours late and trading reached a record volume of 12,894,650. Angelo felt as if a mallet had just imbedded itself into the pit of his stomach. All his investments had turned to dust in the wind before his very eyes. Now what? His dreams, like the stock market, had taken a nose-dive. On the verge of breaking down and slobbering like a snot-nosed brat, Angelo got a flash of brilliance. "With so many people bankrolling my election, I got nothing to worry about…that is…unless I lose the election." He thought for a moment. "Hah! Ain't gonna happen. This son of a great manipulator is gonna make damned sure of it."

Incumbents took the wrap for the economic conditions. Tuned in to voter wrath, Angelo LaRosa put on the pressure. Waging a series of blistering attacks, he blamed his opponent for everything that went wrong since the days of Eve. Poised in front of the equestrian statue of Paul

Revere in the North End, he demanded, "What happened, my honorable opponent? Earlier this year, Boston bragged the highest blue-collar wages and per capita retail sales in the nation. Over a twelve-month period during 1928-1929, the number of boot and shoe establishments fell from 948 to 817! And textiles lost ground at a similar rate. Where were you, my honorable—and I use that term, honorable, loosely—opponent when the nation was on the brink of disaster? No, wait! Let me guess...You were too busy living the high life in Washington to notice the warning signs. Well! My fellow voters...I say this to you! Our current senator is nothing but a miserable worm of an opportunist and crook."

The crowd booed the incumbent. Some held their noses with one hand while shooing away the invisible incumbent with the other. *Hah,* Angelo thought. *Do I know how to work these suckers or what?*

In one particular speech he rode the anti-anarchist sentiment by labeling his opponent a drooling fascist. It didn't matter if it was true or not. Just uttering those words in those times lent a veil of truth to them. The label stuck.

A few days later, Angelo introduced the class-conscious element into the campaign by claiming, "Unlike me, a son of a god-fearing blue-collar worker, our current senator is a city slicker. Everybody knows the way those guys look down their noses on common folk like us. Our illustrious senator is by no means an exception."

It was not long before the incumbent ducked a cloudburst of rotten tomatoes every time he appeared in public. A month before the election was the last time anyone saw the man.

Down and dirty campaigning won Angelo the U.S. Senate seat in November 1929. Clasping his hands over his head before jubilant constituents, the new senator from Massachusetts grinned scornfully. *Ah, sweet victory.*

Unfortunately, the celebrations died down much too soon for Angelo. His enthusiasm waned as quickly as the full moon on a cloudy night. He familiarized himself with the new job, but that went quicker than anticipated. So the Senator-elect grew restless with too much time on his hands. He tilted back his office chair, and crossed his feet on top of the desk. He stared out the window at the wintry landscape. It was spitting snow. Mindlessly he fondled a pencil with the fingers of one hand while sipping black market hooch with the other. "Gonna be a bear of a winter." He spoke to no one. "January and Washington's too damned far away. Can't wait to leave this miserable city in the rear view mirror. Then watch out world, Angelo LaRosa's on his way. Things are going to change in one big hurry."

Damned Heather. He couldn't get over the tantrum she had that morning. She begged to stay behind with the kids, sniveling on and on how it wasn't a good thing to uproot children from friends and family. Her face got all red and puffy from crying and her nose was running. Disgusting. He broke the pencil in half and threw it at the window. "Damn, I hate that crap." He stood up and scratched his groin. "Well, that's just fine and dandy with dear ol' Angelo. That leaves the door wide open for countless possibilities. And you can bet your frigid ass, my dear Heather, this new Senator plans to explore each and every last one of them quite thoroughly. Yep, from the very moment I set my sweet little feet on Washington soil, I'll be a man of action. Broads vastly outnumber men there, so I hear. Hah!"

* * *

New Year's Eve, 1930. Angelo picked up his spanking new Pontiac Big Six. He cruised out of the dealer's late in the afternoon making headway to Maverick Square. Parking in front of Packard's Drug Store, he strutted in and purchased a pack of cigarettes, which was only a ruse. He really wanted to show off his slick new machine and be the center of attention once again. The strategy worked. When he came out of the store, a good dozen or so gawkers ooh-ed and ah-ed around the midnight-blue machine.

Angelo slouched against the rear quarter panel and thumped the cigarette pack against the butt of his hand. He zipped off the red strip and tore off the cellophane and paper, letting the wind take away the pieces. He rammed the pack against the back of his hand until several cigarettes jutted out. As the Senator-elect lit up, he imbibed on the envious stares he was getting. Those two-bit idiots thought he was the luckiest son-of-a-bitch in the world.

An hour or so later he drove out to the Captain's house. The first words out of Joseph's mouth were "Where did you come up with the money for such a fine piece of machinery?"

None of your God damned business, Angelo itched to scream. *You know full well that damned shack in Orient Heights has me mortgaged up the ying-yang.* Christ, Mama even made last month's mortgage. Funny thing, she asked him not to tell anyone. Oh well. Needless to say, it was no secret that his stocks had taken a nose-dive. And most of his meager savings went into getting himself elected. Shit, what a hole he had dug for himself. Forget about it, worrying to death over it gets nowhere. The special interests that kept his election coffers filled would put him back on top again once he arrived in D.C. Won't take long. He'd make damn sure of that. Angelo stiffened. "I financed the full amount. Eight hundred ninety-five dollars and no cents."

"Financed a car?" Joseph catechized. "Never once did I ever borrow so much as a dime. My success came about through hard work and the grace of God, not the handouts of others or credit. Surely you have not given enough thought to this purchase.

"Yeah, Pop, I have. GM's got time payment plans now. The rate's nothing to sneeze at, either. No reason not to take advantage of it."

"You should have spoken to me." Joseph pursed his lips and shook his head. "Bad idea. Bad. Bad.

Angelo turned his back to hide his hostility. *Too fucking bad what you think, old man. Did it anyway, like it or not.* Running his hand through his hair, Angelo focused on the impressive midnight-blue Pontiac. It took his breath away. His palm glided over the smooth Fisher body smartened by concave belt molding and flaring 70-inch fenders. There was something sensual about it that gave him instant gratification. And sitting behind the wheel, Angelo felt an awesome sense of power and control. Yes, that machine was worth every penny.

Somewhere around a quarter to eight, he arrived home. Heather was in the bedroom, sitting at the vanity. The fragrance of the rose water that she smoothed all over her freshly bathed skin filled the air. She barely acknowledged him. What did he think? She'd come rushing into his arms and they'd make wild passionate love all through the night? Shish. That would be the day. "Kids asleep?" he asked.

"Yes." Her voice was soft, succinct.

Angelo mixed himself a drink. Just to breathe some life into the room, he stirred it loudly with the glass swizzle stick. He swigged it down in one gulp. "Want one?" He raised the empty glass.

"No. Thank you."

He shrugged then made another for himself, leaving it untouched as he stripped for a shower. Angelo took no notice of the drapes only partially closed. He had gotten used to Heather's deterrent to sex. "Picked up the Pontiac," he said.

Heather remained impassive.

He slugged down half of the drink and slammed the glass on the dresser. Damned bitch. She didn't want him to buy a new car anyway. Big surprise. She never liked anything he did.

"Sitter here yet?" he muttered.

"She'll be here at nine."

Angelo scowled at his wife. Wish she'd soften up, be more talkative and attentive. Don't seem like any big deal that she's a senator's wife. His eyes slitted. Still in all, Heather looked pretty good. He fidgeted. She got her figure back pretty quick after having those brats. He leered salaciously. How long had it been since he got a good piece? His eyes rolled in thought. That night, just after the election, yeah, that was the last time. On that stinking floor of the bathroom at campaign headquarters with…Damn. Who the hell was that starry-eyed slut anyway? Oh, yah, that money-wielding supporter's kid from Beacon Hill. Angelo scratched his head. Must've been nuts. That whore's ugly as the day's long. Couldn't help it though. Too much time had passed since that September day when Pop walked in and caught him humping Miss Flaherty. By election time, juices were at the brink and needed release.

Just then Heather dropped a brush on the vanity. Retrospect disturbed, Angelo cleared his throat as his mind cleared itself of Miss Flaherty. Ah, his wife was gorgeous, sitting there with all that honey-colored hair cascading in waves over her satin camisole. Light blue was perfect for her and the feel of satin always made him horny. If only she wasn't so damned frigid. Look at that skin, so velvety smooth…white as the driven snow. And those long, sleek legs. He imagined her firm breasts that climaxed the satin into peaks.

By now Angelo had gotten himself all worked up. He grabbed his robe. Holding it waist-high in front of himself, he crossed the room. He massaged her shoulders. He knelt down and kissed the nape of her silky neck. His hot breath spike Heather's skin into goose flesh. She inched away. "Not now."

"We got time," he cooed. His arms encircled her. His hands cupped her breasts. His fingers kneaded.

"No," she insisted and wriggled to free herself. His fingers dug into soft tissue. "You're hurting me!"

The hormone-driven male refused to let go. He lifted her to her feet and yanked her against him. Hardness parted her legs. "Come on, Heather," he demanded. "See what I got for you." His tongue slathered across her shoulder blade.

"Not now!"

Her indignant tone ignited a time bomb that had ticked inside Angelo for much too long. His dark brows came together. Incensed, he spun her around and glared into her blue eyes. There wasn't even a hint of passion. He shook her ferociously. She flopped back and forth like a rag doll. "Well, OK then, if that's the way you want it." He snatched her up in his arms and carried her to the bed.

Heather kicked and screeched, "No, Angelo!"

"Yes, Angelo," he mocked her. "Yes, yes!"

"My diaphragm..." She lurched away but his hand clamped onto her wrist.

"You don't need it."

"But..."

"I said you don't need it," he thundered and flung her onto the bed. Forcing himself into her, she screamed and he laughed, "Hah! If there's a kid outta this, everyone will get the impression that we still do it. But you wouldn't like that one damn bit, would you now, my sweet Heather?"

She bit his hand. He yanked it back. A fist formed. "No," Heather screeched.

"Yes, Goddamn it. Yes," he bellowed as his fist pounded her head. Once. Twice..."Son of a bitch!" Unexpectedly Angelo rolled off Heather. Clasping his hands behind his head, he stare at the ceiling. He had come too soon. Heaving a disgusted sigh, he muttered, "What poor luck I have to be married to such an ungrateful bitch." Angelo vaulted out of bed and headed for the shower, making no attempt whatsoever to cover his nakedness. He made sure that Heather heard him talking to himself. "Sickening. Absolutely sickening. My own wife, frigid like a god damned dead fish." The bathroom door slammed. His lust quelled. Yet there was no real satisfaction. "Things gotta change."

When Angelo came out of the bathroom, Heather had returned to the vanity. This time, a dark-green chenille robe, cinched tightly about her waist, covered her. Dried blood caked her swollen lip. A welt ripened on her cheekbone. She ignored his presence. *No big surprise*, he thought. Wait, did he hear her wince? He glanced at her. "For Christ sakes, woman, look at you. What the hell's wrong with you, anyway?" he spat. Pacing back and forth, once or twice, Angelo stopped and leered at

Heather, silently brushing her hair. One hand gesturing, he blasted, "You ain't goin' nowhere with me tonight. Not looking like that! Forget about it!"

Angelo finished dressing. As he swaggered to the door, he shouted, "I'll tell everybody at Mizzulo's that one of your precious little brats got the bellyache and you can't possibly tear yourself away." Then he whined sarcastically, "What a good mother." He waited for a retort. Her swollen lip trembled slightly, but Heather remained silent. If only the bitch would stand up to him once in a while. Throw something, a glass, one of the brats' toys. Anything! Instead, she slouched on the vanity like a jellyfish. "Whimpering bitch," Angelo muttered and slammed the door.

The driveway light reflected brilliant pointed stars off the midnight blue Pontiac. He stopped to gloat. "Hah! What a magnificent machine!"

Angelo slid into the car as if it were a woman and yanked the door shut. He groped for the pack of cigarettes on the dashboard then sat there, rapping the pack against the palm of his hand, admiring the creamy leather interior. He stuffed a cigarette between his lips and started the engine. Shifting into first, he popped the clutch and rammed the gas pedal to the floorboards. Tires peeled out as the Pontiac leapt forward and sped off into the black night.

One hand controlled the wheel as Angelo searched his pockets for a match. None. He remembered the stick matches he had earlier stuffed between the cellophane and the cigarette pack. Two fingers fished around until several fell out onto his lap. He struck one against the steering wheel and bent his head to light the cigarette. He looked up. "Holy Cow!" The outside edge of a curve was closing in on him. The cigarette and lit match dropped to the floor as he jerked the wheel. The car skidded sideways around the bend. His heart pounded. He blocked it all out with a roar of laughter. "Hah! No car holds a curve like that! Just wait till the next one, buster!"

Angelo struck another match, this time a cigarette glowed. His foot laid on the gas pedal. "Ah-hah! There it is, the second curve, dead ahead.

This'll be a cinch!" The farthest thing from his mind was slowing down. Headlights! Exploding from beyond the curve, they blinded him. He spun the wheel. Neither his mind nor foot went for the brake. The oncoming vehicle swerved; its horn blasted. By a hair's breadth, it skimmed past. Angelo glanced in the rear view mirror. The transitory vehicle fishtailed near the outer right edge of the road. "Shudda bought a big ol' Pontiac, my friend."

He rolled down the window and flicked the half-smoked butt into the night. Glowing embers disintegrated like exploding firecrackers. He left the window open and took in the brisk ocean air.

"End of the road coming up, sweetheart. Sorry, gonna hafta slow ya down a bit. Gotta head on over to Maverick Square, ya know. Great big crowd waitin' there just for good ol' Senator Angelo LaRosa."

For the first time since leaving Orient Heights, he hit the brakes. Nothing. The pedal went all the way to the floorboard. He pumped it. "Damn. No brakes." The butt of his hand came down violently on the steering wheel. "Brand fucking new car and no God damned brakes!" He jerked the hand brake erect. The cable snapped. "Shit."

Ahead, the stop sign distorted, bloating into a liquid red demon… advancing…ominously closing in on him by the second. Nothing deterred its course.

Angelo threw in the clutch and down-shifted. Metal ground against metal. The car slowed, too little…and much too late. The midnight-blue Pontiac sped though the intersection, licking the rear bumper of a black Caddie. Beyond, the twelve-foot wooden barricade of the rail yards rose up like the gates to hell. Angelo shielded his face with both arms and hollered, "S-o-n o-f a b-i…"

The car accordioned into the barricade. The gas tank ruptured spewing fuel that ignited and shot flaming fingers, like those of a famished beggar seeking sustenance, into the black night. Splinters rained as molten iron meteored through the freight yard, bounding, yawing.

White-hot wreckage that was once a midnight-blue Pontiac plunged into the Chelsea River. Water sizzled giving rise to billowing steam that went nearly unnoticed in the starless New Year night.

Chapter 26

"Kill all Presidents," Joe Zangara shouted as he opened fire on President-elect Franklin Delano Roosevelt who was just finishing a speech in Miami's Bayfront Park on February 15, 1933. The hale of bullets missed the mark as angry bystanders wrestled the Jersey bricklayer to the ground. A smiling FDR stood up and waved, but when the dust cleared, Mayor Anton Cermak of Chicago, who had stood next to FDR was dead.

Late the next night in his palatial home outside Boston, Phil Buccola hit the ceiling. "Can you believe it? That damned immigrant botched the hit. Well, as far as I'm concerned, the commission's out of it now. Gonna take Roosevelt down, myself."

"The mob hired that Zangara fella?" Armand feigned ignorance.

"Whaddaya think, eh LaRosa,?" Buccola snorted inches from *il capo*'s face. His breath stunk of bathtub gin and stale cigars.

Maintaining a cool exterior, Armand felt the puke rising inside. These temper tantrums were getting nastier by the day. For a man who controlled such a sizable organization as Boston, Buccola possessed little self-control. The most insignificant things set him off and when they did, God bless the poor schmuck who got in the way.

Chewing the defiled end of a stogie, Buccola raved on. "Roosevelt's the driving force behind the repeal of Prohibition. Cermak was, too. At least that guy's outta the picture. Those two dimwits have been promising great reforms and are out to collect taxes on liquor sales."

Armand shifted. "Improves the economy. That's what got 'em elected. Still, it sounds the death knell for the organization."

"You can bet your Italian ass on that," spat Buccola. "Roosevelt's gonna legalize 3.2 alky and that's only the beginning. Sales of moonshine, bathtub gin, white lightning, they're all gonna dry up. Smuggling ain't gonna be lucrative anymore and all that'll spill over into other family enterprises. Kiss those speakeasies of yours good-bye, LaRosa."

Armand's skin crawled. Like a speeding locomotive, changes were coming down the line. Nothing and nobody stood a fat chance in hell of stopping the inevitable. The Mafia, Phil Buccola in particular, was not going to give up a forty-million-dollar industry without a fight. Wait a minute, where's Buccola going with all this? Attempting to wheedle more information, Armand ventured, "This ah Zangara fella…never got wind of him before."

"Yeah, well. That was supposed to be the beauty of Luciano's plan, and let me emphasize, supposed to be. A triggerman not known to the cops can get closer to the mark. The day Capone ordered Cermak and FDR out of the picture, Lucky had Zangara waiting in the wings, all primed and ready to go, and nobody knew him from Adam."

"You knew about Zangara?" Armand asked.

"Hey, I'm not the idiot New York makes me out to be."

Armand arched his eyebrows as if agreeing with Buccola, but the reality was quite opposite. Without a shred of doubt, he believed that Don Vito had Phil pegged right.

"Zangara came to this country eight years ago," Buccola said while snuffing out his cigar. He swilled down a double shot of straight gin as if summoning up courage to accomplish some hidden agenda. "Kept his nose clean all this time, too. Gotta give the guy credit for that."

Armand nearly jumped out of his skin when Buccola struck a match on the back of his chair to light up another cigar. He had let down his guard. That wasn't healthy. Appearing unflustered, Armand reached into his breast pocket for a cigarette. If only he could shake out this uneasiness. He lit up. After taking a bogus laid-back drag, he got up and crossed the room to the bow window draped with ruddy brocade. An early March snow squall raged outside. *Must be an omen of things to come. Damn, here we go again. Buccola's plotting another rise to the top by blowing away FDR. Well, not to worry. That idea's gonna hit the dust, just like before. Gonna see to it the second I blow this joint.*

"Know what I think, LaRosa?" Buccola asked as he strutted up next to Armand. He exhaled a cloud of smoke that fogged up the window.

Armand continued to stare indifferently at the blowing snow.

"A rat's running loose in the organization. That's how come Zangara failed. But," Buccola said with a self-satisfied look plastered across his face, "with Cermak outta the picture, we can fix the rest."

Like most people, Armand had thought the crusade against the underground had come to an abrupt end right then and there. Actually, the assassination of Mayor Cermak produced the opposite effect. Within hours, the Feds arrested eighteen former Capone associates including Machine Gun McGurn and William 3-fingered Jack White. Every suspected member of organized crime felt the pinch. Worst of all for would-be assassins, the guard around Hoover and Roosevelt tightened so much that penetration became virtually impossible.

"So what's the plan?" Armand tactfully prodded as he sat down on the window seat and crossed his legs. He casually smoothed out the wrinkles in his blue serge suit then pretended to delight in his recently purchased calfskin oxfords by twisting his foot side to side. At all times he knew exactly where Buccola was and what he was doing.

"Roosevelt's coming to Boston, June 17th. By special train, right into South Station. We're gonna blow that bastard to kingdom come," said Buccola while firing an invisible Tommy gun.

Thirty-five minutes later, the boss of the Boston rackets struck another match, this time on the window ledge while watching Armand get into his car. Lighting up another cigar, he blew rings of smoke high into the air and imagined that the rings of smoke were ropes. "Nooses tighten around yellow dog's neck," he seethed. "The clock ticks. Hear it? Tick. Tick. Tick."

* * *

Suffolk Downs, two days later. Armand met up with Rom, now a full-fledged detective in the Boston Police Department. An undercover state trooper by the name of John was with him. The trooper was connected to the Feds and other law enforcement agencies beyond state level. It didn't take long for Armand to conclude that John was nothing but an out-and-out blow hard. Long-winded monotone soliloquies irritated the hell out of the Mafia *capo*. "Jesus Christ! Will you shut up?"

"Jeez, Armand," Rom bristled as his eyes ping-ponged between his brother and the trooper.

"Hey! Whaddaya expect? I don't have all day, ya know. You guys wanna know Buccola's plans for FDR or not?"

John, a gritty military type, thick-bodied with closely cropped brown hair, kept his mouth shut for a short time. Armand had gotten out only the barest facts before the trooper started spouting off again. Armand rolled his eyes and turned his attention to the horses at the starting gate. Perhaps it was wiser to pay more attention to John, but Armand felt it wasn't necessary. Besides, that guy's voice made him want to puke last Sunday's dinner.

"Bootlegging's on its way out, fellas," John droned on and on. "So organized crime's steppin' up gambling operations, narcotics traffickin', labor racketeerin', prostitution, and kidnappin'—you name it. Makin' up for all that lost income somehow, I suspect. And if you keep up on what's going on, you know that Lucky Luciano's put together an interstate syndicate that's got strong political connections, too. Murder Inc. serves as his enforcement arm. Why, just last month they took out Congressman Godwin in DC. And remember that cop, murdered in

Revere not too long ago? Well, Murder, Inc. got him. But what the heck, that cop was dirty anyway. Just like Godwin—playing both ends from the middle. Didn't fool nobody though. Both sides of the law were wise to him all along."

"Newspaper accounts say it's unknown if Godwin jumped or fell from his hotel window," said Rom.

Armand's eyebrows arched. How did Rom manage to interrupt Mr. Know-it-all?

"FBI knows for a fact that the Chicago mob took Godwin out. He knew too much about the deal going down in Miami and got scared that the money they paid him wouldn't keep him from blabbing," John countered in one long breath. "Mafia thinks the woman, the one who shoved Zangara's hand into the air when he popped off the shots at FDR, was FBI. Just so happens, only connection she had was the bad luck of sleeping with Godwin a few months ago in Miami. She's come up missing, you know. Probably sleeping with the fishes, as you wise guys put it."

Armand shot a dirty look at John. This guy was not winning any points. The horses crossed the finished line. Armand sighed and tore up his betting slips. Hopefully John had finished his incessant yapping, too. Armand dropped the pieces to the ground and turned around. Leaning against the rail on his elbows, he scanned the sea of faces. How many scoundrels were hobnobbing among the law-abiding people here today? Sure was hard to tell.

Armand cursed himself. What the hell was he thinking when he got linked up with Aldo and the family in the first place? Back then he didn't have the slightest inkling that the Mafia was destined to become such a widespread problem, so out of control, so dangerous. The old-time Mafia was just a group two-bit hoods but things had gone far beyond simple arm twisting, aimed at helping one's own. Organized crime had evolved into a despicable disease that now infected everybody and everything. It thought nothing of destroying its own kind, which went against the reason the Mafia existed in the first place.

Not only did the mob exploit and destroy adults, but also kids were falling under its control. With the ever-increasing sale and distribution of narcotics, Armand foresaw *babania* as a scourge on generations to come. Cops, judges, they all looked the other way, so the problem was sure to grow. Nothing new about that. Crime paid better. Armand was the perfect example. Yet things had become so destructive that he no longer wanted any part of it. No matter what the cost, he had to climb out of this snake pit. But before he did, he had to put down Phil Buccola.

Rom and John started back to the clubhouse. Armand reluctantly followed. He had other things to do but needed to know what the cops were going to do before making plans of his own. As they ordered beers, he asked, "How are we going to stop FDR's assassination?"

"Don't worry about it," said Rom. "Now that John knows what's going on, it'll get taken care of."

"Got a glitch," said John, eyeballing Armand while sucking the suds off his brew. He wiped his lips with the cuff of his shirt.

"What's that?" Armand asked impatiently. That long-winded trooper certainly was short on all social graces.

"A snitch by the name of Charles K. O. Elkins slipped up to an undercover. Says Buccola's gunning for you." John belched.

"Me?" Puzzlement sheeted Armand's face. He didn't know anybody by the name of Elkins. And he had just met with Buccola. Except for this FDR thing, the guy seemed his normal deranged self. He certainly didn't show any sign of being ticked off at Armand. "How come?"

"You squawked to Don Vito about something or other. Buccola wants your ass for it. What's the poop on that?"

Rom and Armand exchanged knowing glances.

"Aw, nothing," said Rom cracking his knuckles.

* * *

The next few days, Rom sniffed around the station house, trying to get the lowdown on K. O. Elkins. Meanwhile, Armand set his hounds on Elkins' trail. In a coffeehouse down the street from Paolo's barbershop, the two brothers brought each other up to speed.

"The riot squad's got Elkins under scrutiny," said Rom. "He's a small-time hood, an empty suit. Hijacks slot machines, fences, shakes down speakeasies—stuff like that."

"Yeah, I came up with the same kind o' dirt." Armand twisted up his face. "Barkeep at my place in Southie told me K. O. came by one day a while back and tried to shake us down. Elkins certainly didn't do his homework. Else he'd have steered clear of my place. The pisser didn't know what hit him, his ass was out drying in the street within seconds flat."

"So, what's to be done about the info he slipped?" Rom scratched his head.

"Shish, I don't know," Armand passed it off. "Elkins is just slime. Don't worry about it."

"You sure about that?"

"Sure I'm sure. Listen. A couple of runners tracked Elkins down for me. Last night we cornered him 'n laid him to a brick wall. The sucker squealed like a stuck pig, but he had nothing new to say. The little sleaze operates on rumor, that's all."

"How is it he knows Buccola is out gunning for you?" Rom asked.

"Says he ran into some wise guy in a downtown bar one night. They got to yakkin' it up and the guy tells Elkins how he's a part of Buccola's organization and all. After a while the guy asks Elkins if he knows me. Elkins says yeah, he heard my name once or twice but didn't know me personally. Well, bottom line is the guy hints around that my days are numbered. Elkins knew nothin' more than that."

"Better watch your back," Rom cautioned. "Buccola's out to be top dog again. Gonna get a whole lot nastier this time."

"Eh, don't worry about it, *piccolo fratello mio*," Armand sloughed it off. "Don't make much sense though when ya come down to it. What's the connection between Buccola and an independent like Elkins?"

* * *

The day before FDR's train was due in at South Station, Aldo Messina showed up at the South End speakeasy. "Aldo," Armand shouted as joyfully he embraced his old friend from the boat days. "For crying out loud, what're ya doin' in Beantown? Weather too hot for ya down there in Miami?"

"The President's coming." The answer was chilly, resolute. So was Aldo.

Armand suddenly wanted his old friend to get his ass out of Boston and back to Miami. His insides curdled. Aldo couldn't be involved with Buccola's sick plan to eliminate FDR, could he? Well, maybe. In the past he had a tendency to let himself get sucked into tight spots. That's good ol' Aldo for ya. Unfortunately, that meant that there was a very good chance that he'd go down when the Feds put the screws to the assassination attempt. Armand was going to have to save Aldo from himself just like in the good ol' days. Motioning for his old friend to take a stool at the bar, Armand asked, "Drink?"

"Yeah, throat's parched," Messina scowled. "Trip was hell."

Armand leaned over to warn him about Buccola's tricks when the bartender interrupted. "Phone call for you, Mr. LaRosa. Says it's urgent."

"OK. Set up a round, will ya?" Armand slid off the barstool and glanced at Aldo who was studying his fingernails. "Lemme take that call. Be back by the time the booze gets here."

On the opposite side of the bar, Armand picked up the phone, "Yeah?"

"LaRosa? Armand LaRosa?" The male voice sounded panicked, out of breath, insistent.

"Yeah, yeah. Who's this?"

"K. O. Elkins. Something's up."

"What's that?"

"Can't tell ya right now. Got the goons tailin' me. Meet me at the Gem."

"The Gem Theatre? East Boston?"

"One hour."

The phone went dead. Armand pulled the handset away from his ear and frowned at it. Slowly he set it back on its cradle. What did Elkins need to tell him that was so all-fired important? Catching the time on his watch, he had to get on the road straight away 'cuz the car needed petrol plus traffic's a bitch this time of day. This stunk. There's his old friend sitting across the bar and…Their eyes met. Messina's face contorted. Armand managed a faint grin. He wanted to catch up on things. Not only that, he wanted to keep Aldo occupied and out of the clutch of the FBI when this FDR thing went down. *Il paesani* also needed some educating about that conniving bastard, Phil Buccola.

Armand rounded the bar and hooked half his rump on the barstool. He swilled down the drink the barkeep had left and said, "Gotta go. A business associate's got a hot deal. Catch up with ya tonight?"

Messina grunted and signaled for another drink.

"Where ya gonna be?"

"Around."

* * *

Armand parked in front of the Gem Theatre. He checked his watch. Five minutes late. He thought about Aldo back at the bar. Hopefully this wouldn't take long. There's scads to catch up on. No sign of Elkins—only a couple of dowagers on foot, dressed in black with white kerchiefs. Down the street in front of Bud's Market, a box truck blocked one lane of Meridian Street while the driver unloaded wooden crates filled with produce.

Slowly Armand lifted the door handle. As he got out of his car a scrawny black and white mutt pranced up to him. "Hungry, ain't cha boy? Sorry, got nothin'. Hit me up later, 'K?" Armand patted the dog's head then crouched down to scratch behind its ears. "Whaddaya think there, fella? Should ol' Armand go into the Gem or wait it out?" He stood up and stretched. "Where the hell's Elkins, anyway?

"LaRosa."

Armand swung around. The muffled voice had come from the alley next to the theater. Coattails disappeared around the corner. "K. O.?" Sprinting into the alley, he caught a glimpse of a face peeking out from the back corner of the building then disappear. That ain't K. O. Intuition signaled, "Trap!"

Armand wheeled around. A couple of hard-bitten thugs in dark trench coats had him cornered. "Going somewhere?" sniggered one.

Spinning back, he came eyeball to eyeball with the psychotic black eyes of a towering pock-face. A huge head set directly on immense muscular shoulders overshadowed like black wings of Satan. Armand stepped back. The cold hard end of a pistol barrel jammed behind his right ear. *Well, there's at least three of 'em.*

Gritting his teeth, Armand half-turned and feigned submission by slowly raising his hands. Unexpectedly, he ducked, catching the hard-bitten jackals off guard. Quickly they recouped and set upon their prey. The element of surprise on his side, Armand wormed through them, first shoving one against the brick building then deflecting another with a right hook to the jaw. A scar-faced brute ran up and blocked the escape route. From out of nowhere the black and white mutt set upon the enemy of the man who had taken the time to scratch its ears. Ferocious growls intensified as its snout latched onto a pant leg and thrashed back and forth.

Armand crouched low. *There's four.* He moved like a hunted fox. His teeth cast determined grit. His arms spread out to his side with fingers taunting the enemy to come and get him.

A slow grin appeared on the fiend. baring a silver eyetooth and a grotesque assemblage of yellow-coated teeth. Kicking the dog off his leg, scarface took the challenge with an airy swing. The mutt yelped as it impacted the wall and fell to the ground. Sidestepping the blow, Armand did not have time to look after the animal, for another burly goon came in for a tackle. As he leaped over the guy, he cussed, "Crap! Five of 'em!"

Coming down hard, Armand stumbled; his right hand caught his fall. He staggered to his feet in time to glimpse an outline of a giant hand beneath a yellowed handkerchief as it jammed into his face. Chloroform! No! Armand fought tooth and nail. Unconsciousness girdled his brain. *Six.*

As their victim sagged to the ground, the six gangsters snatched him up and surreptitiously scurried down the alley where a black Buick waited with its engine revving. Four of the jackals stuffed Armand into the Buick then hopped in. Two others got into the Caddie behind them. Itchy drivers floored the gas pedals.

Hobbling with the aid of a walking stick past the entrance of the alley, a bent-over white-haired man was minding his own business. A noise caught his attention. He turned. His head sprung back. Two cars were lurching straight for him. He gasped. As quickly as his feeble legs could carry him, the old coot tottered out the way. Just in time. A heartbeat later the Buick and Caddie hurtled across the sidewalk and into the street. The old geezer leaned on his cane, leering at the vehicles maneuvering a sharp left turn then fishtailing down the street. The tailgating Caddie with its rear bumper missing and crimped license plate sideswiped a Model T parked in front of Packard's Drug Store. A few blocks beyond, the two cars whipped around the corner and disappeared. The old man shook his head and tottered off, mumbling to himself, "Humph. World's goin' ta hell in a handcart. Yep, shur is."

* * *

Shortly after 2 AM, neighbors of a speakeasy in Southie heard a loud thud. A woman had just opened her bedroom window for air and saw two men in light suits with white flowers pinned to their lapels. They wore no hats. After dumping a lifeless form unto the street in front of the speakeasy, they jumped back into the black car. Tires screeched. Next thing she knew, the car whipped down the street out of sight.

Rom LaRosa was just going on duty. The radio on the watch commander's desk squawked as he passed by. Something was going down in South Boston. The address flagged his attention so he asked, "Picked up a stiff?"

"Looks like it," snorted the sergeant.

"Got a name?"

Glancing down at his paperwork, Sarge mumbled, "Says here, Charles K. O. Elkins."

Rom's blood ran cold. He made a mad dash for his desk where he dialed Armand's number. No answer. He called the Captain's house. Nobody had seen Armand today. He tried Paolo's barbershop. No answer. Rom slammed down the phone. "Where the hell are you, Armand?"

He immediately put the word out on the street then paced his office and cracked his knuckles. Back and forth. Again and again. Hours passed. The telephone rang. Rom jammed it to his ear. "Yeah? Yeah. Be right there." He slammed down the phone and darted out of his office. With siren blaring, he sped off to East Boston where Armand's car had turned up in front of the Gem Theatre. A flatfoot who was standing guard next to it stopped talking to a couple of delivery men when he saw the cruiser zipping directly at him. Screeching to a stop, Rom jumped out and ran up to him. "Any sign of him?"

"Nope. Car ain't locked, but no sign o' struggle. These guys ain't seen nothin' neither."

Rom's eyes probed the street, the building, the parked cars, the cars that passed. Nothing hit him. He stepped over to the door of the Gem and read a sign aloud, "Closed for renovations." He shaded his eyes against the glass. Nothing in the empty expanse except a step ladder and tools. Hopelessness took control. He backed up and yank on the door handle. Locked. He tugged on it. Perhaps the door might change its mind and unlock itself if he insisted. No dice. He slammed a flat hand against it and spun around. Heaving a sigh, Rom walked back to the edge of the sidewalk. His eyes squinted, dissecting the street for the slightest of clues. The hair on the back of his neck bristled. He cracked his knuckles. "This don't look too good. Nope, not too good at all."

Rom patrolled the street. Twice, he passed the alley and glanced into it. The third time, something caught his eye. What's that? His eyes narrowed. It glittered in the sunlight and seemed insignificant, but yet for some reason it made his skin crawl. Gut feelings spurred him on as he took long, anxious strides towards the object. He strained to make it out. Something gold. His heart sank, a cufflink. Part of the set that Mama gave Armand several Christmases ago. Those things never left his wrists. And making it official, the raised onyx initials, A. L. Dread washed over Rom. He stood above the link peering down at it. Picking it up meant he accepted the worst. All at once he snatch it up and raced back to the squad car. The radio cackled following his alert. "All cars scour ten mile radius of city. Report without delay individual matching the description of Armand LaRosa or any other person or thing out of the ordinary, no matter how minor. In particular anything remotely linked to organized crime.

Meanwhile, detectives searched the Gem Theatre and the surrounding buildings, attic to cellar. They came up empty. In the back alley Rom noted the obvious signs of struggle. Armand had put up quite a fight. One comforting thing, there was no blood. "What the heck are all these dog tracks? Armand doesn't have a dog." The tracks suddenly disappeared. Rom discovered an indentation in the soil near the wall. He studied it, then the wall. Fur. The dog had been thrown against the wall and had fallen to the ground. It was injured. Only three paw prints led away from the spot and crossed a trail of heel marks that dug into the ground down the alley. Rom followed the mix of human footprints. There had been six assailants. Examining tire tracks, he concluded that two cars had waited behind the building. The rear end of the second car was definitely out of line. He followed the tracks around the back of the building and out the alley on the other side. Back on the street, the detective put together the scenario and concluded that the work belonged to Phil Buccola. "Dammit, Armand. I warned you that power-hungry Buccola meant business." His own words stabbed his gut over and over again. "Watch your back, Armand. Buccola wants to be top dog again. Gonna get a whole lot nastier when he makes his move this time."

Rom stood there, helpless, sizing up the dingy brick walls. The sun was going down, the alley grew darker by the minute. There was nothing else he could do. Unexpectedly he felt a tongue licking his hand. A black and white dog. Rom squatted down and scratched the mutt's ear. "Time's running out there fella, and I'm plumb outta ideas. Bet you know what happened here."

The mutt nuzzled Rom's hand, insisting that the closed fist opened. Sniffing the cufflink, the dog whined plaintively. Anxiety overwhelmed both man and dog. Not knowing where his brother was, Rom was unable to save him from a fate both brothers had predicted in their own dissimilar ways. He wished he had told Armand what really ate at him the day he had warned about Buccola. Losing Angelo was losing one too many brothers. Yeah, it was more than enough.

Chapter 27

Unable to escape the stink of raw fish that nettled his sinuses, Armand thrashed his head side to side. The putridity acted like smelling salts, plucking him from a chloroform-induced sleep. He never could stomach fish, cooked or otherwise. Alone, bound and gagged, his bones ached. His head throbbed. A filthy oil rag that smelled of dirty hands and engine oil dug into the corners of his mouth. Spit had saturated it and was dribbling down his cheek. How long had he been out? Pins and needles jabbed his left hip and down his leg. Gotta sit up. He wriggled. Impossible. Ropes don't give an inch. Desperate for relief, Armand wormed across rotted linoleum to the horizontally planked wall. Bracing his head against it, he slithered up into a seated position and scrutinized the room. Scrap lumber criss-crossed two side windows, allowing very little light to enter. Or else it was nighttime. Table, chairs, sink, broken dishes. The thugs had him cooped up in an abandoned apartment.

A horn blasted and vibrated the entire building. A signal device of some sort. A ship? All went quiet. Jingling. Armand squinted at the paint-laden door. The brass lock was brand new. Again jingling came from beyond it. And another sound of a door opening and closing. A store was downstairs. A fish market. The building was probably one of several that lined the docks just off Marginal Street, that is, if he was still in East Boston. Most were weathered two-story shacks with peeling paint, if painted at all. Armand recalled one fish store in particular. God, did that place stink. Scales layered the floor inches deep. Some years back, he had slid ass over teakettle across that floor. The jerk behind the counter found that quite amusing. Armand had to walk home all slimy. Anyway, *Mamacita* was happy; she got her damned codfish. Humph. Wouldn't it be ironic if that's where he was right now? If that were true, he knew exactly which way to run when he figured a way out of this hole.

Footsteps! Armand zeroed in on the glass doorknob below the recently replaced lock. Chipped and held in place by only one screw, it began to vibrate. Someone was coming up stairs. Closer, louder, heavier. "Brace yourself, LaRosa." The slimy gag muffled his voice. "Got the feeling this one's gonna be a doozy."

"Open it."

Buccola! He's got enforcers out there. How many?

Keys rattled noisily as one jammed into the new lock and jostled around until the tumblers fell into place. The glass knob rotated precariously until the door burst open and smashed into the wall. "Wait here," barked Phil Buccola. A flashlight beam blinded Armand. Footsteps tromped toward him. "Thought you was home free, didn't ya, LaRosa?" snickered Buccola "Hate to burst your bubble, but time's come to even the score 'tween you and me."

Armand's vision cleared. He maintained a calm front, but inside, all he wanted to do was wipe that egotistical smirk off Buccola's face.

"Got wind of you and Don Vito conniving against me over the Sacco and Vanzetti deal. Didn't believe it at first but…" Phil shrugged with a dumb look. "Sure, it took me a while, but this time I got it all together. Nobody's gonna stop me, not even the Don. Know why? 'Cuz this time I ain't told nobody what I got in this head o' mine." He tapped the flashlight against his temple. Wandering about the decrepit apartment, he waved the flashlight, inspecting everything but touching nothing. Fingerprints would link him to this place. "Couldn't figure out for the life of me why in all these years your speakeasies never got raided. Then it came to me. In the middle of the night! Well, don't cha know? I sat straight up in bed and hollered, 'That bastard's also working for the cops.'" Buccola chortled, "Scared the hell out of the old lady." Abruptly he stopped and flashed the light back at Armand. "That's it, ain't it, LaRosa? You and your flatfoot brother and the Don are in cahoots. That's why all these years, the law's turn a blind eye to your establishments." He bent over Armand and twisted up his nose. "Don't cha know, LaRosa? Nobody shakes down Phil Buccola? Sooner or later ol' Phil gets wind of it and evens up the score. For crying out loud, you certainly haven't forgotten Frank Wallace, have ya?"

Oh yeah, Armand remembered that bloody ambush very well. A couple years back, Wallace, the head of an Irish gang, put the squeeze on for the North End territory. Sure that he had the upper hand, Wallace demanded a sit down to clarify his new domain of power. Just before the meeting, Buccola set his dogs on Wallace, ambushing him and his associates. Gunned down every last one of them in cold blood. The cops had no doubt that Buccola did the work but everyone clammed up. Nobody knew a thing. No one saw a thing. As it turned out, not one person ever got pinned for the murders.

"Aldo Messina's back in town. But you already know that, don't cha, LaRosa?" Buccola mocked in a slimy belittling tone. "That's all my doing, in case you haven't figured it out yet. I convinced the dimwit that you got designs on taking over the Boston and New York rackets. Then you're on to Miami. I made up a cock-and-bull story about how you were planning to bump off him, Don Vito, and me."

So that's what Aldo's doing here, thought Armand. *Shit! He's so damned gullible. Always will be. Gotta get out of here and set him straight.*

Buccola sat down on a rickety chair in front of the boarded-up window and scratched his head with the flashlight. "Hey, you're really gonna love this one. I went out and hired an independent by the name of K. O. Elkins. Linked the mangy bastard up with Messina down in Miami for the sole purpose of filling his head full of lies. K. O.'s got no connection to any family so Messina believed the snitch. And then, what do you know? Messina comes to me. Can you believe it? He actually came to *me! Phil Buccola!*"

His finger poked about his front teeth as he tried to suck out leftovers. "Pfft. Naturally, I tells him I caught wind of what you was up to and I already had a plan put together. Pfft. Pfft, pfft. Told him if he didn't believe me, get a feel for it from you himself. Knowing what *paesani* you two have always been I expected him to do just that. Yup, Messina ate it all up, hook, line, and sinker. So I got one of the boys to tail him. When Messina left Miami, I had K. O. picked up and the minute Aldo met up with you, I had the snitch make a phone call to you. That way you didn't have any time to set Aldo straight."

Armand leered at Buccola. He didn't believe a word of it. Not only that, he and Aldo had been friends much too long for Aldo to believe such lies. Well at least now Armand understood the connection between K. O. and Buccola.

"Meantime, FDR bites the dust and you, LaRosa, you're gonna take the heat for it. Got it all worked out. Getting rid of Roosevelt will keep my new organization lucrative. Never heard of anything sweeter, eh, *cane gialla*? But you and FDR are only part of the set up. Don Vito's on his way out and so is Aldo. With no more zips in my way, I got clear sailing, all the way to the top. *Capo de tutti capi*, that's gonna be me, the strongest of all the five families!" Buccola roared with laughter. He stopped. His eyes flared with red-hot rage. He stomped towards Armand and landed a powerful kick directly in the groin. Watching Armand writhe in pain, Buccola howled once again with laughter. He went to leave the apartment but as he reached for the door handle, he hesitated. "Where's my damn brain?" Buccola whacked the butt of his hand against his head. He faced Armand and casually pulled a Cuban cigar from his pocket and stuffed it between his teeth. "Something else, LaRosa. Your brother, the Senator?" Buccola struck a stick match on the door and lit up his cigar. His mouth rounded. Circles of smoke wafted into the air. "Had the brakes altered."

Hatred seized Armand. Buccola killed Angelo? Vile loathing exploded. Battling the bonds that held him back, Armand wrenched his mouth out of the mucky gag and thundered, "You God damned son of a bitch. You're a dead man, Buccola!"

The boss stepped back. The violent outburst from a man he had just kicked in the groin momentarily alarmed him. He pulled himself together and smoothed his clothes. "Hey, whaddaya want from me? I ain't gonna have no senator in Washington representing my territory but giving favors to New York."

"Angelo never did anything against you," Armand bellowed.

"Like I said, too much of a risk. Besides, Senator LaRosa wasn't the Mr. Nice Guy everyone pegged him for."

"What the hell are you talking about?" Armand demanded.

"The fixers witnessed an interesting little domestic scene." Buccola took several thoughtful drags on his cigar, ignoring Armand struggling with his bonds. "Politicians, they really know how to hoodwink the public with all their smooth talkin', don't they? Amazing thing is, they get themselves elected anyway! Can you beat that, LaRosa? What a racket those guys got."

"You're full of shit, Buccola!"

"Fact of the matter is, a ruckus flared up inside Senator Angie's house. While one fixer monkeyed with the new Pontiac, the other sneaked a peek through the bedroom window. Drapes were wide open, imagine that? Well, lo and behold. There's the good ol' senator, man-handlin' his woman. Then he jumps her. Against her will, let me add."

The story sickened Armand. Turning away, he squeezed his eyes shut; his heart pounded with pent-up anger. With icy clarity the pieces fell together. That night when he drove *Mamacita* and Pop out to Orient Heights, they expected to find just the baby-sitter. Instead there was Heather, all bruised up. She claimed she had tripped over one of the kid's toys and fell down the stairs. The instant *Mamacita* told her about Angelo, Heather went nuts. Hysterical-like. Screaming like a banshee. It was almost as if she was laughing.

Lost in his thoughts, Armand was not paying any attention to Buccola who had gone to the door and was turning the knob. He stopped and leaned against the door. "Nearly lost my fixers at the stop sign. Before Angelo's car rammed into the barricade, it clipped their Caddie. Only lost their bumper though. Plate got mashed a bit too, but they hammered the thing out and put it back on the car," he snickered then left the room.

One last time, Armand heard Buccola's voice. "Don't let the yellow dog outta your sight."

"Sure, boss," replied a voice in the hallway.

Buccola's heavy footsteps faded down the stairs as three enforcers came into the room. The last one slammed the door and turned a shiny brass key, leaving it in the lock. "Light up the joint," he grunted as his gunboat feet shuffled across the room, headed for Armand. Big and solid with one ear missing and only half a nose, he was the only one of the three men that Armand had not seen back in the alley. Without a word Half-nose untied the prisoner.

What a relief it was to get rid of those bonds. Painfully Armand got to his feet and rubbed his wrists. Linking his fingers together, he stretched his arms frontward then up. His head rotated in circles as he opened his mouth wide and rolled the hinges of his jaws that filled his inner ear with crackling noises. He kicked the kinks out of his legs and executed a couple of deep knee bends.

One of the other two henchmen kept an eye on him while the other got up on a wobbly old chair and twisted a low watt light bulb that hung unsheathed from the ceiling. The first guy was the ugly scar-faced giant who had blocked the escape route behind the Gem Theatre. Only in nightmares had Armand seen such depravity. Now, with arms crossed, a dirk in one hand and a blackjack in the other, Scar-face was taking no chances. He grinned sadistically, exposing the silver eyetooth that Armand had seen before.

The second burly thug, who had tried to tackle Armand back at the alley, got down from the chair after dim light illuminated the apartment. On his right hand he now wore brass knuckles and began to strike them repeatedly into the palm of his left hand. His swollen spider-veined nose was that of an alcoholic. Tackler gave the false appearance that this whole mess bored him, although Armand had no doubt that the thug sorely wanted his ass for that bungled tackle. So this was not the time for heroics. At least he was out of bondage. That gave him the ability to scope out the situation and figure out the options. If only one chance presented itself, Armand was determined not to squander it. Able to move and speak, he was now the master of his own destiny. "Gotta use the can, 'K?" He scrunched his face and grabbed his crotch.

"Make it snappy," scowled Half-nose.

Deciding that their prisoner posed no further threat, the three enforcers settled in. Half-nose reached into his pocket for a flask of bathtub gin. He chugged some down and wiped his lips on the back of his sleeve. He cleared his sinuses without a handkerchief while Tackler and Scar-face dragged an old table to a spot in front of the door. A deck of cards landed in the middle of it as the three pulled up broken-down chairs. More flasks appeared.

In the bathroom Armand gazed up at the sagging water-stained ceiling while urinating. "That bumper," he thought out loud envisioning the one he had picked up the morning after the wreck. "Should've known right then and there it didn't come from a brand new Pontiac. Dammit, Angelo. What the hell were you up to that night?"

Buttoning up his fly, Armand scoured the room for an escape route. Rat droppings littered the shelf next to one of the three windows. His fingers pried the thick wooden slats that covered the broken panes. Spikes held them securely against the casing. They wouldn't budge. He tried the other window. Same thing. He pressed an eye against the opening between the planks. Beyond the right side window was a two-story shack not ten feet away. Out the window at the back of the room, he saw only endless darkness. The left side window revealed another two-story shack across the way. He was able to look to the left down a short alley. Against a murky nocturnal sky, a halo surrounded a gas light at the street. He backed away, trying to convince himself that this building was the one at the dock off Marginal Street. A sinking feeling came over him. This time he had really crossed the line and there was no going back.

The ancient wall faucet above the chipped porcelain sink jumped when Armand turned it on to wash his hands. After he shut it off, it continually dripped making rust tracks over time that ran into the decaying drain. He tightened the handle. The leaking continued. "Shitty plumbing," he spat. Holding up his dripping hands, Armand looked around. "Great. No towels." His face twisted up as he swiped his hands, front and back, up and down his pant legs while his attention wandered to the water closet. "How could I have ever been so damned stupid? Letting those idiots sneak up on me like that? *Stupido*!"

Water seeped from the metal ring at the base of the wooden water closet and trickled down the old lead pipe. Staring at the stream of water, he gnarled. "Well, that ain't *never* gonna happen to Armand LaRosa again! And you can take that to *Banca Italiana*."

He stomped over to the windows and tugged on each one of the slats. Not one of them budged. Ramming the side of his clenched fist against the casing, he spun around and crossed his arms over his chest. He studied the way they intersected, the bulging muscles, the hair on his forearms. Damn. His mind was so empty.

He sighed and glanced around the bathroom. Incredible web of pipes. "Someone without a clue played plumber." His eyes fell upon the stream of water that trickled down the decayed lead pipe. Following the stream up to the water closet, his head twisted this way and that all the while analyzing the primitive contraption. "A bit rickety." Suddenly

Armand uncrossed his arms and came to attention. "Wait a minute, what if..." He dashed across the bathroom and grabbed onto the lead pipe near the hopper. He gave it a good yank. The badly eroded connection easily gave way. Twisting the soft, pliant feed pipe toward the broken window, Armand jammed it through an opening between the wooden slats. Water cascaded into the alley below and flooded out to the street. Without adequate water supply, the wooden hopper gurgled and choked. He glanced at the door and held his breath. He listened. Did the creeps on the other side hear all the noise?

A fist banged against the door. "You comin' outta there or what?"

"Yeah, yeah. Hold your horses," Armand shouted while yanking off one of his socks and stuffing it into the gurgling exit pipe. That quieted things down. He ripped off a good one. "That oughtta add a little atmosphere." He opened the door and pretended to wipe his hands on his shirt. "Crapper don't flush right. Hear it? Dumped a good load in it. Chloroform will do it to ya every time. Go in there at your own risk."

The enforcers twisted up their faces while their hands fanned away the odor that drifted their way. Smelling that stink, not one of them was about to go into that bathroom. "Fercrisesakes, close the damned door," screeched Scar-face.

Armand pulled the door shut and dragged an old crate up to the table. Across from him Half-nose squinted through his own cigar smoke while dealing out cards. The door to freedom was behind him. "You in?" Half-nose asked.

"Sure, why not," replied Armand. "Don't count on collectin' bets though."

The three henchmen smirked and belted down more gin.

"How about a swig?" Armand asked.

Scar-face bared his silver tooth sadistically then slid his flask across the table. When the prisoner took a couple long slugs, Scar-face took offense. His grin disappeared as his open palm beckoned for the return of the nearly empty flask.

Armand belched. He tossed the flask back and ventured, "Haven't seen you fellas around."

"Not from here," said Tackler.

Armand rearranged his hand. Out-of-towners. Buccola's got the bases covered this time.

Time wore on. The plumbing got louder by the minute. Luckily, inebriation dulled the enforcers' senses. It also loosened their tongues. Armand took advantage of the situation and pumped them for information.

This morning, FDR's motorcade was going to pass the Lafayette Square Fire Station in Cambridge. A member of his own entourage would conveniently lose his soft hat in the breeze. That signaled a marksman on the roof of the fire station to do Roosevelt. The cops would find Armand later shot dead. Some fine upstanding citizen, who just happened to be squeaky clean, would claim he overheard Armand bragging in a downtown bar about how he had shot FDR, the finest president these United States ever saw. The citizen became so outraged that he waited in the back alley and when the dirty assassin came out, he plugged him. The instant hero would have his picture splashed all over the newspapers and lots of Phil Buccola's money lining his pockets.

"Gotta take a piss," said Half-nose slamming down his cards. With both hands he shoved himself away from the table.

"Take my advice. Go outside." Armand showed no urgency.

"Can't wait no longer."

"Open that door and whew! You'll be sorry."

"Buccola will have my ass, if he finds out I left this room," spat Half-nose. He threw open the bathroom door. Moments later, he shouted, "Hey, what the hell is this?"

Tackler and Scar-face dropped their cards. Their chairs tipped over as they rushed to the bathroom. Half-nose stormed at Armand and lifted him by the collar. "That ain't crap clogging the plumbing," he growled and hurled Armand across the table.

Landing on his stomach, Armand lifted his head, sucking for air. Suddenly his eyes narrowed. Right in front of his nose was the key, still in the lock. He lunged for it then twisted the key as he turned the glass knob. The last screw fell out and the door popped open. Armand scrambled to get off the table and around the half-opened door, but Half-nose locked onto his ankles. He fought to stop himself from being dragged back. The table slid to the side. The door opened and slapped against the wall. Rolling over, Armand kicked again and again until one leg was free and he dangled off the table by one leg. His fingers grappled for the doorjamb. Yanking and twisting, the shoe came off his other sock-less foot. Free at last.

Halfway down the stairs Tackler and Scarface jumped him. The three tumbled to the bottom; Armand ended up underneath, pinned.

Back in the apartment, Half-nose kicked the door shut. It didn't latch. The last screw and knob assembly were scattered about the floor. He grabbed Armand by the neck and bellowed, "Waddaya tryin' to do, LaRosa? Don't ya know you ain't goin' nowhere? And think about it, who's gonna pay any attention to water runnin' out a fish market? My suggestion to you…" He bellowed as he rammed Armand's head into the wall. "Give it up."

Stepping back, Half-nose motioned to Scar-face and Tackler who immediately came at their prisoner scowling. Armand made attempts to evade them, but there was nowhere to run. Tackler nailed Armand to the wall while Scar-face two-fisted him like a punching bag. It was impossible to weather the barrage. Blackness overtook Armand as he sank to the floor.

Tackler and Scar-face continued to kick, making more racket than a pack of starving hyenas awaiting the demise of their next meal. Nobody heard Rom and John kick open the unlatched door. It landed on the rickety table that immediately collapsed. Gunfire lit up the apartment as cops charged across the table and into the room. Half-nose, Tackler, and Scarface fell to the floor; the glassy stare of death veiled their eyes.

"Come on, Armand. Wake up. It's over," Rom said frantically while his hand jostled his brother's chin.

"Yeah," Armand coughed. Blood oozed out his nose, mouth, and ears. His hand fished about the air, searching for Rom. Through a semi-comatose haze, he wheezed, "Help me up…will ya?"

"Gimme a hand," Rom said to John.

As they lifted him to his feet, Armand spat out the blood and swiped his sleeve across his mouth. Speech was almost impossible. "Time's it?"

"3 am." Rom answered.

"Roosevelt," sputtered Armand.

"What?" John asked urgently.

Armand faded in and out of consciousness.

"Armand. Come out of it." Rom shook his brother. "What about Roosevelt?"

"Goin' down in front of Lafayette Fire Station. Riding with Roosevelt…" Armand choked on his own blood. "Hat flies off…Hit man…on the roof."

Rom and John exchanged anxious glances. John made a move toward the door but didn't want to let Armand drop. "I got him," said Rom. "You handle FDR."

John let go of Armand and dashed out the door. Rom sagged under the weight.

"Hairiest odds…been in…quite a while," Armand groaned.

"Forget about it. Let's get you to the Doc," said Rom.

They stumbled down the stairs and out into the dark street. Armand peered at the fog-shrouded pier and gave a weak laugh. "Look at that. Never did leave East Boston after all."

"Yeah," Rom panted. "East Boston Wharf."

"Hey, a black and white mutt horned in…"

"Waiting for you back at Mama and Pop's."

"Promised the mutt some food."

Just then the shadows moved. A dark figure stepped out, leveling a semi automatic.

"Aldo," Armand coughed.

Like a rabid badger, Messina growled—low, uncompromising, and deadly. "Gig's up, LaRosa. Taking over the family ain't in your future."

"You know me better than that," Armand faltered. "Don't be crazy."

"Don't call me crazy," Messina roared. "You had the chance to get it all out in the open, back at the bar. But no, you're too damned busy with all your hot deals to talk. Now I got nothin' ta say ta ya."

"But, Aldo, K. O...."

"Shut up!" Messina let fly. Armand took a direct hit. The force propelled him backward onto the ground. A bullet grazed Rom's left shoulder. Another shredded hip flesh. His teeth gnashed against the pain as he spun around and fell into the corner of the fish store. Struggling to get his wind back he made out the shadow of Messina hovering over Armand whose hand extended toward Messina. Rom made out Armand's stricken expression as Aldo raved on like a lunatic. The detective's hand slithered beneath his uniform and seized the cold metal of a .38 service revolver. Not in time. Aldo pumped another round into Armand. "Aargh," Rom grimaced with anger-laced pain. His finger squeezed emptying the .38 into Aldo. The spent gun clicked. The finger squeezed.

Messina staggered into the street, his semi-automatic swung in Rom's direction. Shots rang out as bluecoats filled the street. The semi-automatic flew into the air and Messina went down face first into the gutter behind Rom's black and white.

Rom pitched the empty gun and slithered over to Armand. He lifted his brother's head onto his lap. Armand coughed, "The key...in my watch pocket...Take it."

Rom faltered.

Armand grabbed a handful of his brother's shirt. "Take it, *piccolo fratello mio.*"

Rom fished around and found a small brass key. He held it up and Armand weakly blinked. "Boston Savings in Southie...Broadway...7." His lips quivered with a faint smile. "Lucky number, 'ey?"

Armand gulped one last breath. His eyes rolled then capsized into the dark abyss of death.

"*No!*" Rom's defiant voice denied heaven. His cheek fell upon Armand's head. Tears drenched the sable hair that gray had yet to streak. Crimson streamed off to the sidewalk and trickled into the storm drain.

The dawn came, another day that the sunlight failed to pierce the thick clouds hanging over Boston. Crowds gathered around South Station. At 8:00 a.m. five sleeper and parlor cars, a dining car, and a combination car screeched to a halt. Cheers erupted. Flags waved. But FDR slept. This was his first vacation since entering the White House. He was not eager to rise—so went the press release issued later that day. However, behind the scenes the Secret Service had informed FDR of the assassination plot and told him to stay put for a couple hours until they got a handle on the situation. The President finally appeared at 10:00 a.m. and the crowd went wild when he shouted, "Happy Bunker Hill Day, Boston!"

Thousands had come to pay FDR homage. An additional ten thousand milled around waiting the start of the annual Bunker Hill Day Parade in which another six thousand marched. Throughout the clogged streets of Boston, police were vastly outnumbered as the presidential motorcade got underway. Passing Lafayette Square Fire Station in Cambridge, a smiling FDR stood and waved. The seat beside him was empty. No shots rang out from the rooftop. FDR lived. Armand LaRosa did not.

* * *

The next afternoon, the sun shone brightly. Laden with sadness, Rom and Maria Avita climbed the stairs of a brownstone in South Boston.

Hesitating at the front door, Maria Avita straightened herself. Taking a deep breath, she glanced at her son as if to say, *Go ahead. This thing must be done.* Rom lifted the knocker three times.

The door cracked then slowly opened. Taken aback by the unexpected visitors, Kathleen leaned against the doorjamb. Her swollen red eyes widened. Her hand gripped a white silk handkerchief against her mouth. She was clad in a black frock with organdy neckwear and cuffs, 42-gauge black silk hose, and black oxfords.

"May we come in?" Maria Avita asked, managing a weak reassuring smile.

Kathleen stood aside. As Rom passed he awkwardly removed his hat and nodded. By the look on her face, he could tell she remembered him from that night he had asked Armand to intercede with Don Vito on Vanzetti's behalf. If only he had known she was still in the picture. In the living room he stood with his mother, both hoping to find the right words.

"Please," said Kathleen motioning to the sofa. "Sit down."

Rom cleared his throat and said, "We have come at Armand's request."

The mere mention of his name caused tears to flood down her cheeks. So many times in the last twenty-four hours her sorrow had rained without comfort. This time Maria Avita got up and went to the Irish woman and took her into her arms. Rocking side to side, the old lady wept.

Rom turned away and choked back his grief. His only consolation was the written words scratched on an ordinary piece of white lined stationary, "This is the hand of cards the Man upstairs dealt for me. Life just played out the game." Looking back at his mother and Kathleen, he drew a deep breath to speak. His voice trembled. "Armand gave me the key to a safety deposit box before he…uhm. Letters were in there, one for Mama, one for you." Handing a sealed envelope to Kathleen, Rom continued. "Mama's letter spoke of you. He loved you with all his heart and soul but thought that mixing Irish blood with LaRosa would cause great anguish. He wrote that Mama and Pop have two other grandchildren—a boy, Aldo…" Rom choked. "Oh, God…"

"And a girl, Angelatina," whispered Maria Avita.

Kathleen pulled herself away from the old woman. Her eyes searched the timeworn face. "Armand told you? Why?"

"You are LaRosa. He wrote in my letter that you have no family. He did not want you alone in this world," Maria Avita faltered. "I am so sorry that my son did not bring you to us before this terrible thing. I wish he had."

"The LaRosa family wasn't the only reason Armand kept you and the children a secret," said Rom. "He was afraid you might one day be a vendetta target."

"I understand. Armand explained how your family experienced vendetta first-hand," said Kathleen. "His involvement with the Messina family and Don Vito…He wanted out…But there was no way."

"I see why my son loved you," Maria Avita patted Kathleen's hand. "Stand beside me at my son's funeral. Please? With your children, my grandchildren."

"But your husband…" Kathleen started.

"Sh-sh-sh, do not concern yourself with my Joseph." Maria Avita repressed the anger that soured her insides. This was not the time nor place for such anger. Still, it was such a shame. That old man and his holier-than-thou attitude had caused so much unhappiness in the family. Perhaps even more so than Father Sandro. "Over time Joseph has learned to accept *religiously* every person who comes into the LaRosa family. He will not go against me in this matter, I assure you. You and the children are LaRosa. That is that. Now, if you please, Kathleen, I would like to meet my grandchildren."

Chapter 28

Disenchantment with the priesthood had soured Vincenzo against the Church. Lacking any sense of direction, he dawdled away the days that turned into years. For a short time Angelo's campaign had lured the recluse from his self-imposed subjugation. The platform that befriended the common man and questioned the self-serving motives of the socially elite sounded promising. Senator Angelo would cleanse the world of these parasites. His death that New Year's night crushed Vincenzo, sending him back into the invisibility of bedroom walls.

Still, his compassion for the human condition remained. It bothered him that the LaRosa family barely felt the pinch of the Depression. But who was he to judge? He took advantage of their economic well-being and seldom worked. When he did, it was because his father was desperate for an extra hand. That did not suit Vincenzo at all. It did not matter that Joseph had backed off from condemning Maria Avita for Father Sandro's death. His sanctimonious overtones still poisoned the air at times. It sickened Vincenzo that the religious zealot could not find it in his heart to forgive Mama. Actually, it was abundantly clear that the old man had never forgiven Vincenzo either. By not becoming a priest, the son had failed miserably to fulfill one of his father's dreams. How strange that Joseph had not taken Angelo's death harder than he did. Certainly the election of Senator Angelo LaRosa had fulfilled another dream. The old man should have been devastated that the accident stopped Angelo from following through. "It is God's will," Joseph had said succinctly.

To Vincenzo it made no sense at all that there were so many deaths in the family. Why did God take innocent little Francesca? What did she ever do wrong? And Angelo, the brightest star of all. The newly elected Senator could have done wonderful things for his own people, for humanity, too. Not at all like Armand, all mixed up in the Mafia. That talk that he worked undercover for the cops seemed a bit hokey. That had to be a line Pop thought up to save face. And speaking of saving face, how come Pop allowed Armand's Irish wife and bastard children into the Captain's house? Wasn't that going against the grain?

So it was that Vincenzo remained secluded in his bedroom with only his thoughts. Maria Avita did what she could to draw him out into the world. The only thing that met with any success was asking him to run short errands for her. One day, in the midst of one such errand, he was ruminating the perplexities of life when he stumbled across scores of people down on their luck, lined up outside the mission next to the Relief Station. The lines had been there for quite a while, but this time, eyes, fixed on nothing, caught his attention. They languished in the vast expanses of hunger and despair where only hopelessness filled the future, for in the factories few wheels turned and few chimneys smoked. His steps slowed. At the door of the mission, Vincenzo stopped. A voice within called, "Enter…Enter."

Not until late that evening did Vincenzo return home, without whatever it was that Maria Avita had sent him out to get. Joseph wasted no time reproaching his son. "Where on God's green earth have you been? Your Mama has been beside herself with worry."

"The mission."

"For heaven sake. What were you doing there?"

"Working."

"Working? Are you out of you mind?"

"Now Joseph," interrupted Maria Avita. She laid a calming hand on her husband's forearm.

"Bah!" Joseph shook her off and stormed out of the room. "*Cafone*!"

Maria Avita sat down next to her son. She studied his demeanor. Nothing ruffled him. Not even his father's insults.

"The homeless, Mama," he said. "They wait for turn to sit through sermons just for free meal and bed at night. I want to help them."

Maria Avita nodded. "In this life we often find ourselves compelled to lift a hand so others, unable to help themselves, can survive."

First light the next morning, Vincenzo took off for the mission. He sidestepped a deluge of dirty water thrown from a third story window of a row house. The whiff of sewage filled the air. He looked up. An old lady wearing a white bandanna was hanging out the window with an empty pail in her hand. "*O Dio mio, Signore. Mi dispiace*," she cried; her hand slapped her forehead.

Waving her off, Vincenzo crossed the street. At the corner a beggar was selling apples. Vincenzo had often seen men selling whatever they could get their hands on. Until today though, he had never really paid any attention. "I take one apple, *per favore*." His hand dipped into his pocket then held out four bits. "Keep change."

"Thank you, sir, thank you very much." The weather-beaten man bowed several times. Tears welled in his beleaguered eyes as he said, "God bless you. And my family will bless you, too."

Vincenzo's heart bled for the beggar and his family, wherever they were. How long had it been since they last ate? By the look of the man, he had not eaten very often. Suddenly the opulent breakfast Vincenzo had eaten this morning churned in his stomach. He could not bring himself to take one single bite out of the apple. He gave it to a little girl in the long line of people outside the mission. She smiled up at him. Those beautiful chocolate eyes made Vincenzo feel a little better. But still, farms were so full of food, so Vincenzo heard. What good was it though? These people had no money to buy anything. Sure, farmers could give their food away, but that did not pay the mortgages on their land. It had come as no surprise when Vincenzo read in the paper that they had formed mobs to stop foreclosures. Meanwhile, the beggar who sold the apples, his family, and the little girl with round chocolate eyes went without food. "Ah, Senator Angelo," lamented Vincenzo. "If only you live. These things you fix."

At the mission homeless adults and families received six meals and two nights lodging. Teenagers got only two meals and shelter for just one night. In addition young people found vagrancy laws harsher than older transients did. Hardly fair, the system did serve a purpose. The government wanted to force youngsters to go back to their families. A quarter of a million children left home during the Depression, hopping freight trains that ran empty except for them and other down-on-their luck individuals. They all sought the elusive better life or adventure. Most families however did not want their older children back; there was not enough food nor money to go around, the reason many kids left home in the first place.

Many youngsters who came into the mission had hardened with road life. Most lacked respect and good manners. Every so often though, one showed up who didn't fit the mold. What was a kid like this articulate and seemingly well educated one, doing so far away from home and the family that loved him? Vincenzo posed this question to one such kid who pulled into town, half-starved, and smelling like a skunk.

"I shipped out for adventure, that's all," Johnny Fisher shrugged. His finger shoved his cap back on his head. Seasoned and wary, he seemed to brag but a note of defeat laced his voice. "I was well brought up, that's a fact. Never had it hard, 'cause my dad was the county doc. But I got the itch one day. Said I'd be back before supper. Instead I left a note in the mailbox and hopped the Santa Fe West. I was gonna be a cowboy. Well, that wasn't about to happen, so now I criss-cross the country 'cause I'm too ashamed to go home a failure."

"Holy smoley, that weren't nowhere near what happen ta me, no way, no how," blustered Johnny's road mate, Stinky Reese. A lanky boy with unkempt hair the color of straw and clothes, snagged and full of holes, draping his stunted frame, looked like a scarecrow in a mown field. "Ol' man kicked me out 'cuz the bulls ran me down one day that I skipped school. Same night he traipsed down ta da hoosegow 'n says ta me, 'Don't cha bother comin' back home no more when dey decides ta let cha out. Go fend fer yerself, ya tink yer so garl-dang smart.' Yep, dat's da very words he says ta me." Stinky paused. Picking at his filthy broken fingernails, his eyebrows arched up and down several times before he continued. "Jes' as well. Mean son-of-a-bitch...always beatin' on my mum and me. Real bad. Scrabble-ass poor ta boot, dat was us. In my mind anythin's better 'n dat, so I hits da road and don't never look back. Sure's humiliatin' though...ol' man yellin' at me like that 'n front o' everybody 'n all."

After their one night at the mission, Stinky, his hat cocked to one side, and Johnny, his cap pushed back on his head, shuffled off down the lonesome East Boston Street. Vincenzo stood at the door of the mission and watched. What was going to happen to them? Bent with life like old men, their hands were stuffed in their pockets, collar to the wind. Trash mixed with dirt whirled around the boys as they turned the corner and vanished from sight.

Some time later, Vincenzo got a post card from Johnny and Stinky. They had hopped the Santa Fe back to California and intended to catch up with the Great Northern heading east. Summer was a good time to ride the northern rails. "P.S. Saw a man kilt for the shoes on his feet.-S.R."

Months passed and the two boys crossed Vincenzo's mind less and less. One day, Stinky Reese strutted into the mission. He was alone. Penniless and half-starved, the teenager hid it well. Hat cocked to one side, he gave the appearance that his luck was about to change any day now. In a matter-of-fact voice he said, "Johnny's gone an' got hisself kilt."

Vincenzo detected pain beneath the kid's tough exterior. "*O Dio mio.* What happened?"

Stinky heaved a sigh and said, "Onest, da train lurches 'round da bend. We was top a freight cah and Johnny weren't holdin' on ta nuttin, 'cuz me 'n him, we was headed ta da back o' the train. Bucked off, Johnny was. Jes' like a bronco in da rodeo."

Stinky Reese left the mission the next afternoon. Vincenzo never saw nor heard from him again.

One wet, gray day in March, the cops collared a lean-bodied woman and a couple of children, raw-boned and stomachs beginning to bloat from starvation. Eva and her two children, Mary, and Adam, had been hiding out at the rail yards near Chelsea Creek, waiting for a westbound freight. When brought into the mission, Eva poured out her heart. "My husband got killed yesterday, just outside of Worcester. We were all hiding behind the water tank waiting till dark, so the bulls wouldn't catch us. A slow moving freight came through. 'This is the one,' he says and we all started running at it in a line. Suddenly there was lanterns and bulls with shotguns all over the place. 'Hurry,' my husband hollered and got a handhold running. But he lost his footing then his grip on the grab iron. Right in front of my eyes, my husband rolls under the train."

"Bulls no arrest you?" Vincenzo asked.

Eva shook her head no. "Must've felt sorry for me and the kids. They told me to get the hell out of there and don't come back."

"But you hop another train," said Vincenzo.

Her head nodded as she swilled down the remainder of her plate of Yankee pot roast. "What else was I going to do?" she asked and wiped her mouth on her sleeve.

Vincenzo handed her a napkin. She looked at it for a moment. Chagrin colored her face. "I'm sorry. I forget all my manners."

"Don't worry about it." Vincenzo wished he hadn't embarrassed Eva like that.

"We was in the middle of nowhere with no food, no nothing. Amazing the way things change. Wasn't long ago, my husband had a good job making tractor parts. He worked that job since getting outta high school. But the plant closed down, and there were no other jobs to be had. So we hawked everything. Didn't get much though, everybody in the same boat and all. I had nice things I collected over the years, especially baskets I wove myself. Those I really liked. And all my kitchen gadgets and clothes went. The children's toys. Everything. We got nothin' now, not even him.

"How you eat?" Vincenzo asked.

"Sometimes nice folk invited us all in for a sit-down. Then we was home free for a day or two. But most times, my husband knocked on doors and asked for work." She tried to clean the caked dirt from her children's faces.

"No you bother do that, you get baths when tub she's free," said Vincenzo. When the woman smiled gratefully at him, a place inside him filled like a stomach that had not known food for a very long time.

"Pay was usually food. When that didn't happen, we stole food from markets." She paused. Pain wrinkled her face. "Night my husband got killed, me and the kids started walking. It was so dark and I was scared to death, but I didn't show it 'cause I knew the kids were scared, too. We spent the rest of the night and the next day in a big ol' barn. I got real homesick and I missed my husband." Eva didn't cry. Children of the Depression understood the futility in it. "I feel so ashamed of everything, but there weren't much other choice. Listening to the preacher's sermon here, trying to save my soul, makes me even more ashamed, 'cause I know in my heart that me and my children will do anything just to survive. Even against everything I know is right."

After they bathed, Eva laid down on the cot next to her children. Within moments they were all sleeping like the dead. Vincenzo pulled the green army blanket up to destitute mother's chin. Her sleeping face twitched a slight smile as she drew the blanket up to her nose. Peering down upon the three peaceful faces, Vincenzo felt an ache fill his breast until he thought he could breathe no longer. He simply could not imagine that this woman with two children actually hopped freight trains. And under the cover of darkness? How frightened they must have been when bulls stuck flashlights and guns in their faces. Suddenly Vincenzo could see that Eva and her children needed him. Even though his salary was not the greatest, it was theirs. He used very little money anyway. Living at home cost him nothing and having few friends, he rarely went out after work.

That evening when Vincenzo got home, he asked Maria Avita if she knew of any flats for rent. Abruptly she turned from the cast iron stove where she was preparing his meal. Sauce dripped from the ladle she held in her hand. "Why Vincenzo, are you moving out? You know you don't make enough money at the mission for a place of your own. How are you going to buy food..."

"Mama, stop. No for me. *La donna e due bambini* came to the mission. They stay two nights, then they go out on street."

"Oh." Maria Avita said. Relieved but still worried, she put the spoon in the sink and bent down to wipe up the sauce on the floor. "What does this woman mean to you? You have never gotten involved before. What is so different this time?"

Vincenzo shrugged. "Eva, she different. That's all."

Maria Avita stood up and straightened her back. "Well, if she doesn't have money, how is she going to pay rent?"

Vincenzo looked down at the floor. "*Non sapere per certo*, but I help with my wages."

Maria Avita studied her son. As usual his shirt was buttoned wrong. She turned down the burner on the stove then wiped her hands on her apron as she stepped over to him. She buttoned his shirt the correct way, all the while scrutinizing his tranquil face. "My son Vincenzo, a man of few words, never asks anything from anybody. He sets about his business every day, coming and going. Nobody ever knows if he is in the house or not." After fastening the last button, she patted his chest.

Vincenzo smiled down at her. Was it his imagination or was she shrinking with age?

"If you feel you really must help this woman, there is a way," she said. "But you must swear to tell nobody."

"*Si*, Mama."

His docile face melted her heart. "I have some money…" she stammered. Should she wake the sleeping monster again?

"Father Sandro's money," Vincenzo said.

Their eyes met. "How do you know this thing?" she asked.

"I piece with time. In beginning, I wonder…*moltissimo*. Why we live in such a fine house? Pop do good but no can pay for all we have. Most immigrants struggle long, long time.

Maria Avita nodded. If it weren't for Father Sandro's money, the LaRosa family would have had a very hard time. She and the children might still be in Italy. The priest would have been found and then she…An electric shiver bolted through her.

"Pop, he no know, *si*?" Vincenzo asked.

"Your father finds such things troublesome," she said flatly.

Cognizant of his father's parochial mentality, Vincenzo let it go.

And so it happened that Eva and her children were no longer homeless. They moved into a second-story flat on Porter Street. Eva did what she could to bring in money and Vincenzo faithfully turned over most of his earnings to her. Quite often he didn't come home until the early morning light pulled off the speckled blanket of night.

As time marched on more than twenty states declared bank holidays in an effort to stop panic withdrawals. In New York Governor Lehman closed all banks and stock exchanges. Within days, banking operations across the country ground to a halt. The economic life of the nation stood at a standstill as Americans awaited Roosevelt's solution.

On March 2, 1933, Joseph, Maria Avita, and Vincenzo settled around the brand new Philco radio that Joseph had purchased on sale for $49.95. The six-leg cabinetry of walnut with oriental wood pilasters and genuine rosewood inlay was an elegant addition to the LaRosa living room. They listened intently to FDR's first fireside chat. The illuminated dial mesmerized them, as did President Roosevelt's reassuring voice. The worst was over, he told his Sunday night listeners. "The only thing to fear is fear itself."

Joseph wanted to believe those words. But the future worried him. So far, the LaRosa family had made it through these hard times relatively unscathed. Still in all, his company's lack of growth gave him much concern.

The next morning the Boston Banks received permission from the federal government to re-open. Bostonians cheered in the streets and even the Boston City Council passed a resolution praising "the summary, intelligent, and courageous action taken by President Roosevelt and Governor Ely."

March 4, 1933, FDR stated, "Our greatest primary task is to put people to work." The Civilian Conservation Corps showed evidence of his commitment. Within no time, Vincenzo noticed a great reduction in the number of young people seeking shelter and food at the mission.

Chapter 29

Suffolk Downs, New England's first major horse racetrack, opened in East Boston in 1935, adding tremendously to the already lucrative numbers racket entrenched in the Boston area. Runners, disguised as bread delivery drivers, shopkeepers, and other ordinary folk, took verbal bets from street gamblers. Possessing extraordinary memories, they rarely wrote down bets. If the cops nabbed them, written material became evidence to use against them in court. Meanwhile, spotters set up vantage points in houses on top of Orient Heights. Binoculars came in quite handy for scanning the odds boards.

Opening day, Joseph and Maria Avita entered the clubhouse with Orazio and Carlotta Bascuino. Odors of fresh-cut wood, oil paint, varnish, and newly waxed floors wafted throughout the building. Everything sparkled—floors, windows, chrome tables and chairs, even the glassware on the previously set tables. Joseph waved his hand in a grand swooping circle and said, "Mark Linenthal, ah, such a fine architect. He designed this whole track." Dressed in his lucky suit and finest hat, he carried in his pockets everything lucky that he possessed and had even said a little prayer this morning for good luck, despite the fact that the Church frowned on gambling.

"Everybody has heard of Mr. Linenthal, Joey," said Orazio. "But it is still hard for me to believe that all this was designed and built in less than three months." His brown suit with a white button-down shirt, brown hat, and shoes were typical of the old country. Unlike Joseph, Orazio had not changed his style of dress since the days when he was a young businessman in Italy. The clone of his father felt no need to change.

Joseph scrutinized the streamlined, modernistic features. "This international style is a rarity not often seen in neighborhoods of Boston."

"Let's sit over there. At the finish line," Orazio pointed and hurried toward the table.

The two couples had just taken their seats when the band began to play the Star Spangled Banner, so they got to their feet once again and placed their hands over their hearts. Every time Joseph heard the National Anthem, he grappled with his decision to come to America. Did life truly improve for the LaRosa family? Fine days like this convinced him that indeed it had. At other times great doubt overwhelmed him. Would he have lost a child to a freak accident like the flood of molasses? Or live to see two sons die violent deaths? If he had stayed in Italy, would Father Sandro still be alive? And would Joseph have ever dared to question his God's wisdom during so many times of unholy despair? He felt a tug on his sleeve and turned.

"The band has finished playing," whispered Maria Avita.

Embarrassed to see that he was the only one left standing in the crowded clubhouse, Joseph hastily took his seat only to endure a nervous waiter who buzzed over him like a hungry seabird hovering above a school of anchovies. This was the young man's first day on the job and it showed. As a result, confusion about the order delayed him at the table. Joseph strained to see around him as the horses loaded into the starting gate and the race got underway. "My good fellow, would you please step aside?" Joseph chided then stood up. "What is that I see? My rider fell off his mount coming out of the gate?"

Orazio's horse never even showed up at the finish line. It had taken a liking to the infield grass. The jockey whipped the horse's rump and kicked its withers, but the animal had its own mind and continued to graze. The two men frowned. They looked at each other and shrugged.

Uproarious laughter broke out as they tore up their betting slips and threw them high into the air. The pieces fluttered down like confetti and landed everywhere. The clumsy waiter wore several pieces all day but nobody told him. After all, he did seriously mishandle their meal.

Throughout the afternoon, Joseph lost all bets. Orazio fared only slightly better with one horse coming in on a show ticket. The merriment dissipated, vexation mounted. At the end of the eighth race, Joseph belched, "Ah, ya sommanabitch!" Gesturing to the sky, he ripped off his lucky suit coat and threw it to the floor.

"Do not speak in such a manner," cautioned Maria Avita. "Remember, this is a public place."

"Ah, forget about it." His face swelled red with frustration. "Buncha ol' plugs anyway." He looked so comical that the others could not help laughing. Failing to appreciate their humor, he nearly blew his top but instead turned his chair away in a huff and sulked.

"You are being very silly, my husband. Everyone has fared poorly this day," whispered Maria Avita.

His eyes shot daggers at her then at Orazio and Carlotta who avoided all eye contact. Not wanting the day spoiled by a loser, they directed their attention to the horse in the winner's circle.

Maria Avita placed her hand on his. Her soft eyes gazing into his, her voice soothed him. "Orazio lost every race too, but he still has a good time."

Always unable to resist her charms, Joseph came to his senses. He turned his chair back to the table and kissed her hand. "Sorry, *Angelatina Mia.*"

In a heartbeat the four friends were knee-deep in revelry again. Knowing full well how Joseph dwelled on the negative, Carlotta quickly changed the subject. "The wedding invitation for my niece's son, have you gotten it yet, Maria?"

"*Si.* It came in the mail yesterday. I am looking forward to meeting Michelo and his bride. We will have such a wonderful time. It has been a very long time since..." Maria Avita hesitated.

Joseph read her painful expression. There was no escaping the deaths of Francesca, Angelo, and Armand. Their loss overshadowed every LaRosa get-together. Quickly he finished her sentence. "Er, it has been a very long time since we have seen the inside of the Maverick Hotel."

Orazio pretended to study the racing form, but in his heart there was also great pain. Both the LaRosas and Bascuinos had lost children. Getting over such a loss was impossible. He wished he knew of a way to ease the burden.

"Orazio and I are glad that the bride's family chose the Maverick," said Carlotta. "They are from Revere, you know."

"We thought it strange that the boy's time will be in East Boston," said Joseph. "Your niece still lives in Medford as does your brother. Am I not correct?"

"*Si.* Anna is married and owns the house next to Stephano."

"We have not seen your brother only once or twice in all these years," Maria Avita said. "I'm afraid I would not recognize him if I passed him on the street. Anna, too."

"Orazio and I manage to see Stephano and Anna once or twice a year. Distance keeps us from more than that," said Carlotta.

"And Stephano refuses to drive," grumbled Orazio. "So I am the one who must always drive all the way out to Medford and all the way back."

"My brother is sickly," Carlotta said.

"Just an excuse," Orazio retorted.

Carlotta quickly stepped in. "His wife passed on only a few years off the boat. Stephano took it very bad and after the influenza took his son, he closed himself up in that house. Anna refuses to go anywhere without her father and that is why it is especially wonderful that you will be there. You can meet my niece, Anna, and her son, Michelo. Anna has not set foot in East Boston since she arrived in America. I hope Stephano will be there, too."

* * *

An exquisite autumn morning set the stage for the wedding. Brilliant reds, oranges, and yellows bedecked the trees that lined the sun-drenched street leading up to the church. Not a cloud interrupted the azure sky or amber sunbeams. The air was crisp and easy to breathe, invigorating to the senses. "A perfect day," said Maria Avita. Her eyes darted about, admiring every minute detail. "Isn't this street *magnifico*?"

"*Si*," said Joseph. "Such a day should have been ours, *Angelatina Mia*."

She squeezed his hand. Their eyes met. Age had stolen some of the hazel from his eyes, but in them she still saw that handsome young suitor of long ago. "Being married to you, *mi amore*. That is most important to me," she said.

Ushered to their seats on the groom's side of the church, Maria Avita pondered her life with Joseph. Wedding rituals with fancy gowns and decorations were truly wonderful. Although, thinking back on their courtship in the countryside of Salerno and their little hillside cottage above the Tyrrhenian Sea, she regretted nothing. That life so long ago in Italy belonged to her and Joseph just as their life together in East Boston. It was their own personal story, unlike anybody else's. Now another young couple was beginning their own special story that nobody else could ever share. Her heart leapt with excited anticipation for Michelo and Jane. She hoped their life together brimmed with as much love as Joseph and hers.

The wedding march began. Shoes rustled upon the plank floors as everyone got to their feet and faced the rear of the church, craning their necks for the first glimpse of the bride on the arm of her proud father. She wore a chapel-length satin dress with white stockings and slippers. The veil that obscured her face cascaded over her shoulders and fell into a flowing train that drifted along the red carpet like powdered snow. As

Jane approached the altar, Maria Avita strained to see the groom. His back to her, he stood slender and straight in a black tuxedo. His hair was light brown with highlights of gold. A good part of the hour passed before the priest raised his hands above the newlyweds presenting Michelo and Jane to their family and friends. As they faced the congregation, Maria Avita gasped; her trembling hands shielded her mouth. Electric current bolted through her as goose flesh mutilated her skin and her hair stood on end. The room swirled faster and faster, like a carousel gone crazy. Those eyes, that face. "Father Sandro!" she heaved. Her knees gave way and she collapsed onto the kneeler.

* * *

Her eyelids rippled then slowly opened. She was in her own bed. Joseph was sitting next to her. His hands clasped her left hand against his lips. Anxiety wrinkled his face. "*Grazie Dio*, you have come back," he murmured, kissing her hand again and again.

She smiled.

" What happened, *Angelatina Mia*?"

Before she could speak the doorbell rang downstairs. Moments later, Vincenzo showed Doctor O'Shea into the bedroom.

"Just a spell. I will be all right, I assure you," she murmured, but the doctor kept badgering her with questions she did not want to answer.

"What have you eaten this day?" he asked.

"Nothing," Joseph interrupted. "She was too excited over this silly wedding. Scurrying around like a mad woman let me say. And that Mass, too long, much too long. Know what I mean?"

"Well, that explains it then, plain as the nose on your face." The doctor backed away and took a big drag of air. As he packed his stethoscope into his black bag, he puffed, "I, myself, get that way when my stomach is empty. But from now on, young lady," he shook his finger at her, "You will eat before leaving this house!"

The next day, Carlotta came in through back door of the Captain's house without knocking as usual. The smell of fresh coffee, sausage patties, and sunny-side-up eggs sprinkled with fresh pepper tainted the air. Joseph and Maria Avita were finishing a late breakfast. Carlotta stopped short. *Look at that. He waits on his wife. A rarity indeed.* Maria Avita, still in her bedclothes, was sitting at the table, wearing his robe that covered her like a blanket. Her salt and pepper hair was still braided from the night. Carlotta hugged her friend around the shoulders and said, "Jane insists that you and Joseph have a piece of the wedding cake," she said placing cubes of cake wrapped in snow-white napkins on the table. "Are you feeling better today, *amica mia*?"

"*Si*," answered Maria Avita. Her voice was dull. Her withered fingers traversed the names embossed in silver on the napkin—Jane and Michelo.

Joseph pulled out a chair for Carlotta. "Sit. Sit. I will pour you a coffee."

Carlotta winked at Maria Avita while motioning with her eyebrows at the man clumsily moving about the kitchen. Her friend, smiling ever so faintly, looked somewhat better than yesterday after fainting right at Carlotta's feet. "I heard what you said in the church," whispered Carlotta.

Maria Avita picked up her napkin and wiped her lips. Behind the napkin, she mumbled, "What was that?"

"Father Sandro."

Maria Avita stirred. "Sh. Joseph is coming."

"Things are well with you, Carlotta?" he asked as he carefully poured her coffee. His hand shook making the cup and saucer jiggle.

"*Si*." Carlotta smiled.

"And Orazio?"

"He waits for you at Mizzulo's."

Without a word Joseph moped back to the stove and set the coffeepot on a low burner. Maria Avita gave a weak chuckle. "Go play cards, *mi amore*."

Carlotta spoke up, "I will stay until you return."

Joseph threw off his wife's white apron and grabbed his hat. In a flash he kissed his wife a feathery good-bye then bolted out the door.

Maria Avita gave a frail laugh as she labored to get to her feet. "Let's sit in front of the fire. These old bones don't warm like they used to." She shut off the flame under the coffee pot and trudged into the living room. Listlessly she poked the embers in the hearth. Would that *diavolo* ever stop haunting her?

"Does Michelo resemble Father Sandro that much?" Carlotta asked as she positioned another log on the fire.

Steadying herself on the mantel, Maria Avita did not face her friend. "*Si*. Michelo is his twin." She shivered.

"Orazio and I left Italy before Father Sandro was assigned to the parish."

"So you never met him." Maria Avita went to Joseph's chair and drew off the afghan from the back. Wrapping it around her shoulders, she sank into the chair.

Carlotta sat in the chair next to her and picked at a hangnail. "Michelo does not know that Father Sandro was his father. He thinks his father died at the hands of Giolitti enforcers. A terrible thing, Italy traded the Black Hand for the corruption of Giovanni Giolitti."

Sandro? Michelo's father? No matter how many times those words echoed in her head, Maria Avita could not believe it. She leaned towards her friend and whispered, "Michelo's father?"

"*Si*." Carlotta stared at the flames that seemed to taunt her.

"Why did you not tell me?" Maria Avita weakly protested. "You know that terrible thing I did and my reason for doing so. Surely Orazio told you that night when Don Vito sought his revenge against me through Joseph. Why did you not tell me that Sandro fathered a child? Things might have been easier if…"

"I was going to, but Joseph was so sick in the hospital after the vendetta, and you got so run down…" Carlotta took a quick breath. "I just couldn't. When Joseph come home, I think, well, I tell you both right then and there. But he became a madman and you were so miserable because he hardly spoke to you for weeks. And then that dog…So much time went by before you and me got well again. And then…then Angelo…Armand…I…well, I thought it best not to dredge up the past."

Maria Avita reflected on her friend's profile. The fire glimmering on her face made Carlotta look so old and so very tired. Several spindly white hairs that were not there before refused to stay combed and fell across her forehead that still carried the scars from the dog attack. Her ebony eyes sank into sockets surrounded by dark shadows of sagging skin. Maria Avita murmured, "You have agonized over Father Sandro all these years, just as I have."

"But the secret I carried was different from yours," mumbled Carlotta.

Maria Avita gave a faint nod. "Too bad that all of the priest's wickedness had not been exposed, for Joseph, Don Vito, and others might have understood and the LaRosa family would not have endured such vengeful acts.

"I am sorry, *amica mia*," muttered Carlotta.

"We will speak no more of it," sighed Maria Avita.

"You do not want to know about Michelo?"

"I do."

Carlotta drew a deep breath. "I cannot bear the burden of Father Sandro any longer."

"*Si*, neither can I."

"I got a letter from my brother, Stephano, a month or two after you and the children arrived in East Boston. He needed to get out of Italy right away. There was great danger that he might be arrested. Orazio was doing very well at the furniture factory so I begged him to send Stephano money for passage to East Boston. Orazio found employment for him working on the Prison Point Bridge. Stephano was an excellent stone mason. But then his wife died. She was not well when she got off the boat. And then the influenza took his son. Anyway, no flats were available in East Boston, so we rented a place for the family in Medford. The day we met them at the boat, there was no hiding that my niece, Anna, was pregnant. And no husband stood beside her.

"How old was she?" Maria Avita muttered.

"Barely fourteen."

"That priest stalked babies," Maria Avita shuttered.

"That is very much the truth. The next day, Orazio and I drove them to Medford, but that first night they stayed with us. That's when Stephano and his wife told us about Father Sandro. Stephano almost got arrested for murder because shortly after Father Sandro came up missing, the authorities saw that Anna was pregnant and suspected that the priest fathered her child. Many rumors roamed the village about him having his way with girls. Stephano told Anna to lie when the enforcers questioned her. Tell them that the child's father was a young man from their village who left a month before on a ship bound for America. Well, the enforcers did not believe Anna, but since they could not find the body, they had no proof that Father Sandro was even dead. Poor Stephano. They turned his house upside down looking for bones. Pulled up the floorboards, ripped down the walls, everything. Then they tore up the garden out behind the house. Blossoms were just turning into vegetables. All was ruined. And you know the Church questioned parishioners why their tithes were late. Many reported that they gave their money to Father Sandro. He came to all their doors to collect the money himself."

"But I had no money to give him." Maria Avita slowly shook her head. "By what authority did he have to do this?"

"None," said Carlotta. "The Monsignor checked the church accounts. Father Sandro never reported any tithes. The police investigated and found out that before he disappeared, Father Sandro was seen in Salerno. In a bank. The bank said he exchanged Italian money into American—lots of it."

Maria Avita peered out the front window. A flurry of brown oak leaves, ripped from their branches, whirled about at the mercy of the wind that also took Carlotta's voice. Winter was coming. The raw dampness of Italy engulfed Maria Avita as if that night when she had buried Father Sandro were only yesterday. The anger. The blood. The money. *Dio mio,* that unholy money, stuffed in Father Sandro's robe, was the parishioners' tithes. But it came also from Giolitti's pocket, the priest's share for turning in people who received money from loved ones in America. That's why the enforcer's came the first time. They already knew about Joseph's letter, but *grazie Dio*, he wrote that he had sent no money, for they never would have believed her words. Don Vito sent Father Sandro more money—Armand had told her that before he...Mafia money. Maria Avita wished that she had buried it all with that bloody priest. She chewed the thought over then rationalized that Father Sandro's money was penance for all his sins against Louisa. Drained by a nightmare that had never come to an end, she took a deep breath and closed her eyes. Money sticking out of hidden pockets within the folds of brown monk cloth floated through her brain. If not for that money, who knows what she and the children might have faced in Italy while waiting for Joseph to send for them. The worst of the winter was upon them. She did everything she could think of to stretch the food. And there was no wood for heat. The rain...she felt the rain, soaking her to the skin. The dampness lingered...there was no fire to drive it from the house. It would bring disease, and with precious little food left, she and the children would surely starve.

"So," Carlotta sighed. "What do you suppose Father Sandro did with the Church's tithes?"

When no answer came to her question, Carlotta glanced at her friend. Maria Avita had bowed her head. Her hands were folded on her lap. She had drifted off to sleep.

Chapter 30

On a Tuesday afternoon in late September 1937, Seth motored out to Cambridge to evaluate three adjoining lots for a duplex that LaRosa & Sons Construction Company had on the drawing board. Rom tagged along, or so he thought. Actually, Seth had skillfully timed the trip to coincide with his brother's day off work. Something more important than building sites topped the agenda. He parked the car in front of the middle lot. Broken soda and beer bottles, rusted bicycle and car parts, bald tires, and wind-deposited trash littered all three lots. "Look's like the neighborhood dump," said Rom, glancing around. "Looks like a marketable area though."

"I think so," said Seth and pointed across the street. "Nice park over there, great for kids."

Rom nodded. "Neighborhood's well kept. Noticed a nice little mom-and-pop store back at the corner."

"Yeah." Seth got out of the car. "Probably a good idea to pick up all three lots."

"The house you're putting up in Medford just about wrapped up?" Rom asked.

"Be outta there in less than a month, and nothin's on the horizon till spring." Seth stood there with hands on his hips, swaying side to side. "A project like this will keep the company going for quite some time."

"The trouble is permits. Takes forever these days." Rom leaned against the car and crossed his legs at the ankles.

Kicking a tuft of sod, Seth glanced at the park across the street and said, "Foundation's got to be poured before frost sets the ground."

They tramped about eyeing the perimeter. "Gotta frame up at least one of them pretty darn quick, too, or the crew'll work out in the weather," said Rom.

After weighing the enormous amount of preliminary work against time constraints, Seth shook his head. "Timing's not right. Tsk. Still, it's a good project." He stretched and glanced at the park across the street. "Sure, I can get at least one of the building in the works before snow flies."

"This, I've got to see," Rom chuckled dubiously.

"Hey listen, I've got Pop's faith on my side and Mama's pluck to see that things get done in the shortest time possible."

The two men stuffed their hands in their pockets and hiked the boundaries of the three lots. "How's Mama doing today?" Rom asked.

"*Mezza mezz*," Seth said.

"Well at least I haven't heard Pop harping about that damned priest lately."

"Yeah, that leech Sandro should've been out of the picture long ago. Hard enough getting over losing three kids. Can't imagine doing that."

Back at the car they leaned against the hood and gazed at the people in the park across the street. Barely a breeze whispered through the crystal fall air. Abruptly Seth stepped out into the street and motioned to his brother, "Come on. We got no hurry."

Rom frowned, *what the heck?* He hesitated then followed his youngest brother to a bench next to the swings. Elderly folks, parents watching over their children, and others just whiling away the day occupied the nearby benches. For several moments Seth delighted in the musical clamor of youngsters at play. Without looking at Rom, he said, "Glad you came with me today."

"Why's that?" Rom asked and turned his face up towards sun. His eyes closed. He wallowed in the unusually warm sunshine.

"Over there. See that girl?"

Blinking out solar floaters, Rom skewed his eyes on a young Italian wench. What struck him the most was the uninhibited sparkle in her jet-black eyes and long tresses that suited her light olive skin. Her elbows stabbed the air as she tied a crimson ribbon around disobedient locks to contain them behind her head.

"Who is she?"

Seth shrugged. "Don't know. First time I saw her was a couple of weeks ago."

Rom straightened. He glanced at his brother then at the girl then back at his brother. Rom lit up. Seth was feasting on that girl. It was not at all hard to read his mind. Rom had sat at that very same table the first time he got an eyeful of Rachele. "Been out here quite a few times, haven't cha?" Rom teased.

Seth continued to gape. Totally smitten, stars filled his eyes. The girl with the sparkling jet-black eyes was the most dazzling creature he had ever seen in his entire life.

Rom elbowed him, "Hey! You been sitting here before or what?"

"Once or twice," Seth breathed.

"Can't get her out of you mind, huh?"

"Those girls with her? I think they're her sisters. Takes good care of them, too."

"Pleased to see you finally showing a little interest in the fairer sex. Just about given up on my baby brother ever tying the knot."

Seth punched his brother's arm. Rom grasped his arm and laughed, reminded of that day long ago when baby brother had let everyone know who was boss and made it perfectly clear that picking on him about *his* Margaret was a definite no-no. Rom wished he had been there when she died. Maybe he could have helped the kid from taking it so hard. Only twelve years old when it happened, Seth had vowed that he would never love another. Throughout all these years he dated on occasion, but all amounted to one-night stands.

"You want to meet her? Is that it?" Rom asked.

Seth nodded.

"I don't suppose you know her name."

Seth shook his head no.

"You hoodwinked me into coming here today, didn't cha?"

A sheepish grin crinkled Seth's lips. Puppy dog eyes pleaded.

"You want me to do all the work, don't cha?"

Seth shrugged.

The next afternoon, Rom showed up out of the blue at the Medford construction site. The day was exceedingly hot for late September. He had overdressed that morning and had been peeling off clothes all day long. Down to his strappy undershirt, Rom still sweat like a pig.

"Rom! What are you doing here?" Seth beamed, thinking that his brother tracked down that girl already. Terrific!

Rom grabbed Seth by the arm and dragged him away from the hired hands. He yanked a white handkerchief out of his pocket and wiped his brow. "That girl's no good for you. Find another."

Seth's smile vanished. His hand dropped to his sides. A second later, his lips pursed as his dark brows joined across blazing eyes. "Why? What's wrong with her?"

"She's only sixteen."

"So what? Courting a woman that age isn't uncommon these days."

"Yeah, yeah, yeah, I know that. Just forget about it, OK?" Rom declared. Pacing impatiently, he stopped himself from cracking his knuckles. He was trying to break himself of the habit. It drove Rachele crazy.

"No, I won't," Seth insisted. "She's the one. There's no doubt in my mind."

"I said forget about it!" Waving off his brother, Rom started for his car.

Seth bounded after him. He latched onto Rom's arm and spun him around. Getting right in his face, he shouted, "You're not going anywhere until you tell me what's going on."

Rom rolled his eyes then shook himself loose. His hands jammed into his hips. Isn't anything easy anymore? He kicked the ground and said, "Name's Emma Benedetto. She's adopted and don't know it."

"What's so terrible about that?"

Rom scuffed his foot.

"Pop'll raise a ruckus. That's it, right?" Seth demanded.

"Nah." Rom tilted his head sideways and rubbed the muscle tightening his neck. "Mama's made permanent changes on that front."

Seth put his hands on his hips. He twisted around and took a step away. His eyes squinted off in the distance as he tried to make sense of all this. His weight shifted from one leg to the other. Coming up empty, he faced Rom again. With outstretched arms Seth demanded, "Then what the hell's the problem here?"

"She's Vanzetti."

Seth's eyebrows arched.

"Vanzetti…" he stammered. "You mean Vanzetti of…"

"Yeah, that Vanzetti." Rom huffed and started to pace. This time, he didn't stop himself from cracking his knuckles.

"Whew." Seth backed off. "Well, uhm, that's not her fault. Nobody chooses their parents."

"Except, my dear brother, in this situation, Don Vito did," countered Rom. Sweat poured off him. "Come on. Let's sit in the car. This blazing sun's making my head explode."

Silently Seth tramped behind Rom. He gripped the door handle then hesitated. "Vanzetti's been dead ten years now. Does anything that happened that long ago matter anymore?"

Rom's eyes narrowed. Seth had struck a nerve. "If you remember right, I guarded Bartolomeo Vanzetti," Rom said curtly and slid into the driver's seat. He offered a stogie to Seth but got waved off. Rom lit one up and sucked in a full chest of smoke then blasted it out the window. "I respected Bartolomeo beyond words. We talked many, many hours. He did not deserve what happened to him. Don't you ever forget, that man still matters to me a great deal. Always will. Not only that, he matters very much to countless others. The electrocution of Sacco and Vanzetti will never be forgotten. Take my word on that."

"Sorry," Seth mumbled. "I was way out of line."

Rom rubbed the pinkie finger of his right hand back and forth across the finger grips of the steering wheel. Bartolomeo never left him. Neither did Armand. Nor Angelo and Francesca. Damn! What did it matter if a person was good or bad? There's no stopping fate. He closed his eyes and faced the heavens. V*anzetti? You listening? Your kid lives. And my kid brother wants her. What do I do about that, 'ey paesani?*

Seth stared out the car window thinking he shouldn't press the issue. On the other hand he deserved some kind of happiness in this life. And so did Vanzetti's kid, for that matter. Much to Seth's relief, Rom began to speak. "One night, Vanzetti asked me to get a hold of Don Vito. He had some sort of request. If the Don failed to acknowledge him, Vanzetti was going to spill his guts about something or another."

"How come he asked you?"

"He had it all pieced together. Armand was my brother and he was connected to Don Vito. Vanzetti refused to deal with anyone but the Don. He hated Buccola, but why, I haven't a clue."

"Buccola must've gotten steamed about that."

"Whew, you can say that again. It's one of the nails in our brother's coffin."

"But Armand knew protocol demanded that he must go through Buccola to get to Don Vito," said Seth.

"Yup. He did just that, but then the Don ordered Buccola to give Vanzetti anything he wanted and Buccola blew his top. He resented New York interfering in *his* territory. Essentially he was the Don's puppet. So it seemed he washed his hands of it all by throwing it onto Armand's shoulders."

"What did Vanzetti want?"

"A husband for his lady-love and a father for his illegitimate daughter in exchange for his silence."

"And Don Vito went along with it?"

"Sure as shootin'. Now, get this. Part of the deal was that nobody was ever to know that Vanzetti fathered a kid, not even Buccola."

"Knowing Buccola, even though he claimed he wanted nothing to do with Vanzetti and New York, I'll bet he got bullshit that the deal kept him out."

"Bet on it." Rom took another drag on his stogie. "Buccola, that bastard. Someday, that scum's going down. I hope I live to see the day."

"Dammit Rom. Let it go. Mama and Pop can't take burying another kid."

"Don't worry about it," Rom shrugged it off. He chewed on the inside of his cheek. *After Mama and Pop pass on, Buccola? You better watch your back.* Rom cleared his throat. "Don Vito sent Vanzetti's woman to Italy where she married a guy by the name of Benedetto. He's cousin or something to the Don, can't say for sure though. Then all the papers got forged. The marriage was dated several years before the actual date. At the same time a couple of Don Vito's goodfellas broke into Plymouth Town Hall and destroyed the kid's birth certificate. A bogus certificate fixed the files in Italy. It named Benedetto as her father."

"So Emma thinks she was born in Italy but she's actually American born."

"Uh-huh," Rom grunted and looked skyward once again. *There, Vanzetti, your paesani violated his oath of silence. Mi perdonerai se?*

Seth waved his hand. "So, hey, if nobody knows, including Emma, what's the problem? Nobody ever needs to know. I'm sure as hell not gonna tell her. She deserves a fair shake, just like everyone else."

"The problem as I see it is Don Vito. He's not about to relinquish his hold on the Vanzetti kid. Yesterday at the park, did you happen to spot two guys sitting on the bench by the water fountain?"

"No."

"Well, I'm a cop. I spot things like that. One of those guys, I remember from Armand's days. He's Mafia, real trouble."

Seth searched his mind. The guys on the park bench. He drew a blank. "Look, I don't care about them." His hand waved impatiently then slapped his knee. "I intend to meet this girl with or without your help."

Rom rammed the butt of his right hand against the steering wheel. His eyes rolled. "Damn. There's no stopping a pig-headed LaRosa." Reaching into the back seat for his shirt, he took a piece of paper from the pocket and threw it at Seth. "Here," Rom fumed. "Show this to Pop. Tell him you want to get hooked up with this girl. He'll jump up and down and drive backwards all the way to Benedetto's house in Cambridge. You'll be in Emma's arms in the blink of an eye."

Seth picked up the paper. Scribbled on it, the name and address of the first girl to stir his heart since Margi. The next Sunday, he found himself in the Benedetto parlor seated next to Emma. As tradition dictated, her parents and his parents, visiting at the kitchen, kept a watchful eye on every move Seth and Emma made. The couple was not to be left alone unless marriage vows were spoken. Side by side on the sofa, both were much too nervous to speak. Instead, they passed the afternoon listening to conversation drifting in from the kitchen about Mussolini and how he had conquered Ethiopia for Italy. The event dramatized the ineffectuality of the League of Nations from which Italy had recently withdrawn membership. When Mussolini pillaged Ethiopia, 50,000 Italians paraded through the streets of Boston chanting, "*Il Duce, Il Duce, Il Duce*." It was the longest afternoon Seth spent in quite some time, but it was worth the pain. Things finally got off the ground with Emma.

The next week, LaRosa and Sons Construction Company bought the three lots in Cambridge. Winter was late in coming, so preliminary work got underway fairly quick. Seth made sure of it. This way, fair weather days, he got to see Emma at the park with her sisters. And when it stormed, he got to see her, too.

One wintry afternoon in December, Seth and Emma went to see Walt Disney's "Snow White and the Seven Dwarfs" with her two sisters, Lucia and Gabriella in tow. Afterward, they stopped at a soda fountain where Seth gave the sisters a handful of nickels to feed the jukebox. He slid onto the bar stool next to Emma. Amplified music soon covered up the conversation.

"Know what a juke is?" Seth quizzed.

"No," she giggled.

"It's what southern inns are called that have these music machines in them. Juke joints."

Emma giggled.

"Seems everywhere you go these days, there's one playing." Seth hesitated. "Emma, for heaven's sake, what are you giggling at?"

"You look so funny sitting like that. Your legs are so long." Emma covered her mouth with her hand. Her eyes sparkled impishly.

His eyes shot to his legs. One twisted around the pole of the seat; the other jammed between the metal foot rest and the bar. He was twisted up like a court jester. Mortified, he quickly straightened himself into a more dignified position.

"What can I get for you two?" asked the soda jerk.

"Two root beer floats, my good man." Seth winked at Emma.

"You're such an imp," she jabbed. "Oh, that's a nice song. You like it?"

Seth nodded, "'Ole Buttermilk Sky,' a Hoagy Carmichael tune. I like most kinds of music. Good thing, 'cause my father and his friends have always been aspiring opera singers in their own right. They sing in the house, the street, the job, everywhere. It doesn't matter."

"My Papa's the same," she giggled.

The relationship between Emma and Benedetto intrigued Seth. It took a special person to take on a child not his own. But knowing that she's the daughter of such a notorious individual? Whoa. What must that be like?

"You're close to your father?" he asked.

The music on the jukebox had stopped and Emma immediately turned her attention to her two sisters who were arguing quite loudly over the selection for the last nickel. At the same time the bell over the door jingled. Two men dressed in long overcoats and hats pulled low on their brows came into the Soda Fountain. Seth squinted. Eyeing them up and down, he recognized Don Vito's baby-sitters. Since Rom had warned him of their presence, Seth noticed that they were always tailing Emma. As the gangsters walked past an empty window seat, she cried out to her sisters, "Hey you guys, Mama won't like you making such a fuss in front of all these folks."

The Don's men faltered. Was their charge yelling at them?

"Oh, I'm sorry," said Emma quite seriously. "I was talking to my sisters over there."

The two men gave nervous chortles and quickly stole to the table in the corner where the light was dim. Taking off their trench coats, suit jackets flapped open, exposing chest holsters with handguns in the pouches. Seth shifted.

Emma focused back on Seth. "Yes, my Papa and I are very close. He's strict. Well, so is my mother. She's worse than him. But I don't mind. The old ways are OK with me. How about you and your father?"

Seth had lost his train of thought, triggering a resentful response that resonated through him. Those rogues were part of the reason Rom had done his best to discourage any contact with Emma and now they won't let her be. Something's got to be done about them.

"Seth?" Emma nudged him. "Seth, what are you looking at?"

Blankly he peered back at her. Suddenly he realized he had not heard one single word she said. What in the world were they talking about?

Oh, yeah, fathers. "Er...yeah," he stammered, "Our whole family's very close-knit...course two of my brothers, Angelo and Armand, passed on. My sister, Francesca, too."

"Let's not talk about sad things," she said quickly.

"Good idea. Marriage is a better subject."

Emma blushed. "We haven't known each other very long. Perhaps, it's best to wait a little longer."

"I don't want to wait, Emma," Seth whined. "You'll be seventeen in February. Not long after that, I'll be thirty-one. If I'm ever to have children..."

"Children?" Her mouth dropped.

At that moment the soda jerk set two root beer floats on the counter in front of them. Emma immediately poked the ice cream into the soda. She studied her handsome suitor while sipping the delicious concoction. He seemed more like a teenager than a thirty-year-old.

"Why haven't you married before now? Hasn't any girl ever caught your eye?" she asked.

"Once. A long time ago," replied Seth soberly.

"Didn't work out?"

"The influenza got Margi...I mean Margaret." He stared into his root beer float. Remembering his Margi was still incredibly painful. Nobody's made him feel the way she did. Until now. Until Emma.

She saw the sadness spread across his face and wanted him to smile again. Why did sad things keep trying to ruin this day? Well, that was not going to happen, not if Emma could help it. After all, only a moment ago Seth had spoken of marriage. When strains of "Once In A While" filled the room from the jukebox, she touched his hand and gazed into his eyes. "Dance with me?" Her voice was like a soft summer breeze at midnight. Her midnight eyes became fathomless pools into which he sank deeper and deeper. All reality was lost. His heart beat for only Emma. He took her hand and led her to the dance floor. She was in his arms, but not too close. The two gangsters in the windowless corner never entered into his mind, but those nosy sisters of hers did. When he found his voice, he ventured, "I'll ask Pop to speak of marriage to your Papa, if that's all right with you?"

"It would please me very much."

His eyes grew wide and round. Through quivering lips he choked, "Really?"

Emma nodded bashfully. Their eyes met. For a long lingering moment, the world stopped. All of a sudden, Seth lifted his head into the air and let out a war whoop. He grabbed the girl around her waist and twirled her until they both became dizzy.

Her two sisters stopped what they were doing and scrutinized the insanity. Tearing themselves away from the jukebox, they rushed over to the couple. When Emma announced the news, her sisters jumped up and down screeching like two-year-olds.

The table in the dark corner grated on the wooden floor as Don Vito's men jumped to their feet and recoiled, poised for action. Their hands gripped their weapons beneath their black suit coats. When the hullabaloo died down on the dance floor, they settled back down in the dark corner. The threat had gone completely unnoticed.

Chapter 31

Silver moonbeams streamed through the open window casting shadows that frolicked across walls of delicate pastel motif. Zephyr fanned the slumbering man's cheek and toyed with locks of disheveled sable. He twitched then swiped at the airy pest. Awakened from a lover's deep repose, he lifted himself up onto one elbow. The mystique that sheathed the room held him spellbound as the night train droned a lilting strain while worming through the city. Transparent white Priscillas flitted in the playful summer breeze that passed at will through the open window. The figure of a young woman knelt at the sill. Her forearms cradled her head as she slept. "Margi?" his melancholy heart called out. "Is it really you?"

Heavy with sleep, Seth peeled off the pale yellow chenille bedspread. His legs dangled over the edge of the bed as he balanced there, straining for a better look. Was the diminutive figure kneeling at the windowsill his long-lost love? He blinked hard. His insides thundered, harder, faster, louder. Yes, it was true. Heaving himself out of bed, Seth hastened to the window and looked down upon her. Eager fingertips brushed against each other, yearning to reach out, but fearful that just a mere touch might vanquish the maiden, long absent from his existence. Trembling with anticipation, his fevered palm brushed her cool silky shoulder. When she did not disappear, he drew closer. Essence of honeysuckle filled his senses as feathery chestnut tresses, tussled by the playful breeze, brushed against his naked chest. Love, eternally unrequited, overflowed. "Never go away again, my own sweet Margi."

Scooping her into his arms, Seth held the maid close to his breast as he brought her to his bed and gently laid her down. He drew up the blanket then knelt down beside her. His hungry eyes feasted on every minute detail of her face that he had never forgotten. That pouty mouth, that diminutive nose, those eyes bordered by thick lashes that could persuade the devil to do good. She looked so much like…His entire frame shuddered. "Emma," withered from his trembling lips. Seth wobbled to his feet. "No." The sleeping figure was not Margi. His head swayed side to side. "No, this cannot be." He tottered backward and bumping into the wall, slithered to the floor. Burying his face in his hands, he moaned, "How could I have possibly thought Emma was Margi?"

His arms clamped about his knees as he stared at his bride. Only yesterday she had taken his hand in marriage. Her veil could not hide her ebony eyes. She was everything that this empty shell of a man had longed for, that his body needed, that his mind adored.

This room. It was his and Emma's. He had no right to taint it with the memory of Margi. His eyes drifted. An array of white daisies and red tea roses, arranged in an unadorned jade vase on the mahogany dresser, reflected in the etched mirror. Ecru doilies, which Emma had tatted herself, accented all the furniture. Her white satin gown draped the bedroom chair next to the door.

The door. Few hours had passed since he had hesitated on the other side before opening it up and standing in awkward, bashful silence as he connected with her innocence. At seventeen Emma had never known a man. She blushed. Her trembling finger fussed with the top button of her white eyelet gown, still unfastened. He had gone to her and cupped her delicate hand in his, brushing it across his freshly shaven cheek. His lips pressed into her open palm as her eyes reached into the depths of his soul, giving rise to passion long dormant. "I waited a man's lifetime for you," he cooed. "And now that your are here, I will love you and cherish you for all of God's lifetime. You will find me here always, my sweet Emma. Count on me to care for you forever."

He drew her to him. Her arms clasped about his waist as she snuggled against his chest. He lifted her chin. Eager lips met. The man and woman found each other and locked in intimate embrace. He became she. She became he.

Seth shook off the memory and buried his head in his arms to hide his shame. So much time had gone by before Emma had come into his life and conquered the monstrous void that Margi had left behind. Emma brought him back to the living. Now...now, he betrayed her with images of Margi. Oh God, how could he be so cruel? Overwhelmed with guilt and needing to banish himself from his sin, he got to his feet and threw on some clothes. Before leaving he stood over his sleeping bride for a brief moment. "I love you, my sweet Emma," he whispered and with a kiss he said, "Good-bye."

Outside, the early morning light glowed in the East. The fiery red orb, held in limbo by the jealous night, had yet to rise above the horizon. The air was stagnant. Destiny decreed this day to be a scorcher.

Seth got into his car and noiselessly closed the door. Torn between staying and leaving, he sat there for eternal moments before slowly backing out the driveway. His thoughts muddled, he drove around aimlessly. He was at Jeffrey's Point, that is, what was left of it. Like a giant parasite the airport was gradually sucking the lifeblood from its host. The beach, where ever since Seth had memory he and Margi had played, was now filled in, making way for another runway. Not far from there, he came across a secluded section of beach that bulldozers had not yet claimed. Gentle waves crested and overturned into misty foam before licking the shoreline. How many times did he frolic in surf like that with his Margi? Like snowy feathers of the dove, her carefree laughter tickled his ears. His empty heart smiled. Ebony eyes laid bare his soul as his fist tightened around a handful of long dark tresses, matted by the sea. His heart skipped a beat. Breathing seemed unnecessary.

"Run!" screamed a voice in his head.

Seth bolted. He ran through the school yard and out into the street. His arms felt so heavy. What was wrong with them? He looked down. "Margi," he gasped. She was draped across his arms. Oh God, she's limp—and so…so sick.

"Run, Seth. *Run!*"

He took up the vigil on the steps of the Bascuinos. Margi's inside. The Spanish Influenza was ravaging her body and Seth could do nothing. Endless hours passed. The doctor! Margi? Dying? Dead? Margi's gone? *No!* Grief consumed his entire being as Seth fled through the streets of East Boston.

"Run."

Never touch her again?

"Run!"

Never look upon her sweet face again?

"*Run! Fast!*" So Malavita, who held Margi in his grip, would never overtake him. He could not bear to see the ogre take his Margi away forever.

"Seth?" A hand nudged his shoulder. "What are you doing here?" Again a nudge. "Seth!"

Through a wretched haze of despair, he perceived the shadow of his mother. Her face wrinkled, anxious. "My dear Serafino. Why do you sit here on Bascuino's front stoop?"

"Where's your car?" asked a second voice.

Seth did not answer, only blinked at a form within the fog.

"Come on, Mama," said Rom. "Grab his other arm. Let's get him back to the house."

Slouched upon the kitchen table, Seth wallowed in a morbid stupor as Rom poured a glass of wine and set it in front of him. Seth made no move to pick it up so Rom wrapped his brother's hand around the glass. Seth did not drink. Holding his brother's fingers against the glass,

Rom pressed the glass to his lips. The wine tasted bitter as it lingered on his tongue.

Maria Avita sponged her son's fevered brow. Fright pasted her face. Vacantly he peered into her eyes and murmured, "She's dead, Mama."

"Who is dead, my son?"

"Margi."

Maria Avita stepped back. Clutching the face cloth to her breast, she exchanged anxious glances with Rom.

Seth muttered, "Emma looks like Margi."

Maria Avita sank into the chair next to him. She took his hand in hers and said, "*Si*. In many ways."

"Listen to me, *piccolo fratello mio*," Rom said massaging his brother's shoulders. "Emma is not Margi."

"It's a mistake, Rom," Seth moaned. "I shouldn't have married Emma."

"Now, why do you say such a foolish thing?" Maria Avita asked.

"She's too young for me."

"The girl is not too young for you," boomed a voice behind them.

Maria Avita and Rom turned, but Seth remained fixed, confused, and silent.

"Joseph," exclaimed Maria Avita with questioning eyes.

"Nobody showed up at Mizzulo's." The old man threw a deck of cards on the table. Ordinarily he would have taken his frustration out on his loved ones, but this time, his voice remained calm. "Could use a coffee, A*ngelatina Mia*."

While his wife set about making a fresh pot, Joseph pondered his youngest son who bent over the kitchen table like a feeble old man. The conversation he had just overheard disturbed him to no end. Joseph had known that day Margi died, it did not set well with Seth. But after all these years, her memory had loomed again? Now? After Serafino had finally married? This was truly beyond all comprehension.

Joseph sat down and reaching for the chair that Seth was sitting on, he dragged it away from the table until the father and son sat face to face. He grasped Seth's jaw in one hand and with the index finger of the other, pointed to his own eyes and commanded, "Look at me, Serafino."

Seth remained catatonic.

"Look at me," the old man demanded and jostled his son's jaw.

Seth began to come around.

"Now, hear me. Thirty years blesses you with maturity and wisdom that earns you much respect. But the heart that beats within your bosom, it is the only part of you that has refused to grow. The influenza, the scourge of your childhood, stunted it. For that reason I see that you are the same age as Emma. Your heart must now take seed and ripen with hers. It is time, *caro figlio mio.* For your sake, for Emma's sake, release Margi Bascuino from your soul."

* * *

Around noontime Rom and his fellow flatfeet tracked down Seth's car. "It was out at Jeffrey's Point," said Rom. "What the heck did you do, hike all the way to Bascuinos front porch from there?"

Seth shuttered. "I have no idea."

With his father and mother's guidance, Seth sorted out his relationship with Margi and Emma and came to a new understanding of himself in the process. For his own survival and the survival of his marriage, he had let go of Margi, not forget, just let go. While driving home that afternoon, he formulated a plan of action. From now on, whenever Margi crossed his mind, he was not going to deny her memory. Emma was the perfect person for this. Not only because she was his wife, but also because she had a unique way of looking at things. From the first time he saw her, she had diverted his attention from the grief he had carried for so many years. Nobody else had that effect on him. The next thing he must do is get himself and Emma out of Boston for a few days. It would do their marriage a world of good.

Emma was delighted. The unplanned honeymoon was right up her alley. So Friday morning, just as the night sky brightened to rose then golden, and the birds woke to greet another dawn, the newlyweds motored off to New York City. They spent the entire afternoon together, aimlessly wandering the streets of New York and exploring Central Park. When they returned to the hotel, they indulged in fragrant baths, foot and back rubs, and bubbly champagne. That evening, Seth took Emma to see Rachmaninoff in concert. The Russian composer mesmerized the audience with romantic and haunting melodies.

Seth was always aware of the two Mafia watchdogs who kept track of Emma but found it particularly galling that they had followed her to New York. When the hounds showed up outside the theater, that was the last straw. How dare the Mafia cast a pall on this special evening? "Wait here, Emma," he whispered. Appearing poised and in full control, Seth marched over to the two men. "I'm fed up with you guys tailing my wife," he snarled through gritted teeth that feigned a smile. "Back off! Hear me? I'm her husband, now. Which means that from here on out, Emma is my responsibility. Go tell that to Don Vito. Inform him that Seth LaRosa will have it no other way!" He stood there like a pillar of alabaster, staring down the two men in black. Slowly, they backed off and took their leave.

Emma sidled up to him and took his arm. "Did you know those gentlemen?"

"I thought perhaps I did, my sweet Emma, but I was mistaken," he smiled and stepped towards the street with his hand raised to hail a cab.

Emma yanked him back, pleading, "Come on. What do you say? Let's walk. The music still plays in my head and this is such a heavenly night."

Once again, those abysmal dark eyes overpowered the man. So naïve, yet she bedazzled him every time and got her way. "Quite a performance, huh?" he said.

She nodded. "No wonder Rachmaninoff is your favorite composer. Did you see that icy concentration on his face when he played 'Rhapsody on a Theme of Paganini'? Who would think such rich music comes from a stern man like that? I felt romantic and melancholy, all at the same time. I feel as if I've been cleansed, like as if I just came from church."

Seth laughed. "So who's your favorite composer, now?"

"Well, it used to be my Papa."

Away from the bright lights, Emma pointed towards the sky. "Look at all those stars. I especially love that one, the bright twinkly one right over there."

Seth recognized the star. As a desolated youth, he had slouched against an oak tree on Eagle Hill and gazed upon it during endless solitary nights. The essence of Margi hovered there while the haunting resonance of the night train spirited up from the rail yard below. Steel rails clacked while the fitful whistle moaned then faded in the distance.

"What's wrong, Seth?" Emma asked.

"That star. I've always look upon it as if it were Margi smiling down on me from heaven."

Emma squinted up at the star. Pondering its mystery for several moments, she asked, "If I die, will you make me a star, too?"

"Emma!" The question pierced Seth like an arrow straight to the heart. His soul could not bear to lose her. "Don't be silly. No one's gonna die."

"Well, I think we should name our baby girl Margi."

"You can't be pregnant already."

She scrunched her shoulders. "But when I am, it will be Margi or Adam or Samuel or Timothy or…"

"Wait a minute. You got this all planned out, haven't you?"

Snuggling up to her husband, the young bride giggled, "Uh-huh."

After a late breakfast the next day, the newlyweds toured the Bronx Zoo. Unexpectedly, hot breath spiked the hair on the back of Seth's neck as a low monotone voice growled, "Don Vito wishes to speak with you, Mr. LaRosa."

Seth searched out Emma. Alone, fifteen feet from of him, she ogled a pair of lion cubs. She's too far away. The Mafia goons could easily snatch her. Wait a minute. He straightened. The goons stood within inches of him. They didn't want his young bride, they wanted him. Without facing them he blustered, "Don Vito and I have nothing to discuss."

"At your convenience, *Signore* LaRosa, or Don Vito's. It is entirely your choice," grunted another voice.

"What does he want from me?"

"Only Don Vito knows."

Emma smiled over her shoulder at Seth. She started prancing toward him. Quickly he said, "OK, OK. Be outside my hotel tonight. At two. I assume you already know the place, right?"

Without further conversation the men dissolved into the woodwork. Seth shook off jangled nerves, vowing that Emma must not get so far away from him ever again. Nothing, nobody would ever take her from him. Every day she filled him with more joy than the day before, more than he had ever felt. He was the luckiest man in the world to have her.

"Who were those gentlemen?" she asked.

"Wanted directions to Central Park. That's all."

*   *   *

The clock in the hotel lounge struck two as Seth crossed the deserted lobby. A sleepy doorman jumped to his feet and opened the door. As Seth stepped into the night, heavy mist peppered his face. He expected the lights and the bustle of cars and pedestrians, but somehow it still surprised him. A black limousine shimmered at curbside. The motor purred while windshield wipers slapped time. A black suited chauffeur leapt from the car when he caught sight of Seth and hurriedly opened the rear door. In silence the driver and passenger motored away from the downtown area. Less than a half an hour later, the limousine took a right onto a dismal street that Seth remembered as if it were only yesterday. Ancient trees, like druids of old, cloaked the street lamps, obscuring the way and creating a solid canopy that kept out light even during the day. Rolling past towering hedges that concealed a fortress wall, the limousine turned into a narrow breach where an ornate cast iron gate swung open to allow entry into the compound without stopping. Tires thumped onto the cobblestones and rumbled up the circuitous driveway. Outside the mansion, a doorman waited. The car had yet to come to a complete stop before the rear door opened for Seth.

Inside the mansion a man wearing an expensive suit and shoes in which one might see his own reflection motioned to Seth. Don Vito's *il consigliere* appeared much older, but Seth would have known him anywhere. As they ambled through a maze of dark hallways, Seth remembered the only other time he had been in this house. It was so long ago that it seemed only a dream now. The place had aged gracefully but just like back then, was incredibly dark and gloomy, perhaps more so now than before.

The door to the study was open. Behind a familiar mahogany desk, Don Vito slouched in an imposing tapestry armchair. Seth hesitated as with barely a click, the door closed behind him. The shadows of his brothers and Antonio Messina standing beside his father Carmelo haunted this place. A grandfather clock throbbed. Apathetic forms of over-stuffed furniture distorted the room. Not one iota had changed. That was not the case for Don Vito who looked incredibly old and haggard. Wisps of white sprouted from a nearly bald pate that sunk halfway into bony shoulders. It seemed a great chore for the old Sicilian *Capo de Tutti capi* to breathe, more to speak. His voice was raspy and barely audible when he spoke. "Your message regarding your new bride has reached my ears."

"I meant no disrespect," said Seth.

"*Si*. I know that well. I have come to expect it from the LaRosa family. I know a great deal about all of you. The youngest son of Joseph and Maria Avita LaRosa is the only one who chooses to follow in the father's footsteps. Joseph, the builder of fine homes, is a pious man."

"He is."

"You also keep your father's faith. Still, your Mama's instinct to protect those who have sprung from her bones also thickens your blood."

Seth shifted his weight from one leg to the other. Was that good or bad?

"In some cases, such as your Mama's, such instinct is an admirable quality. Age has given me the wisdom to recognize that quality that lesser years had blinded me to." Don Vito paused to regain his breath and ponder the past. "Your brother Armand. He was also a curious mixture of your mother and father. My family survives because of him. The day before he was lost to us, he telephoned warning me of a person by the name of K. O. Elkins. The mucky link between Elkins and Phil Buccola bothered Armand. He knew that Buccola can be trusted no more than a rabid dog. I am grateful that I heeded his intuition and put my soldiers on alert. Buccola's assassins came over the walls of my compound late that night. They met with swift justice." Angry labored breath disturbed the silence that engulfed the room. "Not much longer will Buccola walk this earth."

Seth stood straight and confident on the outside. Inside, that was another matter. All this stuff about Mama, Pop, Armand, Buccola. What did any of it have to do with him? Should he ask or what?

"The secret of Vanzetti I take to my grave. You, me, and your brother Romeo, we are the only ones now living who have knowledge of it. Even the guards I assigned to watch over the girl all these many years were given no reason for their assignment."

"I am pleased, Don Vito," said Seth bowing his head slightly, but his voice seemed hollow and out of place. "Nothing can be accomplished by my wife's knowing."

"You will see the guardians no longer."

"Thank you, Don Vito."

"If your woman ever learns of her past, will you tell her that Don Vito regrets the death of her innocent father? And that his tormented soul gave him no rest?" Faded eyes searched Seth's youth. The elder nodded slightly when the younger returned a flicker of compassion.

Pity stirred within Seth. Why did the Don carry such heavy guilt?

"I am old," Don Vito continued. "My heart beats weak and sick. These eyes of mine yearn to once again contemplate the beauty of my homeland. This business of ours," he gasped for air and slowly opened the desk drawer. "It has not turned out as I planned so long ago. Our people have not benefited. Greed and violence has taken over. It is the pitiful legacy I leave."

"You are going back to Italy?" Seth asked.

The Don took a black leather pouch from the drawer and placed it on the desk in front of him. "*Si.* Arrangements have been made."

Seth had seen the pouch once before, a long time ago. "So what do you want from me?"

"Nothing." Don Vito ran his fingertips over the leather pouch and played with the flap.

"Nothing?"

"*Si.* I wish to give you this." Opening the leather flap, the Don emptied the pouch on top of the mahogany desk. Metal clanked. The silence shattered. "I wish you to have this."

Seth stepped closer to the desk. His eyes narrowed. "Why?"

"It is a symbol of all that is good. And also the wickedness wrought by it. Remember the difference, Serafino LaRosa. Times will come when you may wish to hold it in your hand to weigh good against evil. Let it guide the path that life takes you."

Gingerly, Seth picked up the object. It was heavier than he expected. He glanced up at Don Vito. But the old man had turned away. Barely audible words drifted back. "Sandro's crucifix. My gift to him the day he was ordained."

CHAPTER 32

It was one of those January mornings when the sub-zero air was so clear and crisp, it crackled. Crystal icicles refracted the unbridled sunshine that infiltrated the wintry aura and streaked through the bedroom window. Joseph squinted as his eyes opened from a night of resplendent sleep. His chest swelled with chilled air that invaded the deepest reaches of his stagnant lungs. Every tissue banished the torpid night as he stretched out his aging bones and crooked his back, pressing for the ultimate extension until every last cell gave up its lethargy. How good it felt to be alive on such a splendid day. Snuggled in a cozy bed piled high with quilts, Joseph wished he could cuddle between the warm sheets with Maria Avita to spend hours of quiet, untrammeled time. He clasped his hands behind his head and envisioned a breakfast tray laden with steamy coffee and luscious home-made cinnamon buns. But the incessant tick, tick, tick of the wind-up alarm clock disturbed his fanciful illusions. He rolled over and grappled around on the night stand for his spectacles. Winding the chilled metal around his ears, he gawked at the time. "Holy mackerel! I must get up straight away or I will be late for the eight o'clock Mass. For heaven's sake, where is that woman? She should have gotten me up by now." One foot landed on the icy floor. He drew it back and winced. The mystery unraveled, Joseph chuckled, "Downstairs, rekindling the ashes of the night fire. *Angelatina Mia* has lost track of time once again."

Wrapping a chilled robe around his warmth, he hustled to the closet and picked out a suit. As he dressed, the fabric further chilled his skin. He clasped his hands together and breathed on them. He listened. Like so many Sundays too numerous to count, Vincenzo had not risen for church. It was perplexing indeed. For someone who had once aspired to the priesthood, Vincenzo lacked all devotion. And that woman, Eva. Why did he not marry her after all these years? Well, no matter. At least he came home last night.

How different his sons had turned out. Rom, a cop, walked on the side of justice. Armand, police informer, Mafia *capodecina*, worked in obscurity in an effort to equalize the good and bad of these trying times. Angelo, the politician, played both sides from the middle, his own selfish ends in mind. Paolo, an honest man and excellent barber. He earned more than an adequate living for himself and his family. It mattered nothing that he was slight of body and strength. Seth, strong as the day is long, followed in Joseph's footsteps both in work and faith. "Ah, Serafino." An inkling of a smile lifted one side of the patriarch's face. "And Emma, his beautiful bride."

No doubt that at this very moment the newlyweds were readying themselves for church, just like Joseph and Maria Avita. Seth and Emma reminded the old man of the early days when he and Maria Avita were just married. It seemed like forever ago. He could not remember a time when she was not in his world. Life had begun when she came to him. A strong, faithful wife, Maria Avita devoted her entire life to him and her family. It mystified Joseph how she faced every trial that life presented her with remarkable resiliency. He detected that same quality hidden deep within his new daughter-in-law's ebony eyes. Running his hands through his hair, the color of winter wheat, satisfaction clashed with selfishness, for he wished that Seth and Emma had chosen to live in East Boston, closer to him. Brighton was so far away. Still, the house they had purchased in Brighton was everything they wanted. So, if the place made them happy, it also made Joseph happy.

Yes. God had blessed this old man with a good woman and a long life. Fully dressed, he still shivered. He leered at the cursed door that did not open. "That old woman plays much too long with the fire. I should go down there and stoke it myself."

An empty stomach pestered him and he was grateful that today he was not receiving the sacraments, for he would not have to wait until after Mass to eat. This growing-old business made him less and less tolerant of the slightest discomfort. Chilled to the bone, he rubbed his hands together. Where was his morning coffee and biscotti? She usually brought them by now.

Opening the bedroom door, Joseph stood in the hall. He listened. The house was cold, silent. "Hmph," he frowned then plodded past Vincenzo's door to the landing above the winding stairway. His expression softened. "Well, there you are, *Angelatina Mia.*"

He scratched the back of his head while pausing to soak up the image of his wife sitting below in his club chair. She was staring into the embers of a half-kindled fire, having given up all attempts to revive the infernal thing. Her head was bowed slightly, her hands folded. *She must be in prayer. Perhaps now is not the time to disturb her.*

She was not wearing her robe, only a muslin nightgown that draped to the floor and covered everything except the toes of her feet. "You will catch your death without a robe," Joseph called as he stepped off the last stair. With every step he became more and more irritated that she ignored him. For heaven's sake, she didn't even look up. "We will be late for Mass. You must hurry, *Angelatina Mia.*"

Again no answer. He rounded the chair. She made no move, her gaze remained fixed on the stubborn embers. He touched her hand and his world forever shattered. Cold, inflexible. Maria Avita had flown away with the angels.

* * *

The day after the funeral, Joseph stared blankly out the bedroom window. He could not bear to look at the room where so many years he shared union with Maria Avita. It was so empty without her. Now the bed was just a place to lay his miserable brain until the long sleepless night transcended into day. The house was no longer a home. It had become a hollow frame of memories that he could not hold in his arms.

Snow had fallen during the night. The blanket of white gave the garden below a sense of purity to her passing. Like wisps of snow swept away by the wintry blow, Maria Avita had been taken from Joseph. What on earth was he going to do without her? Melancholy shrouded his heart beyond any that he had ever known. The old man heaved a sigh. His shoulders slumped as he hobbled to the boudoir chair and collapsed into it.

Across the room, Louisa and her daughters were sorting through Maria Avita's things. Clothes would be donated to the immigrants' relief charities. Jewelry and other keepsakes were already spoken for, mementos for family and friends. Watching the somber task that he had no stomach for, Joseph wished he were somewhere else. It did not matter where, just not here. This life was too much; he wanted no part of it. Regardless, Louisa had insisted she needed him here. The old man knew that this was just as painful for his only surviving daughter as it was for him. Maria Avita and Louisa had been everything to each other. They had shared women secrets, to which men were not privy. His weary eyes became overcast. Louisa was the spitting image of her mother. She moved like Maria Avita. She thought like her mother. Even her voice belonged to her mother making the young, innocent bride of his youth live on in his heart. How his arms ached to hold her. *Lord? At least one more time, let your humble servant Joseph enfold his arms about Maria Avita in the cold hours before dawn. He needs to draw strength once again from their union. His body has become so heavy. It cannot function without her.*

The desolated old man languished upon an ocean of grief. His every moment, his every thought, his every breath drifted with sorrow's ebb and flow. Why did Maria Avita leave him alone like this? How would he survive without her? His chest tightened. At that moment the pain that had tormented her after he left her alone in Italy so long ago struck home. Even though she had the children to cling to, just as he did now, there was no comfort without one's mate. No comfort existed without *Angelatina Mia.*

So many decisions Joseph had made through the years caused him regret. And some he didn't make. He could not run from the facts that confronted him; his bad times resulted most often from his own distorted religious beliefs and reluctance to give up the old ways. He was a man beset by his own stubbornness. What did that get him? Only pain. Pain inflicted on others that more often than not ricocheted off them to sting Joseph even worse. Through all his bullheadedness, Maria Avita had stood by him. Good times and bad, she was always there listening rather than judging. His eyebrows lifted as Joseph chewed over that thought a second time, *well, that is not entirely true. She never tolerates anyone doing harm to her family, even me, her sanctimonious husband. Holy saints in heaven, that woman can fly off the handle! Father Sandro had no idea what he was up against.* Joseph smiled. *Even when you are so far away, Angelatina Mia, you are still in my heart, in my soul, lightening my load.*

"Here, Pop," Louisa said softly. "I found this in the back of the bottom drawer."

The ancient cigar box was wrapped several times with shipping twine and several overlapping square knots fastened it securely. The faded label read, *Manual Garcia Alonso Cigars, made by the Garcia Factory. Sold by Eastbrook and Eaton, 211 Washington Street, Boston.* Joseph swallowed. His mouth was parched. "What is this?"

Louisa shrugged. "Looks like something of importance. I shunned opening it myself for that reason."

Joseph played with the knots. They refused to budge and the twine was too tight to ease over the edge of the box. Throwing his hands up, he mumbled, "I will need scissors."

Louisa scurried out of the room. Her footsteps faded down the stairs. Not a moment later, he remembered his pocket knife. By the time his daughter returned, he had already severed the twine, wrapped it around the palm of his hand, and was opening the box. His eyes grew wide. Louisa gasped. His mouth dropped. "Money! Where the devil did all this come from?"

* * *

One day late in springtime, Seth and Emma drove Joseph to the Sacred Heart Cemetery in Malden. Maria Avita and Joseph had purchased the family plot when *Malavita* stole little Francesca. He would have preferred it to be closer to East Boston but Maria Avita loved it here, way out in the country. Disturbed by human presence, sparrows fluttered out of the shrubs up to the safety of treetops and noisily chirped in protest. The men doffed their hats as they approached the grave site. "You've done a fine job, Pop," Seth murmured.

Emma nodded, "Mama surely smiles when she looks down upon this place. It's so green and peaceful. And all these flowers, her favorite."

Choking back the dull ache that rose in his throat and robbed him of breath, Joseph mumbled, "*Si.*"

Falling into silence, all three blessed themselves. With Seth's help the old man got down on his knees. His hand reached out to touch the marble headstone. Cold and impassive, it lacked the warmth of Maria Avita. His fingers raked the furrows in her name. Rigid and sharp, the etching was not at all soft and lithesome, the way her name floated from his lips and drifted upon the breeze. Joseph bowed his head as Seth offered up a faltering prayer. "May God grant that the rose Pop placed in your hand blooms as long as the memory of you that lives on in our hearts."

Joseph heaved a sigh. "Amen." His eyes wandered to the graves of his family. On the left of Maria Avita was Armand, her oldest son, cut down by the friend of his youth, the very person who started their oldest son on a way of life that eventually brought demise for both. Sweet, frail Francesca was resting on the other side of her mother. Joseph could still feel the penetrating sparkle of her button eyes, the color of the cinnamon rose. How small her hand was in his. He could still see her nimble little fingers tatting a baby's bonnet. But that terrible flood of molasses had snuffed out the life of his Francesca and that of Joseph Belladonna, the youthful immigrant who had covered her body with his, an insignificant shield against raging *Malavita*. The noble youth had found eternal rest next to Francesca at Maria Avita's insistence. A great deal of searching failed to locate any relatives. Joseph still avoided the North End, especially on hot summer days, for the odor of molasses continually haunted the back streets and alleys. Only once did he set aside this aversion. That was when he campaigned for Angelo and saw a thing no father should ever see. Now the North End meant nothing but pain. Angelo, Joseph's shining star and hope for the social advancement of his family and the Italian community, lay next to Armand. Angelo…college graduate, Senator. Such a waste. So consumed by ill-begotten obsessions. Funny, Armand never set foot in a single classroom, but he did much more good than Angelo.

A hand patted Joseph's shoulder. He looked up. His youngest son whispered, "See you back at the car."

After Seth and Emma slipped away, the old man began to murmur, softly, secretly, the way he used to in the darkness while the children slept beyond the homespun in the two-room cottage overlooking the Gulf of Poliscastro on the Tyrrhenian Sea. "I miss you, *Angelatina Mia*. More than Italy's hillsides miss the rain in the parching heat of August. How hard it was to lose our children. But losing you…it is beyond any strength I am able to call forth."

And it seemed as though at that moment Maria Avita touched him. Her velvet skin warmed his as her nose nuzzled his ear. She snuggled close. Her arm draped across his naked chest. He smelled the soft essence of her raven hair. He could hardly hear her breathing, for she had drifted off to sleep.

"The stonemason has done a fine piece of work, did he not, *Angelatina Mia*?" His whispered words choked off his air. "And these evergreens, they will give color when the snow falls. Impatiens and roses grow this summer, and next year, I will see to it that you have more."

Silence surrounded him. A soft breeze brushed his cheek. "The money in the cigar box," he sighed. "I used it all for this fine marker. And that picture of you...the one that I have carried with me all these years...you know the one. You smile only a little...like the Mona Lisa. I gave it to the stone mason so he might carve your face into the statue."

The bell in the church steeple tolled twelve. "I should go." Joseph faltered. The weight of his broken heart was too much to bear any longer. His hands clasped his face. "*Cara* Maria Avita *mia, mi manchi molto*. I am dead inside without you." And Joseph wept...loud...inconsolably.

After a time, he dried his eyes with the back of his hand and labored to his feet. He took one last lingering look at the life-size statue that marked the graves and remembered a world so much younger and innocent. His God had provided him strength to endure the struggles that had come their way, but Maria Avita was the one who had taken charge, bringing the family through each and every trial.

The statue knelt on one knee, robes cascading over arms as hands clasped in prayer. Unfocused eyes turned downward. A trace of an ethereal smile lightened its bearing. The wings, partially extended and intricately detailed, gave airiness to the feathers. In his mind Joseph beheld Maria Avita. "May St. Anthony watch over you, *Angelatina Mia*, until I weep no more and hold you in my arms for eternity."

About the Author

K Spirito has always been a history buff. She loves to browse though microfilm of old newspapers, especially at the Boston Public Library. Noting stories of human interest, both significant and otherwise, she weaves them into works of historical fiction.

She enjoys traveling, in-line skating, sailing, kayaking, and Mexican train dominoes. She believes she was born of gypsies (although she was not) because she wouldn't mind one bit living a year or two in New York City then moving on to Montreal then San Diego then Rome then London then…

K Spirito holds a Bachelor of Science Degree from Franklin Pierce College in New Hampshire and also an Associate in Arts from L. A. Pierce College in California. In the '60s she built power supplies for the Lunar Excursion Module that now sits on the moon. She transcribed *Five Little Firemen* by Margaret Wise Brown and Edith Thacher Hurd into Braille for the L. A. Public Library. She was a licensed Cosmetologist and owned a hair salon.

She and her husband of thirty-five years managed to get four children through high school; two went on to college. They are now blessed with one granddaughter and three grandsons.

K Spirito's goals are to continue her education and become the best storyteller she can be.

9 780595 131303